JAM

YAHTZEE CROSHAW

DARK HORSE BOOKS
Milwaukie

Cover design by Tina Alessi

Published by Dark Horse Books
A division of Dark Horse Comics, Inc.
10956 SE Main Street, Milwaukie, OR 97222

DarkHorse.com

Library of Congress Cataloging-in-Publication Data

Croshaw, Yahtzee.
  Jam / by Yahtzee Croshaw. -- 1st Dark Horse Books ed.
      p. cm.
  ISBN 978-1-59582-957-3
1. Jam--Fiction. 2. End of the world--Fiction. 3. Prophecies--Fiction. 4. Brisbane (Qld.)--Fiction. 5. Humorous fiction. 6. Fantasy fiction. I. Title.
PR9619.4.C735J36 2012
823'.92--dc23
                                                                    2012023323

First edition: October 2012

Printed by Offset Paperback Mfrs., Inc., Dallas, PA, U.S.A.
10 9 8 7 6 5 4 3 2 1

This book is dedicated to Google Street View for reminding me what the building on the corner of Creek and Ann looked like. Thanks for saving me the bus fare.
—YZ

DAY 1.1

I woke up one morning to find that the entire city had been covered in a three-foot layer of man-eating jam.

I didn't notice straightaway. Our apartment was on the third floor, so the day began as a fairly ordinary one. I got up at around eleven a.m. to go job hunting. I tried to take a shower, but the hot water was off. Then I tried to have some cereal, but the milk was off. The whole refrigerator was off. I fingered the light switch: nothing. The power was cut.

None of this was any cause for concern. I glanced over at the increasingly urgent utility bills pinned to the corkboard by the front door. It wasn't that we couldn't afford to pay them; it was just that none of us ever really got around to it.

At that point Frank emerged from his bathroom, wearing his gym clothes and with gooseflesh dotting his arms and shoulders. "Hot water's off," he said, through his teeth.

"Power's off," I replied.

"Oh, christ." He ripped the most recent payment demand from the board. "Was it off when Tim got back last night? Do you know?"

"No. He got back late. I was in bed."

"I'll give them a call when I get back," he said, waving the bill. "Don't worry about it."

"Thanks. You going to the gym?"

He pointed to the word *GYM*, emblazoned brightly on the front of his vest. "Yep."

"I'll come down with you."

He raised one of his thick eyebrows at me. "You gonna sign up?"

"No, no," I said, quickly. "Just get breakfast somewhere."

"When are you going to do it? I get a discount if I recommend someone." He prodded my stomach in his good-natured but nonetheless painful way. "You should start working that off soon as you can. Your twenties only last so long."

"I know. I'll sign up," I protested. "At some point."

He raised a disbelieving eyebrow and I followed him out into the stairwell that led down to the courtyard. He immediately parked his thick buttocks on the handrail with a short whoop of glee and slid down the first flight of steps, swinging around and starting on the next without waiting for me. He was already at the bottom by the time I reached the top of the last flight.

So I was just in time to see him get eaten by the jam.

He was looking back at me to shout encouragement, so he didn't notice it until he was on top of it, flopping bodily onto the three feet of wobbling red that flooded the bottom of the stairwell. "Urrgh," I heard him say, in the disgusted tone of one falling victim to a messy practical joke. This quickly became "Arrgh" when he realized the jam wasn't letting him go, and that in turn became "AAAAARGH" when he saw his legs, immersed in the semitransparent goo, stripped of their flesh over the course of a second.

The rest of him summoned a burst of effort from somewhere and his torso strained at the ropy red strands that wrapped him like festive ribbons. He reached his last remaining arm out towards me, and his terrified eyes met mine. Then the jam shot out several more tentacles that fastened around his wrist, eyes, and mouth, and he was yanked back with a desperate gurgle.

His wristwatch, iPod, and fillings slowly floated to the surface, with a motion that seemed reminiscent of a satisfied belch.

I very, very slowly turned around and went back up the stairs.

I must have let myself back into the flat. The next thing I knew, I was sitting rather stiffly on the living room sofa with my fingers drumming on my knees, staring at the Master Chief figurine Frank kept on top of the TV. After a while, the finger drumming didn't feel right, so I clutched my thighs instead. That didn't feel right either, so I gathered my hands over my crotch. That felt even less right. Nothing felt right.

Finally, I stood up slowly, holding my stomach in case it hurled itself up my throat and out my face, and opened the blinds that covered the balcony doors. The balcony looked out on the courtyard, but we generally kept the blinds closed because Frank (Frank, who was dead) would always complain about sunlight on the TV.

It was a pleasant, cloudless Brisbane day. The sun beamed cheerfully across the balconies of the vacant flats opposite. I slid the balcony doors aside, and felt a warm breeze play gently on my face. What a lovely day. By now Frank, Frank who was dead, would have reached the gym, probably flirting with the receptionist on his way to the locker room. If he hadn't been dead, that is.

I kept my gaze focused on the clear blue sky and stepped forward until I could clench my hands around the railing. I took a deep breath. Then I looked down.

The jam had filled the courtyard and foyer and pushed the water out of the swimming pool. Where it touched the walls, little tendrils snaked their way upwards like searching fingers. There was an overpowering stench of strawberries.

From my vantage point I could see into some of the ground-floor apartments. All of them were half-filled with jam, the top halves of TVs and stereos poking up like electronic islets. The occupants were nowhere to be seen.

I went to the far end of the balcony and craned to look through the main entrance doors at the street outside. I couldn't see much, but it looked like there was jam there, too. It was only then that I remembered that a main road was barely fifty yards from the complex, and yet I couldn't hear any traffic noise.

Please stop noticing things, went my brain. *I'm having trouble finding room for it all.*

I rapped my knuckles against the other set of balcony doors behind me, the ones that led into Tim's bedroom. I had been knocking continuously for close to five minutes before they finally slid aside.

"WHAT?!" yelled Tim. He was naked save for a pair of cargo shorts he was still zipping up, and his blond hair was unshowered and still chaotic from sleep.

"Juh," I said.

"What?"

"Jam."

"Jam?"

"Jam."

His baggy, sleep-deprived eyes glanced left and right, confused. "Are you saying there's a jam?"

"There is jam, yes." I pointed. "Down there."

He stepped out of his room dubiously and leaned over the balustrade. His eyes bulged, and his mouth spread gradually into a grin. "Holy shit. That is so awesome." He bent his entire top half over the rail, trying to look out into the street. "It is jam, isn't it?"

I took up position next to him, supporting my face in my hands. " 'S got seeds."

"Yeah. Whiffs a bit, doesn't it. Has Frank seen?"

"Frank's dead."

Another long silence passed, during which neither of us moved.

"When did that happen?"

" 'Bout ten minutes ago."

Tim stood upright and coughed. "So, of the two important things that happened this morning," he said, enunciating slowly and carefully. "One being jam, the other being Frank dying, you felt jam was the one worth mentioning."

"The jam killed him," I said, finally getting the words out. "He was eaten. By the jam."

"Ah. Right." A pause. "Actually, no, not right. Back up. What happened?"

I gave an account of the morning's events. Tim slowly nodded in bafflement after each significant word, drinking them all in one by one but not quite connecting them in his head.

Eventually, he ducked back inside his room and picked his dressing gown up off the floor. "I think you're going to have to show me," he said.

I led him in silence down the stairwell, stopping at the same place I'd stopped before, at the top of the last flight. The jam was where I'd left it, flooding the ground floor, pulsating slightly and slopping gooily below the fourth step.

"Is he in there?" asked Tim, squinting.

"It dissolved him." I waved a hand uncertainly at the heaving mass. "He's dead."

Tim peered forward, examining the small collection of objects that were still bobbing on the surface at the foot of the stairs: a few coins, a key ring, and Frank's phone with the Mr. T plastic casing. "Hmm," said Tim thoughtfully, before pulling off his left thong and hurling it in.

The jam extended a couple of elongated peaks of itself to welcome it. The sole rapidly shriveled away to nothing in the grip of the corrosive red ooze, while the plastic toe strap popped free and drifted over to join Frank's pocket change.

"Likes rubber but not plastic," Tim said to himself. "Okay. What else do we know about it?"

"It liked Frank."

"Likes human bodies. We should be taking notes."

"Tim?"

"Yes?"

"Frank's dead."

"Yes, I gathered that." Tim looked at me. "Are you all right?"

"I . . . don't know. I feel a bit numb."

He pulled off his dressing gown and wrapped it tightly around his hand until there was a foot-wide cloth fist on the end of his arm. Then he made his way carefully down the stairs, one at a time, stretching his covered hand towards the jam. He stopped a few steps before the surface. I noticed the jam had gone rather still and quiet, as if anticipating something.

"Er," I said, twiddling my fingers. "What are you doing?"

"Give me a hand."

He wrapped his arm around my right wrist as I clung to the banister with my left. He leaned even closer to the jam and began dabbing at it with the dressing gown. I felt myself inhale sharply.

"It's all spongy," he reported.

As he examined the jam's texture, he failed to notice a large section of jam in front of him start to rise from the surface like a tombstone being pushed out from under the earth. After a few false starts I found my voice. "Er, Tim . . ."

"Sort of feels nice, actually."

It stopped growing when it was about six feet tall, then stood quivering back and forth uncertainly. "Tim, there's . . ."

"Reminds me of that fat girl I—"

"TIM I AM RAISING MY VOICE NOW TIM."

He looked up just as the monolith of jam began to fall forward. I hauled him backwards as hard as I could and we crumpled together onto the stairs less than a second before the jam slapped like wet pizza dough against the tiles, inches from Tim's feet.

He smiled nervously, trembling from the adrenaline. "Holy shit," he breathed. "It tried to eat me."

"I told you, it ate Frank," I said. I took a deep breath. "Frank's dead."

DAY 1.2

Noon had just passed and we were back on our balcony. I sat on the floor with my back against the balustrade, fiddling with my phone and eating a sandwich as some token acknowledgement of lunchtime. Tim stood next to me, leaning on his elbows. He had been staring silently at the jam for some time, the relentless tapping of his fingers his only perceptible motion.

"I'm not getting through to anyone," I said, hearing the same apologetic recorded voice for the fourth time. "You want me to try your mum?"

"This," he said, finally, "is the greatest thing that has ever happened to us."

I peered up at him, plastic screen still fastened to my ear. "You what?"

"Seriously. We have been elevated to the status of kings."

I stood up and followed his gaze. "By jam?"

"Think about it. Last night, we were nothing. A freelance musician and an unemployed, two faces among billions. But you know what we are now?"

I glanced left and right, thinking. "Both unemployed?"

"We're survivors. By the simple act of living this long we have been marked by fate." He leant forward and tried to see into the street for the eighth time.

"I can't reach your mum, either," I said.

If Tim was worrying, he hid it well. He tipped back and touched down again. "We need to know how far the jam's spread."

"There's no traffic noise," I said, helpfully bringing up something I'd noticed earlier.

His foot tapped rapidly as he thought. The damp slaps of sweaty skin against tile echoed off into the yawning silence. "Could be covering the whole city," he said, knuckle to mouth. "The whole country. Maybe the whole world." He inhaled excitedly at the thought, grabbing my arm. "We could be the last human beings on Earth! This apartment could be the last beacon of civilization in a total jampocalypse!"

Somewhere in the complex, a door slammed.

From our position we could see across the courtyard to the four levels of walkways that the residents in the other half of the complex used to access their lift. A patter of footsteps slowly grew louder before stopping somewhere on the second floor, then we heard the owner halfheartedly slapping the elevator call button.

"There's someone else in here," hissed Tim.

"Sorry," I hissed back.

He leant over the balustrade again. "Oi! Survivors up here!"

We heard the call button being slapped a few more times, with increased urgency.

"Lift's not working," I called.

There was a momentary pause as the person on the second floor internally debated their options; then a female face, wearing a baseball cap, appeared at the railing. "Why not?"

"Jam," said Tim and I in unison.

"It's jammed?" she said. We pointed, and she finally looked down into the foyer. "Oh. Oh my."

"Don't touch it! It eats people!" warned Tim.

"It ate Frank," I added.

"Okay, hang on," said the girl. "I'll come up the stairs."

She vanished from sight, and we heard the door to the front stairwell open and close.

"Do you know her?" I asked.

"Seen her around, I think. Be nice. We might end up having to rebuild civilization with her."

"What, all of it?"

"We could set up somewhere in the central business district," he thought aloud. "Where the tall buildings are. We'll gather some materials and build the major settlement on the upper floors of the tallest one, in case the jam rises. We'll expand as necessary to settlements on shorter buildings and connect them with rope bridges. We'll have to forage on the remnants of the previous civilization at first but we'll aim for total reliance on food grown in the rooftop gardens within one to two years. Sound good?"

I coughed. "How are we going to get out of this flat?"

"Yeah." He glanced at me. "What? Oh, right. Wait there." He disappeared back inside.

The stairwell door on the third-floor walkway opposite our balcony opened, and the girl trotted out. She was wearing a Starbucks uniform, and had dirty blond hair tied back in a ponytail. "Hey!" she called, waving. "Where'd all the jam come from, then?"

"Er, you know about as much as we do right now," I called back, scratching the back of my head. "It's been there since we woke up and it ate our flatmate."

"Yeah, you said that. Does it really?" She wrapped her arms around her waist and eyed me, shifting her weight back and forth. "I mean, I don't want you to think I'm . . . gullible, or anything. No offense, but you could be anyone."

I looked at the jam again. I could swear that bits of it were trying to climb the walls. "We didn't put it there," I said.

"No, I wouldn't have thought you did, I just thought you might have been being, you know, opportunistic."

"What?"

Tim stumbled back out his balcony doors, closely followed by a trail of bed sheets, then a corner of a mattress making a halfhearted attempt to come with them. He was clutching the carry case for my laptop under one arm, which he began knotting to the first sheet.

"What's that for?" I asked.

"Weight," he said, simply, busily knotting the sheets together. He noticed the Starbucks girl on the other balcony, and waved momentarily. "Hi."

"I was just saying to your friend," she said. "I'm not saying you don't seem trustworthy or anything but I'm just going to head down and check for myself . . ."

"DON'T!" said Tim and I together.

"Give us one second," he said. He'd knotted the sheets together into a long rope, and was letting the laptop bag dangle off the end, testing the weight.

"Er, Tim, is my laptop in there?" I said.

He rolled his eyes. "It wouldn't be much of a weight, otherwise, would it."

"I'd really rather you—"

"I am not going to waste any time hunting around for heavy objects you can bear to part with. Your laptop will be fine. It's a padded bag."

"All right, just . . . be careful."

He paid it over the rail and swung it back and forth, building up momentum. "We'll get across to the rest of the complex and figure it out from there," he muttered. The makeshift grappling hook was spinning around and around, gathering speed. "Journey of a thousand miles begins with a single . . . STEP."

He let go, and the laptop bag sailed through the air towards the opposite balcony. It bounced off the railing, then the three of us watched it fall into the courtyard and plop into the jam.

Tim was wrenched off his feet as something pulled hard on the bed sheet rope, and his head collided sharply with our balustrade. He released his grip and the jam sucked the knotted bed sheets in like a strand of spaghetti.

The silence rolled in again. Somewhere in the distance, a crow cawed.

"Jesus, did you see that?" said the girl.

"Huh," said Tim, shakily standing up and clutching his temple. "Right, then. We'll add that to the list. People, rubber, and cotton."

"I guess you were right," said the girl. "I've got some sheets at my place. You wait there."

"Tim," I said, after she'd disappeared back downstairs. "I'm a bit upset about the laptop thing."

"Well, it . . . wouldn't have done you much good if civilization has fallen, would it."

"Tim, your head's bleeding."

He touched the red line that was drooling down his forehead and inspected his fingers with dazed wonder. "So it is. Just bashed it a bit. It's all good." He rubbed the rest of it off and absent-mindedly wiped his hand on his cheek.

"Hey," said the girl in the Starbucks uniform, as she reappeared across the courtyard shouldering a thick coil of white cable. "I found this extension cord. The jam stuff probably won't like it so much."

She spun the plug end around her head a few times and let it go. I was able to lean forward and grab the wire just before it dropped out of reach.

"I'll go first," said Tim, taking up the cable in both hands. He tried to put his foot on the rail, but missed.

"Er, maybe I should, actually," I said, tactfully removing the wire from his unresisting hands and giving him the plug. "You just stay here, relax, hold onto this as hard as you can, and, er . . ." I attempted to recall some of the first aid they taught me in the Cub Scouts. "Just try not to go to sleep."

"Yeah, yeah," he said, nodding rapidly. A few small drops of blood spattered onto my chest. "I'm okay, I'm okay. You go first. Go."

"Ready," said the girl. She'd tied her end of the cable onto the handrail and was clutching the socket end with one foot braced on the knot. Tim entwined the cable in his hands and leaned back as hard as he could.

I hopped up onto the rail, let my legs dangle over the jam, and several rounds of second thoughts hammered across the back of my mind. The fall would have been only arguably survivable even if the floor weren't covered in flesh-eating, strawberry-scented death. There must have been twenty feet of depressingly thin air between our balcony and the walkway opposite. I was quietly impressed by the length of the extension cord.

I swiveled around, putting my back to the jam. That helped. Then I hugged the cable to my chest, crossed my thighs and ankles around it, took a deep breath, then another one, leaned back, and inched backwards with my buttocks until I slipped off the edge.

My heart rattled a steel mug against the bars of my rib cage for a split second as the cable sagged, then it and Tim's upper-body strength took my weight. I was dangling from the line like a sloth, staring up into the beautiful clear blue sky. The sun was directly overhead, and I screwed my eyes shut. That helped with the glare, but now my imagination was attaching all sorts of horrible images to every wet sticky noise the jam made as it idly flexed below me.

Once I was assured that the cable could hold me, my only concern was getting across before my muscles completely gave out. I should probably have taken up Frank's offer to sign up with his gym before he'd gotten himself killed. Pain was already worming its way through my chest and groin, but the adrenaline was dampening it nicely.

"Don't look down!" suggested the girl. "Nearly halfway now."

I was actually starting to impress myself when I felt something jogging the wire, and my entire body tensed up into something like a giant conker on a piece of string. I looked up, and saw Tim on our balcony. He was standing with hands on hips, and he wasn't holding his end of the cord.

"Where's the plug?!" I squeaked.

"It's all right," he said. The trickle of blood from his forehead had almost reached his mouth. "I put it back in at the wall." Then he fainted.

The sudden realization of upcoming death burst in my ears with the faint crunching sound of my weight pulling an extension cord out of a wall socket. Then I was clinging to a line that was shifting extremely rapidly from horizontal to vertical. My back slammed painfully against the side of the second-floor walkway, and my hands slipped from the cord.

My thighs reflexively tightened around the socket as my arms dangled down towards the jam. I tried to bend my torso, to get my hands back on the cord, but pain stabbed hotly in my back muscles. Just one visit to the gym, I thought. Just one, and maybe I could have done a single sit-up.

"Oh my god oh my god oh my god oh my god," I heard Girl chanting.

"Can. You. Pull. Me. Up," I said. I'd had to force every word out through a layer of terror that wrapped me like duct tape.

"Oh my god. Hang on." I felt myself being lifted about a centimeter, then descending back again with a gasp of effort from above. "Oh my god. No. Can you reach the thing? On the thing?"

I looked around. The handrail for the first-floor walkway was six feet away. I stretched my hands towards it and only served to dishearten myself further. I squeezed out the words, "Too. Far."

"Okay. I'm going to try swinging you. Try and grab it when the—" she suddenly let out a little shriek. "Oh my god!"

"What?!"

"Nothing, it's nothing! Don't look down! I'm going to swing you now."

So obviously I looked down (or from my perspective, up) and saw a column of jam rising from below to greet me like a questing finger aiming to pick the nose of God.

That was the moment I cracked. All the tension and horror that had been building inside me like foam in a shaken-up Pepsi can finally burst out and I started screaming. I was swinging stupidly back and forth, wailing like a foghorn, spraying spit and tears as I went.

All my energy that wasn't being blasted from my mouth was focused on keeping my thighs clamped tightly around the extension cord as I gained momentum. I swung towards the railing and thrust out a hand. Still a good two feet of clearance. The subtle slithering noise of the stretching jam was getting louder and louder. I swung again. Still short by a foot. Out of the corner of my eye I saw the jam phallus wagging back and forth to follow my movement like a curious cat.

I swung back and forward again. I felt a couple of my hairs brush the jam, then get yanked out by the root. My scream shot up another octave, and I thrust my arms forward with all the strength I had left.

My hands clamped around the railing. The finger of jam curved over too far and collapsed back into the quivering mass, defeated.

"Is everything all right?" came the girl's voice.

"AAAAAAAAAAAAAAAAAAAAA," I replied.

"Stop screaming!"

"SORRY! I mean, sorry!" I clung in silence for a few seconds, panting and feeling the blood thumping around my head.

"I'll come down and help you," she said, panting. "Hang on."

"Could you be quick please? I think I'd like to pass out for a bit."

DAY 1.3

"Tim!" I called, once I'd been helped back onto something approaching solid ground, and after I'd climbed back up to the third floor, clutching the handrail probably more tightly than necessary. "Tiiim!!"

I was starting to worry when his hand finally appeared above the balcony rail and dragged the rest of him into view. His other hand was clutching his bleeding head. The red smear running down his cheek was the only color in his face.

"Tim," I said. "Before you do anything else, find some cloth and wrap it around your head. Tightly."

"And drink some orange juice," said the girl in the Starbucks uniform, who had introduced herself as Angela.

Tim emerged from the flat a few minutes later shakily clutching a juice carton and with an entire toilet roll secured to his forehead with a dressing gown cord. "I'm all right," he insisted, taking a generous pull. "I'm fine now."

"I'm going to throw the extension cord over again," said Angela. "Tie it to something really sturdy over there. Do you think you can do that for us?"

The toilet roll quivered as Tim nodded rapidly. "Jeff," he said. "You're near Don's place. Go scout it out. We'll meet you there."

"Don?"

"You know. Don Sunderland. Number 38. The place with the rooftop balcony. We can see the whole city from there. Remember? We came to his housewarming?"

I glanced down the walkway at the various apartment doors. I took a few steps towards 38, then stopped and turned back. "Tim, are you sure you're all right now?"

"Yes, Jeff, I'm fine."

"Only my name isn't Jeff; it's Travis—"

"Travis! Yes! I know! I'll be fine!"

I left them to it. I made my way down the hall and around the corner to the door for number 38. I walked slowly to hide the fact that my knees were still trembling, partly from the adrenaline comedown and partly from the recurring shooting pains in my groin. Each time my thighs brushed together I could almost feel the cable still carving a white-hot line across my inner thighs.

I was in the expensive part of the complex, the upper stories with the views of the city, for executives who liked the idea of having an inner-city address but wanted to spend as little time as possible on street level. They were good for entertaining, judging by the loud music that would often drift across the courtyard at three a.m.

I tried the door to 38, but the handle didn't move. Locked.

Don Sunderland would have gone to work, of course. If the jam really had spread across the whole city, he would almost certainly have been eaten. Eaten, like Frank had been. Frank, who was dead. And now Don, who was also dead. Frank and Don. Don and Frank. Dead and dead.

I was testing my emotional state like I'd probe a loose tooth with my tongue, but it wasn't coming out the same way it had done while swinging for dear life. Now everything felt like it was happening on the other side of a thick pane of glass. I wondered if this was one of those coping mechanisms they talked about on TV.

I rattled the handle again but it wasn't going to see things my way. I thought about going back to tell Tim, but I already knew what he'd do, and I didn't want to seem helpless. Experimentally, I took a step back, then threw myself shoulder first at the lock.

The impact shuddered its way through the door and up my arm and rattled around in my pain receptors for a few seconds. The lock hadn't moved. I heaved a sigh. The residents here were clearly paying for good home security.

The hallway here was narrow and didn't offer much of a running start. I had a better idea: I sat down, planted my feet on the door, and braced my back up against the opposite wall. I filled my lungs, clenched my fists, and pushed.

Some of the tendons in my legs were threatening to burst clean out of my body and wriggle off down the hall like angry snakes when I heard the crack of wood and paint and a section of door the size of a tea tray gaped open with a sprinkling of shards. I was quite impressed by the lock, which still hadn't moved, but now I could get my hand through the ragged gap I'd created and unlock it the civilized way.

I stood up and opened the door, remaining in the threshold for a moment to admire my handiwork. I was actually quite impressed with myself. Look at me, I thought. I'm adapting. The first vestiges of civilized society have been smashed aside in the postcrisis world and I'm not even regretting it much.

I stepped into Don Sunderland's living room. The blinds were all closed and the lights were off, but I caught a glimpse of a fastidiously neat lounge/coffee table/television setup before something heavy and wooden smacked across the back of my head and I couldn't see anything for stars.

On the way to the floor I caught a glimpse of a furious Don Sunderland standing behind me in a T-shirt and boxer shorts, clutching a freshly deployed baseball bat.

"Jesus Christ!" he hissed breathlessly, visibly trembling. "Who the hell burgles people at one in the afternoon?!"

I rolled over like a wounded bear, clutching the back of my head. "Duuuoooonnn," I moaned.

"Get up, you piece of scum," he growled. "I want to hit you a few more times."

"Don, it's me!" I scuttled away from him, displaying my hands and trying to look harmless. He looked doubtful. "Travis! From number 30!"

"Travis who?"

"W-we came to your housewarming! Tim, Travis, and Frank! You asked us to leave!"

He stood in silence for a few moments, breathing heavily, the end of the baseball bat bobbing up and down. "Why the hell did you break my door down?"

I was half-lying, half-sitting on the floor, backed up against Don's fridge. "I didn't know you were in!"

"Oh, well! I guess that makes it perfectly acceptable! Sorry to be inconvenient!"

"Haven't you looked outside?!"

"What?!"

"The city's covered in jam!"

There was another thoughtful pause. Then he made a frustrated noise and lowered the bat. "Ugh. Okay. Travis, was it? Concentrate on my voice, Travis. I want you to tell me how much you took."

"I'm not . . . Don, I'm not . . ."

He'd picked up his phone from the kitchen counter and was frowning at the screen. "Christ, there's never a signal when you need one, is there. Stay with me, Travis. Try to stay awake."

I got up and ran. I pushed him aside, knocking him onto his sofa, and made for the stairs to the upper level. I heard him swear behind me, but kept moving. Faced with a number of closed doors, I picked one at random and found myself in an extremely clean bathroom that smelled strongly of lemon.

I doubled back and made for a different door, but Don's baseball bat appeared between my legs and tripped me up.

My body slammed against another door and it gave way. A light, strawberry-scented midday breeze fluttered against my face as I crawled madly out onto Don's roof terrace. He stepped slowly and deliberately out after me, clutching his baseball bat in two white-knuckled hands.

"For christ's sake!" he yelled. "I do not need this bullshit! I've been working all night, I've only had three hours' sleep, I'm having to deal with crazy drug fiends who don't know how doorknobs work, and—"

"LOOK!" I wailed, attempting to point at everything around us.

"—and the city's covered in jam." He tapped his fingers thoughtfully on the bat as the meaning of his own words ran a few laps around his head. "Well, you still broke my door, you little shit."

The view from Don's rooftop terrace had until recently been worth a ridiculous amount of extra rent, but every wasted cent of that was showing in the lines of his face as he stood grimly at the edge, shoulders arched like the entrance to a monster's cave.

The jam stretched all the way to the horizon. Even the distant hills glinted redly in the sun. Most of the suburbs had disappeared, with only the occasional shopping mall and office building rising from the goo. Most of the city center was intact. You could almost convince yourself that everything was normal if it weren't for the lakes of glimmering red interrupting the rows of buildings here and there, marking where the parks had been.

"The city lies stricken by a carnivorous substance of unknown origin," said Angela, next to me. She was scanning the view with a handheld camcorder. "Who could have caused this? And why?"

The street below us was swamped with cars. They were arranged in neat queues, with no weird angles or crashes that might suggest a panic. Some of them had open doors, but that had only given the jam a quicker route to the vehicles' inhabitants.

"Where the hell did it come from?!" asked Don, mainly to himself. "I came in off night shift at six this morning. Everything was fine."

"Look!" said Tim suddenly. He had now redressed his head wound with a mere three or four layers of toilet paper tied around his head with an extension cord. "It ate all the wooden buildings but not the others. What does that tell you?"

He was answered by three silent looks. Two confused, one openly hostile.

"Wood, rubber, cotton, people?" He waved his hands emphatically. "It eats organic matter! That's how it works! I knew it! It must have gorged itself on the surrounding countryside and that's how there's so much of it now!"

Don was looking at him with a mixture of sneering contempt and sneering incredulity. "You're excited, aren't you? You are genuinely happy about this."

Tim looked him square in the eye and wrestled the idiot grin off his face. "Of course I'm not."

"You are! This is a complete disaster, you fool! People have died!"

"Frank died," I added.

"Exactly! Maybe you didn't have enough of a life for it to matter, but this has destroyed everything I've been working towards for years!" His face suddenly fell and he glanced out towards the city. "Oh, shit, the build! We only just started the alpha!"

"Sounds like you still need to accept that civilization is over," said Tim, with shaky confidence.

Don took a step closer to him and extended a single index finger right in front of his nose. "One! Morning! I personally am not prepared to abandon the concept of society after one! Morning! You . . ." He noticed Angela standing nearby. "Will you please stop filming?!"

"I'm documenting," she explained.

"Stop it!"

She frowned, offended. "Look, every time anything historical happens, all anyone complains about afterwards is how it wasn't documented from the start. Trust me; I'm a journalist."

"You don't need to document me shouting!" shouted Don.

"Yeah, Angela," I said, mollifyingly. "There's probably going to be lots of opportunities to do that."

"All right!" yelled Don. "Everyone get the hell off my terrace!"

"But—" began Tim.

"Off!" He was suddenly holding his baseball bat again, and started shoving the three of us towards the door. "Show's over! Idiot tolerance time is now over and idiots must now leave! Get the hell off my property! I want to be alone!"

He slammed the door. The three of us, packed into Don's narrow upstairs hallway, exchanged hurt glances.

Angela's news-reader voice broke the silence. "As you can see, tempers are already flaring in the remaining outposts of humanity. Can civilized society possibly hold together as tensions rise?"

From behind the door, a muffled voice screamed, "I AM NOT! TENSE!"

DAY 2.1

By the next morning, Don had firmly blocked his ruined front door with his fridge. I'd spent the night on the living room couch of his next-door neighbor, and had heard Don pacing up and down his stairs and opening and closing his kitchen cupboards. He probably had a lot to think about.

We'd realized after being hustled out by Don that his balcony presented the only escape route from the complex. There were other apartments with roof terraces, but we didn't know precisely which ones, and the roof access in the main stairwell was locked with a heavy steel door that no amount of leg pushing would shift. We'd spent the rest of the first day methodically breaking into Don's neighbors' apartments, but we'd found no other roof access doors, just a lot of canned and dried food that we'd moved into Don's next-door neighbor's place, or as Tim insisted on calling it, "Settlement Alpha."

We started our operations on the morning of the second day with number 36. Tim took up the barbell he'd found two doors down and rapped the end of it on the front door.

He sighed when there came no reply. "Well, I guess that's confirmed. Don was the only survivor in this part of the complex." He swung the barbell and his sentence was punctuated by the crunch of wood and metal screaming for mercy.

"You'd think there'd be more," I said, dutifully pushing our makeshift cart, a laundry basket strapped to an office chair, into the kitchen.

Tim made straight for the pantry. "You know, I've been

thinking about that," he said, idly inspecting the ingredients list on a box of Choco Choco Choc Blocks. "Don said he came in off night shift at six and the jam wasn't there yet, right?"

"I think that's what he said."

"Yeah. And we all got up at around eleven, right?"

I opened the fridge door. The lukewarm contents looked salvageable until the smell reached my nostrils and my arm reflexively slammed the door shut. "Around then, yeah."

"So, from this we deduce that the jam hit the city at some point between six and eleven in the morning. What does that tell you?"

I fielded a bag of dry pasta. "Er . . ."

He let my *er* drag on for a few seconds before putting me out of my misery. "Rush hour. I don't think we're going to find many more survivors here. Inner city location, near the bus stop . . . Our complex was mainly for business types with city jobs. They would have all been on their way to work. Me and you, and Angela, and Don, we were anomalies. Go and see if you can find any batteries."

"Right." I passed through into the living room.

"Makes sense when you think about it," he said, weighing up some cans. "Anomalies in the gene pool are how evolution works. Whenever there's a big shake-up, the anomalies are the only things left."

"Tim . . ."

"Like the world was a great big Etch A Sketch . . ."

"TIM COME LOOK AT THIS."

He threw his tins aside and jogged to my side. "What?"

I was too petrified to respond, but I was able to bring up an arm and point to the corner of the room.

"A fish tank?" he said. "No, there's . . ." He was probably going to say *there's no water*, but at that point he noticed the same thing I had, and froze.

There, huddled in a thick layer of dirt at the bottom of a large glass tank, partially concealed between some miniature plant life and a piece of hollowed-out log, was the biggest spider either of us had ever seen in our lives. Its legs were as thick as my fingers and the orange-brown body was the size of two generously proportioned scones.

After a tense silence, I heard Tim exhale as he relaxed. "Is that all? It's just a spider."

"You can't say that's *just* a spider," I said, keeping my teeth clenched.

"Anyway, more to the point, it's dead," said Tim, walking with slightly wobbly confidence towards the tank.

"Are you sure?" I asked.

"Of course. There's no one around to feed it, is there?"

"Do you know how long it takes for . . ."

"Look, if it was alive, it would have moved by now." He leant close to the glass and tapped it with a knuckle. The tarantula jumped back, splaying its legs and raising its arse in irritation.

One second later, Tim and I were both trying to squeeze ourselves into the far corner of the room. "Okay," said Tim, his voice now one octave higher. "It's not dead." He took a few deep breaths and stepped towards the tank again. "Great. That's good. This is a really, really good development."

"Yeah, obviously," I said, eyes fixed on the twitching legs.

"We've found another surviving life form," he said. "We have to take it with us. These delicate, early days might define the entire future of the new society. Humanity has to live in harmony with the animals. We should take it with us."

I was still staring fixedly at the thing. "What for?"

"Come on, man, it's a Noah's ark scenario. Every species is precious now. Even the . . . even this one. We might be able to farm them."

"Er . . . again, what for?" I said. "Wool? Milk?"

He scowled at me, hands on hips. "We are tasked with the salvation of the human race. It's going to be very tough and we are going to have to adapt very fast. That starts with not being scared of something that isn't even particularly big if you compare it to, like, a car. So bring it with us."

"Screw you, man. You bring it with us."

"When are you going to start contributing, Travis? I know you've spent the last twenty years being carried by the rest of society, but you are now an entire quarter of the human race and you can't really coast along anymore. It's going to take more than pushing the office chair around."

"Guys?" came Angela's voice. Her camera appeared around the side of the ruined door, closely followed by her face. "Tim and Travis have been scavenging the rest of the apartments for supplies, and I've come down to tell them about Don."

"What about Don?" said Tim.

"He wants to talk to us. He left a note on his door." She produced a piece of printer paper with black tape on the corners, which she held carefully in front of the camera lens. "Says just to show up at any time before twelve or after one so we don't interrupt his lunch."

"Right, well, let's head up now," said Tim.

"I thought you wanted to bring this thing with us?" I said.

"We can't lump the whole tank around; we'll think of something later." He was already out the door.

I stood where I was and eyed the spider. The words *you can't really coast along anymore* were still burning in my ears. I took one last look around at the kitchen cupboards that were hanging open and the word *opportunity* flashed up in my mind like a traffic light. "Hang on," I said. "I'll meet you there in a minute."

—

Don's door was wide open when I arrived at his place. There was no one in the kitchen, but the cupboards were all hanging open and there were a couple of empty ramen noodle wrappers lying around. I headed upstairs to find my three fellow survivors on the roof terrace. Don was standing at the far end. He had arranged three chairs as audience seating.

"Hello, Travis," said Don, in an awkward attempt at a welcoming tone. He seemed rather paler than he'd been four days ago. His hair was uncombed and he was wearing a faded dressing gown. "Please take a seat."

I did so, between Angela and Tim. Don coughed and produced some indexing cards from his pocket.

"Hello," he read. He moved to the next card. "I have had some time to think about the situation. And I've come to the conclusion." He swallowed with revulsion before continuing. "That we should probably stick together if this really has become some bullshit survival scenario. Do you agree?" We nodded mutely. "Right. Then we need to talk about what . . ." his sentence faltered. His head suddenly flicked back to face me. "What the hell is that?"

"It's a tupperware box," I said, jiggling it with my foot.

"What's in it?"

"Breakfast cereal," I said innocently.

Don's eyes narrowed. "What else is in it?"

It was a large, fairly transparent box, so I felt the answer was rather self-evident, but I took the lid off anyway. Don started. Tim made some kind of involuntary strangled noise, and was on the other side of the balcony with his back pressed against the wall before his chair could even finish clattering to the ground.

"Sorry, sorry," he said immediately. "Just . . . caught me off guard."

"Hey, that's a Goliath birdeater, isn't it?" said Angela, dutifully filming as it twitched uncomfortably in the daylight. "They're supposed to be the biggest spiders in the world. Ridiculously violent, too."

Don stood with mouth agape, forearms rotating uncertainly as he contemplated how best to begin his next sentence. "What is wrong with your head?"

"It was Tim's idea," I said. "He said we need to adapt and learn to stop being scared."

"Yes, I did say that, didn't I?" said Tim, looking a bit white.

"Well done, Travis. I see you punched holes in the lid, too. What great initiative. How did you get it in there?"

"Wasn't easy. I had to use a broom and a dead gecko."

"Hey!" cried Don, slapping his hand on the perimeter wall for attention. "Ow! Hey! Decorum! Professionalism! We need to talk about the plan! Travis, throw that horrible thing in the jam before it sucks someone's blood out."

"No!" said Tim.

"It's not dangerous," added Angela. "I saw it on David Attenborough. The bite's no worse than a wasp sting."

"People still avoid wasps," pointed out Don levelly. "They do not put wasps on little leads and take them to the wasp show."

"I'll be responsible for her," I insisted. "This is how I'm contributing."

Don turned around for a moment and threw up his hands, as if appealing for support from the deathly silent city behind him. "Fine. Have the stupid thing. Look after it and if you're very good then next year we'll get you an anaconda or something. Just put the lid back on before it urticates all over someone."

"Yes, we have to keep it safe, at any rate," said Tim firmly, returning to his seat with shoulders squared and a curiously deeper voice. "Every living thing is precious in the new world."

Don, who had been inspecting his cue cards, now threw them to the floor and put a hand to his temple. "Will you at least concede one thing? This is not an apocalypse. This is one city. Not even a particularly nice one. We are not rebuilding civilization. We are waiting for rescue."

"Rescue?" It was Tim's turn for sarcasm.

"Yes, rescue. There are a lot of other nations in the world that offer disaster relief. That's just how politics works; governments fall over themselves to build up goodwill at times like these. Especially when white people are involved. Remember when that volcanic eruption hit New Zealand? They got so many aid packages they had to start feeding them to the sheep. We'll just wait, get picked up by aircraft, and resume our lives somewhere else. I will find another job with another game studio and hopefully never clap eyes on any of you ever again."

"How about you concede that you might be in denial?" said Tim.

"Don't you pop psychology me, you little bastard."

"Well, look at it! It eats organic matter and turns it into more of itself. There's no way to stop it from spreading all the way around the world."

"It's called a gray goo scenario," added Angela.

I glanced down into the street again. "Red goo."

"Oh, okay," said Don, folding his arms. "So what's it going to do when it reaches the ocean, smart guy? Breaststroke?"

"Look, this isn't getting us anywhere," said Angela, swinging her camera left and right to capture Don and Tim's matching contempt. "Wasn't there a plan we needed to talk about? Getting out of the complex?"

"Yes. No!" said Tim. "We search the rest of the complex. We set up a base of operations. We pool our resources. And when we're ready, we mount an expedition to . . ." He swept his arm across the skyline, then suddenly stiffened. Surprise and concern twisted their way around his face before settling around his open mouth. His hand, still gesturing indistinctly, snapped into a definitive point. "What's that?"

I attempted to determine which particular aspect of the sprawling, jam-drowned city he was referring to. "Where?"

"There! The Hibatsu building!"

Rumor had it that the Hibatsu Corporation had set up their headquarters in the center of our central business district because this had been the nearest convenient country that didn't mandate product recalls until people other than the working class started dying. The law was changed after about three years of patient bureaucracy, but the Hibatsu building remained, the tallest building in the city, eighty stories of rented office space raising a permanent middle finger to socialism.

I shielded my eyes against the sun and tried to see what Tim was pointing at. There was something on the side of the building, fluttering in the wind just below the top floor. Something white and rectangular.

"It's a message," said Don. "There must be survivors there."

"Those ba—YOU BASTARDS!" called Tim, cupping his hands around his mouth. "I BAGSIED THAT BUILDING! THAT'S SETTLEMENT BETA!"

"Can't make out the words," said Angela, her camera making zooming noises. "That other building's in the way. We could see it if we were a few roofs over."

"They're going to mess the whole place up! Grow the wrong food! Match the wrong breeding partners!" said Tim, pacing urgently. "That settles it. We've got to get over there."

"Excuse me, children, but could you at least listen to my suggestion, now you've heard the village idiot's?" said Don.

"Okay," I said. "What do you think we should do?"

"Right!" he slapped his hands upon his hips, filled his lungs, hesitated, then emptied them again. "Right. Yes. My plan. I think the first thing we should do is . . . go to the Hibatsu building, and—"

"THAT WAS MY—" went Tim, spinning around.

"MY PLAN IS SENSIBLE," continued Don loudly. "It's the most obvious point in the city. Where do you think a rescue chopper's going to go to first, the survivors in the massive building that's conveniently closest to the sky or my pathetic signal down here?"

"You made a signal?" said Angela.

Don pointed dismissively at the floor. For the first time I noticed that he had emptied the earth out of some flower pots and spread it out into huge letters that ran across the tiles.

"H-E-P-L," I read aloud.

"I got confused, all right? The sun was out. They'll get the idea. More than what you lot did." He glanced up. "Where's he going?"

I turned just in time to see Tim disappearing over the low wall that marked the edge of the terrace. I bolted over and saw him marching determinedly across the roof of Bar 66 like a homeowner on his way to complain at the neighbors.

"Shit," I said. I kicked a leg over the wall, did something distressing to my testicles, readjusted, and lowered myself gently onto the sticky black gravel below.

"Fine! Meeting over! Get the hell out!" called Don, as Angela fed herself after me. "And take your bloody breakfast cereal!" My spider box landed nearby. The occupant turned some impressive gymnastics and escaped harm. I picked her up and lightly patted the lid in a vaguely comforting gesture before holding her out at arm's length again.

"Don't go anywhere," called Angela, after she, too, dropped onto the gravel. "We're just going to look at the message and come right back."

"I don't know why you're still talking to me when I said very clearly that the meeting's over," sniffed Don, wrapping his dressing gown tightly around himself.

Bar 66 was—*had been* was probably more accurate, I corrected myself sadly—a slightly misguided attempt to create the atmosphere of a traditional English pub in a night-club setting, somewhat themed around the Battle of Hastings. It was also on the corner of the block, so any further progress was impeded by the yawning, jammy abyss of McLachlan Street. This was clearly bothering Tim as he stood at the edge of the roof with his foot on the fiberglass arrow that protruded from the eye of neon King Harold.

"Still can't read it," said Angela, filming towards Hibatsu. "Need to get across the road, I think."

Tim started pacing antsily again. "What's the world long-jump record?"

I pointed. "As far as that parking meter, I think." He seemed disheartened. "The triple-jump record might be far enough."

"Doesn't really help, Trav."

"Next roof's lower down," said Angela, energized by the expedition. "Maybe there's a way we could . . . make a glider?"

Tim considered this. "We'd need the right materials. I think number 16 has a wetsuit . . . Oh, hang about." He was looking up thoughtfully. I did likewise, and noticed the telegraph wire running from a nearby pole to the edge of the roof of the convenience store across the way. Tim pulled his belt out of his trouser loops with a single sharp snap of leather.

"This might be a bad idea," I said, as he stepped onto Harold's arrow and threw the belt over the line.

"This is a good idea," he said, through clenched teeth. He wrapped the belt around his fists. "It's a great idea. I'm adapting. I'm doing what has to be done to survive. I have no fear. None."

He jumped.

"OH JESUS MONSTER TRUCK DRIVING CHRIST THIS WAS A TERRIBLE IDEAAAAAAAAAAA," he yelled as the belt screamed its way along the thick cable, tossing his legs around like a mishandled puppet before his final vowel was suddenly cut off as his body slammed heavily into part of the corner shop's upper wall, which happened to contain a window.

As the echoes of the shattering glass gradually tinkled away, Angela and I stood wordlessly exchanging concerned looks for some time before a hatch was thrown open on the shop roof and Tim hauled himself up, exhaustedly waving his arms to get our attention. His hands were severely reddened, from friction burns and blood.

"Are you all right?" I called.

"Can you see the building?" asked Angela.

Tim nodded to answer both questions, then shielded his eyes to peer into the distance. "No good," he said. "Writing's too small. Angela, can you toss your camera over?"

Angela examined her camcorder unhappily, as if contemplating handing her sick hamster to the tactless vet with the big syringe. Then she stared at a section of the jam that was sucking noisily on the windscreen wiper of an abandoned white-topped Mini. She turned to me. "What's the world camera-throwing record?"

"Not far enough. Also there isn't one."

"Oh well." She heaved a deep breath. "Guess it's my go, then." She climbed up onto the arrow and started taking off her belt.

"I don't think this idea has gotten any better," I said, tugging gently at her trouser leg.

"Look, it'll be easier now; the window's broken. And Tim's heavier than me." She tightened her grip, breathed in, and hopped off before I could come up with a reason for her to stop.

One came to mind a moment later. While Angela was almost certainly lighter than Tim—even if Tim became steadily more emaciated with each day he wasn't living with his mum—Tim had been able to distribute that weight, because Tim hadn't been trying to zipline down while filming with one hand.

She almost made it halfway across before she let go. Either the belt slipped from her grasp or she couldn't outlast the pain from the strap tightening around her knuckles. I didn't get a good look because my hands reflexively slapped over my eyes the moment I saw her detach from the wire.

"Ow," I heard her say. Which seemed like an understated response to being stripped down to the marrow, so I let one of my hands slide down my face.

Angela had landed on top of some kind of delivery van that was part of the modest traffic queue that had been forming at the fateful moment of jam strike. She got to her hands and knees and returned her gaze to her camera's viewfinder. "I'm okay. I'm okay," she said, less for our benefit than for that of the tape. "Luckily, my fall was broken by . . ." she knelt by the edge of the van and filmed the logo on the side. "Bumby Graham's Bakery. And if that's not good advertising, I don't know what is."

"Are you all right?" I asked, before deciding it was a fatuous question. "Do you see a way back up?"

"Hey, there's a sunroof here," she said, kneeling by a black square in what she was using as a floor. "Do you want me to take a look inside? If the bread's still good we could add it to the supplies."

"Pragmatism!" cheered Tim from the opposite roof. "Very important quality! Let's do it!"

"Um," I said worriedly, unheard.

She shoved her elbow through the cheap plastic until a large enough gap was formed, then placed her hands either side of the hole and shoved her face in for a look. A moment's utter stillness passed, then she scooted backwards on her arse, her eyeballs now doubled in size.

The back doors of the van were ajar. The interior was flooded with jam. And Angela sticking her face down the sunroof had been like holding a biscuit above a dog's nose. The jam surged upwards in a squarish column and started spreading out across the van's roof as if it were a thick slice of farmhouse multigrain. She backed right up to the edge of the roof and the jam below her in the street slurped in anticipation.

"There's no bread!" she cried, somewhat hysterically. The ever-growing puddle of crimson was dripping unpleasantly off three of the truck's edges and wasn't hesitating to get the fourth under its belt.

"JUMP!" suggested Tim loudly.

Angela opted to act before thinking and threw herself back towards Bar 66. This time I was a little more prepared, and only one of my hands slammed over my face. Through my third and fourth fingers I saw Angela's limbs wrap tightly around the upper portion of a lamppost that protruded from the redness like a buoy. She shuffled around to film the jam as it claimed the van completely.

"Travis!" called Tim. "Can you reach her?"

"What? Oh. Hang on." She couldn't have been more than six feet away from the King Harold sign. I gripped the protruding arrow, placed my feet on his steel shoulders, and leant as far back as I could. Harold's flailing right arm squealed with displeasure and shifted slightly, and the sudden movement sent hot ripples of fear through my limbs.

Angela was stretching her free hand towards me, her camera arm hooked around the pole to capture my petrified face. There was still a foot of clearance. Below us, the jam made a sort of yawning sound.

Suddenly I noticed a television aerial sticking out of a nearby section of Bar 66's roof. In my mind's ear I heard the word *adapting* in Tim's voice, and a momentary thrill went through me as my very own bit of survival improv came to mind.

I leaned forward again, grabbed the end of the aerial, and yanked once, twice, three times before it snapped off its housing. A few components that some technician long ago had probably worked quite hard to install drizzled down and disappeared into the jam with a sound like the soft patter of raindrops on a car roof.

This time, Angela's hand closed around the metal rod. We hung there silently for a few moments, taking comfort in our firm connection, like God and Adam in that one painting. "Okay," she said. "I'm going to let go of the lamppost, now. Ready?"

"Yes. I mean no. Wait!"

"What?"

"Could you . . . hold onto it with both hands this time, please?"

She tutted as if I'd asked her to stop her dog from weeing on my lawn. With some complex twitching of limb and shifting of weight she managed to get the camcorder strap to slide up her arm so she could wear it like an elbow pad, and put both her hands around the aerial. "Okay, here I go." And there she went.

I wasn't prepared. Her weight almost tore the aerial out of my hand, my hand off my arm, and my arm off my shoulder, in that order. I grimaced as the pain tightened about my fingers. Angela was kicking her legs, trying to find a foothold on Bar 66's gaudy logo, and every movement sent another shock wave through my straining arm. The thought of actually trying to pull her up was almost comical.

"Oh my god! Pull me up!" she cried.

"Ha, ha, ha."

"What?!"

"Nothing! Is there anything you can put your weight on?"

She waved her feet towards the building and I felt something click in my arm bones. "Hang on," she said, needlessly. "Yes. Yes! I think if I swing forward I can put my feet on the—"

A loud, metallic CLONK rang out, and I felt myself shift an inch away from the building. Something that sounded important rattled out from behind King Harold and succumbed to the jam.

"—sign," completed Angela, in a heartbreakingly small voice.

The arrow to which my arm was clinging had almost bent into a complete right angle. The flimsy sheet metal was just rated to support a few neon tubes, not two adults hanging from its top half. It was groaning like a wounded rhino.

I shut my eyes and counted the ways I could possibly survive this situation. One. The sign flips in midair and lands between us and the jam, acting as a raft for just long enough to let us jump onto some other, more permanent platform. Two. An enormous superdense object spontaneously materializes next to the planet Earth and gravity shifts ninety degrees.

I came up with three more and was working on a fourth when I realized that the sign wasn't falling. I tentatively opened one eye, then a second.

"You people," hissed Don through gritted teeth, kneeling on the roof of Bar 66 and pulling the sign back with both hands. "If you people were any stupider, you could use the tops of your heads to catch rainwater."

"You saved us, " said Angela, once the three of us were safely back on the roof of the bar.

"Look, don't make a big thing of this," said Don contemptuously. "Don't think I'm starting to like any of you dipshits. I was just watching you all being complete failures from my roof and, well, you know when you're watching your grandma trying to type, and she's so crap and taking so long that you just want to slap her hands away and do it for her?" He slapped Angela's camcorder away from his face to illustrate the point.

"Don?" said Angela wearily, nursing the hit.

"What."

"Thank you very much for saving us."

He folded his arms and sneered. "You're welcome," he said, spitting the words from the corners of his mouth. Then his gaze shifted to the middle distance. "What's wrong with him?"

Tim was still on the roof of the convenience store opposite, standing stock still. His head was tilted back to watch the sky, and he had one hand held to his lips. He seemed to be contemplating something extremely important but hadn't quite made up his mind as to which emotion he was going to respond with.

And now that Don had stopped talking, I could hear it. A tiny, rhythmic thump coming through the thick quilt of silence. Helicopter rotors.

I followed my ears, and saw it. A gray-green dot in the sky to the east, following the river and getting closer and louder by the second.

Unlike Tim, Don had absolutely no uncertainty as to how to react. He immediately ran forward, jumped on top of a ventilation shaft, and began waving his arms like he was giving a semaphore message that had been generated by randomly smashing a keyboard. "HEY!" he yelled, his voice echoing hugely through the dead city. "DOWN HERE!"

"Don't bother!" called Tim from the opposite roof, who was probably feeling left out. "It won't see us from that far!"

"OH, EAT A *GIANT* DICK! HEEEEY!" He hastily pulled off his dressing gown—revealing austere black boxer shorts and a threadbare T-shirt for something called *Mogworld*— and began twirling it frantically around his head. "SURVIVORS! CHARITABLE ACTS! PUBLICITY! THINK OF THE HEADLINES!"

"Holy shit, it's coming towards us," said Angela, zooming in as the helicopter appeared to rotate and the rotor noise grew in volume.

"Yes. YES!" roared Don. He waved his dressing gown with renewed gusto. "I told you there'd be a rescue operation! A whole city can't get jam packed without someone noticing!"

"Hey!" yelled Tim. "Is that thing heading for us?"

"Yes!" shouted Don. The noise from the helicopter was getting loud enough to drown our voices. "GET BACK OVER HERE! YOU IDIOT!"

"SHOULDN'T IT BE SLOWING DOWN?"

Not only was the approaching helicopter not slowing down, but it seemed to be having trouble keeping a straight course. It weaved and bobbed drunkenly back and forth like a fly sizing up the biggest horse carcass it had ever seen. Don gradually ceased flailing and let his gown dangle forlornly from his hand.

I was able to get a very good look because it descended to eye level, narrowly missed ploughing straight into Bar 66, turned awkwardly, and found a spot to hover just in front of Don's roof terrace, pitching and yawing like a set of wind chimes in a breeze. The helicopter was a very large military gunship generously equipped with missiles. The hull was patterned with green camo and the occasional American flag. It was going to try to land, which would have been a tall order for a skilled pilot, let alone whatever drunkard or cretin was in charge of it.

The gunship tilted down too hard and thrust itself forward too fast. Its nose screamed along the terrace floor, tearing up tiles and patio furniture as it went, before the spinning blades ploughed effortlessly through the roof and upper story of Don's apartment like a circular saw through a wedding cake. Pieces of furniture and infrastructure fountained up out of the chaos like the contents of a woodchipper. I glanced at Don. His mouth was agape.

The engine finally stalled and the tail of the helicopter collapsed down onto the terrace, crushing the picnic table. The rotors continued mincing the building's interior for a few seconds before slowing and stopping, whereupon what remained of the ruined roof collapsed and buried any possible entrance to the apartment.

As the noise gradually faded away I became aware of the sound coming out of Don's open-hanging mouth. "—uuuuuuuuuuuuuuuuuuuuuuuuuuck."

The ensuing thoughtful silence was interrupted by a metallic thud, then another, then a twisted, vaguely door-shaped piece of metal detached itself from the wreck and bounced away. A human figure, dressed in black, pushed itself exhaustedly out, landing quite heavily amid the debris on the floor below.

As the figure struggled to its knees and crawled towards the edge of the roof, I saw that it was a woman, wearing slightly skewiff business attire, a pair of headphones, and mirrored aviator sunglasses with one missing lens. She was filthy, and her hair had almost completely come out of its ponytail.

"Excuse me," she said in an American accent, tottering slightly as she approached us. "Would you by any chance know if anyone's organizing a rescue operation?"

Then she fainted.

DAY 2.2

We found another survivor in the wreckage. Or rather, *I* found another survivor in the wreckage. A round of paper-scissors-stone decided that I would be the one to check the gunship for supplies and unexploded fuel. I squeezed my way through the twisted hatchway into the rear compartment and saw him lying unconscious in the cockpit, half in and half out of one of the control seats.

He was a soldier: a well-built man with a crewcut, dressed in urban camo and some kind of armored vest covered in pouches. I grabbed him under the armpits and pulled. It was like dragging a sofa across a thick-pile carpet, but I managed to shift his massive form over to the hatch and push him out with my feet.

"That's all," I said, crawling out after him into the waning daylight. "Doesn't look like there's anything we can . . . What are you doing?"

Don paused in the act of fiddling with the unconscious soldier's belt and stood, turning his nose up with insulted dignity. "I am taking his trousers."

"That's a bit cheeky, isn't it?" said Angela, who was tending to the female survivor by uncertainly dabbing her forehead with a bit of dry cloth and trying to force bottled water into her mouth.

"Oh, it's very easy to occupy the moral high ground when you've got trousers of your own, isn't it?" said Don, worrying the soldier's boots into his trouser legs. He waved a temporarily free hand at the crumpled gunship and pile of impassable debris that now utterly clogged our only way back inside Don's apartment. "Some of us lost access to all our trousers when American military ordnance smashed through their homes. And are starting to feel the cold up here. This is just the start of the reparations, I promise you that."

"I wouldn't hold out hope for those," said Tim, sitting on the vent.

"America's got deep pockets." Don waved the stolen garment. "See?" A moment's thought passed. "How did you get back over here, anyway?"

"Made a harness," said Tim, gesturing to a slinglike device still hanging from the telegraph wire, apparently made from a ThunderCats bedspread.

The unconscious woman suddenly gave a gurgling cough, and a stream of drinking water geysered out of her throat. Angela immediately started patting her about the cheeks, whereupon her patient swatted her away and sat up. "Wblguh?" she began, then revised, "What's going on?"

"You were unconscious. You were in a helicopter crash," cooed Angela reassuringly. "But everything's . . ." She sounded like she was going to finish with the words *all right now*, but thought better of it after a quick glance at the surrounding city.

"The helicopter," recalled the American woman aloud. She looked around, taking in our faces, but didn't seem impressed. "Okay. What's the situation?"

Her voice was stern and official. The rest of us exchanged glances back and forth, none of us confident that we could deliver the kind of answer she was apparently expecting. "There's a lot of jam around," I said eventually. "And a helicopter just crashed."

She frowned at me, confused, like I'd just asked her the

way to the nearest space station. "Which one of you is HEPL?"

"What?!" barked Don.

"We saw your signal," she said. "HEPL. This is a Protocol outpost, isn't it?"

"It was supposed to say *HELP*," said Don. "It was a typo. Or whatever you'd call it."

"A floor-o?" I suggested.

The growing lines of concern on the American woman's face became even deeper. They were the crags of someone realizing they had committed the kind of miscalculation that ends with exploding space shuttles and grim-faced news readers. "So . . . you're not . . ."

"Not what?" prompted Angela, interested.

The woman's hand suddenly flew to her brow and her eyes screwed up in pain. "Aagh! My head! Where am I? What just happened? I must have been raving up to now." She opened one eye to check the dubious faces of those around her, then noticed the unconscious soldier I'd just pulled out. It was like an exposed wire had been touched to the base of her spine. She jumped like a pony out of the gates and started feeling him for a pulse in every conceivable spot. "Can you hear me?!" she yelled. "Please be all right!"

I knelt down beside her as she began slapping at his colorless cheeks. "He hasn't woken up yet. What's his name?"

"His name?" repeated the woman, freezing in midslap as I put her on the spot. "You want to know his name? I, er . . . I don't remember."

"You don't remember," repeated Angela, rather unsympathetically.

The woman clutched her temple. "Ow. Everything's a blank. Just call him . . . X."

"What about you?" said Angela, adjusting her viewfinder.

"I'll be Y. Just call me Y."

"Do you mind if we switch those around?" said Tim, sitting on part of the wreckage with his chin resting on his hand.

"What?"

"Do you mind if you be X and he be Y? That way we can use your chromosomes to remember which is which."

For a moment the female survivor seemed about to burst into tears of confusion, but she took a deep breath and leveled her quivering mouth into something a bit more neutral. "Okay. I'll be X, and he's Y."

Suddenly the man we had recently christened Y moaned loudly and sat up, his heavy form folding like an overstuffed sofa bed. He clutched at his head. It was like watching a coconut getting stuck between two bunches of bananas. "Sir?" he said, in the way a lost child would say, "Mother?"

"Everything's all right, Y!" said X brightly.

". . . Sir?" repeated Y. This was apparently his default setting.

"It's okay, Y. It's me, X!" she continued, not breaking eye contact or blinking. "I was just thanking these four CIVILIANS for pulling us out of the crash!" She emphasized the word *civilians* like a tourist pointing out an aborigine, waggling her eyebrows at him meaningfully.

He glanced around at us, trying to figure out what page everyone else seemed to be on. "What about HEPL?"

"Yes, that was an odd misspelling of *help*, wasn't it?!" said X, speaking even louder and becoming quite manic. "But it's okay! They were just explaining to me that it was a simple typo and is absolutely NOTHING TO DO WITH ANYTHING THEY KNOW ABSOLUTELY NOTHING ABOUT." Her sentence turned suddenly stern towards the end and if she had stared at X any harder his crewcut might have caught fire.

"Ohhhh," went Y, nodding, clearly still baffled but willing to play along. He looked down and noticed his missing trousers, but apparently decided not to mention it.

"What's HEPL?" pressed Angela.

Y was about to speak when X placed a reassuring hand on his chest and looked into Angela's camera lens, then put on a rather emotionless half smile and fluttered her eyelashes. When she spoke, she sounded like someone reading a prepared statement at a press conference. "I have absolutely no idea what you are talking about. I have never heard of any such organization."

"Ooh, you liar!" said Angela.

Tim, who had been yawning and glancing pointedly toward the Hibatsu building throughout the conversation, suddenly clapped his hands together and swung onto his feet. "Is this going to take much longer? We've got important things to get on with."

"Yes, what are you going to do about my house?" said Don petulantly.

X adopted that winning-smile press-conference voice again and directed it Donwards. "We promise you will receive appropriate compensation as soon as we reestablish contact with our base."

"Oh," said Don, nonplussed. "Well. Good."

"I meant, we have to get to Hibatsu," said Tim, tapping his foot.

Don sighed and got to his feet. "Well. Don't suppose we have a choice, do we? Even if we could get back inside, I can't be certain I even own a bed anymore." He glared at Y as the big soldier experimentally poked the mangled helicopter rotors that were still lodged in the remains of Don's apartment. "Of course, I might have about one hundred smaller ones."

—

Having introduced herself and Y from the arse end of the alphabet, X explained their presence rather hurriedly. Apparently the two of them had been on an American aircraft carrier that had arrived as part of the disaster relief effort. The ship had ventured too close to the shore and been ensnared by the jam, which had quickly absorbed most of the crew. X and Y had made an assuredly extremely exciting last-minute escape on a gunship, with no time to enlist an actual helicopter pilot.

Tim clapped his hands impatiently as the story concluded. "Well, now that we're all satisfied . . ."

"I have some questions—" began Angela.

"SATISFIED," pressed Tim. "I think we were all agreed that heading to the Hibatsu building was going to be our next course of action."

"The building with the SOS?" asked X, eagerly running with the change of subject.

"Oh, yes," said Don, folding his arms. "I've been very eager to hear your plan for how we do that, O glorious leader, bearing in mind the few miles of open streets and tall buildings between us and—where's he going?"

Y had already tied Tim's makeshift harness to King Harold's bent arrow with a long length of rope he'd been keeping in one of the pouches in his vest. He grabbed the wire and slipped his naked legs into the bed sheets with a single, smooth hop. Once he'd ridden safely across McLachlan Street like a baby being tenderly delivered by the stork, X wordlessly stepped up and started pulling the harness back with the rope.

"There's something not quite right about those two," muttered Angela once X had slid out of earshot. "He hasn't even mentioned the trousers thing. I think that's very odd."

"Well, no one else bring it up," said Don sharply, snapping his waistband.

"And you know what? I think she knows more than she's telling." She swung her camera around to capture my reaction to her announcement.

"Well, yeah," I said. The camera didn't move. "Er. My goodness. How dishonest of her."

"Listen to me," said Don, hissing over his shoulder as he hauled the harness back up for his turn. "Do not screw this up. I don't care what their real story is. As far as I'm concerned those people are godsends. They're going to be number-one priority for the rescue efforts. That's how it goes. Your own citizens, then children, then white people, then everyone else. All we have to do is stay close and NOT offend them." He glared pointedly at Angela, then quickly at Tim and me.

"They destroyed your home," said Angela.

He sat in the harness, wrapping it around him. "All the more reason to stay chummy. Maybe they'll rebuild it out of something sturdier than polystyrene." Then he pushed himself off the roof and wobbled down the line.

"Or they'll have us killed for knowing too much," posited Angela. "Look at that Y guy. He could probably stand behind us and cough and our necks would just snap."

"Why are you so paranoid?" said Tim. "They're just more numbers. Ergo, more strength."

"You said the jam would have appeared at around rush hour, right?" said Angela, in hushed tones.

"Yeah?"

"Rush hour, when a large percentage of the population would be clustered about at ground level? Seems a bit convenient, doesn't it?"

"That's . . . kind of the opposite of convenient," I said.

She glared at me. "Not convenient for us! Convenient for them."

"Who?"

"Invaders!"

I glanced down into the street, baffled. "In the jam?"

She grabbed me by the ear and pulled until I was facing the camera again. "Think about it. A weapon that instantly removes all the organic matter in a populated area, leaving the buildings and the infrastructure completely intact. No fighting. You don't even have to raise your voice. Just move in and occupy what's left. And lo and behold, a mere . . ." She quickly checked her watch. "Day and a half after the jam, here come the Americans. With their big *rescue*. Trust me. There's something big behind this." She took an excited breath. "And I'm going to find out what."

Tim coughed. "Angela, there are any number of weapons that remove the people and leave the buildings. Biological weapons and that. Jam seems like kind of a messy solution."

"Maybe that's just what they want you to think," she said, staring into the middle distance.

"So once you've gotten to the bottom of the conspiracy and have the evidence you need to bring the perpetrators to justice," said Tim airily, "whom, exactly, are you going to show it to?"

Angela opened her mouth to reply, but that was as far as she got. She held up a hand for silence as she considered the question.

"And how are you going to get it out there?" continued Tim, regardless. "Write it on a paper airplane? Train pigeons to carry your camcorder footage? It doesn't matter how the jam got here. Civilization gets too large, it finds a way to destroy itself. If it hadn't been the jam it would've been nuclear war or corrosive Vegemite. Who cares? All that matters now is how we rebuild."

From the other rooftop, Don made an extremely loud exaggerated cough to get our attention. He tapped his bare wrist meaningfully.

"All right, all right," said Tim, taking up the harness rope. "Who wants to go next?"

"I'll go," I sighed. I stepped towards him, then froze. "Oop. Hang on. Almost forgot Mary."

"Who?" said Tim.

I picked up the tupperware box, whose occupant shifted sleepily with the sudden movement. "Can't just leave her here; we have to preserve whatever life is left," I said, holding the box as close as I could bring myself to. "That's what you said."

I took a step forward and he took a step back. "Fair enough. I'd just . . . I'm not creeped out or anything. I'd just rather you didn't give it a name. Do you know what? I'll go next. See you down there." He hurriedly threw his legs into the harness and was gone.

"Hey," said Angela, tapping my shoulder. "Travis, listen. You agree with me, right? You think it's important to get to the bottom of all this, right? For history and stuff."

I looked away from the unfeeling black gaze of her electronic eye and sighed. I stared at Mary, trying to think of what would be the best thing to say to avoid any kind of conflict. Mary had nothing to offer. "I don't know."

"But you'll help me get the real story out of X and Y?" She peered out from behind the camera to give me the full effect of her puppy-dog eyes. "If the Americans did this on purpose, that's not something we can just let go, is it?"

Tim had reached the corner-shop roof, so I started busily hauling the harness back up to avoid having to look at her. "But why would America invade Australia?" I said. "It doesn't seem like there'd be much strategic value in it. Unless you're really into Antarctic research stations."

Angela frowned as she thought about this. Then she put on her narration voice again. "Could Antarctic research stations really hold the answer to this mystery? My cohorts seem unconvinced. But who can say anything in a world gone mad?"

"Are you really a journalist?" I asked, pausing in the act of climbing into the harness to voice a question that had been lingering for a while.

"Yes!" she said, offended. "This is my duty. This is what I'm going to do. Some people are going to be the scavengers and some people are going to grow the food and I'm going to be the one who chronicles it all. You know, for future generations."

"That's not really answering my question . . ."

"Yes, I am a journalist," she said loudly, before continuing much more quietly. "Studying journalism is more like being a journalist than actually being a journalist. You have to do a lot of theory."

DAY 3.1

We spent the rest of the second day investigating the convenience store. The jam had flooded the shop level, lured in by the promise of sausage rolls and stale donuts, but there was a maisonette on the upper level from which we recovered a small cache of supplies. Among them we found some bedding and sleeping bags, so we made a rather haggard attempt at camp on the roof to spend the night.

I woke the following morning when I felt Tim trying to step over me. He was holding the supply box we had put together the previous night, containing the pittance of food from the shop apartment and the few tools and implements we had been able to recover from Don's place.

"Tim?" I said, sitting up and laying Mary's box aside, which I had been spooning.

He sat near the edge of the roof, put the box down, and silently motioned for me to come over. "Shh," he added.

"What are you doing?" I whispered, perching nearby.

"I'm going to test a theory," he replied, digging around in the box. His hand came out clutching the jar of crunchy peanut butter that had been part of last night's dinner, along with half a bottle of ketchup and a pack of lemon-and-honey throat lozenges.

I placed a hand to my chin as he carefully opened the jar, shook a generous blob of the stuff into the lid, then held the lid upside down over the street. He watched intently as it tumbled down onto the jam, where it was almost immediately absorbed.

"Hm," he said, stroking his five o'clock shadow like a research scientist.

"What the hell are you doing?" said Don, suddenly revealing himself to be awake and watching intently from his pillow.

"I thought there might be some reaction," said Tim weakly.

"Would that be because you're an absolute cretin?"

"You know. Peanut butter and jam. I thought they might cancel each other out."

"You don't think that's a bit irrational?" I said.

Tim was slightly offended. "Will you look around? The city is being devoured by strawberry preserve. Rationality left us behind a long time ago."

"That's not a good reason to start throwing our extremely limited food supplies to the jam," said Don, snatching the peanut butter. "It's people like you who started cutting hearts out to make the sun rise in the morning. You shouldn't do this sort of thing when X and Y are around; it makes you look expendable."

A moment's silence passed as something slowly dawned on us, one after the other.

"Where're X and Y?" said Don, as the realization reached him.

"I knew it!" shrieked Angela, throwing her quilt aside and hopping instantaneously from a lying to a standing position. Her camcorder was already strapped to her hand, or she hadn't taken it off to sleep. "I knew they were up to something! See if anything's missing! Check your skin for puncture marks! They may have implanted microchips!"

"The harness is gone," I said, checking the wire.

"They're trying to strand us!" yelled Angela, without even taking a breath. "Before we can tell the world!"

"They're over there," said Tim.

"And now they're over there!" added Angela uncertainly.

I scanned the jammy horizon, and now that I knew what to look for, I spotted a blob of brightly colored ThunderCats-themed pattern a few rooftops away, on top of the clothes shop at the junction of Brunswick and Ann. X and Y were at the edge, looking down into the street. At some point during the night Y had taken down the ThunderCats bedspread and expertly cut and stitched it into a pair of pajama trousers.

"That's a bit passive-aggressive of him," I said, as we hurriedly gathered up the bedding and supplies.

"I don't care," said Don, trying to stuff his rolled-up sleeping bag into a canvas wrapper obviously far too small for the purpose. "I'm not giving these trousers up until he specifically says something. It's cold up here."

We started moving along Brunswick Street towards X and Y. The roofs were basically the same height until we reached the last building on which they stood, which was slightly higher, but there were a couple of outcrops and ledges to aid climbing. Compared to how rooftop navigating had gone so far, the trek was almost restful.

Y was standing at the far end of the roof, arms folded and gaze fixed upon the horizon as if daring the rising sun to say something about his trousers. X was sitting at the edge running along Ann Street with one leg dangling off, examining the building opposite, a bar that had been converted from an old bank. It was the nature of the district that any building older than fifty years was either promptly torn down or remodeled into an ironic drinking establishment.

". . . estimate the swarm has receded by between ten and fifteen inches since dawn," we heard X say as we entered earshot.

"What swarm?" said Tim, by way of greeting.

It was a remarkable effect. All Y had to do was turn to face us and the entire dynamic of the scene changed, because suddenly he had the air of a nightclub bouncer. Behind him, X sat frozen for a few seconds before suddenly looking around with what she probably hoped looked like a neutral expression. "Good morning. I trust you all slept well."

"What are you doing?" said Tim.

"Reconnaissance," said Y.

"Just getting some air," said X, simultaneously. She jumped to her feet and got between us and Y before he could say anything else. "And we just stopped here to check on the, er, the substance."

"The jam," said Tim.

The bar was on Ann Street, near the entrance of the mall. The market stalls stood silently choked with jam, their cheerful displays torn apart by its relentless pursuit of fruit, vegetables, and Vietnamese fighting fish in little plastic bags.

"Well, since we're all up we should start making some distance," said Don, jerking a thumb and half-turning in an attempt to spur the rest of the group into following, but Angela and X had now locked gazes—or at least, X had locked gazes with Angela's camera lens—and neither moved.

"You called it a *swarm*," said Angela.

"I . . . don't think I did," said X.

"You so did! You all heard it!" She looked at me.

"You said it was receding," interjected Tim.

"Did I?" said X weakly, but we were already clustering around the edge to see for ourselves.

"Oh, for christ's sake!" complained Angela, throwing up her hands. "Why is no one else calling her out on this?!"

Don, Tim, and I weren't calling her out because we were leaning over to peer at the bottom of the wall opposite. Sure enough, the jam was only coming about half a meter up, with a band of highly polished concrete on the wall above it to mark the previous level.

"It was definitely deeper before," I said.

"Maybe it's pissing off," said Don. "Could it really just go away by itself?"

"That would make sense, if it's some kind of engineered antipersonnel weapon," said Angela huffily. "You'd program it to go away after a while so you could move your troops in. Then you could do whatever you want. You could even go to *Antarctica*." She watched X's reaction intently, but X didn't appear to be listening.

"I wouldn't get your hopes up," said Tim.

"Why not?" challenged Don. "There was a lot of jam, and now there's less of it. I'm calling that a step in the right direction."

Tim snorted.

"Yep, the jam could be all gone by the end of the day," said Don, looking pleased. "They'll be able to rescue everyone on a great big bus."

"You're only setting yourself up for disappointment."

"Aw, what's the matter? You upset because you might not get to start your new society?"

"No!"

"Never mind; maybe you could set yourself up in a nice treehouse and play The Floor Is Lava all day."

X didn't seem to share Don's optimism. She and Y were having an urgent, wordless conversation, backing and forthing a series of facial expressions ranging from concern to confusion to muted terror, punctuated by occasional worried looks at the jam, which continued to burble and fart to itself obliviously.

Following their gazes, I noticed for the first time that the queues of abandoned traffic were becoming arranged more and more oddly the closer we moved to the city center. They weren't in the neat rows we'd seen before. They were scattered and at strange angles, as if something big had swept through and shoved them out of the way. I turned to look northeast down Ann Street, away from the city center, and that's when I saw the boat.

"Is that a boat?" said Tim.

"Don't change the subject," replied Don. "Yes, it's a boat."

It was quite a big boat with big sails, and quite expensive looking. It was painted uniformly white, except for the name *Everlong* written in neat, serifed black letters along the side.

The *Everlong* was floating freely in the middle of a ring formed by the shifted traffic—*floating* being the most intriguing aspect of its description. There was no trace of red goo in the interior and it didn't look like the keel was having any difficulty gliding across the stuff, judging by the brief, strangled snatches of car alarms as it slowly bumped into partially submerged vehicles.

"How'd that get there?" I asked, voicing everyone's mutual thought.

"Maybe it was on the river," thought Angela aloud.

"No one sails on the river," said Don. "It's full of public ferries and condoms. It'd be from the marina if anywhere."

"Who cares? It'd help us pick up speed," said Tim, moving to the northeast corner of our current perch. "Look. We climb down onto the next building, drop onto the overhang, jump off that SUV there, then right into the thing. Sail it straight up Ann to the central business district. Couldn't be more perfect."

"You can't," said X suddenly. Everyone turned to look at her and her shoulders immediately hunched up with regret for her hasty statement.

"And why not?" said Angela, with the wheedling voice of a prosecuting counsel.

"Because. It . . . doesn't belong to us."

Don allowed the silence to go on for a few seconds so that everyone could drink it in. "Erm," he began. "Where exactly was this respect for property when you were landing your helicopter yesterday?"

X moved subtly closer to Y in the way she always did under pressure. "We just strongly feel that . . . employing the boat would not be an ideal course of action."

"You so know something about the jam!" barked Angela, camera quivering. "Just admit it! What do you want this country for? Is it the opals?!"

"Hey!" said Don suddenly. "Hey hey hey hey! Who's that?"

He was pointing across the street. On the roof of the former bank was a small cluster of shapes, silhouetted against the morning sun. I shielded my eyes, and it became abundantly clear that they were people. Two men. They were obscured by shadow, but I could tell that the slightly bulkier of the pair was wearing a baseball cap, which I've never found to be a good first impression. He was also holding something indistinct but vaguely weaponlike in both hands, which was even worse.

Tim raised his arm to shout a greeting, to welcome some new additions to the eventual gene pool of his new society, but thought better of it. The strangers had probably been watching us since we'd arrived, and hadn't made any effort to draw attention to themselves. That was not the behavior of stalwart fellow survivors looking for friends—more like vultures perched on the rocks above a dying explorer.

The peak of the larger man's baseball cap was rotating nervously back and forth, towards us, then the *Everlong*, then back to us. As he scrutinized our party, it became clear that the same two thoughts were going through every head present. Firstly, that a jam-proof sailboat would be an unmixed benefit, and secondly, that eight would be a need-lessly large crew.

As the delicate politics of the situation settled on our shoul-ders, we all stood in silence, gazing at each other from across the chasm of the street, wordlessly trying to ascertain each other's character, wondering who was going to make the first move.

Then Tim and the man in the baseball cap both broke into a run.

Baseball Cap Man's route took him across a few progres-sively lower roofs, then down a covered balcony; then a hop, skip, and a jump over two vans and a postbox and he'd be in the boat. Tim, meanwhile, first had to contend with a rather savage drop onto the next building.

He landed with an uncertain roll and rose up into an awkward limp. Baseball Cap was already level with the *Everlong*, and it was clear now that even a direction as straightforward as "drop down onto the overhang" acquires no end of complications the longer one looks at it, especially with an already complaining ankle.

Pausing the slightest moment to think—a moment that would probably have gone on much longer if he'd been thinking clearly—Tim opted to dangle down from the roof as far as he could, then let go.

I could tell the awning was slightly lower and harder than Tim had been anticipating. He slammed onto it back first like a wrestler being thrown onto canvas, bounced towards the edge, and realized just an instant too late that the SUV he'd pointed out was nowhere near close enough for him to reach. The jam flexed in delighted surprise.

He corrected himself in midair, flailing his arms and legs, and managed to grab the overhang again. The corner slammed into his chest and knocked the wind out of him, but two of his arms and one of his legs found purchase, and he ended up clinging to the top like a quivering limpet.

Then there was a thump, and the man in the baseball cap bounced off the *Everlong*'s extended mainsail and fell back onto the small deck like a sack of potatoes. "Ha!" he exclaimed, holding up two victory signs. "Safe!" Now he was out of silhouette, I could see he was a short man in early middle age, with the kind of deep tan and muscular build that comes from a lifetime working on building sites and beating wives. The indistinct weapon he had been holding throughout was now quite distinctly identifiable as a crossbow, a sporting model with a cold efficiency to its design. He pulled himself to his feet and gestured to his friend on the opposite roof. "Toby! Get down here!"

By then Tim had managed to climb fully onto the bus shelter and was now standing upright, clutching his side. He moved uncertainly towards the boat, but its new occupant hefted the crossbow and aimed it directly at Tim's stomach.

"Don't think so, mate," he said menacingly.

"Don't be stupid!" called Don from the rooftops. "There's six of us and two of you!"

"Well, why don't you all come down and try it, then?" said Baseball Cap, nervously shaking the point of his crossbow in Don's general direction. "I've got enough bolts for everyone. Toby! Hurry up!" Toby, a pudgy teenager, was still struggling his way down the first two rooftops.

"Look, we can work something out," said Tim in a reassuring if rather winded voice. "There aren't many of us left in the city. We need to be able to trust each other."

"All right then," said Baseball Cap agreeably. "Toss over all your supplies."

"Oh my god, he is doomed," whispered Angela to me, keeping her camera on the scene.

"Sod off!" said Don.

"Be serious," said Tim, the diplomat.

I heard X make a sharp intake of breath, and turned to see her looking concernedly down the street with her hands over her mouth. I followed her gaze and didn't see anything unusual—besides all the jam, of course—but I could hear a low rumble, just on the edge of earshot.

"I'm totally serious," said Baseball Cap, breathing heavily down his sight. "Trust starts with you. Anyone wants to ride, it'll cost you food. Or blankets. The chicks can get in free."

Then I noticed something odd about the view to the south. The jam still stretched to the horizon, but the horizon seemed to be higher up than it had been a moment ago. The rumble was becoming a roar. Like the roar of the ocean, but . . . slower.

"TIM!" I yelled, leaning forward as several of my thoughts suddenly came together. "GET TO HIGHER GROUND!"

He took one look at the misbehaving horizon and immediately threw himself at a nearby lamppost. A tidal wave of jam was rolling its way up Ann towards the city center. It was a merciless fifteen-foot steamroller of God and it was coming fast, shoving cars aside in its wake like an ocean liner cutting through the foam.

The man in the baseball cap was concentrating on keeping his crossbow trained on Tim, and by the time he noticed the incoming red wall he was far beyond saving. The boat stayed upright as the massive wave passed by underneath, carrying it another fifty yards down the street, but the jolt threw the man right off the deck and into the jam. Moments later a polished skeleton broke surface, its dissolving arm bones waving in desperate greeting as the wave swept it along.

The rumble gradually faded into silence as the wave left us behind, continuing into the city. The jam in the street was back to its original depth, and the cars and buildings had the glimmering sheen of a recent polish. Tim clung like a sloth to the very top of his sparkling-clean lamppost, which had just barely escaped submersion.

"Uh," said the boy on the opposite rooftop who had answered to Toby. "Boat's all yours." Then he ran.

"Oh no, after you," yelled Don after him. "We insist!"

The *Everlong* had been pushed right up to the junction of Ann and Brunswick by the wave, and we could now climb down the side of the clothes shop and drop in at our convenience, which was something Tim apparently still wanted to do, once he was back with us and had stopped hyperventilating.

"Hey," said Don. "Gamble with your own life all you like. I insist. But don't start adding us to the pot."

"There will be more ripples," warned X.

"How do you know?" said Angela instantly.

"I said, there *may* be more ripples," corrected X.

Angela appealed to Don and me, waving her free hand as if prompting. "Am I the only one who notices when she does that?!"

"It didn't capsize," said Tim. "Not then, and presumably not after however many waves there've been since this all started."

"That guy died," I said.

"We'd be fine if we were below decks. We know what to look for before a wave, now. That douche only died because he was taken by surprise."

"About that," said Don. "I want to point out that we just watched a fellow human being die. I want it noted that I'm a little bit freaked out. Especially by how we're all taking it in our stride at this point."

"You want to hold a requiem mass or something?" said Tim, clearly impatient. "Let's go."

Debate concluded, Tim and Don climbed down, followed by Angela, sliding one handed down a drainpipe. As I lowered myself onto the first window ledge I saw that X and Y weren't following. They were standing stiffly a few yards back from the edge of the roof as if suddenly acrophobic. Y was back in his folded-arms nightclub bouncer stance.

"Are you coming?" I asked.

X put on her diplomatic smile and shook her head a little too fast. "It's our opinion that six is too many for a boat of that size. We'll make our own way and rendezvous with you at the Hibatsu building."

I glanced towards the city. Ann Street ran straight to the central business district and there were plenty of islands and telegraph wires all the way. And they were probably right; the *Everlong* would be crowded enough with four. All in all her reasons were perfectly valid. But she was looking at me like a schoolgirl silently praying that her teacher would believe her hastily fabricated excuse for absence.

"If you want," I said, carefully stepping down onto a window ledge, tupperware box balanced on my shoulder. I resolved not to worry about it, but Mary was watching X and Y carefully, legs tensed with suspicion.

Tim was already on the overhang, clinging to another convenient lamppost and testing the *Everlong* with one foot. The jam seemed to actively repel whatever it wasn't interested in eating, and the fiberglass keel was bobbing on the surface like a weight on a stretched rubber sheet. Tim sucked in a deep breath and stepped onto the deck. Don counted to ten, then, seeing Tim was still alive, joined him.

"There you go," said Tim, crouching by the hatch that led below decks. "Big heavy trapdoor. Good seal. Should be safe."

"Where're X and Y?" said Don.

"Er," I said, accurately predicting his response at the very moment I opened my mouth. "They're making their own way. They'll meet us there."

"What did you say?" said Don in a low voice.

"I—"

"I heard what you said; I was being aghast. You just let them *go*?!"

"Don't yell at me," I requested, staring at my hands. "What was I supposed to do?"

"They could be doing anything!" said Angela, shoving me in the shoulder. "They're probably giving away our position right now!" She immediately started scanning the sky for stealth bombers.

"Look, it's not that big a boat," I protested. "They said they'd meet us at Hibatsu. There's no reason they wouldn't go there."

Don strode over and started jabbing his fingertips into my forehead to punctuate his words. "But what! If! They! Get picked up while we're not around! Genius! You think they're gonna say, 'Oh no, we'd better remain in mortal danger for a bit longer while that random group of thick survivors catches up!'?"

"Who'd want to leave us behind?" said Tim jovially, patting the *Everlong*'s mast. "We've got a boat! We're officially the new ruling class!"

Don loudly smacked himself full in the face with his palm. "Why is every survivor in this city an idiot or an arsehole?"

"The whole working population got wiped out at rush hour," suggested Tim. "Most of the people left would be whoever was still in bed. Students, the unemployed . . ."

"You mean slackers," said Don.

"Not all . . ."

"But mostly. Christ, it probably was deliberate, wasn't it? It's a really smart strategy. Don't kill every single person, just all the useful ones. Leave all the awkward spods to wipe themselves out." He stared into the middle distance. "The geek shall inherit the earth."

"Agh! Damn!" Angela aimed her lens at him and twiddled with the settings. "Could you do another take of that? I wasn't in focus."

DAY 3.2

Don's statement proved prescient, since it soon became clear that none of us knew the slightest thing about sailing. I could just about hazard that the sail should ideally be at right angles to the wind, but that was as far as my expertise went. Fortunately the sail was already unfurled and I found some poles with hooks on the end, so we used them to push away from the corner of Ann and Brunswick and shove the sail around until it caught a bit of breeze.

This meant there constantly had to be one of us keeping the sail in line and one of us holding the rudder, or whatever it was called. These roles went to me and Tim respectively for the first shift while Don and Angela explored below deck.

The wind was light and progress was slow. Once we passed the barren jam lake where the park on Centenary Place used to be and moved further along Ann into the city center, the buildings grew taller and taller and the mood grew bleaker and bleaker as we navigated between the silent, looming walls of concrete and black glass. We hadn't seen any other human beings since leaving X and Y behind. The rooftops were high out of sight, and if there were survivors inside they weren't rushing to say hello.

Tim had been sitting in silence with his hand on the what-ever-it's-called, foot tapping nervously. I'd been feeling rather depressed after being admonished by Don, but after an hour or two of silence I felt moved to start some kind of conversation. "Wonder where everyone is."

"This is where people used to work, not live," he theorized aloud, staring at the buildings. "Not many people come to work before rush hour. Except weirdoes." He looked at me uneasily. "How's the spider?"

Mary's box was sitting on my thigh. I patted it reassuringly. "She's doing all right."

Tim nodded, then frowned to himself. "It's funny that you instantly assumed it was female. I think that says a lot about you."

The deck hatch thudded open and Don climbed into the daylight, gave us one glance of acknowledgement each, and took up position at the frontmost part of the deck, inspecting the encroaching city. A few seconds later Angela emerged.

"Wow, it's really nice down there," she said, probably more to her camera than anyone else. "There's three beds and a kitchen and everything. And a shower. And a freezer like you wouldn't believe. Might even work if we could find the generator."

"Have we passed Creek Street?" said Don suddenly, spinning around with the force of an important realization slamming into his forebrain.

"It'll be coming up soon," I said.

"We have to take a quick detour," he said. "I need to stop in my office on Creek Street."

He immediately turned around and folded his arms before anyone could ask the obvious question, which Tim voiced, undeterred. "Why?"

Don hung his head and hissed a sigh through his teeth. He turned around and looked him square in the eye, prepared to wade into another argument. "I'm going to pick up the build for my current project."

Tim went straight for it. "Are you still holding out hope for the rest of the world?"

"Yes, I'm prepared to assume that the few square miles of jam we've seen do not imply an extinction-level event. You're the one holding out hope. You just can't bear the thought of this not being a proper apocalypse because you'd have to go back to being pointless."

"We can't waste any time," said Tim calmly, determined to be the better man. "Our supplies are low and there might still be people waiting for rescue."

"Some of us are thinking about the future!" barked Don, building up a decent rant speed. "You can't just dig your way out of the cell block and hope everything will turn out for the best! You're going to end up wandering around the nearest town in a stripy prison uniform!"

"What are you on about, Don?" said Angela.

"That build is my entire career!" screeched Don. "You can't do this to me! I'll sue you!"

"How about a vote?" said Tim, looking to me and Angela. "Who thinks we should follow Don's stupid plan to get his thing no one cares about? Show of hands?"

"Don't word it like that!" yelled Don as our arms failed to extend upwards. "You're loading the question!"

"Don, just let it go," said Angela, bored.

Don grunted with frustration and slammed his fist against the handrail. Then he sat in the corner and hugged his knees to sulk and rub his injured knuckles.

"Any luck with the phone signals?" asked Angela.

"Nothing," I said, checking my phone for the umpteenth time.

"Hmm," said Angela with mock thoughtfulness, apparently unsurprised. "That seems strange, doesn't it? No signals even in the city? It's almost as if something's deliberately trying to prevent—"

"Well, I've got nothing because the battery ran out," I admitted, shaking the device. "I was playing *Joogie Bounce*. Sorry. Tim, did you ever get through to your mum?"

"Haven't tried," he said, quickly and with no emotion. "How are we for supplies?"

"Aren't you worried about her?" asked Angela, echoing my own concern. I liked Tim's mum. I was fairly certain I was her favorite friend of Tim's and she could always be relied upon for an ice pop whenever I came around.

"Of course I am," he said. "You worried about your folks?"

"They're all in Toowoomba," said Angela. "So far we only know Brisbane's gone. I'm keeping the worrying sensible."

"Supplies?" said Tim, very deliberately moving on.

"Oh yeah!" said Angela, suddenly pleased. "Check this out." She ducked under the deck hatch for a second and returned with armfuls of sealed cans of food. "There's a chest freezer in the kitchen full of 'em."

"Great," said Tim, with questionable sincerity. "Did you find any fruit? Vegetables? Anything with seeds?"

"Nope, just loads of cans," said Angela, enthusiasm fading. "They're full. And sealed. It's all edible."

"Yeah, it'll keep us going for now," said Tim. "But we really need to think about what we're going to cultivate once we get to the settlement." I heard Don make a little scoffing noise.

"What's in them?" I asked.

Angela met my gaze hotly and I felt myself flinch. "I don't know," she said, with even temper. "None of them have labels. It's like a lucky dip. It'll be fun."

"Hey," I said, having trouble keeping up as thought after thought trundled through my head. "If survivors were stock-piling food in this boat, why would they abandon it?"

"Maybe they forgot to tie it up and it drifted off!" snapped Angela. "Could you please stop asking stupid questions?"

"I've got one more," I said.

She sighed tolerantly. "Well?"

"How are we going to open them?"

Angela looked at me, then at the cans in her arms, then at Tim and Don, both of whom were deliberately taking a marked interest in something other than her. Then she dropped the cans and stormed back down the hatch as they clonked about the deck.

"Is there a can opener or a knife or something down there?" I called. The hatch slammed shut.

"Guess not," said Tim. "Hm." His eyes rolled this way and that as he put his mind to the issue. "Maybe they'd open if we whacked them with a shoe a whole bunch of times."

I didn't answer. Not verbally, anyway.

"Well, I don't know, do I?" he said. "I'm not big on technical details. I'm more of a big-picture guy."

"I know where to get a can opener," said Don levelly, suddenly lifting his chin from its resting place on his knees.

"Where?" said Tim.

"There's one in the kitchen at my office."

Tim considered his next statement like a chess player who had just noticed an incoming checkmate. "There are quite a few places where we could potentially find a can opener," he said, finally.

"Yes, but not all of them are just around the corner. And familiar territory." He patted his dressing-gown pocket as if laying down his winning move. "And buildings which I have the keys for."

"Er, why do you have your keys?" I asked. "You're not wearing your own trousers."

He scowled at me, getting to his feet. "Look, I know I'm not the only person who keeps their spare keys in their dressing gown. It's in case I get locked out when I'm collecting the mail. It's perfectly rational. It doesn't make me neurotic."

"I didn't say it made you neuro—"
"I know! I'm just saying it doesn't!"

DAY 3.3

We took a rather inexpert and bumpy hard right at Creek Street and eventually managed to park diagonally in front of Don's work building. Well, not so much "park" as "allow the boat to slowly drift into a wall."

Creek Street was in Spring Hill, the area in the central business district where all the technology companies based themselves. Don's workplace was in the tall brown office building that dominated the corner of Creek and Ann, but he'd made us turn into Creek Street to park at the rear entrance. The door was wide open and the small antechamber within was flooded with jam. But Don's interest seemed to be on the rather pleasant little second-floor terrace just above, which seemed to be clear.

With the *Everlong* right up against the building, Don was able to jump straight up from the prow and grab the guardrail, but then his upper-body strength failed him, so I helped push his legs upwards until he could climb in.

"Travis, maybe you should go with him," said Tim. He gave me a look that was apparently supposed to mean something to me.

"Whatever," said Don, looking down on us grandly like a dictator speaking to the masses. "There might be some supplies he can carry."

Accepting that I had been volunteered, I was on the prow and crouched and ready to jump when Tim put an urgent hand on my shoulder.

"Keep an eye on him," he said quietly.

"What for?"

"The more he clings to hope that someone's going to rescue us, the more tetchy he gets."

"Really?" I rubbed the lump on the back of my head. "I think he's been pretty consistent as far as tetchiness goes . . ."

"Just be aware that he could crack at any moment. Try to bring him down if he starts, you know, shouting, stabbing things, stuff like that."

"Will you look after Mary?"

He glanced at the tupperware box on the deck of the boat for a second and took what sounded like a deep breath before replying. "Yes. See, it's right over there."

Somewhat satisfied, I pushed myself up into the air as hard as I could and grabbed the ledge, whereupon Tim pushed my feet up a little too enthusiastically. My chin and the palms of my hands hit the balcony floor a little too fast, scattering paper cups and cigarette ends. I rose to my knees and saw Don fiddling with the lock on a glass entry door.

"Hung urn," he said, his cheek flattened against the glass. "It lurcks from insurd but thurr's a wuy you curn—"

"We could just smash it in," I pointed out.

He turned to glare at me over his shoulder. "You do not know what the caretaker of this place is like. He gobbed on a potted plant once and I swear I heard it fizzle. Ah, there we go." The door opened outwards, and he patiently held it open as I passed through. "You're welcome." He swiftly overtook me and led the way. "Our studio's just around the corner. Try not to scuff the walls; they stain."

"Er, Don," I said, remembering Tim's words. "How are you feeling?"

"I'm fine," he said automatically, before pausing in midstride for a moment. "Actually, no, I'm not fine. I'm homeless, everyone I know is dead, the Internet isn't working, and I will be eaten if I ever touch the ground. But under the circumstances I think I'm holding up pretty well. Do I even want to know why you ask?"

"It's just . . . Tim said—"

"I wouldn't pay much attention to what Tim says," he interrupted archly. "I don't think Tim is entirely on speaking terms with Mr. Reality right now."

"How do you mean?"

A tinted glass wall with a set of double doors divided the hallway from the reception area of Don's studio. The glass was etched with a rather disquieting close-up of a fantasy barbarian's groin and the words *Loincloth Studio Australia*. Don started fumbling through his keys for the right one. "There is a certain kind of failure, Travis," he said, "who thinks they're looking forward to the apocalypse. They lead empty, sad little lives but refuse to take responsibility. They tell themselves they were just born in the wrong time. So they think a complete breakdown of society will solve all their problems." He jammed a key savagely into the lock. "And once Tim realizes he hasn't gotten any less useless, I wouldn't be surprised if he crack—"

As he tried to turn the handle and the key at the same time, the entire locking mechanism tumbled away in his hands, along with a few shards of glass. The door fell open inwards with an eerie creak.

"Someone's broken in," he muttered.

"Looters?"

Don didn't reply. He turned around and walked purposefully back down the hall and around the corner. While I was wondering if he was expecting me to follow or not, I heard another tinkling of broken glass, and he returned carrying a two-handed fire ax.

I stood out of his way as he stalked quietly into reception, then followed behind him without a word. It occurred to me that he had known exactly where to find the ax, as if he'd spent a lot of time thinking about scenarios that involved him storming into his office wielding a large-bladed weapon.

The reception area didn't show any signs of looting. The desk was undisturbed, even to the tupperware lunchbox full of rotting lasagna. The leather sofas were still in place. A snack machine and an arcade cabinet stood like unbroken monoliths. And no sound could be heard coming from the two narrow hallways either side of the desk that led to the rest of the studio.

Don needlessly put up one hand for silence, twisting the ax head nervously in his other. "Stay here," he hissed from the corner of his mouth. "I'll take a look around."

"Righto," I whispered back. He disappeared into the offices.

I passed ten minutes sitting on one of the leather sofas, fidgeting with my thumbs. After recrossing my legs for the fifteenth time I thought about going to find him, but I didn't want to be in the way, and he had an ax. Then I thought about going back to Tim and Angela to ask for advice, but I hated to give the impression I couldn't make decisions on my own. Frank had accused me of that a few months ago, right after he told me to stop calling him at work every time the doorbell rang.

Idly I stood up and stepped over to the snack machine, taking a closer look at the contents. It was one of those automat-style machines, with each item in a separate compartment, and I noticed that one of the compartments contained an apple. Five days in an unrefrigerated lobby had taken its toll, but it was fruit, the very thing Tim had said we needed most.

Yes, I realized. This was me being decisive. The other snacks could be added to our short-term food supplies, but the apple could be the foundation of the new society's barter economy. We'd have an orchard on the roof of Hibatsu and maybe he'd name it after me.

All I had to do was get inside the machine. I tapped a few of the buttons, but without power all they produced was a tinny rattling. Then I kneeled, pushed open the output flap and tried to get my arm up into the machine, but that was even less successful, and after suddenly recalling a gory health and safety video I was once shown while doing temp work at a manufacturing plant, I withdrew as fast as I could.

I looked around for a solution, and found myself staring at the full-sized plastic warrior that stood in frozen battle pose in the corner of the waiting area. Specifically his sword, which appeared to be real—or at least genuine metal, since I doubted any *real* sword would ever have a foot-wide curvy blade carved with skulls.

I removed it from his unresisting hands and immediately confirmed my theory by the way my knees started trembling every time I tried to lift it off the floor. I dragged it across the room, doing irreparable damage to the carpet, and hesitated when I reached the machine. I wondered if it wouldn't be a good idea to go and find Don, after all, and ask if this was all right. But then I remembered something else Frank had said: "Better to seek forgiveness than permission." Those had been his exact words before he slammed the phone down.

I stood to the side of the machine, shifted my grip, and took a few deep breaths. Momentum would probably do most of the work on this one. I took one more deep breath, then spun on my heel and yanked the sword through the air.

For an instant the room blurred past in a horizontal smear, then the impact shook the pommel out of my hands and I

continued spinning for half a turn before getting hurled into
the floor. A massive, splintering crack rang out and echoed
through the halls. The sword bounced off and skidded into
the room. Various pieces of broken plexiglass trickled from
the front of the machine.

Once I was back on my feet and the room had stopped
swaying I stepped back over and peered into the hole,
impressed with myself. I reached in, mindful of shards, and
carefully worried the apple out.

"What was that?" came a voice. A voice that didn't belong
to Don.

I dashed across the room, apple in one hand and pulling
the sword along with the other, and hid behind the first piece
of cover I came to, which turned out to be the overlarge thighs
of the plastic barbarian.

I thrust the apple protectively behind my back as the owner
of the voice came closer. Their movements didn't sound like
normal footsteps. They sounded like weird, slithering thuds.
A shadow appeared on the wall that didn't seem to have much
in common with a human silhouette. For a heart-stopping
moment I thought that the jam must have acquired the ability
to climb to this height, and had gathered the necessary intelligence to take human form and voice.

Then it came into the lobby. It wasn't jam, but it was just
as terrifying. It was humanoid, about six feet tall and with
two arms and two legs, but its body consisted entirely of a
glistening black substance that trailed viscously from its
limbs. It was grotesque, but I couldn't look away. I felt cold
sweat run down my back, and tried to shrink further into my
clothes.

The thing's featureless face tossed left and right, as if
sniffing the air, and it seemed to notice the smashed vending
machine. It lumbered over and ran one black flipperlike

appendage over the ruined front of the vending machine.

Oh god, I thought. Whatever it is, it's found my scent. On top of that, my hastily adopted crouch was starting to make my legs ache. My knee twitched, bumping the back of the barbarian's leg. It wobbled on its feet, and the black slime creature spun around at the noise.

Instinct took over, and I dove behind the sofa. The monster didn't seem to have seen me, but I was shaking more and more violently as it stomped towards the barbarian, closer and closer to me.

I tried to push myself silently along the carpet with my feet, but when its quivering mass was within six inches, I panicked. My limbs moved of their own accord and I bolted away, shoving the sofas aside as I went, not daring to look behind me to see if the creature was following. I was still gripping the hilt of the sword and the blade made an ugly tearing noise as it dragged along the floor.

I headed past the reception desk and down one of the halls to a junction, where I slowed to consider my options. There was another of the monsters. It was in a small kitchenette at the end of one of the passages, rooting through the drawers and cupboards for who knows what. This one was black, too, but with patches of white and dark green. I took a sharp left turn and kept running, boosting myself with the massive sword's momentum.

Soon I found myself in the main office space of the studio, a huge room with a strip of windows facing the street and thirty cubicles arranged into a neat grid, the occasional monitor-mounted action figure or Star Destroyer dangling from the ceiling in colorful defiance of conformity.

A third monster was crouching under one of the desks. It hadn't seen me, but as I came in, my sword banged against a radiator, and the monster looked up. My blood ran cold as it slowly stood upright like Godzilla rising from the ocean. This one was mostly green, and seemed to be wearing a Woolworths carrier bag on its head. It was the last straw in an ongoing sequence of absurdities that finally made my nervous system throw up its hands and refuse to go on.

I stood petrified as the latest monstrosity lurched towards me, one shapeless limb outstretched. But as the beast passed in front of one of the offices, the door suddenly flew open and Don came out in midair, swinging his ax overhead and screaming at the top of his voice.

He'd chosen his moment a little too early and the blade embedded itself in the carpet a few inches in front of the green slime monster's quivering feet, leaving Don still clutching the handle, bent double and within easy attack range. I darted forward and swung my sword at the advancing demon. Seeing me coming, Don abandoned his attempt to stand up and stayed down.

About halfway through the blade's arc, it occurred to me that no one in their right mind would sell replica fantasy swords that were also sharp and efficient weapons. An instant later the sword's flat edge bounced off the creature's misshapen shoulder, knocking it off its feet and sending me spinning in the opposite direction.

"What's going on?!" I wailed, dizzy.

"They took my build!" raged Don, jerking up and down in a futile effort to get the ax out of the floor. "They took my bloody bastard build!" He glanced at me. His red unshaven face and sweat-matted hair were only marginally less disquieting than the blob monsters. "LOOK OUT!"

I heard the thud of footsteps behind me again. I was already swinging the sword even before I looked over my shoulder. The black one from the lobby was there, close, but not close enough. My blade whistled freely through the air and the creature shoulder barged me aside as my spin reached its three hundred sixtieth degree. I went flying into one of the cubicles like a *shuriken*, tripped on something expensive sounding, and lost consciousness when my head smashed into a quarter-scale Iron Man figurine.

DAY 3.4

When I woke up, I was sitting in one of the wheeled office chairs. My wrists were being tied together behind the backrest, and my ankles had already been tied to the shaft under the seat. There was an Iron Man–shaped ache in my face.

I looked up, and immediately regretted it. Two of the glistening swamp monsters were in front of me, talking amongst themselves. They were leaning against the window with their armlike limbs folded, which seemed an oddly casual pose for bloodthirsty hell beasts. The third one was behind me, still securing my arms.

"What are you?" I said, voice trembling.

"I'll tell you what they are," snarled someone to my immediate right. "They're on the right path for an ax in the center parting, that's what they are."

Don was also secured to a wheeled office chair. He had considerably more bindings around him but they were hastily tied, so he'd probably been struggling while they did it. That went some way to explain his furious, boggle-eyed stare and gritted teeth.

"Are you—" I began.

"DON'T even say it," he barked. "Don't even ask me if I'm all right. I don't know how much inanity I can tolerate."

The one that had been putting the finishing touches to our ropes—the black one I had seen in the lobby—shambled to his fellows and the three of them went into some kind of whispering debate. Occasionally one of them would turn and look at us thoughtfully. It was clear the subject of their conversation was our eventual fate.

I slowly leaned towards Don's chair. "Are they . . . human?"

He looked at me, anger at our captors swiftly replaced by sarcastic contempt for me. "Yes, Travis, they're human. Those other things are desks. The things we're sitting on are chairs. Stop me when you get confused."

"What happened to them?"

He spoke loudly and slowly as if to a foreigner. "They wrapped themselves in bin liners."

What I had taken for the wet glisten of slime was, in actuality, reflections of light off a wrinkled, plasticky surface, and I could see strips of gray and black going around parts of their body that were probably duct tape. They were humans. Humans who had wrapped themselves in several layers of garbage bags. I wasn't immediately sure if that was better or worse than their being swamp monsters, because at least the swamp monsters would have an excuse for looking that way.

"Yeah, we're talking about you," said Don confrontationally, noticing that they were watching our conversation. "Come over here and we'll do it to your face." He clacked his teeth suggestively.

The man wearing the Woolworths carrier bag on his head seemed to have been wordlessly nominated the leader of the trio. He strolled towards us while the other two watched worriedly from the background. Then he held up a hand to reveal an internal hard drive, which he turned over and over in front of Don's snarling face.

"Calm down, dude; you'll give yourself an aneurysm," said the Woolworths man. His voice was surprisingly young and nasally. Not teenage, but definitely on the fresher side of his twenties. "Why are you so crazy about this?"

"It's mine!" yelled Don. "It's my build!"

"Hey, did you work here?" said one of the other plastic-bag wearers, who sounded equally as young. "Did you work on *Interstellar Bum Pirates*?"

Don's furious response derailed on its way to the mouth and he sputtered in confusion for a second. "N—what? No! That wasn't even a Loincloth game!"

"Man, *Interstellar Bum Pirates* was so awesome," said the leader. The hard drive glistened in the light. "Is that what this is? I heard they were making *IBP 2*."

Don wound his temper back in with superhuman effort and tried to sound rational. "Even if it was, which it isn't," he said, his voice like the sizzle of a spark moving along a dynamite fuse, "there's nothing you can do to access it."

Some of this seemed to penetrate, but it didn't dampen the leader's mood. "Nah, it's all good," he exclaimed. "We'll take it back to base and put it on display and all the awesomeness will come off it and we will marvel at the glory."

"What the hell?!" barked Don, back at full volume.

"Er, it's ironic," explained the leader mockingly.

"Dude, I told you it'd be a good idea to check this place out," said the second one.

"Yeah, man, I think this calls for an ironic high five," said the first. The pair immediately thrust out their arms and slapped the backs of their hands together. Then, with no further discussion, they started heading for the exit.

The third, who still hadn't spoken, didn't move at first, but glanced between us and them a few times. "Erm . . . are we just . . . leaving them tied up, then?"

His colleagues didn't even look at him. The Woolworths-bag wearer just sniggered while the other said, "You just don't get irony, do you, Martin."

After Martin, embarrassed, had scurried after his fellows, I sat waiting patiently while Don screamed and bounced around on his chair for a few minutes. Eventually, he gave a last few halfhearted barks of anger and sunk back into his seat, his head bowed forward, defeated.

I coughed. "Did you really make *Interstellar Bum Pirates*?"

His head shot back up again, hateful energy renewed, but he managed to stop himself before he exploded again. He screwed his eyes shut and took a few deep breaths, then answered in a moderate if quivery tone of voice, "No."

"Oh, that's a shame. Me and Tim used to play that co-op. It was really—" I tailed off when my words were competing with a loud roaring noise coming from outside, like a subway train driving past. "What's that?"

"Another tidal wave," said Don nonchalantly.

"What?!" I hopped up and down a few times, hoping I could vibrate myself free.

Don smashed his chair into mine like a dodgem car to calm me down. "Look, if the other wave didn't get inside the building then this one won't, will it? Focus on something important." Sure enough, the roar swiftly faded into the distance and we remained undigested. His own words made him realize something, and he spun in his chair to show me his wrists. "Have I been tied up with strips of plastic bag?"

I checked behind his back. "Yeah. A blue one."

"I thought so. I've got an idea. We have to get to the kitchen."

That was easier and considerably less embarrassingly said than done. To make the chairs move we had to toss our heads back and forth and thrust our hips forward to wheel down the hall towards the kitchen, inch by humiliating inch. Don made better speed, but I managed to stay close enough behind to keep talking.

"WHAT hapPENED in HERE?" I asked, voice modulating oddly with each push forward.

"GOT as FAR as my OFFice. DIDn't SEE aNYone. GOT my HARD drive OUT of my CASE when ONE of THEM came IN." He paused for a moment to get his breath back. "I HID unDER the DESK and he TOOK the HARD drive. I don't know WHY. I guess they're atTRACted to SHIny OBjects. I only NOTiced after he'd LEFT. Then I ran OUT of the OFFICE and THAT'S when I RAN into YOU again."

Once we were in the kitchen, the tiled floor was a lot easier to navigate on casters than the carpet. Don rolled himself over to a crumb-stricken gas stove and turned his back to it. "Tell me when I've got the front hob."

I looked. "No, you're just grabbing the knobs, there."

He blinked. "I meant the knob that controls the front hob."

"Oh! Yeah, that one."

He turned it. By some miracle the jam hadn't affected the pipes, and the stovetop started hissing gas. After a minute or so of effort Don grabbed a barbecue lighter from the counter. It clicked emptily as he pulled the switch, but it created enough of a spark to ignite a predictably large fireball on the stovetop.

"Where do you think they came from?" I said, as he gingerly held his wrists towards the flame.

"I don't know. Ow. But they took my build so wherever they are, we're going to go there and keep setting fire to things until they give it back."

Finally, the plastic strips stretched unhappily in the heat and he pulled his hands apart, then untied the rest of his bonds. "Right. I need to see if they took anything else important from around here. Can you do a check for supplies and meet me on the balcony?"

"Could you untie me first?"

He stopped on his way to the door and rolled his eyes. "Oh. Whatever." He snapped the plastic from around my wrists and left me to take care of the rest.

Once my legs were free I glanced momentarily at the door he had gone through, then turned back to the kitchen counter and turned off the stove. Then I rooted through all the drawers and cupboards until I found a shiny white-handled can opener glittering invitingly in a cutlery drawer. I tested its weight in my hand, and felt immensely proud of myself.

I came out onto the front balcony with a plastic sack over one shoulder and the apple in the opposite hand.

"What's in there?" said Don, pointing.

I jiggled my two prizes. "Food from the snack machine in here. And the apple's important so it gets its own hand."

"Whatever. There's a problem."

He pointed into the street and it didn't take long to realize that the problem was the *Everlong*, namely that its current location was not immediately apparent. "Where's the boat?"

"Must have been that last wave." He hit the balcony rail and I jumped. "God damn it!"

"Couldn't Tim and Angela come back for us?"

"They'd have to figure out how to sail the boat first." He drummed his fingers anxiously. "And before that they'd have to figure out how to stop being retards."

There was nowhere to climb onto from the balcony, and the wave must have pushed all the vehicles out of the street, leaving us without steppingstones. Navigating across the rooftops was no longer tenable now the area was transitioning to the business district; fifty-story skyscrapers stood side by side with older ten-story buildings like fathers and sons at the urinal together.

Something in the jam caught my eye. "What's that?"

The surface of the jam was never even, since it remained at an approximate depth of three feet regardless of the rising and falling of the ground underneath, but a strip of it leading from the front entrance of the building was disturbed strangely. It seemed to be divided into three parallel furrows that grew better defined the further they went from the building, like the wakes of three small boats.

"The plastic men," growled Don ominously. "The ones that took my build. They can move through the jam."

"That must be what the bin liners are for," I said.

"Yes, that was pretty obvious, Travis; keep up. We need to find a way to follow them."

Our eyes met. Then our gazes simultaneously traveled downwards, taking in each other's unsealed, nonplastic clothing.

About twenty minutes later Don and I rendezvoused in the emergency stairwell that led down into the jam-filled lobby. We had agreed that he would search levels two and three while I covered four, five, and six.

"Couldn't find many bags at Loincloth," he said. "They were all gone from the kitchen."

"Yeah, I saw them rummaging around in there," I said. "I found a whole bunch in the clinic upstairs." I waved the roll of yellow bags marked *biological waste*. "And I emptied all the bins and took the liners that weren't ripped or smelly." I waved a slightly damp wad of plastic in my other hand.

Don produced three rolls of duct tape and tapped them rapidly against his palm like a nervous tambourine player. "Right. Good." He looked into the jam, which was rubbing itself into the bottom of the next flight of steps, then looked away and covered his face. "No, not good. This is stupid. All it'll take is one tiny rip and we're spreadable."

"So more than one layer, I'm thinking."

We dressed in silence from the abundance of yellow medical bags the roll provided. Starting with two as stockings, then two with the ends opened up as shorts, then one with two leg holes as a sort of nappy, then one with three holes as a sort of vest, then two for each arm. We taped up the joins until our knees, elbows, and waists had tripled in size. Then we added a second layer.

"Mum always told me not to do this," said Don as he readied one of the smaller, transparent bags. "Shows what she knew, the bitch." He pulled it onto his head and sniffed disgustedly. "Where the hell'd you get this?"

"Just a waste paper basket," I said honestly, neglecting to mention that it had been in a women's bathroom.

He took a few experimental breaths, then snatched the bag off, gasping for air. "Okay. Okay. Mum may have had a point. It's going to need a breathing hole."

"But . . ."

"I know, I know, but it's only three feet deep; it shouldn't even come up to head height." He wriggled his finger through the bottom of the bag, then pulled it back on. He seemed a lot more comfortable, even though a single tuft of hair stuck stupidly upright from the hole, fluttering in time with his breaths. Satisfied, he taped up the join around his neck and shoulders.

I followed suit, and my world quickly became a very warm and moist place with a constant orchestra of crinkling plastic. Don started making his way down the steps toward the jam, but the determination slowly faded from his gait until he stopped with one foot hovering six inches above the shimmering red surface.

"We have to get moving quickly or we might lose their trail," he said, mostly to himself. His foot didn't move.

"Uh," I coughed. "Don, I'm not questioning you or anything, but . . . are you absolutely sure that getting your hard drive back isn't totally, totally, 100 percent not just a tiny bit unnecessary?"

"Yes, I am sure," he said, not looking away from the jam. "It's my best work. It's a new dimension of interactive entertainment." His teeth clenched and his voice grew in volume. "Thrills! Spills! Epic adventure! FUN! FOR ALL! THE FAMILY!" He screamed and thrust his foot into the jam. "AAAAAAGH! CHRIST THAT FEELS WEIRD!"

He watched his leg as he brought it in and out of the goo a few times, but it didn't seem to come back any shorter. He brought his other foot forward and waded into the lobby until the jam level reached his crotch. He winced. "Aaaah haahh. Hah. That's quite nice, actually. Come on."

"Hang on." I tied up the plastic bag into which I'd just placed my sack of food supplies, then suddenly noticed the apple lying where I'd left it on the top stair. "Oh. Damn. I left my apple out of the bag."

"Ugh. Well, just hold it, then. Hurry up. I'm not waiting for you."

As Don turned and stomped away, the fear of being left behind overtook my fear of the jam. I clasped the apple tightly in one hand and walked forward. The sensation of my legs sinking into the jam was unlike anything I'd felt before. It couldn't decide if it was repelled by the plastic or attracted towards the juicy filling, so it compromised with a rhythmic squeezing sensation, like being play bitten all over my body by a horde of toothless puppies. I was shorter than Don, so the jam reached my crotch quicker, and that experience was everything it had been hyped up to be.

Between my weight and the jam's repelling effect, my feet weren't actually touching the ground. I was moving through the jam by cycling with my legs and using my sack of supplies as a makeshift oar. Don was making faster progress because he wasn't holding fruit and could use both his arms, so by the time I stepped very, very carefully through the broken glass in the front entrance, he was already at the street corner, waving me forward.

The stuffy interior of the anti-jam suit wasn't at all improved by direct sunlight. Little reservoirs of sweat were pooling uncomfortably all over my body and I was starting to feel like a carnival goldfish. But Don was making good on his promise not to wait for me, and I was forced to push through my growing exhaustion. Being stuck alone with nothing but two questionably reliable bin liners between me and the jam was not an attractive proposition.

I emerged from the large front entrance doors into Ann Street and my hope lifted. The *Everlong* hadn't been pushed far—it was only about fifty yards ahead. I slogged towards it with renewed vigor, but I couldn't see any sign of Tim or Angela on deck, and they weren't answering Don's cries.

It was requiring more and more effort to keep moving. Pain nipped at my legs, and the sweat was starting to pour. It seemed like the jam grew thicker with each step.

I glanced down. No. Not thicker. Deeper.

With the next step, the jam came up to my belt buckle. Three steps later, it was three inches higher. For a horrible moment I thought that the entire surface of the jam was rising, but it was followed by a considerably horribler moment when it became apparent that the deep spot was limited to a very short radius around my waist.

Jam was crawling up my body inch by inch, unconcernedly pressing and massaging my stomach and spine as it went. I called Don's name but he was too far ahead, and more to the point there was a plastic bag on my head, so I was shouting for the sole benefit of my own ears.

My rising coat of jam was starting to tickle my armpits. It gripped me around the middle like a glistening fist, and dragging it along with me was halving my speed with each step. I raised my apple over my head. Don was a speck, and there were still forty yards to the *Everlong*. I was on my own with this one.

I'd have to think about this laterally. I searched my panicking mind for what I knew about the jam. It was red. Okay, that would do for a start. It was red and sticky and smelled like strawberries. It very quickly absorbed any organic matter that touched it. And when it was near something it could eat . . .

. . . then it slowly extended bits of itself towards it. That was what it was doing. It had the scent of something. I thought of the breathing hole in the top of my head bag. Was it reaching for that? Logically going through the facts step by step was proving difficult. The jam had closed over my shoulders and terror was grabbing my conscious mind by the lapels and metaphorically shaking it back and forth.

Then I looked at Don again. He was still wading nonchalantly along and wasn't having any of the same problems. He had a breathing hole in the same place. So it couldn't have been that. The jam was after . . .

I looked straight up. I was still holding the apple in my raised hand. Its bruises caught the sunlight prettily. I waved it left and right experimentally, and the tube of jam pulled my torso this way and that in time with the motion. It wanted my apple.

The jam was around my throat, making it harder to breathe. I could feel its clammy tendrils slithering up my chin. I gritted my teeth. I wasn't going to let it take the apple, which had become, by then, far more than just bruised flesh and seeds. It symbolized the future of humanity's self-sufficiency. I could still see Travis Orchard in my mind's eye. If I didn't do something fast, it would have to be a memorial garden.

I tried to turn my neck to look around, but the jam held it in place. I used all my strength to tilt my entire upper body and swivel my eyes around. I spotted a nearby alley with a tall wrought-iron gate leading into some kind of car park. If I threw the apple just right, it would be speared on one of the gate spikes and be safe until I could come back to pick it up. This was about the absolute best-case scenario, besides perhaps suddenly acquiring the ability to fly, but it was all I had.

I made to wind my arm for the throw, but the jam had already snared my shoulder and it refused to be pulled back far enough. I waved my elbow back and forth, trying to worry my arm out of the jam's grip just for long enough. The jam covered my mouth, pushing its way between my teeth slightly, and my tongue tasted it through the plastic. Desperate, I summoned all my strength and poured it all into one last yank.

My arm came free. I almost fell backward with surprise. I was about to follow through with the throw when I noticed that my face was free, too. The jam was retreating of its own accord. Within seconds it was back at crotch level.

Then it kept going. It retreated straight past my thighs and came to rest just below my knees. I stared at it, feeling ridiculous, as if my trousers had fallen down. It wasn't just around me this time—all the jam in the street had become lower than usual.

By the time I remembered with a start what a dropping jam level had heralded in the past, the rumbling sound had already penetrated the plastic over my ears. I looked behind me.

This wave was smaller than the first one we'd seen, barely seven feet, but it compensated with speed. Vehicles and debris were being thrown around like grit in a blender. I broke into a run and had almost covered another yard before the wave hit.

The jam slammed into my back and yanked my feet from the ground. With the remarkable boost to energy that only comes from imminent death I was able to keep my legs cycling fast enough to stay on the surface and my head firmly bowed, with the breathing hole pointing forward into the nonjammy air.

As I passed the crest I was launched into the air, tumbling like a rag doll. The wave was moving so fast that it had moved on by the time I started to fall.

Spinning end over end, my vision a blur, I caught a glimpse of a sign hanging from a lamppost coming straight towards me. I spread my arms, and an advertisement for an allegedly upcoming music festival slapped me full in the face. I slammed my arms and legs closed like a set of mantraps, and I wasn't falling anymore.

I wobbled to a dazed standstill, and a few moments of peace passed before I realized that the jam now appeared to be above me. My precious apple, which had landed between my right wrist and the plastic sign, rolled out of my grip. I craned my head back as if I could suddenly persuade myself to evolve a chameleon tongue in the next few seconds, but could only watch helplessly as it rolled through the air in dreadful slow motion and plopped into the jam. It ate it in an instant, chomping obnoxiously.

"NOOOOOOOOOOOOOooooooooooooooo!" I wailed, the noise bursting from my lungs without my brain having any say in the matter.

"YEEEEEEEEEeeeeeeeeeeeeees!" came the echo.

I twisted around. The *Everlong* was barely ten yards away. Don was on deck, slamming closed the hatch under which he had been sheltered from the wave.

"Are you quite finished faffing about?" he yelled.

After a few minutes, I was able to untense my muscles for long enough to slide down the lamppost. Don hauled me up onto the *Everlong*'s deck and I kneeled gratefully on my first solid horizontal surface in what felt like years, lovingly running my fingernails along the cracks.

"Mary!" I realized.

Don had been standing at the front of the boat, gazing out into the city. He turned his head. "And?" he prompted.

"And, Tim and Angela," I added quickly. "Where are they?"

He turned back to the city. "Your girlfriend's in her box below deck. I tripped over it on the way down."

"What about Tim and Angela?"

"I dunno. I haven't looked everywhere yet." He suddenly gripped the rail and thrust his head forward. "There's the trail!"

"I'm just going to see if they're down there," I announced, but Don was busy grinding his teeth at the jam.

It was dark below decks. Something must have happened to the battery, or the generator, or whatever the power came from. I had to keep the hatch open to see. Mary was at the bottom of the stairs, twitching unhappily as the darkness suddenly went away. I picked her up by the handle on the lid and held her like an old-fashioned lantern as I ventured further into the kitchen.

I tripped on something, rustling the noisy plastic outfit I was still wearing. I knelt, felt around at the obstruction with my hands, and after some examination, concluded that it was a drawer, wrenched from its housing.

As I adjusted to the darkness, I saw that all the drawers had been pulled out and their contents dumped on the floor. The cupboards and the chest freezer were open. The curtain had been torn down from the shower. The mattresses had been thrown around. Either burglars had come and ransacked the place, or someone had gotten really, really hungry.

That thought made me hesitate. As a party, we hadn't had a meal since yesterday evening, and that had been mostly sandwich spread and cough sweets. How long would it take for starvation to drive Tim and Angela to madness? Had they torn the kitchen apart? Fought and fallen into the jam? Had one eaten the other? Going insane was a gradual process, I knew that, but it only takes an instant for the concept of cannibalism to switch from *unthinkable* to *justifiable* to *breakfast*.

I moved into the master bedroom, a private chamber with a double bed and a low ceiling that was constantly bumping the back of my ears. It was deep within the boat and far from the deck hatch so by rights it should have been pitch black. But somehow there was enough light to see all the disturbed bedding and raided cabinets.

Looking around, I saw that light was spilling through the cracks in the wardrobe. Something bumped the doors gently. I could see enough of a silhouette to tell that there was something moving in there.

I held Mary towards it like a pistol and she reared up, ready to strike. I started slowly edging forwards. I tried not to make too much noise with my breathing, but the rustling plastic bags all over my body rendered that effort somewhat moot.

When I was barely inches away from the door, I heard a whispered voice coming from within. "I'm in the cupboard," it was saying, quavering with fear and grief. "The things have come back. Back for me. It's all gone to hell here. I can hear them right outside the door." A pause. "I just hope they can't hear this."

"Angela?" I said.

There was a long pause. "I said, I hope they can't hear this."

"I can hear this."

There was a shorter pause. Then the wardrobe door suddenly flew open and I was dazzled by a mounted light on a handheld camera. Something shoved me around the middle and I fell onto my back, clutching Mary's box to my chest. The light shone in my eyes again, illuminating a plastic fork that Angela was preparing to jam into my throat.

"Travis?" she said, stopping her fork with the plastic points tickling my Adam's apple. Her torso was pressing the tupperware box painfully into my chest. Mary hissed jealously between us. "Why're you dressed like a swamp monster?"

"They're just bin liners!" I plucked at one of my sleeves to show her.

"Oh," she said. Then she said it again two more times with increasing realization, glancing aside. She rocked back, heaving a sigh of relief while keeping the camera on my face. Then the lens snapped sideways. "Please tell me that's food."

Before I could answer she bounded over to the sack of vending machine snacks I'd somehow managed to hold onto up to now. I'd left it on the floor and it was spilling cupcakes, one of which Angela grabbed and attempted to inhale.

I watched her carefully over the top of Mary's box. "Angela?"

"Whaff?" she said, cheeks stuffed like a hamster's.

"You've been really hungry, right?"

"Yeff?"

I glanced back at the chaos in the kitchen, and chose my words carefully. "I'm not accusing you of anything. I think there have definitely been a lot of mitigating circumstances lately. I just want to know what you did with Tim."

She looked at me expressionlessly, cheeks bulging, then swallowed. "Tim's gone. The monsters took him."

I nodded. "Do the monsters ever talk to you when nobody else is around?"

"I mean, the guys in bin liners, I guess. There were three of them. Came out of nowhere. They took all our cans." She suddenly grabbed my arm urgently. "They took Tim!"

The penny finally dropped like a manhole cover into a vat of porridge. "They came through here?"

"I don't understand where they could have come from, unless they were somehow able to walk through the . . ." She ran her camera gaze over my plastic yellow jumpsuit, then did that same thing again where she said "oh" three times. "What happens if it gets ripped?"

"There's another layer."

"What happens if that gets ripped?"

"Er." I thought about this. "Death?"

"Not a perfect system, is it."

The floor suddenly tilted a few degrees. Angela and I both looked at the wall when we heard something large and metal grinding against the outside like a horny robot.

The *Everlong* was moving, or at least trying to. I stumbled through the wreckage in the kitchen as the hull tilted left and right, as if trying to wriggle through a gap slightly too small for it. I trotted up the steps and another lurch almost threw me headlong into the jam.

The sail had caught the wind and was trying to pull the *Everlong* out of the little cluster of overturned vehicles that the jam waves had formed at the crossroads of Ann and Edward Street. Logistically this was turning out to be as straightforward as maneuvering to the front of a packed lift.

"Steer the bloody thing!" yelled Don. He was trying to keep the mainsail in place with his leg and push away from an overturned Volkswagen with one of the boat hooks.

I ran over to the stern, ducked under the mast, and grabbed the rudder. Holding it steady, I was able to keep the boat in line long enough to get free of the throng without splitting the entire hull open.

"Don?" said Angela, poking her camera out the deck hatch. "What're you doing?"

"I'm going after my build," he said, putting his weight into the sail and baring his teeth. "It's a matter of life and death. If I can't get that build back then it is officially the end of my life."

"Build?" asked Angela, looking at me.

"The guys who took Tim took something of Don's," I said. Don made a noise that was halfway between a snort and a dry heave. "I think they were the same guys. They had bin liners on." I glanced down at myself. "I don't know how common that is, though."

"Don't you dare try to change my mind!" snarled Don. "I can still see their trail and we have to follow it before another wave wipes it out!"

"No, no, sounds like a plan," said Angela.

"Yeah, makes sense to me," I added.

Don did a double take. "What?"

His angry glare put me on the spot. I checked over my words but couldn't see any part of them that could make him incredulous. "I said, it makes sense."

He looked between the two of us a few times, then pushed the sail away from him savagely. "Are you people retarded?! We're barely two streets from Hibatsu, I want to delay us who knows how long to get one measly hard drive back, and you're both perfectly fine with this?!"

"But it does make sense," I whined, cringing. "We can rescue Tim as well."

"So you don't want to do this?" ventured Angela.

"Of course I want to do this!" barked Don. "It's just . . . oh, stop talking." He took up the sail again.

Turning down Edward Street put us firmly in the city's primary shopping district. The buildings were divided into shops and boutiques of every color and variety, punctuated by the occasional eatery. This neighborhood would have been particularly crowded at rush hour. Maybe it was my imagination but the jam seemed slightly thicker around that one really popular coffee place.

Something about the area creeped me out. The air was as still and quiet as always, but this time it was a deliberate stillness: not of death, but of alive things trying to keep very quiet. The sun was setting, the brightly colored shop fronts fading against the dusky blue-orange sky, and that wasn't improving the atmosphere any.

Angela was sitting close, trying to hug her knees and film at the same time. I leaned over and whispered out of the corner of my mouth, "I think we're being watched."

"Yeah, I know. He's over there." She pointed.

I didn't have the benefit of a camera with a night-vision setting, so I didn't notice Y until we were right next to him. He appeared to be stranded on the rain shelter outside the clothing-alterations place. He must have been trying to get our attention, because he had taken off his camo shirt and was twirling it over his head like a stripper who didn't know he was supposed to let go.

Don slowed the boat as best he could and Y did an impressive standing leap onto the deck, landing in an alert crouch with one knee and one hand on the floor.

"And where the hell have you been?" said Don, hands on hips like a schoolteacher.

"They took m . . . They took X," said Y urgently, standing to his full height. His imposing size was even more apparent now his muscles were exposed.

"The bin-liner men?"

"That way." He pointed at the upcoming turn that led into the Queen Street Mall. It seemed to be the same way the trails were leading us, but it was becoming harder and harder to see the furrows the plastic-covered thieves were leaving behind as evening rolled on and the light faded.

"They took Tim, too," I said. "And our food."

"*Coincidentally,*" said Angela, with deliberate emphasis. She made an attempt to give Y a sidelong look which was aborted rather drastically when he turned out to not be there anymore. "Where's he gone?"

Don and I were still engaged in keeping the boat moving, but we glanced around helpfully. "I dunno," I said. "Did he go below decks? I didn't notice him move at all."

"He must've," said Don dismissively. "It's not like he can put on some giant wellies and go on ahead. Don't bother him. If you offend him, he might leave again."

Angela backed down sulkily, and we sailed on in silence. All the street lights were off, and in the twilight all the ugly, jagged modern-art installations became like the grasping branches of a haunted forest. I glanced at Mary when I heard her skitter agitatedly in her box. I wasn't an expert in arachnid care, but she definitely seemed a little thinner than I remembered.

"Hey," I said. "What do spiders eat?"

"Depends on the breed," replied Don without interest.

"Okay. So what do Goliath birdeaters eat?"

He turned his head very, very slowly to look me in the eye before responding. "At an educated guess, I'd say, Christmas pudding and milkshakes."

"Are you being sarcastic?"

"No," he said, sarcastically.

Finding a bird for Mary to eat would be problematic. There were some chicken Cup-a-Soups among the vending machine spoils, but we didn't have a kettle. I couldn't remember the last time I'd seen a living bird or heard one calling; those that hadn't been eaten by the jam had probably fled the city. I glanced up at the rooftops just in case, but all I saw was the silhouette of a vaguely humanoid shape that backed away when it noticed me watching it.

I was about to speak up when something struck the hull heavily and the boat gave a dangerous lurch. Angela grabbed the mast to stay on her feet. "Sorry, that was me," I said sheepishly, yanking on the rudder. "Didn't see the fountain. Because of the dark."

Visibility was continually worsening and it wasn't going to get any better any time soon. Angela frowned into her viewfinder. "Maybe it's time we stopped for the night."

"Yeah, genius," said Don, pointing forward. "Or maybe we could just go investigate that light up ahead."

I peered around the sail to see. As we approached the crossroads of the mall where Queen Street met Albert Street, I could see a flickering orange light on the corner.

A metal rake was sticking out of the jam with what I think were discount children's pajamas wrapped around the end and set alight. And it wasn't the only one. As we drew nearer and could see down the length of Albert Street, I saw another three makeshift torches outside the south entrance to the Briar Center, the largest shopping center in the CBD. There was another entrance some distance further up Queen Street, and sure enough I could squint my eyes and spot a couple of flaming specks in front of that, too.

"I think the bin men must've gone to the Briar Center," I said, as quietly as possible.

"All right," whispered Don. "We'd better try for a stealthy approach."

As the *Everlong* was passing the center of the crossroads, there was a loud metallic *clang*, and the boat lurched violently to a halt. We had gotten caught on the artistically designed archway in the center of the mall. The very tip of the mast had lodged itself between two metal plates that had been finely cut into the geometric shapes thought to best express the creative soul of the city.

Don and I both grabbed different parts of the boat and pulled as hard as we could, but that just resulted in more squeaks and groans as our efforts shook the entire structure. "For crying out loud!" shouted Don. "This is why I petitioned against building this thing!"

"They heard us!" said Angela. She was lying on her stomach, peering into the darkness with her camera on night-vision mode.

There were sloshing noises coming from the jam on two sides, the kind that people in plastic bin liners might have made while wading towards us. I felt something cold and metal, and I realized I'd unconsciously backed myself up against the central mast. Don appeared to have had the same idea.

"Outsiders," came a hissed voice from the north that made the fear crawl up and down my limbs.

"Outssssiders," returned a female voice to the west.

The plastic people were close enough that I could see the orange firelight reflecting off their bags. There were two of them, one coming up Albert and one from up Queen, slowly gliding towards us with their arms outstretched. Angela gave a yelp and joined us at the mast.

"We are the plastic men," intoned the male one in a menacing monotone.

"We're totally gonna get you guys," added the female one.

"Yeah," confirmed the first. "You'd better be totally bricking it."

Bricking it would certainly be a good phrase to describe my intention when the one from Albert Street reached the boat and placed its amorphous hands on the side in preparation to climb inside.

And then Y was there. One second the plastic man was boarding us; the next Y was grabbing him around the head and hauling him out of the jam with a wet slurp. A flick of the wrist later and the plastic-covered man slammed face first into the deck, knocking him senseless.

It must have been too dark or the plastic too opaque for our other attacker to see what was happening, because she was still coming slowly towards the front of the boat making ghostly *wooo* noises. Y hauled her inside by the arm the moment she touched the handrail at the prow, and rendered her unconscious with some kind of exotic open-hand blow to the neck.

Only then did Y turn to us, expressionless but for the merest hint of a scowl. All three of us were frozen, leaning tightly into the mast as if roped there.

"Is there a back way into the shopping mall?" he asked. It was the longest sentence I'd yet heard him say, and his voice had taken on a bit of an action movie hero growl. He was clearly in his element.

Don and Angela appeared to be temporarily mute so I took the initiative, speaking carefully in case a hasty word might offend him. "If you go to the end of Queen Street," I said, "there's a little escalator goes into the department store."

He glanced up the street, then back. "Wait here."

"Right you are," I squeaked. "Sir."

He jumped sideways, springboarded off the *Everlong*'s handrail, and grabbed one of the legs of the archway. He shimmied rapidly up and out of the range of the meager torch light, although we heard his boots thundering across the sheet metal overhead.

After silence fell and we could be certain he'd moved on, Don slowly outstretched a finger and turned Angela's camera to look him in the eye. "Of course, you realize what we're not going to do."

"And what's that?" she asked in a monotone.

"We're not going to do what he said and wait here."

"Er, why aren't we doing that?" I asked politely. "I ask because I was the one who told Y we'd wait and I really don't want him to think I lied to him . . ."

"Y isn't going to get my build back," said Don.

"I agree," said Angela. "Not about the build—Don's totally insane—but I want to see what's going on inside that shopping center." She tapped her camera. "For posterity."

"You don't have a plastic covering," I tried.

"Then lend me yours if you're so bent on staying here."

"I'm not staying here alone!" I said.

"Well, I guess that's decided to everyone's satisfaction," said Don, clapping his hands as Angela bent to start pulling the plastic bags off of one of our two unconscious guests. "Let's go hang out at the mall."

DAY 3.5

The three of us waded single file through the Albert Street jam, towards the shopping center's main entrance. I was balancing Mary's box on my head and Angela was now geared up in the green and blue ensemble the female boarder had been wearing. We had tied both boarders to the prow rail on the *Everlong*, and while it probably wasn't the soundest idea in the world to physically attach untrustworthy strangers to our only means of transportation, no better alternative had come to mind.

As we drew closer to the flaming torches at the Briar Center's entrance, we saw two plastic men standing to rigid attention. Don, who was taking the lead, immediately stopped and turned on his heel. "This is never going to work."

"Well, not if you jinx it like that," said Angela, filming the entrance. "If we believe it'll work, it's more likely to work. It's a psychology thing."

"You know who told themselves that?" said Don. "The Children's Crusade."

"Why don't you think it'll work?" I asked.

"Because every one of these bastards I've seen has been wearing normal garbage bags." He glanced down at the canary-yellow biological waste bags we were wearing. "We're going to stick out like . . . like Travis at a Mensa meeting."

I wasn't sure what that meant but it sounded like an insult. "Hey!"

The Albert Street entrance to the shopping center was on the corner of Elizabeth Street, providing access to the ground floor and an escalator up to the food court on the second. It was a stone's throw from the local community college, so most of the time when I'd passed by there'd been a lot of kids sitting around, chatting or buying food, wearing trendy T-shirts bearing utterly mystifying but apparently hilarious slogans, or black leather trench coats and knee-high studded fetish boots in bold defiance of the climate.

The kids weren't there now. The main way through to the ground floor was blocked off by huge metal shutters. Copious torch light was spilling down from the second floor, but the escalator wasn't working. Jam ran all the way up the unmoving steps in a glistening slope. The central business district was built on fairly hilly terrain, so the bottom three levels of the mall all had direct access to a street, and consequently jam.

The two guards were either side of the escalator, both wearing entirely black bags tied up with black tape, so it was good to see fashion traditions remain. They both held cheap plastic broom handles with the heads removed and kitchen knives taped onto the end. As we drew towards the light, one of them brandished his weapon and held up his free hand. "Halt! Who goest there?"

"Friend!" returned Angela, only thrown for a second.

"Oh, don't encourage him," said the other, shorter guard. "He's been doing the medieval-guard thing all day."

"Dude, I'm making, like, an *ironic* statement," said the first guard, covering his mouth as if to whisper but speaking at a normal level. "I'm saying that we've basically gone back to medieval times 'cos there's no electricity but we haven't really?"

"Yeah, man, that's *ironic* as hell," conceded the second guard. Whenever they said any form of the word *ironic* they put a peculiar emphasis on it, rounding out each vowel and rolling their heads sarcastically, as if they were trying to say the word in as ironic a way as possible.

"Can we come in, then?" said Don.

"Yeah, man," said the first guard, as if it were a stupid question. "Few new recruits showed up today; we'll be doing the ceremony soon."

We passed between them and started squelching our way up the narrow escalator. Halfway up, the shorter guard suddenly turned and called after us. "Hey, are you guys new?"

All three of us stiffened. In the soundtrack of our lives, a jarring chord played. I looked to Don and Angela, but they weren't turning around. I was the nearest to the guards. It was up to me to say something that would deflect suspicion.

I looked over my shoulder. "Yes."

"Thought so. I like the yellow. Looks hideous." He made a curious gesture with his plastic-covered hand which I think might have been an okay sign. "Very ironic."

The Briar Center was built around a central food court packed with whatever fast-food franchises could afford some of the most lucrative spots in the city. Five levels of shops looked voyeuristically down upon the main dining area, with the cinema at the very top, a paradoxically overpriced place that had presumably long ago written sticky floors into its mission statement.

Speaking of which, the jam was everywhere. The jam flooding the three levels with street access hadn't deterred the residents at all: the Briar Center had been the social hub for the city's least employable, so its colonization after the rush-hour genocide had been virtually inevitable. Just from a single glance I saw easily twenty or thirty individuals going about their business in the jam, all swaddled in plastic bags.

There were many variations of color and transparency but none quite as hideous as our choice of yellow. Plastic men waded confidently through the jam. Plastic women stepped as nimbly as the thick substance would allow. Some were dragging small plastic children, only their heads emerging from the surface like uneven mushrooms.

"This is all a bit Innsmouth for my liking," commented Don, as we endeavored to look like natives. "And look, I said this would happen. Not a square inch of yellow to be seen."

"I'm not in yellow," said Angela, panning left and right, missing nothing. "Anyone asks, I'll say you're my prisoners."

"We don't even know what they do with the prisoners!" said Don. "They might take us straight off to be cannibalized!"

"Look, do you want to rescue Tim or what?"

"Is that a trick question? I'm going after my build. Then I'm going straight to Hibatsu. You can meet me there if you're not too busy being a casserole or anything."

A translucent glass dome high up in the ceiling provided illumination during the day, but now that it was night naked flames were taking that particular workload. Every spare plant pot and litter bin contained a makeshift torch like the ones outside. The ventilation had never been good in here even when the electricity worked; now the air was hot and thick with foul-smelling smoke.

"Do you see that?" I said, as we moved into the larger open area of the food court.

"Of course I see that," snapped Don. "We're facing the same direction and I'm in front of you."

What we saw was a cluster of flaming torches arranged in a circle in the most open section of the dining area, where most of the plastic people were apparently gathering. At the far side of the circle was the coffee stand, which had been converted into some kind of stage, with a collage of plastic shower curtains forming its backdrop.

Tim was sitting on the stage with his arms around his knees, alongside a few other worried-looking, ragged survivors, presumably picked up today. X was there, too, glancing around with the kind of thoughtful scowl that implied that a lot of faces were being committed to memory.

As we drew closer to try to get their attention, one of the plastic men stomped out onto center stage, blocking our view of Tim. He was tall and skinny, and the clear plastic bag on his head revealed a pale face and greasy black bangs. "Hey!" he called to us. "Where'd you guys come from?"

"They're my prisoners!" said Angela quickly, caught off guard.

"Oh, are they? Could you have brought them up a bit later, do you think?" He had a nasal, high-pitched voice. "Only I don't think we're quite as inconvenienced as we could be just yet."

"What?" said Angela.

"Oh, just pass them up here. Coming prebagged now, are they?"

Under the eyes of a mall full of plastic men there was nothing we could do but obey. Don and I clambered up onto the makeshift stage as the pale young man watched with arms folded. Tim reacted to our appearance with a silent start, then noticed Angela. He seemed to be about to make some kind of greeting when X, still glancing in all directions, slapped a hand over his mouth.

"What the hell's that?" demanded the pale man, pointing.

"That's my spider," I said, hurriedly taking up Mary's box and clutching her to my chest.

He threw up his hands. "Whatever! Just sit with the others and wait for the cue," he ordered, acting more like a theatrical director arranging extras than a sinister cult leader preparing sacrificial victims. I scuttled to Tim's side and Don sat Indian style beside me, resting his cheek on his fist. The director eyeballed us as we settled down. "Any more surprises you'd like to spring on me in the seconds before we go on, hmm? Any heads of state coming to visit?"

"N-no, that's all," I stammered.

"Fantastic. Thanks for contributing."

"Well, this is going swimmingly," muttered Don through his teeth. "Do you think we could be buggering everything up any faster?"

The audience space was rapidly filling up with tottering plastic-bag golems of every shape, size, and color. Just as it was reaching capacity, Don tensed up and grabbed my upper arm.

"There he is," he hissed.

"Who?"

"The arsehole who took my build."

He wasn't difficult to spot. Most of the plastic men wore bag suits of one color, so the thief's patchwork outfit and Woolworths headdress stuck out like a jellybean in a box of raisins. He was right next to the aisle in almost the exact middle of the seating area. We must have walked right past him on our way in.

"Perfect," said Don quietly, glancing around. "Once whatever-this-is is over we'll go and have a word. Assuming we're not being eaten."

Once the entire plastic community had been assembled, the skinny bloke with the bangs held his pencil-thin arms out for silence. "Your attention, please," he said. His voice wasn't quite as commanding as he'd hoped, and he had to repeat himself a few times with increasing volume and petulance before the background noise quietened down to a rustle of plastic. "Tonight's ceremony would like to begin, when we're all ready. Hail Crazy Bob."

"Hail Crazy Bob," replied the audience, throwing their heads back.

I looked up where everyone else was looking and saw a mysterious figure standing alone on the highest level of the complex, head and shoulders silhouetted against the torch light, wearing what was unmistakably a crown. He was looking down upon us and waving a hand benevolently.

"And hail Princess Ravenhair," continued the director, although the word *priest* started to feel more appropriate. "Noble avatar of Crazy Bob on Earth and bringer of His message."

A plain, slightly overweight blond girl of around twenty—Ravenhair was presumably *ironic*—climbed up beside him. In addition to the prerequisite plastic bags, she was wearing a glittering silver cape made from strips of aluminium foil taped together. The priest backed away, golf clapping, to let her take center stage.

"Brothers and sisters," said Princess Ravenhair rapturously, eyes shining behind her rectangular glasses. "Today is the third day of the new era. The era of the Plastic People, chosen by God to be the forebears of the new race, chosen to be the only ones 'gainst whom the Jam of Satan would be powerless . . ."

"They're all bloody mad," said Don, not quietly enough. All eyes fell upon him as Princess Ravenhair stopped, offended.

"Something you want to add?" said the lanky priest spitefully. Until then he had been watching the princess with doe-eyed adoration.

"You're all bloody mad," said Don at full volume, not a man to be intimidated by twenty-year-olds with bad hair. "The jam's not powerless. It just can't eat through plastic."

Something halfway between a groan and a patronizing snigger went up from the audience. Princess Ravenhair smacked her forehead. Someone near the front went, "Someone doesn't get it," in a singsong voice.

"Oh, really?" said the priest in a tone of voice just shy of a shriek. "We, like, totally didn't know that! We were just, um, wearing these things for some completely unrelated reason! Thanks for clearing that up for us!"

"Yeah, we're *ironically* worshiping," said Princess Ravenhair, doing that eye-rolling, vowel-rounding thing. "God. We're just trying to have a bit of fun with the idea. We're not, like, an actual cult or anything."

"Are you happy for us to continue, then?" said the director. The two of them were standing either side of Don and looking down at his seated form like kindergarten teachers addressing a child defecating in a sandpit.

"Please do," said Don, sarcastically.

"Lo," cried Princess Ravenhair in ecstasy, sweeping right back into the swing of things. "Three days it has been, since our people came, tempest-washed, to the shores of this land of plenty. Five days since the pact with Crazy Bob, keeper of the Keys of Security, was founded. Hail Crazy Bob!"

"Hail Crazy Bob!" cried the plastic people, casting their heads back again to receive another hand wave from their savior. My neck was starting to hurt.

"And it is with great pleasure that we welcome the newest members of our family." She gestured magnanimously to us and the other kidnap victims, and the priest ceremoniously placed an armful of multicolored bin bags and duct-tape rolls in front of them. "You guys already in the yellow bags can just sit out of this bit, I guess. Have you anything you wish to say on your arrival?"

"Why did you kidnap us?" said Tim suddenly, finally breaking his thoughtful silence. "We've been looking for settlements. We'd probably have joined anyway."

"We can no longer take chances with recruitment," said Princess Ravenhair, looking at her hands and shaking her head. "Too often are our members found unworthy by God, and are taken from us by the grasping arms of Satan."

Tim scanned the ceiling as he deciphered this. "Their bags get ripped?"

Princess Ravenhair's priestly manner vanished, and the audience groaned again. "Yes, their bags get ripped. We're not actually saying it really is God or Satan or anything. God, you're so weird." She coughed and straightened her hair. "Wear, now, your sacred robes of brotherhood, and verily make sure the joints are nicely sealed."

I leaned sideways towards Don and whispered, "Do you think this is how all religions start?"

Don wasn't listening. He was scrutinizing the hard-drive thief in the Woolworths bag, considering the best angle of approach. It was hard to tell with the bag, but it seemed like the thief was staring back. I wondered if he'd recognized Don's voice. Considering how much Don had been yelling at him in our first encounter, it wouldn't have been too hard.

"We have one more matter to address," said the lanky priest, stepping out into center stage again with his hands gathered solemnly behind his back. "Bring forward the accused!"

From behind the "curtain" emerged two large specimens in ugly gray bin bags, each holding one of the arms of a smaller, sweating young man with an overgrown hipster goatee and an olive-green bag ensemble. "Will someone please tell me what I've done?!" he said, bewildered.

"Silence! Robert Something-or-other, you stand here accused of . . ." One of his hands came around from behind his back holding a scrap of white bin liner that someone had written on with black felt-tip. "Of a blasphemous act of theft:

Stealing the last individual yogurt with strawberry pulp on the bottom from our benevolent Lord Crazy Bob, who had, quote, 'set it aside and been really looking forward to it.' "

"I didn't know it was his!" protested Robert. "I could only get a meat pie for dinner and it'd gone off!"

"So you admit your crime against the Most Holy!" cried the priest.

Robert looked around at the pitiless plastic faces all around him, terror glistening in his eyes. He leaned towards the priest and hissed just loud enough for everyone to hear. "You said we were only worshiping him *ironically*!" he desperately emphasized.

"Yes, just as you wronged him *ironically*," said the priest, doing the emphasis with practiced ease and placing a friendly hand on Robert's shoulder. "And just as we now punish you *ironically*."

The priest's other hand came out from behind his back, clutching a vicious little switchblade. He swung it across Robert's front in a swift, wide arc. Robert flinched, but the swipe did nothing but cut a long slit in his plastic wrapping.

The nature of his punishment became immediately clear to me and Robert simultaneously. He was still babbling apologies and pleas as the two guards wordlessly flung him into the aisle. He landed full length in the jam and rolled madly around for a second, trying to hold the slit closed with his hands, before there was a wet sucking noise, his head bag filled with red, and his bags settled emptily onto the surface.

"What the hell?!" chided Tim. "Why'd you kill him? You're mad!"

That contempt-filled groan went up again, and the priest clicked his tongue. "Do you think you people will get it on the six or seventh hundredth time? We're being *ironically* evil."

"But he's *actually* dead!" pressed Tim.

"Ugh," the priest waved a hand dismissively. "I wouldn't expect your generation to understand sophisticated humor. Now, if no one has any other business to raise . . ."

"My lord!" cried a voice from the audience. Every plastic-covered head in the room turned to face the origin with a loud, joint rustle. It was the man in the Woolworths bag. "I've got something."

"Well?"

"I've come to donate a relic to the church," he said. "For, like, worshiping and being sacred and stuff." He held up his shining prize. "This hard drive."

"What's so holy about a hard drive?"

Mr. Woolworths bobbed it a couple of times, perhaps to speed the thinking process. "Uh. It's a, er, final link to, you know, the world that used to be. Technology and all that jazz." The priest cocked an unconvinced eyebrow. "It's an *ironic* present."

"Oh, well, why didn't you say so sooner?" said the priest, snatching the trinket and holding it up reverently. "Oh, Crazy Bob, accept you this sacred offering of obsolete computing hardware? Clasp you this bounty to your holy bosom, to be never again sullied by the impure hand of Man?"

The heads went back again. On the topmost floor, the mysterious silhouette of Crazy Bob offered a thumbs-up.

"So shall it be so," said the priest, handing the hard drive gingerly to one of the big guards who had thrown Robert. "It shall be moved to His Museum of Relics and protected for eternity from harm. Hail Crazy Bob!"

"That little sod," muttered Don under the inevitable chant, with equal parts hatred and wonderment.

"That concludes the ceremony," said the priest, needlessly; the audience was already chatting amongst itself and moving to leave. "Newcomers, make yourselves beds in the department store. Queue up here tomorrow at eight for your daily rations. Raiding parties to form at twelve. Look forward to working with you all. Hail Crazy Bob!"

"That little sod," grumbled Don for the seventeenth time, about an hour later. He seemed to be in something of a trance.

We had followed the shambling crowds of plastic humanity into the department store, which took up a significant percentage of the upper four levels. The bottom level was jam struck, but that had only been the menswear department, which had little use at present, given that fashion for both sexes had taken a sudden turn in the direction of crinkly kitchenware.

Like most of the rest of the plastic people we were camping in the homewares section. All the beds, mattresses, and sleeping bags had been claimed by our new peers, but there were plenty of soft objects around we could lay our heads on. Tim found a beanbag, and I was making do with an old sack stuffed with a large quantity of designer lingerie.

The plastic people weren't so numerous that we couldn't be nicely spaced out around the store, and the five of us had claimed a little private corner in the shadow of a bank of display refrigerators. Our little survival party would have been wholly reunited, were it not for . . .

"Y," said X, after we'd all finished exchanging stories. "What happened to him?"

"He went off to infiltrate the center alone, for unknown reasons," said Angela sniffily, implying with her pronunciation of *unknown* that the reasons might be less unknown to some individuals than to others.

"I have to find him!" X said. "After that, we can leave and move on to Hibatsu."

"Why?" said Tim. His voice was outwardly casual, but the word hung heavy with implications.

"I am not leaving without him," said X, narrowing her eyes. "Those are my terms."

"I mean, why? It's a settlement, isn't it? That's what we were going to Hibatsu for. They've got food. Supplies. Facilities. A decent staging point. It's safe."

"Safe?!" I squawked.

"Well, for a given value of safe, anyway."

"These people are absolute nutters," said Don. "They took my build."

"They killed a guy!" I pointed out, exasperated.

"I got the whole thing on camera," said Angela proudly. She hadn't taken her focus off X for the entire conversation. "Clear as day. Could be the next Zapruder film."

"Look," said Tim, in a level and sensible tone that failed to calm anyone down. "So they've got slightly irrational policies. You could say the same about marijuana being illegal. Didn't make you want to live in a country with no police, did it?"

"They don't murder you for possessing marijuana," said Angela, turning her camera on him. "I sort of agree with X," she said, grimacing as if the words tasted bitter in her mouth. "Maybe we should just find Y and get out of here before—"

"No!" Don had been slumped down in his seat, anger simmering on a low boil, but now he sprang up like a bear trap. "I am not leaving this place until I've gotten my build back. Or they directly threaten my life."

"You're all free to do whatever you want to do," said Tim pointedly.

"What're you doing?" said Angela, filming X again.

X turned to Don. "Y's definitely in the mall somewhere?"

"Assuming he's not jam bait," he said.

X looked at each one of us in turn, giving various degrees of untrusting scowl. "I'm not leaving until I find him."

"Neither am I," said Angela instantly. "Travis, what do you want to do?"

I looked up, surprised at suddenly being consulted. "Er . . . I'll just do whatever everyone else is doing."

"Oh, will you," said Don, frustrated. "What a bold and respectable position. Just go to sleep, Travis. Maybe the personality fairy will visit you in the night."

I went to sleep anyway. Just to show him.

DAY 4.1

It was probably early when I was woken by a sound. Weak morning daylight was filtering into the store from the dome in the main mall, and most everyone else on the floor was still asleep.

Don, Tim, and X were all there, lying sprawled over their improvised furniture, but I didn't see Angela. And Mary was awake, pawing restlessly at the side of her box. Then I heard the sound that had woken me again—a gentle fluttering of wings.

I rolled over and followed the sound until I spotted the source. One of the plastic people's living spaces had been set up just a few yards away, with a few pieces of bedding and personal belongings lying around. The human occupant was absent, but there, on the floor, was a birdcage.

Inside the cage was a blue-and-white speckled budgerigar, preening itself unconcernedly to greet the new day. From out of nowhere the words *Goliath birdeater* shot to the forefront of my mind, and I glanced back at my restless spider.

Mary wasn't looking any healthier, and this was certainly an uncanny bit of providence. I climbed quietly off my sack of lingerie, crept into our neighbor's territory, and placed Mary next to the bird's cage to let the two examine each other. Mary raised her forelegs in excitement, but the budgie hadn't even noticed her.

I looked around, but not a single plastic person was stirring or looking in my direction. I asked myself: was this really the right thing to do? Well, no, obviously. Not at all. Feeding a stranger's pet to yours is extremely hard to justify without the consent of the owner (or indeed the consent of the pet), especially when party A is a cute, smooth-feathered budgie full of the zest of spring, and party B is a big, hairy tarantula that would send most people dashing for the heaviest broom. And yet, of the three alive, conscious entities present, one wanted to be fed, and one wanted to feed the one that wanted to be fed, which made a clear majority.

The budgie was still cleaning its feathers without a care in the world. What exactly did budgies do? Sit in cages, mostly, occasionally squawking. Spiders keep a home clean of pests, and if people break into your house you can throw a spider at them and certainly give them cause to hesitate. Spiders were much worthier of life than budgies.

This particular budgie also seemed to have no equivalent food shortage. A dispenser on the side of the cage was generously filled with seed. That was the other thing budgies did: eat seeds. Seeds, which Tim had said would be vital for cultivating sustainable crops in the new society. I thought back to that single precious apple I had nurtured, and which had been cruelly snatched from me. Here was this selfish little bastard necking seeds like water. When you looked at it that way, budgies were probably one of humanity's biggest threats right now. This was just a devious, food-stealing crow with blue feathers.

I opened the cage door, held the tupperware box sideways against it with the lid loosened, took another glance around for witnesses, then swiftly pulled the lid away. Mary wasted no time. The budgie couldn't have been particularly attached to life, judging by the way it didn't struggle much. Probably hadn't been very happy. I kept my gaze on the middle distance, trying to avoid watching Mary having breakfast.

"What the hell was that?" said Tim, sitting up.

I quickly tipped Mary back into her box and nonchalantly sped back to our sleeping area. "Hmm?"

"Sort of a squealing noise . . ."

"I don't hear anything." I patted my knees rapidly for a moment. "Did you have any nice dreams?"

He looked at me sleepily, raking his unkempt pillow hair back into place. "What's with the feathers?"

I brushed them off my thighs and crossed my legs. "What do you want to do today?"

He seemed confused, but decided not to pursue the issue. He crawled around our living space gathering up his plastic bags. "I want to head down and talk to whoever's in charge of the food around here. Want to come for the walk?"

"Oh, yes, yes, sure," I said, trying to casually gather up the feathers and fling them in the general direction of the empty birdcage I'd left a few feet away.

I was eager to get away from the scene for a little while, and let Mary sleep it off for a bit, so once we'd put our bags back on I followed Tim through the store towards the escalators. It was surprising how quickly the displays were becoming untidy and unwelcoming now that no one was maintaining them, and the flaming torches everywhere weren't helping matters, either. The mannequins in the children's section were starting to look like Victorian chimney sweeps.

We stopped at the top of one of the escalators (now technically a staircase) and noticed a couple of residents standing in some disorganized attempt at a queue. They stood out, because they weren't wearing plastic bags. It was clear then that the majority of the mall's residents were under twenty-five, and there wasn't a single one wearing a T-shirt without some hilarious ironic slogan.

They were passing wadded-up plastic bags down to a plastic man standing waist deep in the jam at the bottom of the stairs, who passed their protective gear under the jam for a second before sending it back. This, presumably, was the laundry.

Tim and I wordlessly took advantage of the service after a mutually unpleasant smell check of our own gear. "Better check it all for rips," said Tim, after we'd gotten it all off.

I hunted through my own ball of crinkling plastic and tape. It seemed intact for now. "Not a perfect solution, is it," I said, for conversation's sake.

"Certainly not a permanent one," he said, distracted. I gave him a questioning look. "There're limited amounts of duct tape. And it loses its stickiness after a while. Especially with the amount we're sweating on it."

Once our coverings had been freshened up, we bagged back up and headed down the stairs, politely nudging past the laundry technician. My heart quickened for a second as the goo wrapped itself warmly around my lower body.

Sunlight was shining through the skylight, so a lot of the torches had been temporarily extinguished and the air was a bit less thick. But the mall didn't look any better under natural light. The plastic men had already ransacked most of whatever the jam couldn't eat. Most of the shop windows were smashed, and iron shutters had been crowbarred aside and left where they lay. Someone had tried to persuade the jam to pipe through the water feature outside Captain Toys, with evidently disastrous results.

The plastic people who were up at this time in the morning swam unconcerned through the jam like half-submerged, plastic-wrapped corpses bobbing along a canal, occasionally pointing out looting or vandalism to each other and tutting with ironic disapproval. Like us, most of them were heading for the food court.

"Funny, isn't it," said Tim, as we descended the escalator into the crowded food court.

I glanced briefly at the food court full of carnivorous jam and the many grown men and women in plastic bags and tape trying to look dignified. "What is?"

"I was just thinking, this whole situation. It's, like, the one apocalypse no one called."

"How do you mean?"

"Well, you know, every major culture in history has believed itself to be living in the end times," said Tim, with a strange, wistful smile. "It's human nature, or something. People said it'd come from nuclear war, or overpopulation, or a climate change, or zombies, or whatever. Doomsaying was its own industry. No one called this. Not jam."

"Suppose not," I said, unsure what else I could add.

"And you know the funniest part? All the survivalists, all the people who seriously did think the end of civilization was coming, they all set up their compounds in the wilderness. Where all the plants are. They'd have been the very first to be eaten. It's funny, isn't it."

"It's ironic," I commented.

The look he gave me could have pinned something to a notice board. "Please don't."

"Well, it is."

As we descended into the food court, we saw the plastic people gathered near the same stage that had played host to last night's ironic execution. The original intention had presumably been to form a queue, but time and diminished patience had caused it to spread out into something closer to a mob.

The gangly young man with the whiny voice who had taken the role of priest suddenly shuffled out onto the stage, nervously fiddling with his hands. "All right then, quiet please," he said. "The divine protection of Crazy Bob again brings its wondrous bounty. Hail Crazy Bob."

"Hail curmleburm," went everyone else halfheartedly.

"So it's lucky-dip time again. Won't this be fun."

The grumbling plastic devotees who shuffled wearily towards the stage didn't seem to think so. At this point I noticed a row of half-submerged shopping trolleys piled full of (predictably) plastic bags. The two lackeys pushed the trolleys through the jam towards the crowd with tremendous difficulty, looking like a pair of bag ladies who had taken their title a little too literally.

"Plenty to go around, one bag each, let's keep this moving," said the priest, handing out bags to those infuriating morning people who had managed to be first in line. "All you choosy Susies feel free to hold us up as long as you like. It's not like any of us have anything better to do."

It was likewise for want of anything better to do that Tim and I joined the back of the column and stood in line for a handout. The safe assumption was that this was the food rationing, and my stomach was echoing the impatient grumbles of the queue. I'd never been completely certain what, exactly, amounted to a "balanced diet," but I was fairly sure I hadn't been anywhere near one lately.

As the priest handed Tim his bag, he held onto it for a second longer and looked him meaningfully in the eye in a sort of *don't-make-waves* kind of way.

"I got one of those ready-made sandwiches," I reported, peering into my bag once we had moved aside. "And a Mars bar. And a Capri Sun. You?"

Tim showed me an undersized plastic bottle half-full of water, and a rather soggy-looking shrink-wrapped microwave-ready meal. Either shepherd's pie or cottage pie—I've never been sure of the difference. He looked at me, and I was made very uncomfortable by a momentary flash in his eye.

"Excuse me," he said, turning on his heel and addressing the priest again.

The priest, not in the least bit surprised, paused in the act of handing out the rest of the rations. "Would you excuse me, everyone? I think I hear Mr. Important speaking." He straightened up and put his hands on his hips. "Can I help you?"

"This is thawed," said Tim. "It was frozen, and now it's thawed."

"Well, lucky old you. Now it'll take less time to cook."

"It'll have thawed days ago. It'll be rancid now."

"Oh, well, I'm very sorry you're dissatisfied with the room service here. You know, supplies are limited. The supermarket was beneath jam level; we only have whatever was sealed in plastic at the time. We don't HAVE to ration food to every epicure who might come to stay." He flamboyantly turned back to the queue in an uptight attempt to end conversation, which Tim chose not to notice.

"What are you going to do when the supermarket runs out of food?" he asked.

"Gosh, I don't know," huffed the priest. "If only we were in, say, the middle of a city, where there might be plenty of other shops and restaurants."

"So you're going to loot."

"Yes." He looked at Tim balefully. "We'd leave some money, but no one ever seems to be around."

"What will you do when they run out? What are you doing about crop cultivation? Water filtering?"

The priest had done that flamboyant turn to signal the end of the discussion three times now, and the effort was starting to show. "Well, when it becomes necessary, we will follow the divine direction of Crazy Bob. Hail Crazy Bob."

"Hurm," answered the hungry crowd.

"Can I talk to Crazy Bob?"

The priest froze for a moment, then looked at Tim, the side of his mouth curling in an impish half smile. I remembered last night's casual execution, and I felt renewed fear for Tim. "You seriously want to actually talk to Crazy Bob?"

"Yes," said Tim, uneasily, like a man who had just looked down and seen train tracks under his feet.

"Well, he won't be up at this hour," said the priest, suddenly all smiles and friendly service. "But you're free to go up and request an audience whenever you wish. After the morning scavenge, perhaps. Hadn't you better be leaving for that around about now?" He pantomimed checking a watch that wasn't there.

"The morning what?" said Tim.

Angela materialized from the nearby crowd and tugged at his sleeve. "Everyone has to go out into the city and look for more supplies during the day," she whispered informatively.

"Just a simple courtesy in return for membership, entirely optional if you don't want to be part of the family," said the priest. "Like the guy last night. He never really wanted to be part of the family. What was his name again?"

"Let's go," insisted Angela, still tugging on Tim's plastic. I started doing the same with his other arm. The air between Tim and the priest crackled with malice and I could hear bestial murmurs from the members of the crowd who hadn't been fed. It seemed prudent to get away while the metaphorical tide was still swelling.

Thankfully Tim nodded his agreement and turned away with us, but not before giving the priest one last wary glare, a promise that the matter was not closed. The priest replied by displaying his palms in ironic benevolence.

"Well, good morning to you guys, anyway," said Angela as we headed away from the food court. "What'd you get in the lucky dip?" From her own breakfast bag she produced a wrinkled ice-cream wrapper, opened it slightly, and attempted to suck out the now-liquid contents.

Tim glanced back at the stage for a second. "I'm a little concerned with the administration of this settlement," he said distractedly.

"Mm. Noticed that," said Angela, jiggling her camera. "That was Lord Awesomo. He's pretty much in charge."

"He doesn't seem to have planned much in the way of long-term survival."

"And he killed a bloke," I said.

Tim looked at me oddly. "Why do you always go on like this whenever someone dies?"

"Well, anyway," said Angela. "Point is, you shouldn't make an enemy of Lord Awesomo. Everyone does what he says."

"Why?" I asked.

"I dunno. As far as I can tell, it's because he's popular, and everyone's afraid of not being cool anymore."

"Where are we going?" asked Tim suddenly. Angela seemed to be leading us on a very specific path, through one of the narrower corridors on the ground level that went past the bookshop.

"Oh, this is where we meet Sergeant Cuddles for scavenging duty," she said.

"How do you suddenly know all this?" I asked.

"Hey. Journalist, remember?" She jiggled her camera again. "I've spent the whole morning on reconnaissance."

"Journalism student," corrected Tim.

"So?" she said defensively. "That made it easier, if anything. I told everyone I was filming for a project."

Our destination turned out to be the bookshop, which had been full of wooden shelving units and good, old-fashioned organic paper before the jam had obligingly cleared it out into a ready-made meeting center. It was directly opposite a short staircase, one of the smaller side exits up to Queen Street. A collection of plastic men were arranged into three uneven rows, standing to attention somewhere within their baggy plastic shells. We quietly joined them.

Sergeant Cuddles turned out to be an overweight young man wearing coke-bottle glasses over his transparent face bag and a wide-brimmed drill sergeant's hat constructed from plastic bags and cardboard. He was striding back and forth in front of the first row of men, hands behind back, raising his chubby leg so high with each step that it rose above jam level like a battered sausage bobbing in a deep fryer.

"A-all right, maggots," he began when everyone who was going to be there had arrived. "Expect you think you're ready to, to represent us out there on the, er, scavenging grounds. Aren't you!"

He was trying as hard as he could to bark, but just didn't have the voice for it. He lost confidence in the shriek midway through the first syllable and dropped down to the level most people use to order drinks in a crowded bar.

"Yes, sir," said the recruits, in rather sloppy unison.

The sergeant coughed self-consciously. "I can't hear you!"

"Yes, sir," repeated the recruits at precisely the same volume, after a moment's unspoken debate.

"Well, you're wrong," said Sergeant Cuddles weakly. "Probably. Never mind. Today we'll be heading up Queen Street towards the river, left on George away from Hibatsu, and looting along the length of George right up to the bo—to where the botanical gardens used to be. Anyone got a problem with that, you . . . stupid . . . silly . . . bastards?"

"Not really," said someone.

"Seems reasonable," said someone else.

"What's going on at Hibatsu?" said Tim.

Angela nudged him in another example of a don't-make-waves kind of gesture, but Sergeant Cuddles had already turned to look at him. He strode slowly and deliberately up to him, perhaps to give him time to think of something to say, then stood nose to nose, the sergeant's round belly pressing against Tim's midriff.

"Where are you from, recruit?" asked the sergeant.

"Er," said Tim. "Fortitude Valley."

"You know what they say about Fortitude Valley, don't you!" demanded the sergeant.

"Er," said Tim again. "The night life is good?"

The sergeant opted to abandon this line of inquiry. "You think you know better about how to spend the morning, do you?"

"No, I was just asking what's been going on at Hibatsu." A pause. "I'm just asking."

"Oh really?" said the sergeant, his voice heavy with sarcasm. He glanced around uncertainly as he tried to think of how to follow that up. "We never go near Hibatsu. Never."

"Why not?"

"Because. I said so."

"And who are you again?"

The sergeant reddened in equal parts anger and embarrassment. "I'm the sergeant!" he whined, apparently stamping his foot. "Lord Awesomo appointed me in charge of supply gathering! The order came from Crazy Bob!"

"Was this one of those *ironic* things?" asked Tim, neatly adopting that strange emphasis. Angela nudged him again.

Sergeant Cuddles seemed afraid that he was losing his authority. "I hope . . . you get killed!" he squeaked, then turned quickly away, visibly shaking himself. "Anyway, if no one has any actual objections, let's move out!" He turned on his heel and march-waded towards the stairs. "Left, right, left, right . . ."

The rest of us decided swiftly that, like chafing and executions, the sergeant was going to be another factor of our new lives we were just going to have to deal with. We shambled towards the stairs after him in a disorganized mob.

"Keep in line, please!" commanded the sergeant petulantly as he stepped outside, adjusting his hat to shield his eyes from the bright sunlight. "Left, right, left, right, left—"

He stopped dead with his back to us and stiffened oddly, as if he'd just stepped on something nasty and couldn't bring himself to look down at it.

"Right?" prompted Angela.

Something red and viscous squirted gaily from Sergeant Cuddles's breathing hole, as well as the two small holes where he'd inserted the hooks of his glasses, and his bags swooned emptily into the jam.

Fear beat a tribal rhythm down my spine and rooted my legs to the spot. A shocked glance was exchanged around the group of scavengers like a hot potato.

"He's dead!" I exclaimed.

"You're doing it again," said Tim distractedly.

"What happened?" said someone near the front.

One by one, everyone pushed close enough to the front to witness Sergeant Cuddles's fate, then immediately retreated, hoping someone else would take command. Finally a large, businesslike fellow in a mix of black and sky-blue plastic heaved a sigh and pushed his way cautiously to Sergeant Cuddles's garments, which floated morosely on the surface a few yards into the street. He carefully lifted them up, and a pair of coke-bottle glasses tumbled out into the jam. I felt sick.

"There's a rip," he reported, holding the bags up to the light for all to see. "The jam got in his suit. Through the leg."

"He must have got it caught on something," suggested Angela.

The newly elected point man got halfway through a *yeah* of thoughtful agreement when he realized that he was almost certainly standing within inches of whatever it was that had claimed Cuddles's life. With nothing protecting him from the jam but two flimsy layers of bin liner, the tiniest pin, piece of broken glass, or jagged paving stone was as good as a land mine.

"Keep calm," said a plastic woman in red, who had decided to be next in rank. "Just move away as slowly as you can."

The point man nodded infinitesimally, holding his palms parallel to the jam's surface as if trying to placate it. He very, very slowly lifted one leg, moved it as far away as he could, then planted it down as if walking a greasy tightrope. He kept still for a moment, then, satisfied he was still alive, lifted his other leg.

The jam suddenly flexed oddly directly in front of him. His hand flew to his thigh, then his outfit ballooned madly. Jam streamed festively from the breathing hole in the top of his head for a few moments before his bags flattened.

Tim elbowed me in the arm. "Stop screaming!"

I hadn't even noticed I'd been doing it. I clapped both hands over my mouth.

"Okay!" yelled the woman in red as the other plastic people whimpered and wobbled around in alarm. "Nobody go over there anymore!"

"So which way?!" asked someone else.

The woman in red leaned into the street and looked fearfully left and right. The street seemed to be completely deserted, but the X factor was obviously whatever was going on under the jam. She took a single step into the open, keeping her hand on the side of the mall entrance, then turned hard left and slowly headed north, at right angles to the route the last two guys had taken, keeping her back to the wall.

We watched her, biting our knuckles through four layers of plastic. After she had covered six feet with no incident, she let the air out of her lungs and waved for the rest of us to follow.

For a split second I thought I saw some strange movement in the air surrounding her, too fast to get a proper look at it, just as the jam at her waist pulsed oddly. She flung both arms towards us in panic before the jam flooded her suit with a comical farting noise.

Cramming any more tightly together was a tall order, but we managed it somehow. Another nonverbal election seemed to be taking place before someone at the back said, "What the hell do we do now?"

A shrewd-looking black garbage bag at the head of the group, perhaps realizing who the next logical victim might be, turned around and faced the shopping-center entrance. "How about," he said, "we not do any scavenging today?"

"Seconded," said someone behind me.

Immediately the entire platoon except me, Tim, and Angela about-faced and trooped back down the steps into the Briar Center, chatting amongst themselves.

"Hang on!" I called. Most of them ignored me, but a few halted at the foot of the steps and looked at me expectantly, including the two who had suggested and seconded abandoning the morning's hunt.

"Yes?" said the first.

"People are dead!" I said, avoiding looking at Tim.

The plastic men at the foot of the stairs exchanged glances. "Yes?" repeated the ringleader.

"Aren't you going to . . . you know . . . be upset about it?" I remembered what word I was after. "Mourn?"

"You mean . . . mourn *ironically*?"

"No, I mean just regular mourn!"

They seemed quite amused, like I was a small child confronting a visitor with a foam sword and a colander on my head. "Sure, why don't you take care of that," said one, before they went off to join their fellows.

"What is wrong with these people?" wondered Angela aloud, catching their departure on tape.

"It's almost like a hive," said Tim thoughtfully.

"How do you mean?" asked Angela.

"No concern for individuals." He brushed down his crinkling vest. "I guess one plastic bag looks pretty much the same as another."

DAY 4.2

There was a crowd in the great-hall food court again by the time we got back, this time without even the slightest pretension to being a queue. Our abortive salvaging party had joined a much larger group consisting of all that morning's salvaging parties, most of which seemed to have returned with significantly reduced numbers. Tim, Angela, and I endeavoured to lurk in the background.

Lord Awesomo stood in the middle of it all, his face thunderous as everyone within a ten-foot radius tried to bellow their version of events into his ears. Finally he snapped, picked up a chair, and smashed it repeatedly against a nearby escalator in lieu of a gavel. "All right!" he roared irritably when he'd achieved silence. "One person. Explain what the matter is."

This proved to be the wrong choice of words, because about fifteen individuals immediately nominated themselves the one person. He smashed the chair a few more times. It was becoming severely misshapen.

"You!" he said, pointing at the nearest talkative looter. "What happened?!"

"Jam!" barked the chosen one incoherently. "Jam ate! People! Outside!"

"Okay, not you." Awesomo picked someone from our party who seemed a little more together. "You!"

The plastic person explained the events we had just witnessed, identifying the victims only by the colors of the plastic bags involved.

"Oh yeah," said Awesomo. "I can see how easily you could forget that this happens, like, every day. You just need to refresh your bags every now and aga—"

"No, no, no," interrupted a rather agitated creature with a high voice. "It happens to everyone who tries to go outside."

"And where was this again?" demanded Awesomo irritably.

"The east entrance," said our spokesman.

"And the south entrance," said someone from another party.

"And every entrance," said someone else.

I glanced momentarily at Tim. He was staring fixedly at Lord Awesomo with a plastic-covered hand at his plastic-covered chin, like a serious gambler watching the racehorses reach the final furlong. The skinny leader stood stiffly, arms wrapped around his waist, as the plastic crowd looked to him for some kind of wise leadership. Judging by the growing spark of panic in his eyes shining through his permanent expression of ironic contempt, he wasn't sure himself where that wise leadership was going to come from.

"Hey!" came a familiar voice from above. Everyone looked up to see Princess Ravenhair on the next level up, leaning over the barrier. "Has anyone seen Whiskers?"

"Is something the matter, my lady?" asked Awesomo flamboyantly, clearly grateful for the distraction.

"I can't find him anywhere. I think he must have escaped. If you see him, could you let me know?"

She ran off without waiting for a response, and everyone turned back to Lord Awesomo. His eyes flicked back and forth a few times, then to the spot where Princess Ravenhair had been, then back.

"Didn't you hear?" he barked suddenly. "Your princess is upset! Everyone must search the center until Whiskers is found!"

And, to my surprise, every plastic person in the crowd immediately jumped to it, each one running to search in a different direction as if they'd each had a spot prearranged. We didn't move. Tim was chewing on his plastic-wrapped finger.

Soon we were the only ones left in the food court besides Awesomo himself, who caught our gaze with a triumphant smile, as if daring us to call him out on something. Instead, the three of us simultaneously opted to drift off in a random direction.

"This isn't right," said Tim.

"What isn't?" I asked, unable to narrow down the possibilities of what he might have been talking about.

"I thought they were just running things a bit dictatorially. But there doesn't seem to be any leadership at all. His decisions don't make any sense."

Angela blinked. She looked strangely pale. "Wait, so putting the search out for Whiskers doesn't make sense, but executing that guy was fine?"

Tim shrugged. "You've got to exercise authority. Could've done it more efficiently, I guess."

Angela boggled. "Are you from space?!"

Tim changed the subject quickly, either not wanting to confront her statement or too perplexed by it. "I'm going to go talk to Crazy Bob. You coming?"

"I'll meet you on the top level," I said. "I'm just going to stop by somewhere. I left something behind."

Specifically, *somewhere* was the spot in the department store where we had made camp the previous night, and *something* was Mary. I'd suddenly realized I'd left her there unsupervised, and the uncertain fate of Whiskers had made me paranoid about some kind of roving pet thief.

I arrived at the store without even bothering to take my bags off. After I rounded a display of refrigerators, the campsite came into view. I could see Mary's box sitting on my lingerie mattress, and she seemed perfectly all right. Probably still dozing after her extravagant breakfast.

"Oh!" came the voice of Princess Ravenhair as I strode over to Mary. I'd been so fixed on the well-being of my spider that I hadn't noticed her. She was sitting sulkily in the little area where I'd found Mary's meal, hugging one of her knees. A single handmaid fully wrapped in olive green appeared to be fanning her with a plastic snow shovel. "Has Whiskers turned up?"

"Er, no," I said, caught off guard. "What . . . what does Whiskers look like?"

"He's the prettiest little blue bird with black speckles on his face."

It was like a jugful of molten lava had been emptied into the hole at the top of my head bag. I felt myself redden right down to the toes. My first attempt to talk came out as a sort of strangled whinny before I could take a deep breath and try again. "Whiskers . . . is a bird?"

"Yeah. I called him that because it'd be *ironic*."

I sincerely wished that Tim was still around. Or Don. Or anyone. I was having to consciously restrain myself from running away. Princess Ravenhair was watching me curiously. I had to say something.

"Were you . . . very attached to Whiskers?" I mentally face palmed at my own words.

She looked at the floor sadly. Her handmaid redoubled her fanning efforts. "My parents got eaten by the jam," said the princess without much emotion. "Whiskers was the only one I could save. He was the only thing that I brought here with me."

I was mentally face palming so much, I could hear things rattling around inside my skull. I tried not to blink or look too psychotic. "Oh dear."

"I knew Gerald would come to the mall because we'd talked about what we'd do if there was, you know, a zombie apocalypse or something." She didn't seem to be talking exclusively to me anymore. "So I headed straight here and he was already setting all this up."

"Who's Gerald?"

She started, perhaps having revealed something regrettable. "I mean, Lord Awesomo." She cocked her head. "Are you new here?"

"Yes," I said unguardedly, hoping this would be a permanent subject change. "I'm Travis."

"The yellow looks horrible."

"Thanks."

"Don't tell anyone I said this," she said, eyeing her disinterested handmaid and lowering her voice. "But, to be completely honest, I'm not 100 percent sure about what G— Lord Awesomo thinks that he's doing, here. With this whole cult thing."

I frowned. "But aren't you, like, the messiah, or something?"

She sighed. "Everything's gotten so *ironic* lately I just don't know where I stand anymore. Travis, do you ever get the feeling you're just . . . going along with things? Without really thinking about what you want?"

I stared at her. I felt myself take a slow step forward and place my hand on the backrest of a chair opposite her. "You know. It's funny you should say that . . ."

Suddenly she flinched again, and her face twisted in disgust. "Oh my god. Is that a tarantula?"

I leapt back, hugging Mary to my chest. "Yaybe," I blurted.

Ravenhair softened after the initial shock, but she kept leaning away from me with the kind of reassuring smile one reserves for insane gunmen. "It's very . . . big."

Mary hissed jealously as I tried to subtly move her box behind my back. "Anyway, I should be going," I said, sidling carefully away. I noticed a blue feather on the floor, and tried to subtly scrape it under a counter with my shoe. "Nice talking to you, princess."

"Deirdre," she corrected. "Erm. You should probably . . . turn around. You're about to back into a lamp."

I found Tim and Angela on the second-highest level in the main mall area, at the foot of the set of curved stairs that led to the cinema lobby. I trotted to catch up.

"Tim," I said breathlessly, once I'd drawn up to his side. "I think I did something bad."

"What?" He glanced down, then yelped and grabbed at his heart. "God damn it, Travis, could you not sneak up on me when you're holding that thing?"

"Sorry." I held Mary's box behind my back as we began tramping up the steps.

"What do you think you did?" he asked.

For a while I'd been quite desperate for someone to share my latest problem with, but I saw he probably had enough problems of his own to deal with. He was still anxiously chewing a finger in deep thought; at this rate, it would probably be worn down to the knuckle by the end of the day. "Nothing," I said. "Never mind."

"So, what are we doing up here?" said Angela, for the benefit of the tape.

"Talking with Crazy Bob," said Tim. "And failing that, trying to get access to the roof, start thinking about cultivation. Because I'm starting to get a horrible feeling that Crazy

Bob will turn out to be a dog or a cardboard cutout or something."

At the top of the stairs was the cinema lobby, directly underneath the frosted ceiling and thus probably the best-lit part of the whole complex, as well as being completely free of jam. It seemed like this would be a prime piece of real estate, but it was nearly deserted. The popcorn and snack counters had been emptied of anything edible and the film names on the display board had all had their letters rearranged into rude anagrams, but otherwise the area didn't show any of the ransacking the rest of the mall had suffered.

Five guards, each in black bags and carrying a makeshift spear like the ones we had met at the south entrance, stood at regular intervals around the perimeter wall. I hadn't noticed them at first because they were as still and disciplined as Buckingham Palace guards, although they all had their motionless gazes fixed suspiciously on Don Sunderland.

Don was almost bent double by the snack counter, examining the glass with his hands behind his back like an interested tourist. Occasionally he took a look around the room at the guards, and it was during one of these that he spotted us.

"Hello, friends," he said, in an insincere, staccato voice. "Come over and look at this extremely interesting exhibit."

He waved us over and I saw that the glass-covered snack counter had been converted into some kind of museum, with a variety of random knickknacks tastefully arranged on the shelves, including an overloaded key ring and an empty yogurt pot.

Don was drawing our attention to what was presumably the newest addition to the display: the donated hard drive, apparently containing the build that spelled Don's entire future employment and happiness. A bit of folded card in front of it read *The Sacred Hard Drive of Bugger D'Klee*.

"The guards won't even let me touch it," muttered Don as we huddled around.

"Have you tried telling them it's for a project?" said Angela.

"How about you guys cause a distraction for a minute?" said Don hopefully. "I'll grab it while the guards are duffing you up and run away."

"Sorry," said Tim firmly. "We're working on creating sustainable agriculture for long-term survival."

Don gave him a very flat look. "You're just trying to get a rise out of me now, aren't you."

"We're going to plant crops on the roof."

"Ah. That would be with all that in-depth knowledge of farming you have, will it?"

Don and Tim were standing practically chest to chest, heads held high as if they were both looking through their nostrils. "*We'll look it up*," growled Tim.

"Don't kid yourself. There's no Google."

"And what exactly do you plan to do once you get your hard drive back, Don?" challenged Tim.

"I'm going to laugh," said Don, after a moment's thought. "Laugh and run away."

"Look, what is it you people want?" said the nearest guard, unable to remain silent any longer. Don distributed his favorite dirty look to everyone in the room, then marched purposefully towards the stairs, nose still held high.

"We want to speak to Crazy Bob," said Tim.

The guard cocked his head. "You actually want to *talk* to Crazy Bob?" he said.

Tim sighed. "Yes. Would that be a problem?"

The guard jerked a black plastic thumb towards the wide set of curved stairs that led up to the actual theaters. "No, no, you can talk to him whenever you like. Right up there, first left, cinema number one."

We thanked him uncertainly and made our way up the stairs. The red carpet had almost certainly been there before, but someone had also been cutting up decorative plastic flowers and sprinkling the pieces tastefully down the steps.

"All the guards are watching us," I whispered, identifying out loud the cause of the hot prickly sensation running down my back.

"Yeah," said Angela loudly. "I'm starting to feel like the lookout that gets sent into the monster cave first."

"Leave the talking to me," said Tim, unconcerned.

At the top of the stairs was the short hallway connecting the five theaters, where the posters and cardboard cutouts advertising upcoming films were displayed. They were still there, but every single human face had a cardboard mask taped over it: the face of a cartoon man with bulging crossed eyes and his tongue sticking out. I wasn't sure, but I could swear I'd seen that face before somewhere.

We took a left and moved on.

Most of the theater entrances were pitch dark, but theater 1 was illuminated with the prerequisite flaming torches. They were neatly laid out down the two aisles of the auditorium, with a clustered handful illuminating what was going on directly in front of the movie screen.

There, a high-backed leather armchair from the most upscale part of the department store had been set up like a throne. Around it were several plastic-covered concubines arranged in seductive poses, each with two pieces of contrasting-colored bin liner over their standard plastic covering in an attempt to simulate bikinis.

Crazy Bob was presumably the occupant of the throne. He sat in a Conanesque slouch, chin supported on one fist and legs spread unsettlingly wide. Remarkably, he wasn't wearing a single plastic bag. He had on a blue maintenance jumpsuit that seemed to be in dire need of a wash, and his face was entirely covered by another of those strangely familiar cardboard masks.

"Okay, how to approach this," muttered Tim to himself as we walked slowly down the aisle. I could understand his uncertainty. There was no way of knowing if a simple hello was acceptable or if anything other than full-on ironic we-bid-respectful-greetings-to-your-most-resplendent-majesty would bring immediate execution for treason.

As it turned out, he didn't get the chance to pick. "You must be Crazy Bob!" Angela yelled.

Tim's shoulders sagged in exasperation. "Fine. We'll go with that."

"No, I mean, 'You must be crazy, Bob'!" she continued excitedly. "Crazy Bob's Mobile Phone Asylum! That's where that character's from! I just realized!"

"Oh my god! You're right!" I said, before recalling the song out loud. "Your prices are lazy / Everything's gone hazy . . ."

Angela joined me for the final line. "You must be crazy, Bob!" Then we fell about laughing.

Tim wasn't joining in. He appeared to be covering his face with both his hands, fingers clawed like two haunted trees reaching up to the moon.

"Wbluh?" emitted Crazy Bob, sputtering himself awake. "Who's that? Speak up!"

Tim's arms instantly slapped to his sides. "Er, Tim," he said, quickly. "My name's Tim."

"Eh?" barked Crazy Bob in the complete opposite of an indoor voice.

"Tim! I just want to talk to you about the administration of this settlement."

The unchanging wacky expression on the two-dimensional face of Crazy Bob swayed left and right. "What are you talking about, you silly fool? Have you brought my tea?"

Tim's brow furrowed. "No." That didn't seem like an adequate response. "There isn't going to be any tea."

"What?!" bellowed Crazy Bob. "Who are you? Get out of here or I'm going to call the police!"

"There . . . there isn't going to be any police either," stammered Tim. "They're all gone. Civilization's collapsed."

"Well then, call the police! Can't you do a single thing without having to be told?"

"Look, sorry to bother you. I was just looking for the roof access," said Tim, returning, flustered, to the point.

"I'm an old man!" replied Crazy Bob.

There was a long pause, then Tim suddenly strode forward and leaned urgently on the stage. "Could you tell me," he said, slowly and clearly like a tourist trying to communicate with a brown person, "where you are?"

"Don't think you can patronize me," said Crazy Bob. "I'm at work." He lifted up a push broom that had been at his feet, holding it like an offering. It was at more or less this point that I noticed that none of his concubines had moved an inch, and were in fact department-store mannequins.

"There are a load of people downstairs," said Tim with admirable patience, "who worship you as some kind of godly leader. Last night someone got killed because they ate your yogurt. Were you aware of this?"

Crazy Bob's eyeholes flashed as Tim raised one of the few topics that could penetrate his consciousness. "Where's my yogurt? Have you got my yogurt?"

"No, I'm saying someone stole your yogurt and your high priest murdered him."

"Someone wants to steal my yogurt? I'd like to see them try!" He wobbled his broom. "I'm not so old that I can't show some young idiots what for! Where you going?"

"Sorry," said Tim as we backed away. "Thought you were someone else."

"I'm an old man!" he yelled after us.

Once we'd backed all the way out of the theater into the connecting hall, Tim spun around, clutched his hair in his hands, and began pacing like an expectant father in a hospital corridor. After he'd completed his third lap and was setting out on his fourth, Angela coughed tactfully.

"Crazy Bob's attitude rang particularly familiar for me," she said to her camera. "My grandfather was the same. I went to visit him once and he thought I was Howard Holt."

"It's a bit sad, really," I commented.

Tim stopped short but didn't turn. "Sad? It's sick. It's like a European monarchy where they skipped all the good kings and went straight to when they're all mad, inbred bastards. Why the hell would anyone run a settlement this way?"

"I think it's an ironic thing," said Angela.

Tim's attention was drawn to an emergency-exit door that had been painted to look like part of the wall, with the unlocking bar on the front cleverly made to look like part of the advertising display for that one upcoming movie about the anthropomorphic supermarket trolleys. He placed his hands on it, then stopped himself. "Are any of those guards watching?"

Angela leant around the corner. "No, they're all keeping an eye on Don," she revealed. "He's standing by the top of the stairs trying to whistle."

Immediately Tim pushed the door open with a wincingly loud *clunk* and hustled us into the concrete stairwell beyond. There weren't any flaming torches set up, but the advantage of narrow staircases is that they're quite predictably laid out. We felt our way up to the highest level and dazzled ourselves with the bright noonday sun after the roof access door fell open to Tim's pushing.

"Hang on," said Angela, bracing the heavy door open with a convenient nearby brick. "I've seen this movie."

"Why's this door unlocked?" I wondered, prodding the bar with one finger.

"Ah, this I did find out," said Angela, kicking the brick firmly into place. "Crazy Bob was the janitor here. And the plastic men borrowed his keys and went through the whole place unlocking all the doors. That's as far as I could tell through all the irony."

Tim was walking the wide, circular roof, completing a circuit around the huge skylight that was currently illuminating the main interior. Occasionally he kicked at the stubbornly solid gravelly floor, and grimaced each time at either the unsuitable farming conditions or a repeatedly stubbed toe.

"So what's the verdict?" asked Angela once he'd completed his first lap.

"Well, we'll definitely need soil," he said, rubbing his foot on the back of his other trouser leg. "I think I saw some unbroken plastic sacks in the home and garden department. Hopefully that'll be enough. And it is summer, so we can probably rely on some rain."

"Er, Tim, maybe Don is right," I said as gently as possible, prompting Tim's eyes to immediately start from his sockets in preparation for an argument. "Maybe we should just get out while we can and move straight on to Hibatsu. These people are all . . . well, they're all mad."

Tim sighed and glanced back at the building under discussion, which loomed invitingly by the river barely a few hundred yards away. We were now close enough to read the banner that was still fluttering outside the upper windows: *Hibatsu Shelter Welcomes Airborne Rescuers!* "I understand your position," he said, his voice sounding a little dubious as he reread Hibatsu's optimistic message. "I just think there's already a settlement here and a good source for supplies. I'm not sure I want to take a risk on another roll of the dice. Hibatsu could be even worse."

He turned to face us and opened his mouth to make another point, but then his eyes boggled and he spun on his heel. He bolted for the edge of the roof, planted his hands on the edge, and leaned forward so urgently I thought for a moment he'd suddenly been seized by the suicidal impulse. "Look!" he shouted. Angela and I trotted over.

"Whoa, look at the jam," said Angela.

The jam was behaving very oddly around the Hibatsu building. While everywhere else in the city it maintained a permanent depth of three feet, rising and falling accordingly with the contours of the ground underneath, for some reason it had commenced the process of sheathing Hibatsu like a gigantic fruit-flavored condom as high as Hibatsu's third floor. It reached its maximum height against the building's outer wall and gradually tapered down to the standard depth. I was reminded of the way the jam had tried to ensnare me as I'd moved through it with apple in hand.

"Well, that's it," said Tim, turning and rubbing his hands. "Definitely not going to take that risk. We're stuck with the Briar Center. That's fine. Most of the work's been done for us; all we need is a change of government."

I coughed. "Tim, don't take this the wrong way, but . . . do you not think you might be taking things a little too far?"

His mouth hung open as he waited for the punch line. "What?"

"Okay, you're taking that the wrong way. I just think, you know . . ." My hands made nervous groping notions as I sought the words. "It is good that you're worrying about it now, but . . . of all the things that are worth worrying about—the lots of things, don't get me wrong—are you sure that you've got them all . . . properly arranged on the priorities list?"

"Priorities?!" spat Tim. "Fine! You do whatever you want. Go downstairs and mess around eating Mars bars and executing people. And six months from now when all the food's run out, come right on up and ask to have some of my incredibly small amount of crops because I had to grow them all by myself! Will you stop filming this?!"

"Sorry," said Angela, zooming out. "For a second there you looked exactly like Lord Awesomo."

Tim wasn't sure how to take that, so he just turned around and stormed back to the stairwell door. I think he was planning to slam it behind him, but the brick holding it open caught him short and he thought better of it, instead stomping down the stairs as loudly as he could.

I watched him go. When I turned around, Angela was sitting on a vent with her phone out. She'd been making a habit of checking for signals whenever she remembered, and as always, there was nothing. She stared sorrowfully at the lack of bars. "Do you think . . . Tim's all right?" I asked, to distract her.

She didn't look at me straightaway. "I dunno. You know him best, don't you?"

"I've never seen him like this before. He's never been so . . . driven."

"I guess that can be a good or a bad thing." The camcorder came out again. "Travis, if this were a film, who do you think would be the main character?"

I flinched as the lens rounded on me again, my eyebrows crashing together like a motorway pile-up. "What?"

"Because, in film terms, it'd be either Tim or Don. It depends. If this is an actual apocalypse, then Tim'd be the visionary hero and we should all be behind him." She was thinking aloud now, taking establishing shots of the skyline. "But if we're just waiting for rescue, then Don's the only sane man. Well. Right, at least."

"Why couldn't I be the main character?" I said. I'd tried to sound stern but it had come out belonging more to whine territory.

Angela didn't even look at me. "No offense, Travis, but you're not exactly dynamic."

"Oh. Charming."

After a few more attempts to work myself into genuine anger, I gave up and left her to her work. I paced sulkily around the roof, kicking up gravel every few steps. I certainly hoped this wasn't the apocalypse Tim thought it was, because I was not the kind of person who had any business surviving. I didn't have any of the skills necessary for postapocalyptic society. Or preapocalyptic society, come to think of it. In Angela's version of things I'd be the guy who goes off to investigate the strange noise in the first act and whose head is getting paraded around on a spike by the second.

I was still holding Mary's box by the handle, and she was pawing at the transparent walls reassuringly. I sat down with my back to a vent and laid her on my lap, rocking her playfully with my knees. "You think I'm the main character, don't you, Mary?"

"What did you say?"

I froze for a moment, astonished at Mary's sudden ability to speak, before it registered that the voice had come from somewhere behind me.

"That's what I thought you said," it continued. It was a woman's voice, with an American accent. It had to be X.

I glanced over at Angela, but she was on the opposite side of the roof, leaning over the wall with one foot in the air to film something captivating down in the jam-filled street. I didn't feel the need to draw her attention to this just yet, anyway.

Carefully setting Mary aside, I rolled onto my stomach and laid my cheek upon the ground. There was a gap of about two inches between the gravel and the underside of the vent, and I could see another section of roof beyond, and two people's feet.

The one closest to me was wearing sensible women's flats wrapped in transparent plastic bags, while the other had army boots with a few inches of ThunderCats-patterned trouser leg visible above.

"I can't believe you'd overstep my authority like that," said X, her shoes turning away from Y's.

"You were out of communication, sir," said Y quietly. I imagined his face angled towards the floor like that of a scolded schoolboy.

"Of course I was out of communication—I was being kidnapped! I've been worried as hell about where you've been and now I find that you're making deals behind my back?"

"Your rescue and extraction has always been my highest priority," said Y. From anyone else it might have sounded romantic, or at least warm, but the way he spoke about X put me in mind of a courier discussing a package. "Once I established you weren't in immediate danger, I sought to prioritize a long-term extraction solution."

"Immediate danger?!" repeated X's shoes, stamping unhappily. "They are executing people down there! For yogurt crimes!"

"I was observing that ceremony," assured Y. "I would have intervened if you had been under direct threat. It seemed to me you were being accepted into the organization."

"This is not an organization I relish being accepted into. I hesitate even to use the word *organization*." The shoes stomped back and forth uncertainly a few times. "Look. I'm sorry. I know you've got everything under control. I just want to get us out of this god damn insanity once and for all." Y kept silent, letting her vent. "I look at what these people have become, and I can't help but feel . . . responsible."

My eyebrows shot up. That one word had revived my dwindling interest in the conversation. There was a lot about X and Y I found suspicious—the code-name thing just for starters—but I'd never taken Angela's claims seriously. Now there definitely seemed to be more to the story.

"You are not responsible, sir," said Y, muddying the issue somewhat. "If anyone should feel responsible, it's me."

Her feet moved closer to his. "Don't ever think that. All right? We're in this together. To the end."

"As you wish, sir," said Y disingenuously.

X sighed through her teeth. "So, these people you made a deal with. Can we trust them?"

"Of the settlements I have seen, they are the most dependable," said Y. "Above all, they are secure. And they have guaranteed me that they have a means of communicating with the outside world. I don't believe they have any reason to lie. They consider my work to be a favor rather than an absolute necessity."

"And once you've fulfilled your end of the bargain?"

"They will accept us immediately."

"What about the others?" said X.

"I didn't mention them."

X's feet paced a little more. "At any rate, they're not our problem."

"They did pull us out of the wreck, sir," said Y.

"That's an emotional response," said X, her tone implying that it was therefore something entirely beyond her understanding.

"As you say, sir." Y's tone had only the merest hint of discomfort. "And the Sunderland issue?"

"I see no reason to draw Mr. Sunderland's attention to that issue at present. He is an . . . unpredictable factor."

I'd been mentally attaching all kinds of pale, black-suited figures to the name of Mr. Sunderland before remembering that Sunderland was Don's last name. My ears were pricking up so hard now they threatened to peel right off the sides of my head. Why was Don so important that there'd be an issue named after him?

"I could easily recover the unit without his knowledge," continued Y.

"I know that. So could I," said X. "My thinking is it might be for the best that the unit not be in our possession if rescue arrives. It creates considerably more deniability. No, my orders stand. Leave it with him, but don't let him—"

"Hey!"

That was Angela. I glanced over to the left, and saw her plastic-covered shoes trotting into view from around the other side of the roof. By the time I looked back, Y's boots had disappeared without a sound.

"Who were you talking to?" demanded Angela, her shoes toe to toe with X's. I heard her camera zooming. "Are you conspiring again?"

X glanced behind her, apparently as surprised as I was by Y's quick exit, but recovering quickly. "I don't know what you're talking about," she said, in that sincere tone people only use when they're being completely insincere. "I just came up to get some air."

"Some *air-to-air missiles*, maybe," said Angela. "Where's Travis? Have you silenced him?"

I felt some kind of rescue was in order, although I wondered which of the two I was rescuing. I carefully crawled away under the cover of the vent, then stood up, turned around, and walked flamboyantly back to my spot, humming loudly. "Oh, hello," I said, waving over the vent. "I was just doing something else over there."

"Well, if that's all, I'll see you guys later," said X sweetly, speed walking towards the exit before either of us could argue about the *that's all* thing.

"You can't hide it forever!" yelled Angela after her.

X didn't turn back, but merely waved coquettishly as if Angela had been blowing kisses. Then she passed through the stairwell door and vanished from sight.

"I wouldn't think it'd be possible for absolutely everything a person does to seem suspicious, but she manages it," said Angela in exasperated wonder. "What was she doing up here?"

I opened my mouth, ready to reveal Y's presence and give a full account of the conversation I'd overheard, but cooler heads prevailed. I wasn't sure where Y was but he'd already established himself to be, like me, unafraid to listen in on other people's conversations—and more to the point, beat them to a pulp. Besides, I didn't think Angela's probable reaction—to run immediately to X and screech accusations like an aggressive swan protecting her eggs—would improve matters.

"Must be the fresh air," I said, finally.

"She knows something," muttered Angela dangerously. "It's only a matter of time before she lets something slip."

I coughed. "She might slip faster if you didn't keep yelling questions in her face."

"Well, what would you suggest? Find someone to seduce her and find out if she talks in her . . . sleep?" Her voice became thoughtful towards the end of her question and she cocked her head, scrutinizing my face. "Travis, have you ever considered—"

"NO. Definitely, never, no."

DAY 4.3

Once we were back inside, Angela wandered off in pursuit of her own agenda, and I returned alone to the department-store entrance, hands in plastic pockets. On the way, it struck me that the entire gloomy atmosphere of the settlement seemed to have had another layer of shadows painted over it. Murmurs of fear and unrest drifted up from the food court among the usual constant background rustling of bin liners.

My bags were getting whiffy again, so I gathered them up and took them to the laundry. While waiting for my turn, I noticed Princess Ravenhair standing at the store entrance, fretfully watching the people around her, fidgeting with imaginary rings on her fingers. To my surprise, her face brightened when she saw me approaching, and she pushed through the crowd to greet me.

"Hi. Travis, right?" she said, so quickly the words blurred together. "You were on Sergeant Cuddles's detail this morning, weren't you? Is he all right?"

"Er, sure, he's fine," I stammered, caught off guard. "I mean, he hasn't gotten any less dead."

"He's dead?!" cried the princess, clapping her hands to her cheeks.

"Well, probably," I said, flustered. "I'm pretty sure the jam ate him. I might be remembering it wrong."

"They're saying everyone's getting eaten by the jam when they try to go outside," she said, voice quavering. "People are getting really scared and angry and they're all looking to me for answers and I don't know what's going on!" She took a deep breath. "They're saying that Crazy Bob has lifted his divine protection!"

"Really?"

She thought about it. "They were probably being *ironic*. Oh, god, I can't even tell anymore." She sat down on an empty ceramic plant trough and buried her face in her hands. "I can't believe Glenn's dead."

"Glenn?"

She caught herself, screwing up her eyes in self-disgust. "Sergeant Cuddles. He was one of the first. The original founders of . . . of all this, along with Lord Awesomo and me."

"I thought you said Lord Awesomo was already here when you arrived?"

She seemed embarrassed. "Well. The thing is. Me and Gerald and Glenn, we all used to post on the same Internet forum. We had this really long thread about what we were going to do when the apocalypse happened. We were all going to meet up here and live off the shops. We kind of assumed it would be zombies, though."

"I think a lot of people did," I said, nodding.

"I don't think any of us know what we're doing anymore," she said, the volume of her voice decreasing gradually. Then she started crying. Not loudly, not the whole wailing thing; she just covered her eyes and shuddered silently into her palms.

I stood twiddling my thumbs for a moment, uncomfortably aware that something was expected of me but lacking the confidence to commit myself. Eventually, inch by inch, I began to sit down beside her, extending my arm for a tentative shoulder pat.

"I just wish I had Whiskers back," she moaned.

My face instantly reddened. I aborted the sitting attempt and returned to standing and fidgeting.

"Sorry, I don't mean to unload on you," she said, recovering and wiping away some dribbly snot. "I dunno, I guess it's just because you're new. It's nice to talk to someone who's got no idea what's going on."

"I definitely am that," I sighed. The laundry guy thrust my plastic bags back at me. I balled them up under my arm. "Erm, I have to go into the store . . ."

"Oh, sure, I'll come with you," she said, hopping to her feet and deftly overlooking my attempt to break off the encounter. I noticed a lot of the plastic people were giving me slightly hostile looks now that I was escorting their princess. Many of them were still wearing opaque plastic bags on their heads, though, so I might have been projecting a bit.

"How's your spider?" she asked as we climbed the stationary escalator, patting the box I still held in my free hand and making Mary start resentfully.

"Good," I said, noncommittal.

"It really is huge. What breed is it?"

"It's a Goliath . . ." I mentally dropped a massive cast-iron weight on my words just in time. "Goliath . . . eater. Goliath eater. Because they eat things."

"Yes, what do you feed it?"

For some reason it was the only thing that I could think of on the fly. "Milkshakes."

"Milkshakes?"

I was committed, now. "Fat and protein. It's really good for them. For their webs." Inspiration struck. "The one thing you mustn't ever give them is meat. They don't eat any meat in the wild. Can't digest it. They get all their protein from beans and coconuts and biting through the tops of milk bottles."

She seemed satisfied, if a little baffled. Thankfully she changed the subject herself. "Isn't that your friend?"

By now we were back in the housewares section, in the wide thoroughfare that led to our campsite, and Tim was walking towards us out of the furniture department. His head was uncovered and he was wearing a particularly eye-catching set of bright yellows presumably borrowed from Don's bag reserve. With his mouth set into a thin line, he carried an extremely large and heavy-looking high-backed leather armchair into the center of the clearing. He planted it down, then turned it to face him and climbed onto the seat, placing his hands on top of the backrest like a lectern.

Satisfied, he stepped back down and picked up a long, narrow lampshade. I watched him curiously as he mounted his chair again and held the narrow end of the lampshade to his lips.

"Brothers! Sisters! Citizens of all colors of plastic!" he boomed through his makeshift megaphone. "Gather round and hear me now!"

A cheering mob of revolutionary insurgents failed to throng around his pedestal, but a few heads turned.

"Have you lost faith in the current administration?" continued Tim, gaining confidence. "Do you live in fear of execution for committing something you didn't even know was a crime? Do you want to live in a society governed in the name of freedom and equality, rather than irony? Well—"

"What are you doing?" said one of the six or seven curious plastic people who had gathered nearby, a tall young man in whites and blues standing with his arms folded.

"I'm starting a political rally," said Tim, lowering his lampshade for a second.

"An *ironic* political rally?"

"No, a real one. Completely unironic. That's kind of the point."

"Oh, right." He nodded thoughtfully, but didn't seem to quite grasp the concept. "Sorry. Didn't mean to interrupt."

Tim raised his lampshade again. "Lord Awesomo doesn't want you to realize that this society is not sustainable," he declared. "Tinned and packaged food will run out. We can't scavenge forever. We need long-term solutions in place now. It's going to take a lot of determination and hard work, but together—"

"How much hard work?" said a newcomer, clad entirely in black.

"A lot," clarified Tim testily.

"Oh. Well, I don't really like doing hard work. I think everyone should do all the hard work for me so I can sit around doing whatever I want. I think I deserve it because I'm so great."

Tim blinked a few times. "Are you being *ironically* reprehensible?"

The plastic man laughed patronizingly. "Course I am, dude. Chill out."

"So you *are* willing to do hard work?"

A moment's silence passed as he considered this. "Nnnnnno."

"Well, that's not irony, is it?" snapped Tim, his patience fading. "Irony means the opposite of what you'd expect. What you just said was just an unusually candid statement of reality."

There was a hostile grumbling among the ranks. Some of the plastic people started unironically hissing. Someone blew a brief raspberry. I glanced at Princess Ravenhair. She was watching Tim intently, something approaching infatuation sparking in her eyes.

"Listen," said Tim, returning to script. "We can't go on like this. This is bigger than any of us. I'm talking about the future of the human race! That's not your property to be messing around with! It belongs to your children. And your children's chi—"

"I hate children," announced a heckler.

"Yeah, stupid little bastards," said another one. "Always sitting behind me on long flights."

"I think they should all be tortured and killed in internment camps," said the ironically reprehensible guy proudly.

Tim's lips were quivering like those of a vomiting man in the brief moment of unhappy reflection between heaves. Half the crowd was jeering and the other half was wandering off in disinterest.

Then, to my surprise, Princess Ravenhair strode forward into the center of the impromptu forum. Everyone fell silent and turned to face her as if she were a glass breaking in a crowded bar.

"Tell me more," she said.

Tim narrowed his eyes suspiciously. "Are you *ironically* interested?"

"No," said Ravenhair with the gravitas of a royal proclamation. "I'm regular interested." The murmuring returned with much less hostility, and the people rallied around.

Now that someone from the popular clique had made it "cool," Tim's rally started gathering support. More and more people joined the crowd as Princess Ravenhair listened intently, perched demurely on a hastily retrieved box ottoman.

I was surprised by how naturally Tim took to his public-speaking role—his last speech I could remember had been at a middle-school nativity play and he'd burst into tears after one sentence. Now, he discussed the supply issue and explained that, while prepackaged food was currently plentiful, farming crops was one of those things that you had to start doing some considerable time before it became necessary. He outlined his plans for rainwater catching and water recycling. He gave a short but poignant explanation of what *irony* meant— prompting one or two people to get nervous and walk away— and that "ironic" religiously inspired murder was still religiously inspired murder.

After half an hour there was a commotion at the back of the crowd. Lord Awesomo had arrived, and his people guiltily parted before him like a plastic Red Sea. "What the hell are you doing?!" he demanded, before noticing Princess Ravenhair among the crowd. "Deirdre? What's going on?"

"I was just idly talking to myself," said Tim, lent confidence by the crowd. "While standing on this chair. Some people happened to be passing and might have accidentally heard some of it. There's no rule against that, is there?"

"Oh, yeah, sure," sneered Awesomo. "Like the Mongol hordes were just taking a Sunday drive through continental Europe. This is a coup or I'm Germaine Greer."

"He was just talking," said Princess Ravenhair. Lord Awesomo glared at her in wordless astonishment. The crowd were watching them both intently, unsure where to place their loyalties.

"And even if there might have been a slightly political edge to my stream of consciousness," said Tim, now well into his stride, "surely the people have the right to choose how they want to be governed?"

"No!" said Awesomo. "I was made dictator for life by divine order of Crazy Bob. Hail Crazy Bob!"

A few people who were hedging their bets echoed the cry in an uneasy murmur, but it was clear Lord Awesomo had misjudged the general mood in the room. Most people returned nothing but a dirty look or, in one case, a cough that sounded suspiciously like the word *wanker*.

"What?!" said Awesomo, hands on hips. "I'm being *ironic*."

"That's not what 'ironic' means," said the guy who had been ironically reprehensible earlier. He made no attempt to emphasize the word.

Lord Awesomo's eyes flicked madly around like a falling climber seeking a handhold. There was a moment's tense silence before he turned smartly on his heel and walked away, mouth held firmly closed in token preservation of dignity.

Once he was gone, the entire room seemed to breathe a sigh of relief. Taking it as read Tim's little speech was over, the crowd separated and drifted away, talking to each other about their political options. A few members hung around to probe Tim on a few of his details and he responded to them all, wearing a large, immovable smile throughout. Princess Ravenhair just sat on her ottoman, watching him with a strange, satisfied smile on her face.

Finally she got up and walked away without a fuss, but passed me on the way out. She touched my arm momentarily and said, "Thank you." Only after she'd gone did it occur to me to ask her why.

Shortly afterwards I decided to slip away, and it was while picking my way through our campsite in homewares that I was startled by a voice. "You're his friend, aren't you."

Lord Awesomo was leaning comfortably on a refrigerator and watching me over his spectacles as I attempted to make my "bed." He'd pronounced *friend* the same way one would pronounce *amateur proctologist*.

"Whose?" I asked innocently.

"Don't be cute. That newbie doing all the rabble-rousing."

"I didn't tell him to," I protested.

"Yeah, but you're close to him." I didn't like the sound of that. "And now something's been picking us off when we try to leave. Maybe you'd be in a useful position to explain how it might not be a whizzo idea to start sowing the seeds of political discord during a crisis situation. Maybe I'd have some nice rewards for someone useful."

I sighed. "I'd really appreciate if you left me out of all this," I said meekly. "I've got a lot of stuff on my plate right now. I have a spider to think of."

Awesomo's eyes narrowed. "You're Travis, aren't you."

I nodded. There didn't seem to be any point in lying.

"Deirdre mentioned you," he revealed, almost accusingly. "She said you seem quite nice. The two of you seem to be becoming quite . . . friendly." The word fell from his disgusted mouth like half-chewed spinach.

"Sorry," I said. "Are you her boyfriend?"

He seemed startled by the question. "What? No!" he blustered. "No! Not at all. We're just . . . I mean, I never . . ." he shook himself. "No. We're good friends. Very good friends."

"Good," I said. "I mean, that you're friends. It's good to have friends. She said you used to post on some Internet forum together?"

"Do you think you understand her?" he said, confrontationally. "You think I'm the nasty one because I killed that guy? She's done that too. Lots of times. She likes to make herself seem harmless, you know, the one who's just going along with things, but she's just being *ironic*."

I swallowed. "Really?"

"She's a user. She manipulates. She was always like that on the board. She got all of us to vote up some Buffy fan fiction she wrote for CreepyShutIns.com and it ended up getting into the daily top ten. She's no different now. If someone has done something to her bird, I would not envy them, I tell you that."

A spider-shaped creeping dread ran a few laps around my stomach lining. "Uh-huh."

"Well, didn't mean to bore you," said Lord Awesomo, clapping his hands and standing upright. "If you'll excuse me, I have some governing matters to attend to. That's a very nice spider you have there, by the way. Goliath birdeater, isn't it?"

DAY 4.4

I lay awake that night, staring at the ceiling, holding Mary's box against my chest. If I rolled onto my side, I would have been staring directly at Princess Ravenhair's sleeping area, and the Princess Ravenhair–shaped mass under the duvet.

If I closed my eyes, and shut out the sound of crinkling plastic, I could almost convince myself I was back home in the flat. The traffic noise through my open balcony door was lulling me into a doze, and in the morning Tim would play some horrible music and Frank would tease me and maybe we'd all go out for lunch and life would be uncomplicated and no one would need to be executed for anything.

I heard a shuffling sound in our campsite, the kind made by someone trying very hard not to wake people who might want them to stop doing the thing making the noise. I lifted my head off my pillow and saw a shadowy figure hunched guiltily in the center of our misshapen circle of pseudobeds.

It could have been a thief or a murderer. I considered crying out. A thief would run away, but a murderer would murder me. On the other hand, the murderer would probably murder me if I didn't, too. That was his whole thing.

Thankfully the debate ended when the intruder experimentally flicked a pocket flashlight on and off, and in place of the hate-filled countenance of the assassin my imagination had furnished, I saw only the hate-filled countenance of Don Sunderland, putting his plastic bags on.

"What're you doing, Don?" I whispered.

The flashlight beam came back on and hit me full in the face, followed closely by a hand, which clamped over my mouth. "Shhhh," he hissed. "Go back to sleep. I'm leaving. Don't get weird about it."

"Wmmm mmml ymm gmm?"

He moved his hand. "What?"

"Where will you go?"

"To the Hibatsu building. Where do you think? Don't see any rescues stopping by this plague pit. So I'm off. I'd say it's been nice knowing you but I intend to spend the next few years trying to forget your names and faces."

Then he was gone, creeping off towards kitchenware on tiptoe, shining his flashlight whenever he felt there weren't any sleepers near enough to be bothered by it.

I lay clutching my bed sheet in my fingers for a moment until something kicked the back of my mind and suggested that now was a good time to go with the first instinct. I threw my bedding aside, grabbed Mary and my balled-up plastic bags, and ran after Don. I tripped on something body shaped and heard someone swear.

"Don!" I whispered, loudly.

He grabbed me roughly under the armpit and dragged me into a little display kitchenette, pinning me to a glass-fronted drinks cabinet. He kept a hand over my mouth until the muttering and consternation in the next room had settled back into ironic snores. "What the hell are you doing?!" he whispered.

"I want to go with you," I said plaintively.

"Are you serious? Why?"

"I may have done a bad thing. I think I should probably get out of here before anyone finds out."

"What do you mean, may have? Did you do it with your eyes shut?"

"All right, I *did* do a bad thing."

"What sort of bad thing?" he asked, in a tone of voice strongly implying that he definitely did not want a detailed account.

I took a look around. No one seemed to be listening, but I leaned close and whispered into his ear so quietly it was barely a step up from mouthing. "I may have fed Princess Ravenhair's budgie to Mary."

He tottered back a step, clutching his temples. His tonsils groped for syllables for a few seconds before his voice found coherence. "That was *you*? I've been random searched three times! I saw them beat up a guy 'cos he was holding a blue feather duster!"

"I'm sorry. I didn't know it was hers. Mary was getting really thin and I thought I could just apologize later." I looked at the toes of my shoes. "Please let me leave with you."

He sighed in irritation. "Fine, but if they catch us, I don't know you. I guess I could use a lookout, actually."

He let go of me and resumed his expedition to the store entrance. Following him was difficult at first, because he moved quickly and every time I tried to keep hold of his plastic coattails he'd shake me off angrily, but when we were far enough from the more populous sleeping areas he turned his flashlight back on.

Soon we were back in the main area of the mall. The ubiquitous torches, routinely refueled with cheap designer clothing and lit in the late afternoons, had fizzled out by this time of night, so Don's dancing pyramid of light was the only break in the pitch blackness. Don waited impatiently while I put on my plastics, but when I started to make for the down escalator the light danced off in the opposite direction, towards the stairs that led up to the cinema.

"Er!" I grunted. Don's flashlight beam stopped and shone in my face impatiently. "The exit's down this way. Isn't it?"

"Yes, and so is the jam," said Don from behind the dazzling

glow. "The jam keeps eating people who try to go outside. Remember? We're going to escape over the rooftops."

"Oh. Right." The explanation sounded perfectly reasonable, but something about it made me scratch my head uneasily. "Is that the only reason we're going this way?"

Don chuckled unpleasantly. "You can be shrewd when the mood takes you, can't you, Travis."

"Your hard drive?"

"My build!" We trooped as quietly as we could up the stairs. "I put a year of my life into that. So going by my yearly income it's got to be worth at least forty grand. That's a sound investment. You could buy a car with that."

Fortunately the guards weren't on duty in the little snack bar that had been converted into the Crazy Bob museum, and the entire cinema lobby was as silent as the tomb. Don crept eagerly forward and splayed his hands upon the glass like an orphan outside a sweet shop.

"There it is," he said, fogging up the glass.

"What sort of game is it?" I asked.

"It's not really a game. It's more of a proof of concept than anything else. For this new bit of hardware our parent company put together."

"Wait, so it doesn't actually do anything without the hardware?"

"No, but don't think that makes this pointless or anything. There's at least one other unit at the head office in Bellevue."

"So what if Bellevue's covered in jam too?"

He thought about this. "Then this is pointless after all. And so is my life. And so is yours. So we might as well kill ourselves."

"Fair enough."

He tapped the glass, and the *bong* echoed loudly through the silence. Both of us glanced around, wondering how deserted this lobby would stay if we kept making noises like that. He found a discarded towel under the slurpee machine, wrapped it around his fist, and brought it down on the display case. The glass wasn't impressed, and judging by Don's reaction, his wrist hadn't been a big fan of the performance either.

I watched nervously as he tiptoed purposefully over to the area where the ticket collector used to stand, where he unhooked a shiny brass bollard from its velvet rope and carried it back to the counter, patting the thin end on one palm.

"Er," I said, as he wrapped the towel around the bollard's heavy end. "Don't think I'm harping or anything, but is this really necessary?"

"That does sound quite a lot like harping," he said, making a practice swing.

"I mean, they're not actually doing anything to the hard drive. They're just keeping it locked up in here. They're not gonna touch it because they've declared it all sacred and stuff. Maybe you could just come back for it once you've sorted out escaping the city and all that."

He seemed to think about it, which made me feel quite proud. "Yes, but they are all complete lunatics," he pointed out. "They might suddenly decide that the hard drive must be smeared in holy marmalade and put in the holy microwave."

"They might just as easily decide to stab our eyes out while we sleep," I said, speaking from my deepest personal concern. "Maybe we should just get out of here now."

He sighed and looked at the end of his makeshift weapon sorrowfully. "I guess you're right. Lead the way, then."

I probably should have expected this, but the moment I elatedly turned around to look for an exit there was a thunderous crash behind me. The towel did indeed soften the sound of the initial impact between the bollard and the glass, but it couldn't do much about the apocalyptic shatter, or the symphony of tinkling shards falling to the ground.

Don recklessly fished his hard drive out of the ruins and held it aloft. "Changed my mind! Leg it!" he said at lightning speed, before sprinting for the upward-leading stairs without even checking to see if I was following.

The shock at Don's sheer audacity planted me to the spot for a few seconds before I heard footsteps from below, and someone yelling "WOO WOO WOO" in imitation of a burglar alarm. I ran after Don, up the staircase leading to the theaters and Crazy Bob's throne room. At the top of the stairs I risked a look behind and saw three security guards, in uniform black T-shirt-and-boxers sleepwear sans bags, arriving on the scene of the crime. Then a hand seized my shoulder like a Vulcan neck pinch and Don hauled me around the corner.

"Don't make a sound," he hissed. "There's like fifty paths we could have taken. As long as nothing—"

"Who are you?" demanded Crazy Bob. In addition to the cardboard mask, he was wearing an Ebenezer Scrooge–style nightshirt and nightcap combo and was holding a candle in a saucer, perhaps all provided for him in the name of irony. He was standing directly between us and the concealed emergency-exit door to the roof. "Are you the idiots crashing around at this time of night?"

"Just passing through!" said Don, displaying his palms.

Crazy Bob stepped firmly into his path. "I ordered a cup of tea half an hour ago and when I say I want a cup of tea I expect there to be . . ."

I glanced fearfully back at the guards in the lobby. One or two of them were peering curiously in our direction. I put a vibrating finger to my lips. "Shushush ushush shush!"

This proved unwise, because Crazy Bob took it as a challenge. "How dare you shush me!" he bawled. "If there's one thing I will not tolerate from uppity—"

Don shoved him. Not roughly, but hard enough to send Crazy Bob's frail form tottering back into the cardboard stand for the upcoming *Interstellar Bum Pirates* movie, breaking it loudly in two. Crazy Bob yelled incoherently for someone to call the police, and he was joined by a chorus of WOO WOO WOOs from the lobby.

Don shoulder barged his way into the emergency stairwell. I made the briefest possible check for injuries in Crazy Bob—superficial, if any, judging by the way he was flailing his arms and legs—and slipped after Don before the door could swing shut.

By the time I'd climbed the stairs, burst out into the open air, and caught up with Don, he was all the way across the roof. He'd stopped because he'd picked the wrong rooftop edge to run for, and there was nothing to jump down into but the jam that filled Queen Street, seven or eight stories down.

Behind us, the stairwell door slammed rhythmically against the wall as our pursuers joined us on the roof. Don and I glanced at them like prison escapees at a spotlight.

"Now what?" I asked.

"I've got this!" he said uncertainly. Feverishly he reached a hand into his plastic neck hole and produced a plastic bag and a marker pen. He threw the hard drive into the bag, tied up the end, and scrawled TO: HIBATSU on the side. Then he flung it with all his might into the jam, vaguely in the direction of the tallest building in the blacked-out skyline. "There!" he yelled triumphantly, a somewhat irrational look in his eyes. "Now there's nothing to worry about!"

The loss of the holy hard drive definitely hadn't given the three plastic men pause for thought. "Seize the heretics!"

cried the middle one, swinging what I think was a gardener's sickle over his head. The sound of WOO WOOs filled the air.

Don's expression froze. "Shit!"

The plastic pursuers were almost on top of us. The ring-leader had already wound up his sickle, ready to embed it in the nearest convenient torso or skull. If they ploughed right into us at this point we'd all fall off the roof, too, but I wasn't sure how to bring that across in the six or seven feet that remained between them and us.

There was a blur in the air somewhere behind the three guards, then the sickle wielder stopped dead as a subtle *thunk* rang out. He looked down as if someone had just pointed out a stain on his jumper, then he collapsed to reveal the wooden shaft protruding from his spine.

The two remaining pursuers met each other's terrified gaze, each waiting for the other to take the leadership role until the next arrow made the decision for them by lodging itself jarringly in the head of the guy on the right. He bit his lip and got as far as "FFFFFFF" before joining his cohort on the floor.

The newly elected leader showed greater shrewdness and made the command decision to leg it. An arrow found its way between his shoulder blades. For a moment, he groped madly as if seeking a particularly resilient itch; then he, too, fell.

Y hopped down from the top of a tall air-conditioning unit some way off to the left. He was holding a makeshift longbow constructed from a strip of wood and a tightened pair of underpants, and he had made himself a little quiver and bandolier from a lady's handbag. He placed one muscular foot on one of his defeated foes in a triumphant pose, letting the moonlight play off his ridiculous chest muscles.

"Mr. Sunderland," he said slowly, by way of greeting. "Mr. . . . Travis."

"You killed them," said Don, disturbed.

"They're dead," I reiterated.

"They were a threat," explained Y.

The pool of blood under the guy who'd been shot in the head had swelled out as far as Don's foot. "For god's sake," he said, hopping to the side. "Why the hell did you . . ."

Suddenly a realization hit Don like a snow shovel to the back of the head and he fell to his knees at the roof's edge. He stretched out a hand towards the barely visible speck of colored plastic drifting slowly up Queen Street. "For god's sake!" he screamed. "Why the hell did I do *that*?"

DAY 4.5

"So it's you, isn't it," said Don, as the three of us made our way across the rooftops to the crossroads where we'd left the *Everlong.*

"I don't understand what you mean," said Y, in that "official" tone of voice he and X used for lying through their teeth.

"Yes, you do. You're the reason why none of the plastic people can go outside, aren't you? You've been sniping them with arrows from the roof. Wooden shaft, so the jam destroys the evidence, but the metal arrowhead's still moving fast enough to cut through the plastic. Quite ingenious, really. Did you come up with it?"

"I don't understand what you mean," repeated Y. The look he gave Don from under his thick brow made Don immediately drop the issue.

By now we were on the roof of the burger place at the mall crossroads, on the corner of Queen and Albert. From here, we could jump directly onto the roof of the horrible archway where the top of the *Everlong*'s mast was still stuck. The boat was precisely where we had left it, if a little battered from the tsunamis.

"Get to the Hibatsu building," said Y, preparing to take his leave. He was breathing heavily, his massive shoulders rising up and down like the tides. "We'll meet you there."

"So you're definitely coming to Hibatsu?" asked Don, still enamored with the potential of American rescue helicopters.

"I will return to Hibatsu when my business here is concluded."

Don blinked. "What do you mean, *return*?"

Y gave us one last dirty look over his shoulder. "When you reach Hibatsu, find a woman called Kathy." His focus shifted suddenly to the middle distance. "Look, over there!"

"What?" Don and I turned and looked, but saw nothing but the night sky. And by the time we'd turned back, Y had vanished.

"Oh, real mature," muttered Don.

"Angela still thinks X and Y know more than they're saying," I said, conversationally.

"Oh really? Does she also think they breathe oxygen and have arms and legs and everything else that's patently bloody obvious?" He stepped up onto the ledge and jumped before he could have time to think about it. He landed with a clatter on a slanting corrugated surface and started sliding down towards the jam for a second before finding purchase with all four limbs like a climbing possum. "Oh god. That was so stupid."

I hopped onto the section of archway beside him, scrabbling wildly until my position was firm, which was even harder with Mary under one arm. He crawled on all fours towards the cluster of geometric shapes where the *Everlong*'s mast was caught.

"Those guys can have as many secrets as they want," said Don, prodding the top of the mast experimentally with one finger. "As long as they're hooked up with rescue efforts they could have planned the Kennedy assassination for all I care. And that's why we have to stay useful to them."

"How do you know we're useful to them?"

"Because we're still alive." He braced his shoulders up against a low section of perspex and started pushing as hard as he could on the mast with both feet.

"Okay," I said, watching him work. "So WHY do you think we're useful to them?"

"Dunno," he said in a strained voice. The mast had barely moved. "I'm definitely not going to ask, in case it turns out to be one of those things where it hinges on us not knowing about it. Maybe it's just 'cos we pulled them out of the wreck and they're giving us backsies."

I thought of Y, that hardened soldier with a torso like one big giant clenched fist, his face its horny-nailed, calloused thumb. The man who could—and did—kill multiple individuals while most people would still be entertaining their second and third thoughts. The man who almost certainly had something to do with the mysterious absence of the two unconscious plastic people I suddenly remembered that we'd left tied to the boat. Somehow I doubted that *backsies* was a word in his vocabulary.

After another two-footed push the mast finally came free with a sudden start, sending Don flying clean off the archway with a yelp. He grabbed the mast with all four limbs, making it creak back and forth, then slid awkwardly down its length, battered by sails all the way to a painful landing on the *Everlong*'s very solid deck.

As I watched him pick himself up, dust himself down, and swear the air blue, I considered giving Don a full account of the conversation I'd overheard earlier between X and Y, the one in which the word *responsible* had been thrown around so intriguingly.

But I didn't, because I remembered that X and Y had referred to something called the "Sunderland issue." Even I could tell that there was a lot going on below the surface, and Don had given me very few reasons to trust him. There was the chance that Don wouldn't have any idea what I was talking about. But that was the best-case scenario. He might know exactly what I was talking about, and once he knew I knew, he'd be under orders from some shadowy conspiracy to cut my throat out while I slept.

"What are you daydreaming about?" he snapped. "Are you coming down, or what?"

I flinched, braced Mary between my knees, and gingerly wrapped my hands around the mast. Then I followed Don's lead almost exactly, sliding uncomfortably to the deck by way of every sail and extruding component on the way down.

"What are you going to do about your build?" I asked, rubbing my tender bits.

He heaved a weary sigh. "It's probably going to drift towards Hibatsu. The river's that way. So we might see it. And anyway, I addressed it, so if the Hibatsu people spot it they'll pick it up for us." He sneered. "That was a good bit of rationalization, wasn't it."

We headed southwest, towards the river and Hibatsu. The wind was light, but there was just enough to get us out from under the arch and close enough to the left-hand row of shop fronts to push ourselves along with the boat hooks. I felt a lurch of guilt as we passed the eastern entrance to the mall, the site of the ill-fated supply expedition. I recognized Sergeant Cuddles's attire being nudged aside by the prow and felt a little bit ill.

I glanced at Don, who was taking the opportunity to strip off his tattered bin liners. "Do you think this is all right?" I said. "Leaving Tim and Angela, I mean."

"No. It's not right at all. We're going to hell. Who cares?" He yanked a strip of duct tape off his wrist and flinched at the surprise hair-removal treatment.

"We'll come back for them, right? Once we've made sure Hibatsu is safe?"

He paused for a moment. "Yes, that was also a good bit of

rationalization. It must be very comforting to be on your intellectual level."

We reached the end of Queen Street without incident and emerged into the central city plaza bordered by Hibatsu to the north, the casino to the southeast, and the river to the south-west. It had once been the site of an attractive little inner-city park where people had come to eat their lunches and walk their dogs, but after Hibatsu had moved in they decided they preferred a paved plaza, featureless but for a handful of modern art installations. People still brought their dogs, but the turds became considerably less accidental.

Now, the plaza was a flat plain of waist-high jam with the occasional modern art island extruding geometrically from the surface. The *Everlong* drifted towards the center of the square.

"What's going on there?" said Don, staring at the Hibatsu building with his hands on the rail. The jam was still risen oddly around the building, as I'd seen from the roof of the mall.

"Yeah, I saw that earlier," I said. "Don't know why it's doing that."

"Oh well, who cares?" said Don. "Might be an arse to sail up the slope, mind. Guess we cross that bridge when we come to it."

"Okay." I looked around. "How are we going to come to it?"

He opened his mouth, thought for a moment, then closed it again. The wind had completely died down and we were officially becalmed. The *Everlong* had stopped right in the middle of the plaza, fifty yards from Hibatsu and more than a boat hook's length from the nearest artwork.

I took up one of the boat hooks anyway. "Maybe if we push off from the ground . . ." I said, aiming the end towards the jam.

"Don't!" barked Don. "It's made of——"

The jam snatched the pole out of my hands and consumed it before he could even say "wood."

"Marvelous," he said, instead.

"Sorry," I said, opting not to look him in the eye. "I think I've been used to stuff being wrapped in plastic lately."

"And did you remember to bring any of our plastic bag stock with us?" he asked, without much hope.

"I didn't expect us to have to run around in broken glass," I said with, I like to think, some justification.

"You . . ." His clawed hands wobbled back and forth rapidly as he sought to conclude his sentence; then he gave up. "I don't even have the energy to be angry anymore. Maybe I need some sleep. Maybe we should just go to bed and wait for the wind to pick up."

"They're watching us," I reported.

He saw them, then. There were figures at the windows of the Hibatsu building on virtually every floor. They were silhouetted against dismal light, so it was impossible to determine any further detail. None of them were making any effort to attract our attention or rush to our aid. They had the bearing of car accident rubberneckers.

"Hey! Help!" called Don, waving both his arms. No one moved, although one or two of them waved back uncertainly, in accordance with standard etiquette for when people on a boat wave at you. "What, are we the cabaret, now? What are they staring at?"

"Maybe there isn't anything they can do for us," I theorized. "The front doors are under jam."

"Well, the least they could do is crack a window and tell us to piss off."

It occurred to me then that perhaps they weren't coming out because there was something they were afraid of, besides the usual fear of the jam, which for me had now settled into a mild, background kind of terror that I didn't really notice until I thought about it. As if on cue, the boat shook jarringly as if something had struck it from below.

"Kraken!" I shrieked.

"Don't be stupid," said Don, clinging to the mast. "We just touched bottom."

"Bottom!" I added. I glanced around, and saw the jam peeling away from the third-floor windows of Hibatsu with a prolonged wet slurp. "The jam's receding!"

Don and I both remembered simultaneously what this meant. "Tidal wave!"

"It's coming from the south!" I announced, looking towards the casino and down William Street.

"No, it's not. It's coming from the north!" said Don, looking back up Queen Street.

"It's coming from two directions!" I wailed, hopping from foot to foot as the rumbling grew louder. "What does that *mean*?"

"It means, take cover twice as fast," suggested Don as he threw open the deck hatch.

I didn't need telling twice, and practically threw myself into the hatch, rolling down the steps to come to rest in the debris of the ruined kitchen. Don followed and slammed the door shut behind him, immediately plunging us into darkness. He braced himself between a wall and the nearest convenient solid object, which turned out to be me.

The wave hit, and the boat took to the air, pushing us to the floor. After a few seconds of fast movement, I thought it might be safe to shift position, which is why I was hurled across the cabin when the mast hit something solid and the entire boat ricocheted in a new direction.

By the time I'd pulled myself out of a pile of broken drawers and shaken the wooze from my head, the boat had pretty much stopped moving. All I could feel was a gentle rising sensation as the jam returned to its usual level.

My eyes had become accustomed to the dark just in time for it to stop mattering. Don climbed swiftly back up to the hatch and shoved it open, allowing the moonlight to spill down the stairs. I saw him step back up on deck, then I heard him make a curious throat noise and sprint all the way to the far end of the boat.

Curious, I poked my head into the open air and saw him leaning back against the railing at the prow. "What's the matter?"

"Geh durber vur traverse!" he gabbled. He swallowed hard and tried again. "Get over here, Travis!"

Baffled, I leaned over to the rail at the rear of the boat and looked down. And down. I felt my stomach swan dive straight down into my feet.

The *Everlong* was right on the bank of the river. Inches away, the jam became a slope worthy of an advanced ski resort. The river was completely packed with jam, although it was impossible to tell if it had absorbed the water or if it was merely floating on top of it.

If the *Everlong* slid off the edge, the strongest wind in the world wouldn't be able to blow us back up, and there weren't many abandoned shopping malls on the river to raid for food. And that was assuming we didn't capsize, which would at least be a much less ambiguous fate. The *Everlong* began to tip towards the abyss.

Seconds later I had joined Don at the front of the boat, madly leaning back over the rail as if trying to puke out the backs of our heads.

"What the hell are we going to do?!" Panic had reduced Don's voice to little more than an uptight whisper.

I looked back and forth. "Die?"

He considered this, then twisted his head around to yell in the general direction of the Hibatsu building. "HEY! HELP!"

Hibatsu was now considerably closer than it had been before the wave. The whole riverfront thing was part of the reason office space there cost so bloody much. The building had probably been the thing we'd bounced off earlier. Specifically that bit of it on the corner with the visibly broken window.

We could get a closer look at the watchers in the windows, now, who were still making no effort to assist. We still had nothing to go on but their silhouettes, but from them I could see that most of them seemed to be bare chested and wearing skirts.

"PLEASE!" entreated Don as the boat slid back another inch. "WE'VE GOT MONEY!"

"No we don't," I whispered.

"YOU CAN HAVE IT ALL!" he continued, unabashed. "WE'VE GOT FOOD! AND BLANKETS! AND PLASTIC BAGS!"

Finally I saw some activity among the Hibatsu occupants around the broken window; then a grappling hook sailed towards us and clattered onto the deck. I say "grappling hook," but more specifically it was the bottom part of an office chair with the wheels removed and a length of blue network cable tied securely around the shaft. Don didn't waste any time in grabbing the "hook" and securing it tightly around the rail. A few more makeshift hooks arrived, one narrowly missing my head.

"Do we have any of those things?" I said quietly, helping Don secure the ropes.

"I'm pretty sure we've got some blankets left," he said, doing that rationalizing thing again. "Anyway, we can cross that bridge when we come to it."

"Seems like there's quite a lot of bridges on this path we're taking."

"Just shut up and leave the talking to me."

My heart almost stopped when I felt the boat tilt backwards sharply, but this time it was from the people on the other ends of the ropes hauling us up the slope of jam towards Hibatsu's third-floor windows. We were being pulled with surprising strength, and Don and I had to hold onto the mast to avoid being pulled off our feet.

"You still got that bag of snacks you took from the vending machine at my work?" hissed Don out the corner of his mouth as he waved and smiled at our rescuers.

"Down below," I said, hoping it hadn't been scavenged and that its contents hadn't turned into anything hideous.

"Go get it. And whatever blankets you can find."

I found the bag where I'd left it in the "master bedroom," cupcakes still spilling from the mouth, just as Angela had left it. The cotton blankets remained, too. With those, the snacks, and the plastic bin liner the snacks were in, technically Don hadn't lied at all. I pulled the sheets off the mattress and made back for the exit.

The boat bumped sharply again and I almost fell straight back down the stairs. Our rescuers had pulled us all the way up to the building. I emerged into the open, dragging our offerings behind me. I boggled at the sight of the people leaning out the broken window to help.

They had the unhealthy builds and pale skin of people with close relationships with desks: office workers who had arrived at work well before rush hour. Their complexions were easy to assess, because they were all stripped to the waist. None of them wore shoes or trousers, and they wore their shirts dangling upside down like skirts from the waist-bands of their underwear. Some of them had drawn tribal designs on their skin with colored markers and printer toner, but they were rubbing off from their copious sweating.

"Er," said Don, as taken aback by their appearance as I. "Hello—"

I'd never know what kind of diplomatic words he had prepared, because then the helpful members of the Hibatsu tribe grabbed him around the arms and yanked him bodily into the building. He was dragged roughly out of sight by some displeased-looking natives, and then the stocky balding man at the window grabbed my arm with a firm, businesslike motion. I barely had time to grab Mary's box from the deck before I was forcibly rescued.

The moment I crossed the glass-fringed threshold into the gloomily lit interior, I was hit with a wave of heat like I'd stepped out of an air-conditioned airport onto the streets of Morocco in high summer. It was quickly followed by a second wave of body odor that forced its way down my nose and mouth like grasping tentacles.

The hands that held my limbs were so sweaty I could probably have slipped right out of their grasp if I'd made any kind of sudden movement, but before I could put this theory into practice I glimpsed a hand holding the butt of a staple gun coming down upon the top of my head. Fireworks burst numbly inside my head and my vision spun around the room like a dervish.

The next thing I knew I was lying on the floor watching an office worker carry Mary's box away from me, her forelegs stretching out towards me in distress. I tried to reach out for her, but a moist hand grabbed my wrist. I heard the harsh screech of sticky tape being pulled away from the roll, and felt my hands and feet being bound to a long piece of metal which had once been part of a computer desk.

I heard someone count to three, then two workers shouldered the metal bar. I tried to get a good look at my surroundings as

I dangled upside down from my bonds, but the poor light and my constant swaying made it difficult. I saw many cubicles, and occasionally suspicious eyes glaring at me from between the short partition walls. A radius of silence extended around me, and all I could hear was the muttering of people picking up their conversations once they were sure I'd moved on.

After hearing a door open and close I felt myself jiggling madly up and down as my two carriers climbed a couple of flights of stairs, then a few more doors opened and closed and I wobbled to a halt. My pole was lowered gently to the floor and I was left lying on my side with my hands and feet still bound to it. I twitched my fingers and toes in anticipation of release, but my two captors had walked away, chatting amicably amongst themselves, and closed the door behind them.

My limbs were held in place by the tape, but from twisting my neck madly around I could determine that I was on the floor of some kind of conference room. I could just about see the large meeting table and uncomfortable chairs from the meager light filtering through the blinds surrounding the room. Everyone's lives were continuing unconcerned right outside the door, and the bustle and hubbub made my little private silence all the more lonely.

After about an hour, which felt considerably longer, I was starting to wonder if maybe they'd forgotten about me. The fast and professional method by which I'd been hogtied and brought here had more than a hint of *routine* about it. Maybe they'd brought in several prisoners today and I'd been lost in the shuffle. On the other hand, if I drew attention to myself, more people might come in and hit me with staplers some more.

After another hour I was getting pins and needles in a lot of inconvenient places, so I finally made a weak little attention-grabbing cough towards the nearby closed door. Nothing happened. I did it again, gaining confidence. I risked a "Hey!" Again, no one, including stapler-brandishing thugs. I found this encouraging.

I was halfway through the first word of "EXCUSE MEEE" when the door finally opened a crack and a baleful eye silenced me. "Excuse me," it said. "Could you keep it down, please. Some of us are trying to work."

"Sorry," I said automatically. "Um!" I added, as the owner of the eye made to close the door again. "I wonder if you could, er, tell me what's supposed to be happening?"

The eye did a complete circle, scanning the room. "Have you booked this meeting room?"

"No? Some . . . guys just sort of . . . left me here?"

"Oh, I see. I'll just go and see if I can find out who's looking after you."

The door clicked smartly shut, and I was alone again. Ten minutes passed. The whole left side of my body was going numb. I was just about to seriously consider making another coughing sound when my discoverer returned.

"Sorry, did you say who it was who brought you in here?"

"No, they were just some guys."

"Do you know if they were from this department?"

"I don't know what this department is. And no. They just pulled me in out of the jam."

"Oh, *Acquisitions*," sighed the eye, as if this explained everything. "They're always doing this. We tell them, it's fine if you want to use our meeting rooms, but you MUST either fill out the booking form OR leave your name and contact details in the space by the door IF your intended use of the room is for less than two hours. I suppose Kathy might know who brought you in. Do you want me to go and ask Kathy?"

The name Y had mentioned registered in my memory. "Yes! Yes, go and ask Kathy. And, um! Er, could you untie me, please?"

"Oh, sorry. You have a visitor access form?"

"No. Can I have one?"

"Yes, of course. We can get one printed out right in our department. I just need to see your NDA."

"Can I have one of those, too?" I asked, my voice becoming increasingly weak.

"Well, that isn't our department. I'll ask Kathy. She might know if you're supposed to have an NDA."

"Er, one more thing," I said, as they moved to leave again. "Is it past midnight yet?"

"Yes, it's . . . er . . . coming up to six."

DAY 5.1

"Thank you."
   "You're welcome."

DAY 5.2

After several attempts I successfully managed to roll onto my other side, which eased my growing numbness a bit, and I was able to snatch a few minutes of sleep before I was woken by voices outside. Then the door flew open and two indistinct figures—probably the same ones as earlier, but I wasn't certain—wordlessly shouldered my bar.

"You really should have left your details," complained the voice of the last person I'd spoken to, coming from somewhere out of my field of vision.

"We did," said the carrier to my front. "We left them with Kathy."

"Kathy didn't say anything to me. And anyway, you're supposed to leave them in the space by the door."

"Kathy said she'd do it." I had a horrible feeling that Kathy was going to turn out to be some kind of invisible tribal deity.

Now that the sun had risen, I could look around and get a slightly better impression of my surroundings. There was washed-out blue-gray carpeting above my head and white ceiling tiles forming a regular grid below my trussed hands and feet. Most of the floor space was taken up with cubicles, and each one had been repurposed into a small living space. Each desk had been partially dismantled and a makeshift mattress, made from clothing and tote bags apparently stuffed with shredded paper and clipped-out *Dilbert* comics, placed underneath.

Just as I was getting a feel for the place, I was brought into the stairwell again, and all I could see was concrete jiggling madly around as I was carried up the building.

"Er," I said, when my bearers had stopped between floors for the third time to get their breath back. "Maybe if you untaped me I could just walk up by myself?"

"More than our job's worth," growled the guy in front, between pants.

"Well, maybe you could just untie my feet, then I could help out with the carrying."

The two of them exchanged glances. "That sounds . . . reasonable," said one.

"Shall we do it?" asked the other.

"What do you think?"

"I'm just happy to do whatever you want to do."

"I'm really not comfortable with taking responsibility."

"I could take responsibility," I suggested.

That seemed agreeable, and the guy behind me reluctantly unstrapped my feet. They swung down and hit the floor painfully, and after a couple more flights, enough feeling had returned to my legs that I could actually bear my own weight. After that, progress was faster, but there was little conversation. They both seemed a little uneasy about breaking protocol.

Finally we reached the very top floor of Hibatsu and emerged from the stairwell into ultraexpensive office space with Japanese-style décor. The residents that inhabited this level must have been upper management, because they wore silk ties as headbands, and sparkling cufflinks on the arms of their shirt-skirts rattled noisily against the varnished pine floors.

My captors took up position on one side of a foreboding black door with a sliding wooden sign nearby that currently read *Meeting in Session*. It was then that I noticed Don on the other side of the door, strapped upside down to a standing lamp between two office workers virtually identical to mine.

"Oh, charming!" ranted Don, his face the color of an angry stoplight. "How come the 'tard gets to stand on his own feet?"

"Did you have permission to do that?" said one of Don's bearers, in the hushed and slightly excited tone of a schoolboy sensing an opportunity to run to the teacher with a cry of *teeelliiing*.

"It was his idea," said both my escorts simultaneously.

The door to the conference room suddenly opened and the head and shoulders of a woman appeared, wearing spectacles, a chaste, functional white bra, and a necklace of paper clips as some kind of badge of authority. "You can bring them in n—" she said, before noticing me. Her gaze tracked down to my feet. "Who untied his feet?"

"Him," said my front bearer, truthfully. The one behind had been the one to actually physically remove the tape.

"I just, er," stammered the culprit, his constant sweating ramping up several notches so that his head resembled a lawn sprinkler. "Thought that . . . it would . . . make it . . . more efficient . . . to carry him up the stairs?"

"Oh," said the woman. "I suppose that makes sense."

"Yes, that's what I thought!" he said quickly, with ecstatic triumph.

"I helped!" added my other bearer.

"We were just about to do it too!" said Don's front bearer, as the back one busied himself with the tape around his feet.

"Hey, it was my idea," I said, hurt.

"You can just take them off the bars, now," said the slightly nonplussed woman. "Just leave their hands tied together and show them in."

Grumbling bitterly amongst themselves, the guards did as they were told and pushed the two of us quite rudely into the meeting room after the lady, pulling the doors shut behind us. She motioned for us to wait by the door, then returned to the sole unoccupied chair.

The top-level boardroom of the Hibatsu building radiated wealth and good taste. The oval meeting table was reddish mahogany polished to a mirror shine. A single circular skylight lit up the surface, as well as the foreheads and clasped hands of the people around the table, while the rest of the room was concealed in shadow. It was the kind of setting at which evil shadow governments certainly wouldn't turn up their conspiratorial noses.

If the members of the meeting were some kind of evil shadow government, then either it was a pretty low-rent one or we'd shown up on laundry day. They were all topless with their shirts around their waists, sweat glistening unpleasantly off their doughy management flesh. Most of them had some mark of importance—a few had paper-clip necklaces like the woman who'd brought us in, others wore layers of countless elastic bands around their wrists and heads, and one man in the center had an elaborate head-dress made from an ergonomic neck rest and several items of stationery.

". . . pleased to report that we were able to get a sample of river water from underneath the jam, and it's drinkable," said a skinny, balding man whose turn it was to speak. "A lot more so than before, I'd say. The jam removed a lot of impurities." The river had contained "impurities" in the same way that Jeffrey Dahmer had had a few minor personality quirks. "We've taken down some air-conditioning vents and we're working on building some kind of well system. We should have a prototype ready by the end of the week."

The man in the headdress nodded. "On that note, I'd like to quickly ask David if there's been any headway in getting the air conditioning back online."

A slight murmur of discontent indicated the importance of this matter, directed at a blond young man with a tanning-bed complexion. "Well, Gary," he sighed. "There isn't much we can do without electricity, but my team has been researching alternatives. One of my engineers proposed a system of fans powered by dogs in giant hamster wheels, but the major issue there is our limited dog inventory. We'll keep looking into it."

Gary, apparently the chair of the meeting, nodded gloomily. "Right then. Item four on the agenda: two refugees recently acquired by Kathy's Acquisitions team. I'm also hearing something about a broken window?"

"Yes," said the woman who'd beckoned us in. "They came here on a sailing boat that unfortunately put its mast through one of the windows on the third floor. We had them brought in because they claimed to have supplies for trade, but frankly I suspect they may have exaggerated their position."

"Hm." Gary tapped his finger against his lips. "It seems to me that we should murder them."

"What?!" barked Don, suddenly alert.

"Oh, yes, perhaps we should get some input from the prisoners on this one," said Gary, turning towards us. "Would you agree that murder is the way forward in this case?"

"No!" yelled Don.

Gary winced, unclasping his two index fingers and rubbing them against each other like mating worms. "Well, you have to understand that you're not negotiating from a firm position, here. With the broken window you're already representing a net loss for us."

"Even discounting the man-hours and sticky tape," agreed Kathy.

"And I hate to be a stickler for the rules but the Hibatsu Survival Settlement Charter clearly states that any individual who cannot reimburse the company in liquid assets must make it up with voluntary existence suspension."

"But . . ." stammered Don. "How are you going to explain that when the rescue teams get here?"

"Mm. Well, we considered that," said Kathy. "Our basic decision was that any contributions we make to this disaster's already quite significant death toll would be comparatively negligible."

Don seemed about to launch into some furious tirade when his head and upward-pointing finger suddenly dropped as if his puppeteer had cut the strings. "You know what? Fine. I have honestly stopped caring."

I started like a dog-show contestant whose entry had just slumped to the floor and started quietly eating its own puke. "What? No! Don't murder us! We must have something to trade! What about that bag of stuff we brought?"

"Oh yes, we have your personal effects here," said Kathy, beckoning to the shadows. An ordinary tribesman without accouterments came forward holding our bag of vending machine snacks and Mary in her box. She poked nervously at the transparent plastic.

"See? We've got food," I said desperately, holding forward a rectangular slice of individually wrapped carrot cake.

"Yes, yes, you've got food in a significantly smaller quantity than the amount we get through in a single day," said one of the managers, bored. Gary nodded to somewhere in the darkness, and two guards stepped forward brandishing swords made from paper-cutter blades. Don seemed to have frozen completely.

"Look, what is it that you want?!" I wailed.

"Plastic bags," said Kathy.

"Dogs," said David the air-conditioning guy.

"Fresh fruit or vegetables," said someone near the back. "With seeds in, something we can cultivate." I thought of my lost apple, and almost burst into tears. I rifled desperately through the contents of my bag, holding out each cake and muesli bar for inspection and receiving nothing but shaking heads.

"I've got a spider!" I declared, options dwindling.

David sat up. "Could it possibly turn a giant hamster wheel?"

"Don't be silly," droned Gary. "Look at that thing. It'd freak out the whole staff."

One of the sword-wielding guards took Don by the arm. Don didn't move, but I could see his eyes bulging, as if some base instinct somewhere in his mind was desperately kicking the backs of his eyeballs trying to spur him to action.

The other guard snatched my quivering elbow and I started violently, my bag of stocking fillers flying from my hand and spilling some of its contents upon the absurdly soft carpet. A rusty paper-cutter blade pressed coldly against the side of my throat and Don and I were dragged towards the door.

"All right, next item on the agenda . . ." said Gary, consulting his paperwork.

"Hang on a second. Sorry, Gary," said the bloke who'd mentioned agriculture. "Is that a banana?"

All eyes fell to my discarded goodie bag. Among the items that had fallen out was one of the bananas I'd found in the vending machine. Several people at the back of the room stood up to get a good look at the oblivious yellow-and-brown crescent.

The swords came away from our throats. "Why didn't you say you had bananas?" asked Kathy.

"Well . . . bananas don't have seeds," I said timidly. "Do they?"

"Jesus Christ, Travis," said Don wearily, covering his eyes. "Well, I've never found one!"

After the meeting broke up, our hands were untaped and the director of Agriculture and Food Distribution, or Philip as he'd introduced himself, insisted on escorting us up the final flight of stairs to the roof so we could see how our contribution to the Hibatsu society would be used.

"We made the troughs from sections of air ducting," said Philip breathily. He was a thin, bespectacled man in his thirties, and he smelled faintly of eucalyptus cough drops. "The soil we gathered from potted plants from all over the building. There was more than enough. I bet you're wondering what we're growing in them, aren't you?"

Don and I stood with shoulders hunched, arms limp, and eyelids drooping, but the man was immune to signals. The handle on Mary's box dangled from my hand, Mary herself inside sleeping on her back.

"Most of the seeds we got from packed lunches," continued Philip. "But you'd be surprised how few of them had seeds in forms we could use. We've got apples there, tomatoes there, and over there is where we planted potato salad. Not holding out much hope for that one, I'm afraid. That's why we're really very grateful to have those bananas you brought."

I was still dubious about the whole banana seed thing, but I wasn't about to challenge anyone over it.

"Hasn't been much rain lately, so we've been watering them with whatever we can spare from the water-cooler stock." He sighed. "The whole settlement is holding its breath waiting for the river-water pumping system. Literally. No one's had a shower in days and with the air conditioning off . . . Maybe you noticed."

Don and I had been making sure to stand several feet away from him. "No, not really," I said diplomatically.

"But once that's ready, life will be much more comfortable. I understand David's engineering team even think they could rig up a hydroelectric generator. But from what I understand, the current design would only generate enough power to run the pump that draws the water up to turn the generator . . ."

"I thought you were just waiting for rescue," said Don.

Philip seemed hurt. "Well, we had a few meetings about it. Basically we thought that it's better to be rescued and feel a bit stupid than to all kill each other six months down the line. And I used to garden as a hobby, so I fell over myself to take this project. Do say something if I'm boring you."

"You're boring us," said Don in a monotone.

"Now then," said Philip obliviously. "I'll be endorsing the placement of the two of you into our happy little family, but you will need to go to Personnel right away to receive a work placement. That's Kathy's department, on the fourth floor. You'll have to take the stairs. Sorry. The elevators were another thing David's team were working on, but they fell down the shaft and broke after he tried to get them working with exercise bikes. And the riders ended up getting terrible friction burns on their—"

He was still talking as we closed the stairwell door behind us. We took a moment to enjoy the silence, then began to descend the stairs. I found myself increasingly disturbed by Don, who walked silently with his hands in his pockets and his face turned down. He didn't even seem irritated by my presence.

"You know," I said, after a cough. "I was kind of hoping, if we came here, we'd finally meet some normal people."

Don didn't reply verbally, but gave a short nasal snort as some kind of automatic response. That was something, at least.

"I mean, yeah, the mall would be full of ironic hipster kids wrapped in plastic bags, that makes sense, but I'd have thought people who work in offices would be sane."

Finally I touched a sensitive-enough nerve that he spoke, albeit quietly and without emotion. "Not the people who get to work before rush hour. Only three kinds of people do that. The suck-ups, the insane, and people who enjoy their work. Actually, make that two kinds of people."

He fell into silence again, tramp-tramping down the concrete stairs ahead of me in a steady, gloomy rhythm like a pallbearer on a treadmill. I felt a strange desire to provoke him, somehow. An angry or sarcastic Don was something I could deal with.

"Lots of stairs, aren't there," I commented, as a sign indicated we'd passed the thirty-fifth floor. "It's the sort of thing that could really make you angry, isn't it."

Finally he looked at me. There were darkening lines under his perpetual glare. "Why do you keep talking?" he snapped, or at least tried to snap. It came out more like a thump.

"Don, are you all right?" I said, voicing my concerns.

"I . . . don't know," he said, stroking his chin thoughtfully. "I was just starting to think that I'm never going to get my build back. And then, when they were going to kill us just now, I felt very relaxed. Now I just feel like I stopped halfway through jerking off."

I decided to stop talking to him, if only to mull that analogy over in my head. We continued in silence down to the fourth floor.

Now that I wasn't seeing the lower-level dormitory/cubicle farm from the underside of a pole, I could detect an air of tension. Workers stood in small groups with arms folded, carrying on private conversations that were promptly suspended whenever we passed through earshot. Had someone been playing a honky-tonk piano in the room, the music would have stopped as we came in the door.

Don asked the nearest resident for directions to Kathy's office, and he answered with sullen passive-aggression, as if we were asking directions to the boudoir of a woman with whom he was in unrequited love. It was a marked contrast from the cheerful toiling of Philip and his small gardening crew on the roof. Perhaps it was something to do with the lack of fresh air.

Kathy's office door was wide open, in an emotionless gesture of welcome. She was behind the remains of her desk shuffling through some indeterminate documents, and ushered us into the room with one hand, without looking at us. Like the cubicles, Kathy's office had an impromptu bed in the corner made from bits of cloth and shredded paper, and two buckets that I didn't like to think about on the opposite side of the room.

"Hello-nice-to-meet-you-I'm-Kathy," she said automatically, practically all as one word. She chose not to bring up her part in our most recent brush with death, so we didn't, either. "I'm the Personnel officer at Hibatsu Survivors, so my job is to make sure everyone in the settlement has somewhere to be where they can be the most productive. And happy, obviously, if possible. So let's just start with some friendly casual small talk. Names?"

"He's Don," I said.

"He's Travis," said Don.

"Right, that will suffice." Kathy ticked a little box on one of her papers. "So what sort of skills do you think you have been developing in the post-jam survival environment?"

I saw Don's eyes rotate around inside their sockets as he mentally backtracked through the last seven days. "I dunno. We've kind of just been making it up as we go along."

"I found some bananas," I said.

"Oh, yes," said Kathy, wincing patronizingly. I'd never been very good at reading the mood in job interviews, but I could tell this one wasn't going very well. The way she was tapping her pen on the desk was making me wonder if the paper-cutter option had been completely discounted.

"And we've nearly figured out how to sail our boat properly," hazarded Don, visibly embarrassed at the exaggeration.

"Well, we have had difficulty finding ways to advance into the surrounding city to find salvage," said Kathy, a finger to her chin. "Apparently it's possible to swim through the jam if you seal yourself in plastic, but that hasn't been a tenable option for us."

"Why not?" said Don.

"Early in the disaster we traded all our plastic bags to another settlement in return for some food supplies. Their representative only wanted plastic bags, duct tape, and green highlighter pens. We didn't really ask why. They seemed to think they were being ironic, or something."

I tried not to think about the sound of a budgerigar attempting to escape from a giant spider in a foot-wide cage. "The plastic people?" I said. "We just came from there." Don kicked me in the ankle.

"Really?" said Kathy, suddenly interested. She had been propping her face on her elbow, but now she immediately sat up straight. "The settlement in the Briar Center? You've been inside?"

"Yeah, we stayed there for a day or two," I said. Don kicked me again, twice in quick succession. "Ow. *Ow.*"

She leaned forward. "Tell me, did you notice any significant changes in the settlement while you were there?" She scanned our blank looks. "Any fresh difficulty that has arisen?"

"Are you talking about how they can't leave the mall anymore?" I asked. "Don, why do you keep kicking me? It really hurts."

Kathy scribbled something on a legal pad. "Thank you; that's all I wanted to know."

"Hey, you know something about this?" asked Don. "Are you working with Y?"

"It's not really my department to say anything. I'm Human Resources; that's more of a Public Relations thing," said Kathy in her practiced, noncommittal tone of voice, making a little note on Don's form. "Well, it's lucky that you have an established profile with the other settlement, and a vehicle, because we were looking for one or two agents to act as our representatives there."

The sound of panicking budgerigar still playing through my memories suddenly took on aspects of a car alarm. "What? You want us to go back to the mall?"

"Yes, just someone to monitor their activities and address resource balance."

"Resource balance?" asked Don.

"Yes. When they have a lot of resources, and we don't have as much, it would be your job to . . . restore that particular balance." She coughed. "We do have just enough plastic bags for the two of you. After we traded most of them away we had someone go around and gather up all the ones that were lining the wastepaper baskets. So is that okay with you both? We don't really have openings in any other departments for your particular . . . skill sets. I'm really not sure what other use you could be."

"But . . ." I was about to explain that we were wanted men, but that wasn't true. Everyone who had seen us steal the hard drive and chased us to the roof had been subsequently murdered by Y. Plus Kathy was tapping on the desk in that slightly threatening way again, and the sound of budgie and car alarm were all silenced by the sound of a paper cutter slamming shut. "Don?"

"Fine, whatever," he sighed. I really was getting worried about him.

"Well, that's just excellent," said Kathy sweetly, making a very definite and forthright signature to conclude the interview. She leaned back, immediately much more relaxed now the bureaucracy was dealt with. "Have to say, you and your boat and your banana arriving now has been quite a stroke of luck. We almost gave up on finding useful things in the stuff that washes up around the building. Do you know what we fished out just before you arrived?"

Someone pulled the plug on Don's apathy and it started the process of gurgling down the drain. He slowly lifted his chin off his hand. "What?" he asked, his voice low and ominous.

"A hard drive. In a plastic bag. And do you know the strangest thing?"

"It was addressed to you," guessed Don, tone unchanged.

"That's right. Very odd. We assumed the Briar Center settlement was sending some kind of message or tribute, but I don't know what they thought we could do with it without electricity. I think Gary's been using it as a drinks coaster."

DAY 5.3

"Well, I have to say, it's lucky they didn't change their minds about letting us in," I said conversationally, once we were back in the *Everlong* and pushing our way through the Hibatsu square with some borrowed metal poles. "After you threw that fit, I mean."

"Drinks coaster," muttered Don. He was standing with one hand at the mast staring fixedly at the retreating Hibatsu building.

"Probably for the best that we get away from the place for a bit," I said wistfully. "Kathy might need some time to get over those papers you ate."

"Drinks coaster," he repeated, like a mantra.

"At least they said they'd give it back if we did what they asked."

"If that hard drive is so much as scratched, I am going to stick it straight up Gary's arse. You think I'm saying that idly. I'm not. I'm going to make a project out of it. I'm going to use forceps and lubricant. What are you looking so satisfied about?!"

"Nothing, nothing. It's just . . . nice to have you back, Don."

He gave me a slightly confused scowl, then turned to gaze at the Briar Center, whose authoritative domed roof was becoming visible over the smaller shops. "Don't know what you've got to be pleased about," he said. "Isn't the mall exactly where you don't want to be right now?"

"What?"

"Remember? You fed their queen's beloved pet to your hairy girlfriend?"

I gazed at Mary, who gave a sort of embarrassed shrug with her legs, and felt my stomach twist sickeningly. In the Hibatsu building the memories of paper-cutter blade being held against my soft, yielding throat had loomed largest in my thoughts, and our activities in the lair of the plastic people had been sprinting down my mental priority list in leaps and bounds. I'd allowed myself to write off that particular chapter of my life, but now that the shopping mall was visible again it hovered like a huge floating asterisk portending some dreadful footnote.

"Well, they'll have forgotten about that by now, right?" I said, partly to convince myself.

"Oh, sure," said Don, bored, standing with arms folded. "One day is about an average statute of limitations for that sort of thing."

"Besides, Lord Awesomo only suspects me, I'm sure. He doesn't *know* anything. And he wouldn't tell Princess Ravenhair unless he'd gain something from it, right?" I saw Don roll his eyes discouragingly. "Well, he wouldn't, would he?"

"No one acts rationally in the friend zone. Creates this weird mix of total moony-eyed devotion and hate-filled bitterness. My mate Dub got friend zoned by one of our lead artists, once. I had to hook him up with my fat slut cousin 'cos I found murder-suicide plans in his desk."

"Anyway, she'd probably forgive me if I explained," I said, refusing to acknowledge him. "She likes me. I think. I'm not sure how much, but . . ."

"Oh, christ. Not you as well. What is it with this bitch? She's got a friend zone like a post office queue."

"She's not a bitch . . ."

"Hey!" hissed a new voice. We were back in the pedestrian precinct that ran alongside the mall, and someone was trying to get our attention from behind the pillar outside the pharmacy.

It was one of the plastic people, but we were already wearing Hibatsu's donated plastic bags so we hadn't broken our cover. The plastic person was female, with a slight build, but she was wearing an opaque bag over her head, so the only other detail I could determine was that she was pinned against the pillar and quivering with terror.

"There's someone shooting at us!" she revealed as we parked our boat near her hiding place. It was then we noticed several splintered wooden shafts bristling from the side of the pillar that faced the mall. "I figured it out! We can't leave the mall because someone's shooting arrows from the roof!"

"Um, yeah, how about that," said Don quickly. "Well, we don't really want to hang around, so . . ."

"How did you get across the street?" I asked.

"There were six of us!" I suddenly noticed a cluster of discarded plastic bags floating on the jam. "We thought we could brute force our way out and figure out what keeps killing us! And we could! But now I can't get back! And I really need a wee!"

"Look, just calm down," I said. "It's okay. We know the guy."

"No we do not!" interjected Don angrily. "He will almost certainly have no qualms about killing all of us! Don't calm down! Continue panicking!"

"Don, why do you keep —" I began.

Then, perhaps to illustrate his words, I heard the sound of whistling wind moments before an arrow lodged itself in the *Everlong*'s deck directly between my feet. Reflexively I

grabbed Mary and threw myself away, landing squarely in
the jam. For half a second I was frozen in terror, not having
checked to see if my fresh plastic-bag coating was airtight,
then I used the remainder of the second to take up position
behind the pillar with the stricken girl.

"HEY!" screamed Don, directing his voice at the bulky
silhouette just visible on the roof overhead. "STOP
SHOOTING, YOU CLOT! IT'S US!"

"You do know him," said the girl, astonished. "Who is he?"

"IT'S US, SOME PEOPLE YOU'VE NEVER MET!"
added Don, after a moment's hesitation. "BUT WE'RE
HUMAN BEINGS SO THAT'S WHY YOU SHOULD STOP
SHOOTING US!"

"Nice save, Don."

"But why isn't he shooting you?" asked the confused girl.
"He shoots everyone else."

"And why'd he shoot at me?" I peered recklessly around
the pillar and tried to get a look at Y's silhouette. His bow
was lowered, and his stance was that of a castle guard
lowering the drawbridge. He must have finally noticed that
it was Don and me. But who else did he think would show up
driving the *Everlong*? *The Sunderland issue*, Y had said.

"We should probably get inside," said Don, hopping
gingerly down into the jam like a man carefully testing the
temperature of his bathwater.

"Riiight," I said, trying to keep one eye on him and one
on Y, who was still watching us, unmoving.

Don had noticed that, too. "HEY!" he called to him. "FEEL
FREE TO GO NOW! DON'T YOUR PECS NEED
OILING?!"

Y wasn't making any motion to leave, or indeed any
motion at all.

"Erm, Don," I said, still not having moved out from behind

the pillar. "Could you stay in front of us while we walk across the street?"

"Oh, fine," said Don, although he was staring at Y too, with growing concern. He backed slowly up to our pillar and I put one hand on his shoulder, holding onto Mary with the other, then the girl did the same to me. After a brief unspoken debate we started marching with the left foot and proceeded slowly across the street like a small, frightened conga. All three of us kept our eyes fixed on Y.

He had an arrow nocked. If I saw him start to draw his arm back I could probably dive to one side. And then the jam would probably get in my breathing hole and I would be killed. But at least it would be vaguely on my own terms.

"You totally know who he is, don't you," said the girl over my shoulder. "Have you told Lord Awesomo? Or Tim?"

"We don't have any idea what you're talking about," said Don loudly, before I could reply. "He's obviously just realized the error of his—what did you say?"

"I said, you know who he is, don't you."

"The bit after that."

"I asked if you've told Lord Awesomo."

"And then there was another little bit."

"Or Tim?"

"That's the bastard. How do you know Tim?"

"You know, he's the leader of the opposition. That whole election thing?"

"Okay, we're under the awning," said Don. "Run."

Run was a command that was impossible to obey in the jam, but we did manage a panicky high-kicking wade until we were all backed up against the display window directly underneath Y's perch. The Queen Street entrance to the mall, from which Sergeant Cuddles had mounted his ill-fated expedition, was just a few yards further south. We kept our backs to the wall and shuffled awkwardly along towards it like mobile firing-squad victims.

"Right, run that by us again," said Don. "What election?"

"Why wouldn't you know about the election?" said the girl, as if the two of them were playing the questions game. "And how the hell did you get out of the mall in the first place? Who are you?"

Our careers as undercover double agents definitely weren't off to a flying start. "Um . . ." I began.

"How about you just shut your face," suggested Don, losing patience. "How about that."

"We've been on a mission!" I declared, inspired. "We were sent on a special investigating mission before any of this happened so that's why this is all completely new to us."

"But why didn't he shoot you?" persisted the girl. We still couldn't see her face but she sounded close to tears. "He shot all my friends!"

"Well, maybe he's only trying to stop people getting out, not in," I said, the interior of my wrapping becoming rather hot and moist with sweat.

"He shot at you, but not you," she pointed out, nodding to me and Don in turn.

I swallowed. The memory of the arrow's impact vibrating the deck between my feet was still fresh. Y wouldn't have missed so far if he'd been aiming for the girl. Something didn't add up.

We were inside the mall entrance, now, and blessedly out of danger. Once we were around the corner Don seized me by the arm and pushed me against a wall. "We can't let her tell anyone."

"Who tell what to who?"

"Her. We can't let her tell all the other plastic people that we know Y."

"But . . ."

"I don't think any group of people would be kindly disposed to anyone who hangs out with the guy who has murdered large numbers of them. It's just a hunch I have."

"I understand that, but what do you propose to do to keep her quiet?" His gaze fell guiltily from mine. "We can't kill her. Surely. Can we? Maybe she'd listen to us if we just explained everything. Honestly."

His mouth twisted as he attempted to swallow that. "Okay, let's just keep on her for now, and make a decision when it becomes necessary." He released me, and I detached from the wall.

"Right," I said. I looked around. "Where's she gone?"

The girl we'd rescued had gone on ahead. Her trail remained in the jam, leading towards the food court. Emitting an extremely rude word, Don speed waded after her. I caught up with him just inside the food court, where the trail became overlaid by a labyrinth of several other trails of varying freshness.

Don said the rude word again. "Where'd she go?"

"What color bags was she wearing?" There were even more plastic people in the food court than usual, all in a state of dull huddled panic thanks to Y's efforts.

"Are you telling me you didn't notice?!"

"No, I don't really notice that sort of thing."

"Oh my god," said Don, exasperatedly pulling at his facial features with his hands. "You've got a brain like a Spam fritter."

"Well, didn't you notice?"

"What the hell are we going to do?!" he cried, dodging the question. "They'll lynch us with flaming torches! And they won't be doing it ironically!"

"Wait, does she even know who we are?"

"We had transparent bags on our heads! She geboddagaboy . . ." His tongue suddenly tripped over an idea as it was on its way to turning on the lightbulb in his head. "Wait a minute. That's it." He made for the nearest escalator and pulled himself up the stairs to the next level, freeing himself from the jam with a disappointed plop. I followed him, bewildered, to a hidden and isolated spot behind an advertising billboard, near the entrance to the department store.

"What are we doing?" I whispered.

"We'll just ambush the next two guys who pass and take their bags," he said. "One plastic man looks pretty much like another, right? And we'll leave them our bags so it's not like mugging at all."

"Couldn't we just ask someone if they'd like to do swapsies? Like a fun game? An ironic fun game?"

"Shush. Someone's coming."

From within the department store I heard the familiar rustling tramp-tramp of two people with plastic bags on their feet walking across polished shopping mall floors.

"Wait for it," he hissed.

"For what? What are we supposed to do?"

"Improvise. Now. GO."

Don immediately leapt out, holding up his hands with fingers clawed, impersonating a lion. I jumped to his side, hefting Mary's box in both hands and preparing to swing her like a club. Mary sprang back on her back legs, ready to do her bit.

Our two mugging victims froze in surprise. So did we, because they were Angela and X. Angela's head bag wasn't transparent, but her perpetual camcorder was unmistakable. She, the journalist, found her voice first. "Where the hell have you two been? No, actually, why the hell did you jump us? Answer that question first, then the other one."

"We just, er," stalled Don, placing his hands behind his back and attempting to reassemble his dignity. "We thought you were someone e—I mean, we thought you were Angela and X, so we thought we'd give you a fun little surprise." He held up his arms in a slightly less threatening way. "Surprise! We're back!"

"Back from where?" asked Angela. "That brings us back to the first question."

"Er . . ." Don waved his hands, extending the *er* as long as he could, before madly looking at me, seeking a tag out.

"To the Hibatsu building," I said immediately. I saw Don face palm with what sounded like quite painful force. "We just went ahead to check it out and make sure everything's all right."

"New question," said Angela. The emotionless black eye of her camera hadn't become any less intimidating. "How did you get out of the mall without getting eaten like everyone else?"

"I'm gonna go on ahead and make sure we get good seats," said X suddenly, breaking off and speed walking away. "I'll see you there, Angela."

" 'Kay," replied Angela with unusual warmth.

I watched X go, her gait a little eccentric as the bags on her feet negotiated around her sensible shoes. "Have you been spending a lot of time with X?" I asked Angela.

She lowered her camera. "Yeah, we've been talking a lot. We've been bonding a bit while we scavenge for magazines to read. I think she's really starting to open up. It's kind of scary. Anyway, don't change the subject." The lens came right back up. "Why weren't you killed when you went out of the mall?"

"Because it's Y," I said.

Don slapped himself again, this time with both hands. His forehead was becoming severely reddened. "Travis," he said with a slightly maniacally calm voice. "You and I are going to have to have a little chat about the importance of keeping certain pieces of intelligence to ourselves."

"What do you mean, it's Y?" pressed Angela.

Don sighed. "Fine! Let's tell the world! Y's holding out on the roof and shooting arrows at anyone who tries to leave! And he didn't shoot us because we're his mates and now we're protecting a murderer which is almost certainly a capital offense! See, Travis, this is how not to do it!"

"It's Y?" reiterated Angela. The camcorder floated hither and thither for a few revolutions as she assembled a jigsaw puzzle in her head, then focused on the top of the escalator where we'd last seen X's retreating form. "That two-faced cow!"

Our expedition to spy on the plastic people was getting more catastrophic by the second. First we had given ourselves away to the very first person we saw, then we had ruined a burgeoning friendship. "But I don't think it's because of a conspiracy or anything. It's just plain self-motivated independent murder, I think."

"Well, that's all right then," muttered Don.

"The truth is getting bigger all the time," said Angela, narrating. "We have to tell Tim about this. It could be just what he needs to swing the election."

"There's that word again," said Don. "What election?"

Angela made off down the escalator after X, and we hurried to keep up. "Tim's challenging Lord Awesomo for leadership of the mall," she revealed.

"Leadership?!" said Don incredulously. "He doesn't need to! We've got an in with Hibatsu, and their settlement's much better run. Slightly less murder."

"Well, he didn't know that. He's won an awful lot of the people here to his side. They're about to have a debate."

By now, I could see what she was talking about. The auditorium in the main food-court area was full to capacity with a writhing sea of plastic-covered bodies, all paying rapt attention to the three individuals on the stage: Tim on the left, Princess Ravenhair in the center, and Lord Awesomo on the right. Each one was standing behind a makeshift lectern constructed from a stack of milk crates.

Lord Awesomo wasn't at all comfortable with public speaking without a veneer of irony. His face glistened with sweat—more than the usual amount that being wrapped in plastic created—and his hands fidgeted with his topmost milk crate when he wasn't toying nervously with the part of his fringe that extruded from his head bag.

I wouldn't have picked Tim as a good public speaker either, but he seemed somewhat more comfortable. He was gripping his lectern rather tightly but he was managing to maintain an approachable smile. I remembered that he had busked a few times in the underground walkway near the train station, so maybe that gave him the edge.

"All right, settle down, everyone," instructed Princess Ravenhair, silencing the nervous crowd. There was a portable whiteboard on her lectern with some questions written in a variety of festive colors. "I know we all want to know what's to be done about the leaving the mall problem, but we'll be hearing proposed solutions as part of the debate."

"Yes, about that," said Lord Awesomo sternly, struggling to survive in a low-irony atmosphere. "Do we really think it's a great idea to be holding elections right now?"

"Hang on," said Tim. "Are you saying democracy should be suspended because of a crisis situation? Isn't that what the Bush administration were proposing at one point?" A smattering of applause from Tim's side of the audience, which prompted him to continue. "This whole can't-leave-the-mall thing has proved quite beneficial for you, hasn't it, Lord Awesomo? A nice, convenient scare to keep the population from getting too uppity? Almost suspiciously so, I'd say."

"I . . . what? Are you seriously accusing me of being in on it?"

"No, I didn't say any such thing," said Tim, springing a trap. "You're the one who brought that up. It's almost as if you're feeling guilty about something."

"You . . ." began Lord Awesomo, before defiantly clamping his mouth shut to stop himself from giving Tim more ammunition.

"Would the challenger like to make their statement first?" said Princess Ravenhair, sensing the mood in the room.

"Probably a good idea," said Tim. He took a deep breath. "I believe the current administration has proved themselves incapable of dealing with the crises the settlement is facing. With the jam consuming any of us who attempt to leave the mall, all Lord Awesomo can offer is ironic jokes and executions." A number of audience members loudly agreed with this sentiment. "And he's done nothing to investigate the hoodlums who just yesterday soiled the holy person of Crazy Bob. Hail Crazy Bob."

"Hail Crazy Bob," went the crowd dutifully, casting their eyes up. The silhouette of Crazy Bob stared down motionlessly from the highest level. I felt a nodule of guilt throb painfully at the back of my head. Beside me I could hear Don's teeth quietly grinding like a tiny lumber mill.

"In addition," continued Tim, speaking faster and faster like a snowball descending a hill. "His leadership has made precisely zero progress into our most pressing issue to date. He has failed to make any headway in unmasking the villain who has kidnapped Princess Ravenhair's beloved Whiskers."

The nodule of guilt at the back of my head suddenly plunged all the way down my spine like a child on a sledge. A fresh coating of sweat further irritated my plastic-covered armpits. At the mention of Whiskers's name, every head had bowed in mourning except two. One was mine, and the other belonged to Lord Awesomo, who appeared to be scanning the crowd.

His eyes met mine, and a sinister smile unfolded on his face. Whatever doubt he may have had that I was guilty of budgiecide vanished when he saw my reaction. It was written all over my face in sweat and an embarrassed blush so vivid it felt almost neon.

"Funny you should say that . . ." said Lord Awesomo, still staring at me.

"Please wait for your turn to speak," said Princess Ravenhair curtly, silencing him with a single glare.

"So when's he going to bring the guilty to justice?" said Tim. I attempted to wave my hands urgently and mouth *tone it down*, but he hadn't seen me. "When will he act in the best interests of the people? I'll tell you when it won't be: it won't be today! If he can't give us answers right this minute, he'll have proven he's not competent enough to keep the peace!"

Lord Awesomo was suddenly a lot more comfortable under the spotlight. His arms were folded and his hips were cocked nonchalantly. He waited until the cheers and chanting had completely died down before he gave a short, unimpressed cough and spoke.

"I know who kidnapped Whiskers," he said.

Instantly the dynamic of the situation turned on its head. The many rapturous gazes aimed lovingly at Tim suddenly flipped over to Lord Awesomo like trains switching tracks. A murmur of surprise and interest broke out and began making the climb to full-on shouting argument.

"Quiet!" barked Princess Ravenhair, in a tone I'd never heard from her before, and the room was shocked into silence. She turned to the smug-looking Lord Awesomo, eyes aflame. "Who?"

This time Lord Awesomo flashed her a winning smile, which only made the situation tenser. "Oh, come on," he said, enjoying his rekindled power. "Maybe most of you haven't noticed, but there's something in this very room that is literally classified as a *birdeater*. It's a difficult connection to make, I know."

"A birdeater?" The princess cast an urgent look around, but thankfully didn't seem to be as well versed in natural history as her colleague.

Don nudged me in the shoulder. "Maybe now would be a good time to pull your thumb out of your butt and get out of here," he whispered. He was probably right, but I was still pinned in place by Awesomo's smiling gaze. Everyone in the room was deer-in-headlights frozen and any movement I made would immediately draw attention.

"What's a birdeater?" pressed Princess Ravenhair.

"It's a kind of spugubduh," said Lord Awesomo nonchalantly, rocking on his heels. Then he slowly looked down and saw a wooden shaft protruding from his upper torso. Almost casually he clamped his hand around the wound, staring at the blood seeping through his fingers with boggle eyes. "Christ," he said, slightly slurred. "Oh, yeah, that doesn't hurt at all."

"Gerald!" cried Princess Ravenhair, running to his side with all animosity forgotten. She grabbed the extruding shaft and pulled.

"Gnnngh! Please keep doing that!" said Gerald, swaying drunkenly. "I think that is doing the world of good!"

"Stop being ironic!" she wailed.

Someone near the front of the crowd suddenly made a startled little *phut* noise; then their plastic exoskeleton quickly inflated with jam. One of their friends suffered the same fate while picking, disoriented, through the empty bags that remained.

Suddenly noticing the angle of entry on Awesomo's wound, I looked up.

The distant shadow of Crazy Bob was still there, but now the distant shadow of a makeshift longbow was visible in his arms. He also seemed to have lifted a lot of weights since I'd seen him last.

By this point the crowd had automatically organized themselves in order of intelligence, with the slower of wit still in the center of the audience seating and the shrewdest already on the outskirts of the crowd, speed wading the hell out of there. Princess Ravenhair was trying to drag Lord Awesomo offstage, and she yelped as another arrow pierced one of the less forward-thinking members of the crowd.

"Out of the jam!" yelled Tim, effortlessly stepping into the leadership role. "Everyone up the stairs!"

Within seconds the four escalators leading to the next, jam-free level were packed with multicolored plastic and hurrying feet, like four giant, neurotic caterpillars. One or two unfortunates were shoved aside and met a sticky end as they fell full length into the jam, exposing their breathing holes to strawberry death. All notion of class had been abandoned and Princess Ravenhair and Tim, carrying the wounded Lord Awesomo between them, were just another screaming part of the anguished queue.

Y was still picking off the stragglers, but with a manual bow and arrow he could barely dent the plastic people's numbers. Don, Angela, and I remained, halfheartedly in cover, while X stood out in the open, staring up without fear.

"Y," she said, barely audible. Actually she might have been saying, "Why?" but there wasn't time to ask for clarification.

"That was Y, wasn't it," said Angela, as we tried to force our way up the escalator together.

"Probably," I said. "I think he might have worked something out with the Hibatsu people."

Her camera turned to me. "Hibatsu? How deep does this rabbit hole go, Travis?"

We followed the natural flow of the crowd. By some unspoken agreement the plastic people were assembling in the residential area on the upper levels of the department store.

I ended up back in our circle of makeshift beds. X was sitting quietly in the center wearing such a deep expression of concern that even Angela hesitated instead of stomping over to throw accusations. Don lay back on a beanbag and stared at the ceiling. Tim was over by Princess Ravenhair, helping a couple of handmaidens lay out Lord Awesomo.

The princess herself was walking totteringly around the nearby area, fidgeting nervously and conversing briefly with everyone she passed. Then she noticed me, and my heart seemed to pump ice for a second as she stomped in my direction before it occurred to me to hide.

"Travis," she said.

"I'M SORRY!" I blurted.

"Do you know what a birdeater is?" she asked. Then, after a pause, "What are you sorry about?"

"I'm sorry," I repeated, "that I don't know what a birdeater is. Really, really sorry."

"That's okay," she said distractedly. Her foot was tapping woodpecker fast. She was wearing the hassled frown of a housewife whose dinner guests should have arrived an hour ago. "Someone said they think it might be a kind of lawnmower. Do you think someone might have done something to Whiskers?"

"Um, how's Lord Awesomo?" I said, attempting to coax her onto a slightly more pressing thread of conversation.

"I can't believe he's known something about Whiskers all this time!" she said crossly. "I'm trying to get more details but he just keeps moaning and being delirious!"

"Um, princess, are you all right?"

"Not really," she said. "I feel a bit numb. I think I'll just . . . go over there for a bit." Eyes wide with shock and apparently no longer able to bend her legs at the knee, she lurched slowly over to a display armchair and sat down—in the lap of its current occupant, but she didn't notice and he seemed to be too polite to say anything.

Angela, who had apparently been recording our conversation, sidled up to me. "Awesomo mentioned birdeaters," she said casually. "Sounded like he was about to start accusing Mary of having something to do with the Whiskers disappearance."

"Maybe," I said quietly.

"How desperate can you get? Literally his only lead is that someone's carrying around a breed of spider that happens to be called a birdeater. In the wild they don't even eat birds very much." Her camera lens remained fixed unsettlingly on my face. "It doesn't automatically follow that you fed Whiskers to Mary, does it, Travis? Travis? Does it, Travis? Why are you turning red, Travis?" She scrutinized my face and body language for a few seconds, camera intruding quite blatantly upon my personal space. "Oh, god."

"It wasn't my fault!" I protested. "I didn't know it was her bird!"

"I'd like to know whose bird you thought it was that made it entirely justified."

"Mary was going to starve!" I was backed up against a chest of drawers, hugging her box protectively.

"What you should have done," said Angela, "was think of it in terms of a kid's movie. If on the one side you've got a pretty little cheerful blue bird who is the only companion to a young girl all alone in the world, and on the other you've got a giant venomous tarantula three times the size with big horrible spindly legs, which one do you think the audience would root for?"

"I like her legs," I whined.

She clicked her tongue. "If Y weren't on a murder spree you'd be in pretty big trouble, wouldn't you."

"What did you say?" Tim had been pacing around the outskirts of Lord Awesomo's sleeping area and had passed momentarily into earshot. "Y's on a murder spree? Oh, hi, Travis, where've you been?"

"You didn't hear it from me," said Angela, tapping the part of her plastic bag where her nose belonged before retreating from the conversation and drifting off to harangue X some more.

"That was Y, wasn't it?" said Tim. "On the top floor where Crazy Bob should have been? He's the one killing everyone when they leave?" He glanced over at Princess Ravenhair, who was still sitting demurely on some uncomfortable person's knee. "That's absolutely perfect."

"It is?"

"We know him. That means we can figure out a solution. This is exactly what I need to gain the hearts-and-minds thing. And now Lord Awesomo's out of action!"

Tim had been making me more and more uneasy ever since I'd arrived back at the mall. I hoped I wouldn't have to cross him off the list of the few remaining things I could rely upon, which was already down to two people and one spider. "Tim, you don't have to!"

"What do you mean?"

I leaned close and lowered my voice. "We went to the Hibatsu building. Me and Don."

"Serious? What's it like?"

"Well, it's full of nutters, but that's kind of par for the course. It's a different kind of nutters. They run the place way better than the plastic people do. Like, crazy well. They're already growing crops on the roof, and they can draw up water from the river."

He winced. "The Brisbane River?"

"It's okay; the jam cleaned it."

"I was going to say, that might explain why they're nutters. So they actually let you in?"

"You have to pay your way, but they accept plastic bags."

Tim chewed on his lower lip. "Well, this is making things pretty awkward, isn't it. I've been working hard on getting this settlement sorted out. I've got a following and I'm this close to taking power."

"How close?"

He glanced back at Lord Awesomo's prone form. "About two inches nearer the heart. I dunno. I'm going to have to think about this. So why does Y keep killing people, anyway? Did he flip?"

However uneasy Tim was making me, we had been friends and housemates for a long time. The jampocalypse had brought on a new, slightly predatory spark in his eye, but he still had the face and the voice of the guy who had stayed up all night with me to drink a whole twelve-pack and play *Ham Fighters 2* after my first bad breakup. I confided everything as fast as possible. "We think Y went to the Hibatsu building and he made some kind of deal with them to let him and X in and I think in return he has to suppress the plastic people and I think Hibatsu are trying to break up the settlement or absorb it or something because they asked me and Don to steal supplies for them but Y shot at me but not Don when we came back so I'm afraid he might be cross at me about something—"

"Okay, okay," said Tim, silencing me with a reassuring pat on the head. "Who else knows all of this?"

"Just me and Don. And I think Angela. And I expect X and Y know it, too."

"Right. Well, don't tell anyone else, okay?" He sighed. "So Hibatsu might be bringing the pressure down on us, eh? Typical corporate thinking, isn't it. Grab all they can and screw the small business. I really am going to have to think about this."

Princess Ravenhair walked past us, and we watched her sit on Lord Awesomo's bed. She started dabbing tenderly at his forehead with what I think might have been a Brillo pad. He seemed to be too unconscious to complain.

"This might be a silly question," said Tim, "but is there a bit of a history between those two?"

"Uh, yeah," I said. "They used to post on some forum together."

"Forum." He snapped his fingers. "You know, ever since we got here I've been trying to put my finger on what this whole society reminds me of. It's an Internet forum. Everyone's got stupid names, makes ironic jokes, and has this weird sort of cult mentality going on. Should have picked up on that sooner."

"Er, what do they want?" I asked.

A growing crescent of plastic people was forming around Lord Awesomo's sleeping area. Those who had removed their plastics or were wearing transparent head bags wore concerned and frightened faces, looking to Lord Awesomo for leadership in a time of crisis. But all he could offer was moans and saliva bubbles, so they looked to Princess Ravenhair instead.

Turning away from her care for Lord Awesomo, the princess started when she noticed the crowd. She looked to me and Tim questioningly. We responded by making prompting gestures with our hands and eyebrows.

"L-loyal subjects," she announced, getting to her feet. Words failed her after that, and it took another four or five eyebrow waggles to get her back on track. "I wish I had . . . more positive news to give you." The few unfallen faces in the crowd fell. "Lord Awesomo's still alive but I don't know if he'll pull through. And we may be facing the fact that we can't move freely around the jam anymore. Whatever it was that was killing us whenever we left definitely seems to have moved inside the mall. And we don't even know what it is."

"I know!" came a voice from the crowd. Two large, gormless-looking plastic men in the front row moved aside and a girl pushed her way forward. A very familiar girl with an opaque head bag and a slight build.

"What?" said the princess.

"I know what's been killing us," said the girl nervously. "I saw it when me and Strike Force Maximum Alpha went outside."

"Saw what?"

"There's a man on the roof," she said breathlessly. "A big man. He's got a bow and he fires arrows at anyone who tries to leave. Then their bags get holed so the jam eats them."

Princess Ravenhair looked back at the shaft still jutting from Lord Awesomo's shoulder, which bobbed uncomfortably with his breathing. "Oh my god . . . Just one man?"

"No, no, I think he's got accomplices," continued the girl. "There were these two other guys when I went outside. On a boat. Dressed just like us, in plastic bags. The guys, not the boat." From somewhere to my right I heard Don, who had been staring at the ceiling and only half paying attention, choke phlegmily. "It looked like they knew the guy on the roof. They called something to him and he didn't shoot at them."

"Where did these two guys go?" demanded Ravenhair.

"I . . . don't know. I got away from them. They're in the mall, I think. Right now. I didn't get a good look at their faces. It all happened so fast."

"What color were their bags?" asked a random onlooker.

"Er . . . well, I don't really notice that kind of thing," admitted the girl sheepishly. Don, who was already trying to subtly push his way out through the back of the crowd on some pretense of being desperate for the toilet, audibly relaxed.

In stark juxtaposition, the princess clutched at her hair, too confused to process it all. "What the hell is going on? Is there some kind of . . . conspiracy against me?"

"Well . . ." began Angela, hearing one of her buzzwords.

"Yes!" cried Tim, taking a step forward. "There is a conspiracy against you. Against all of us. We can't know why or for what purpose, but now we know one thing—it's just a man. Or men. And men can be defeated. Especially when there are so many of us." The crowd seemed doubtful, but they weren't booing him off just yet. "Friends, my opponent in the polls may be indisposed, but I'm not about to declare victory. I swear that I will end the assassin's reign of terror by this time tomorrow, and then I will accept the role of your leader with all due modesty. Under the guiding hand of Crazy Bob."

"Thank you," sniffed Princess Ravenhair.

There was a smattering of slightly disbelieving applause, and a more or less satisfied audience dribbled away, murmuring worriedly to each other about what they were going to eat tonight. Princess Ravenhair kissed Tim chastely on the cheek, offered me a shy smile, then returned to dabbing up Lord Awesomo's brow sweat.

I grabbed Tim's elbow. "What are you doing?"

"I made my decision," he said.

"You're not seriously going to take on Y?"

"Why not? We know him. We saved his life. He'll listen to us. The least we can do is buy some time."

"But what about Hibatsu?"

"I'm going to offer them a truce. No reason there can't be two settlements, right? More than enough supplies lying around for both to become self-sufficient." He was talking fast now, and practically bouncing on his toes in glee. "It makes sense. What are you looking so worried about?"

I cringed. "Tim, I just . . . do you think you're getting a bit too . . . Well, do you think you might be . . . going native?"

"How do you mean?"

"You've been doing the Crazy Bob worship thing a lot."

"Come on, Travis, no true leader genuinely believes the religious part of the ruling system. It's just for keeping the common man in line. It's a feudal thing. You distract the vassals with promises of divine justice so they don't complain about the fiefs having all the groats."

"Okay, I get it," I lied.

"Well, speaking of Crazy Bob, it'd probably be a good idea to find out exactly what Y did with him. You wait here. I'll be back with supplies."

With that assurance delivered, he headed off deeper into the department store. I moved to X and Angela, looking for a conversation that didn't make me want to bang my head against the nearest fridge. X was hugging herself and staring at the floor with more concern than I'd ever seen her display,

while Angela was leaning forward with a tender, understanding look on her face.

"I just . . . don't know what he's thinking," X was saying.

"Mmm," said Angela earnestly.

"He's seen what happens to people in crisis situations. He
swore to me that he wouldn't go the same way."

"What a bastard."

"All I ever wanted of him was to complete his mission. I
didn't expect it to reach this level."

"Sure," said Angela. She shuffled a little closer. "So what
was that mission, exactly?"

"It—" X finally looked at her. "Are you interrogating me?"

Angela leaned back quickly. "Of course not!"

"Then stop filming!"

"It's for therapy!" said Angela desperately, adjusting the
focus. "You can look over it later and see how far you've
come!"

It was to no avail. X looked offended, then stood up huffily
and pridefully gathered her plastic bags around her, before
trudging away alone through the store. Angela leaned back,
disappointed, and noticed me for the first time. "I think I'm
closing in on the truth," she confided. "The friendly-friendly
act is really doing the trick."

"You could just be friendly for reals," I said.

"Maybe when she stops being a big fat fake."

At that point Tim returned, clutching a long, hefty parcel
wrapped in a few newly unwrapped bed sheets, which he
dumped on the coffee table with a metallic, jangling thump,
allowing the cover to fall aside. Don, Angela, and I leaned
in, curious. Don almost immediately leaned back.

"Oh, no," he said. "You can leave me the hell out of this
one. I'm strictly Switzerland."

"I thought you were just going to talk to him," I said.

"Yes, well, we have to get close to him first," said Tim, picking up a circular piece of wood that I think must have been the top of a coffee table before being repurposed as a shield.

I picked up a pool cue with a kitchen knife duct taped to each end. "This doesn't look like something designed for getting close to anyone."

"Where'd you get all this stuff so fast?" asked Angela.

"There's this kid, one of my followers," explained Tim, jerking a thumb behind him. "Was a massive gun nut pre-jam. He's been building weaponry just in case something like this came up. Check this out."

He took up a two-handed device whose purpose was eluding me. It seemed to incorporate two litter-picking devices, a barbecue lighter, and three cans of hairspray. He pointed it at the ceiling and pulled on the two triggers, whereupon there was a snap, and a massive burst of sweet-smelling flame roared briefly into life like Satan's first morning fart. After it had faded away, I noticed that everyone within a twenty-yard radius had dropped into a crouch.

"Okay, I didn't expect it to be that powerful," said Tim, tapping his chin and inspecting the black stain on the ceiling.

"Even better," sniped Don from around knee level. "Nothing says 'I come in peace' like a good incendiary device."

"It'll give him pause for thought and that's all we need," said Tim, not rising to it. "I think I'd better carry this. Travis?"

I picked out a baseball bat that I didn't see myself using, as well as a cricketer's helmet and two tea trays tied together with string that I supposed were intended to be used as breast and back plates. Angela went for the pool-cue spear and the coffee-table buckler.

"Don?" prompted Tim.

"Forget it," said Don, folding his arms. "I'm not playing this stupid game. I've had to put up with a lot of bullshit since the jam came down but I am not doing this."

DAY 5.4

"I am only doing this," said Don, wearing a colander on his head and clutching a toy foam-pellet gun modified to fire ammunition soaked in pepper spray, "to make sure you toss-heads don't bugger the whole thing up like you always do."

"Whatever," said Tim.

"I'm serious. X and Y are still our best bet of getting bumped up the rescue list. I just feel better knowing Y isn't going to be roasted to death by unsupervised shitheads."

After a brief nap and a hearty dinner of cold sausage rolls and chocolate, we were ready to set out on the expedition. We'd originally decided to wait until nightfall in order to have the best possible chance of catching Y by surprise, but by the time we left, a small crowd had formed at the department-store entrance, so, so much for that.

A few of the people in the crowd were holding small banners with inexpert renditions of Tim's head drawn on them, but there was no cheering or applause, and Tim gave no rousing speeches. They were like a solemn peasant crowd, watching their folk hero walking up the steps to a grinning man in a black hood pointing meaningfully at a heavily chipped wooden block.

All the store shutters had been closed except one. "We're going to lock the gate behind you," explained an anonymous plastic man with one hand on the mechanism. "In case they try to come and get us in here."

"Fine," said Tim, nervousness showing only in the way his fingers fondled the shaft of his flamethrower. "When I want to be let back in, I'll give three short knocks followed by two long ones."

The gatekeeper nodded slowly. "Or you could just go, 'Hey, it's me, Tim.' "

"Right. Yes."

The four of us filed out. Tim first, then me, then Angela, then a grumbling Don in the rear. The gatekeeper and an assistant grimly pulled the last shutter down to the floor. The boom as it landed into place reverberated away into the silent abyss of the Briar Center like a funereal bell.

After that, there was not a single sound in the mall. All the surviving plastic people were holed up in the department store. The torches were dark, and the only illumination was a fuzzy moonlight coming down from the ceiling dome, which did nothing but highlight the huge number of dark shadows Y could have been hiding in.

Tim took an unlit torch from an undernourished plant and held it to the end of his flamethrower. A massive gout of flame briefly flooded the near vicinity with orange light before settling into a smaller blaze of wadded-up children's pajamas on the end of a stick.

"What the hell are you doing?!" cried Don, crouching and pulling his colander down.

"It's nearly pitch dark," said Tim.

"You just gave our position away! Remember? There's a sniper around here somewhere you want to invite to a tea party?"

"Oh shit, right." He dunked the burning end back into the soil of the plant. The dried-out brown plant that still occupied the soil immediately burst into flame, and I had to help Tim push it to the floor and stomp it out.

"Well, we're off to a flying start," said Don, slowly and loudly hand clapping in a way that didn't improve the stealth situation at all.

"You know, Don, you're not helping," said Angela, focusing on him angrily. "What now, Tim?"

"We have to go up to the cinema level," said Tim, brushing off Don's comments like biscuit crumbs on a dressing-gown lapel. "The people will want to know if Crazy Bob is all right. Follow me."

He strode off towards the stationary escalators. Almost immediately there was a solid THUD. "GAH," came his voice.

"You all right?" I said.

"I banged my knees on a bench," he replied. "Hang on." THUD. "GAH."

"Hang on, my camera's got night vision," announced Angela, stepping forward. "Is that you, Tim?"

"No, that's me," I said. "Tim's further on."

I felt her move past me, then there was another savage THUD. "GAH," she said. "Man, those things really sneak up on you, don't they?"

"Oh, just light a bloody torch," said Don. "Hardly seems to matter anymore. Maybe we could paint some glow-in-the-dark targets on our faces and hope Y remembers what pity feels like."

The flamethrower coughed violently again and Tim's scowling orange face appeared in the blackness like a lost soul. He took up the flaming torch and proceeded with care. Angela and I followed behind, Angela still trying to find the night-vision button on her camcorder, while Don brought up the rear, doing his best to stay on the outer rim of the circle of firelight.

We reached the base of the staircase that led up to the cinema lobby. Y's last known position, his sniping spot during the election debate, was just a few feet from the top of the stairs. Presumably he'd moved since then, but he had never been predictable, even at the best of times.

"Okay," whispered Tim. He hunkered down halfway up the stairs and we arranged ourselves in a line behind him, like World War I infantrymen preparing to go over the top. "Don, you've got the mace-pellet gun. You go in first."

"Uh, that's a big screw you, good buddy," replied Don, hunched froglike directly below me.

"You're the one who wanted to take him alive. You've got the best nonlethal weapon. All you need to do is get him in the face a few times with mace pellets and Travis can move in and subdue him with the baseball bat."

"Travis can what in the who?" I interjected.

"This thing won't even work," said Don, holding up his multicolored plastic weapon. I was amazed how far toy-gun technology had come; the thing had a stock and a drum magazine. "You're supposed to spray mace in people's eyes. You can't just smear it on them. It's not like VapoRub."

"Look, the least you can do is try it out," said Tim, hurt. "Jamie spent days emptying handbag-sized mace canisters into that thing."

"I can do that just as well from behind something dense," Don said. I wondered how to take that. "You're on point; you go first."

"Okay, I will," said Tim. "And after we've nonlethally subdued him by spraying fire in his face, you can be the one to pat him out. One, two, three."

I couldn't remember if he was expecting me to immediately follow him, so I stayed put and let him run up the stairs and into the lobby alone, waving his flamethrower and screaming. After it died down, I peered my head over the top step to see how much was left.

He was leaning on the snack counter, examining something behind it. Either that or he was steadying himself after having received several barbed shafts to the sternum. Angela did a quick scan with the night vision, then we crept over to Tim, attempting to keep what armor we had between us and the likeliest sniping positions.

"We found Crazy Bob!" cried Angela, naming the individual lying bound and gagged behind the counter. He was still wearing the cardboard mask, with the gag tied around it. I had to wonder what kind of sanity level Y was operating on. She leaned over and fumbled for a pulse. "And he's not dead!"

"At least we know Y doesn't kill people he doesn't believe to be a threat," said Tim.

"What was that?" came Don's voice from back at the stairs. "Did I just hear a reason to stop carrying these stupid weapons arou—"

Falling silent midsentence was so yawningly out of character I immediately knew something was wrong. "Don?" I said.

His voice came a few seconds later, strained and a full octave higher. "Something just ricocheted off my colander. I think I'm going to hide behind this column for a bit."

At the very moment he said the word *bit*, I became aware of a whistling sound, and my tea-tray chest plate shuddered violently, as if I'd been shoved by a gorilla with unusually dainty hands. A slightly bent arrow spun end over end in the air and clattered to the floor.

I sprinted across the open lobby and slid under the first piece of cover I could see—the chest-high wall from which Crazy Bob had looked down upon the lower levels of the mall. I looked behind me and saw that Tim and Angela had simply hopped over the counter and crouched there, a much nearer and sensibler option.

If I looked to my right I could see Don pressed up against the back of the column halfway down the staircase. His face was so pale he looked like a marble bust wearing a colander.

"Y!" shouted Tim from his position of safety. "IT'S US! WE PULLED YOU OUT OF THE HELICOPTER!"

"THAT WAS MOSTLY ME!" I shouted, opportunistically.

The mall fell silent. I wondered if he'd realized his mistake and was preparing some kind of apology. Then I caught a glimpse of movement just above the five-story abyss down to the food court, and one of the long cloth banners that hung from the ceiling fluttered back into place, as if someone had just been swinging from it like Tarza—

Two thick leather soles thudded ominously onto the level below, cutting through my thought processes like a pool-cue spear. At the bottom of the stairs, past Don's shivering form, I saw a thickly built figure emerge from the pitch darkness like a muscle-bound bubble rising from a tar pit.

Y was looking somewhat worse for wear. He was paler even than Don, and both his face and his naked arms and shoulders were soaking wet with sweat. His eyes started from their sockets and rasping breaths sawed in and out of his half-open mouth. If I'd seen him hitchhiking at the side of the road my foot would have reflexively pushed the accelerator to the floor.

He began to slowly climb the stairs towards Don with the lumbering menace of a nightmare monster, shoulders hunched forward and catcher's-mitt hands clenching and unclenching. Don attempted to back away, which proved surprisingly difficult while crouching on stairs.

"Y," he said, trying to sound calm. "How wonderful to see you. We were beginning to worry you might have . . . er . . . gone off your trolley. But I've only got to look at you to know that you're completely rational, am I right?"

In response, Y took hold of a hilt protruding from some kind of armpit holster and withdrew a combat knife easily as long as my forearm.

Tim appeared at my shoulder. "Don!" he called down. "Don't do anything to alarm him!"

"You're worried about HIM?!" called Don back.

"He's not in his right mind! You have to reason with him!"

Y's blade caught the moonlight for an instant. "Reason?!" said an incredulous Don. "Fine! Here's my opening argument."

He swung his toy gun around and held down the trigger. The barrel spun up and a rapid stream of foam pellets noisily filled the air between Don and Y. Most of them bounced harmlessly off his treelike torso and seemed more to confuse him than anything else, until a single pellet found its mark, squishing itself against Y's cheekbone and squirting its payload of liquid pepper spray directly into his madly widened eye.

I heard Angela hiss in sympathy as Y dropped his knife, staggering back and clutching his face. Tim prodded me with an elbow. "Travis! Now! Subdue him!"

In a panic I ran forward, holding the baseball bat overhead like a sledgehammer, and swung it down as hard as I could. He was already bent double, and the bat bounced straight off his pulsating back muscles. I glanced at Tim for further instructions.

"Subdue him harder!" he offered.

I brought it around for a horizontal swing, but it was stopped midway by Y's open palm. His fingers clamped around the end like a Venus flytrap. He wrenched the handle out of my grasp as easily as he'd pull a greasy spoon out of his morning porridge, and I felt the end of the bat rattle disorientingly against the front of my helmet.

Once my head cleared, I discovered that I was sitting slumped on the floor with my back up against an ashtray. Tim and Angela were leaning urgently over the railing, searching the shadows for Y. "Where'd he go?"

"He just jumped straight off . . ." said Angela, obligingly. "Did he land in the jam?"

"No, I think he swung off one of those banners again."

"Recent events indicate that Y may have gone banana sandwiches," said Angela to her camera. "Tim, do you think it's true about the drugs?"

"What drugs?"

"You know, the drugs they give to the military to keep them under control. Maybe he's going through withdrawal."

"That doesn't hold up for a second," said Don grumpily, appearing at her side and uncomfortably adjusting the increasingly moist clothes under his plastic bags. "Military spending's tightly controlled as it is without adding on several thousand tons of smack."

"Well, what other explanation is there for Y's behavior?"

"I dunno. Maybe he's just run out of cigarettes. I looked like that most mornings when I was quitting."

"Did you notice his quiver?" said Tim.

"What?" said Angela, confusedly swinging her camera back and forth. "You think he's got the DTs, too?"

"No, I mean, the arrow pouch on his back. It was empty. That's why he came at us like that, because he ran out." He waggled an index finger sagely. "That means we've got an advantage. We can bring the fight to him."

We watched him scamper excitedly around the lobby until he found what he was looking for: the arrow that had bounced off my chest plate. He brought it over, examining it carefully.

"Bring the fight to him?" said Don incredulously. "I think we should be thinking of ways to take the fight as far away from him as possible."

"He'll need to run off to make more arrows," continued Tim. "If we can figure out where he makes them, we might be able to take him by surprise."

"Nice thinking!" said Angela, taking the arrow off him and holding it up to the moonlight like a cashier checking a banknote. "It's definitely varnished," reported Angela. "He probably carved it from a piece of furniture."

"But it wouldn't be from the department store," said Tim. "Or anywhere else where there are a lot of people around."

"You really aren't listening, are you," said Don. "You're all just tuning me out. This is actually quite liberating."

"Look at this," said Angela, holding the arrow for all to see. It was, indeed, varnished, and the arrowhead appeared to be part of a brass hinge that had been laboriously folded and filed to a point. Angela was indicating a small nodule of wood about two-thirds of the way along the shaft. "Is that a nipple?"

"Do you know, I've fantasized about cutting the throats of every single one of you while you sleep," said Don dreamily, supporting his chin on his fists.

"It's definitely a nipple," said Tim. "Maybe from some arty wood carving?"

"Christ, you people are dense. He's in that exotic furniture shop on level three with all the carved wooden Buddhas in the window."

"He must be in the exotic furniture shop!" said Angela, snapping her fingers. "You know, that place on level three. The one with all those carved fat guys in the window."

The shop was called the Knickknackery, and it had been run by two middle-aged women who had a habit of wearing mystically themed velvet dresses better suited to people with waists around two feet narrower. There were, indeed, Buddha carvings in the window, along with figurines of various religious characters and fertility symbols that had always made me too embarrassed to walk past the place in tight-fitting trousers.

It was one of the shops on the narrow walkway that ran partially around the third-level perimeter, directly above the jam-filled food court. The path was narrow, with just three or four feet separating the shop fronts from the railing, and it was a good spot to bottleneck an invading force, if my experience with strategy games made me any judge. We were practically approaching the shop in single file, in our now-standard formation, with Tim in front and Don at the rear.

Tim held up a hand to stop us a few feet from the Knickknackery's nearest window. The shutters had been forced aside, which had almost certainly been the work of the plastic people, but the partial bead curtain that hung over the doorway was still tangled and swaying gently from someone recently barging their way through.

Tim half turned, back pressed against the window, and patted me on the shoulder for attention. He put a finger to his lips, then moved his hand in a sweeping gesture, then pointed to his eyes with two fingers, then jerked a thumb towards the shop.

"What's that mean?" I asked.

From inside the shop I heard the sound of tools being thrown down, a table being kicked onto its side, and a large, muscular body moving into a holdout position.

Tim's shoulders untensed. "Well, the first bit meant *be silent*," he said. "And the rest of it's academic, now."

"Sorry."

"Y!" shouted Tim. "Listen! We just want to talk, okay? The Hibatsu people put you up to this, right? You can stop killing us. I'm going to take command of the plastic people and I'm going to offer peace to the Hibatsu settlement. Just stop what you're doing, come out slowly, and we'll go back there together to negotiate. Sound good?"

Y made no response. The four of us passed a tense look around. "Maybe he's thinking about it," said Angela.

"Look, we have an opportunity to be uniters, not dividers," called Tim, switching on his newfound politician voice. "If you keep this up, everything that's left of this city will be consumed by chaos. Is that what you want?"

The entirety of the shop window behind us immediately shattered. We threw ourselves to the floor as broken glass rained noisily down and an ornate wooden globe flew over our heads into the jam.

"Okay, screw this," said Don. He immediately scrambled forward to take cover by the other, still-intact window.

"Don't separate!" cried Angela.

"Don't pass in front of the—" added Tim.

It was too late. Don was already framed momentarily in the doorway, and he was immediately hit by one of Y's wooden arrows, fired with lightning reflexes. The arrow struck his shoulder and immediately shattered into strings, failing to even penetrate his plastic armor.

"The hell?" said Don, astonished at his continuing life. "Is this balsawood? You running out of materials in there, dipshit?"

In reply, a life-sized wooden statue of the Virgin Mary came flying horizontally out the door, smacking into Don with the force of a divine wrecking ball. He was flung off his feet and fell backwards over the railing. We heard the squelch of happy jam.

"Don!" yelled Angela.

"I'm okay," came his slightly pained voice. "I landed plastic first. I think I'm just going to wait here. You're on top of this, right?"

"And then there were three," muttered Tim.

"We're certainly putting the pressure on Y," said Angela, on all fours, trying to film into the broken shop window without exposing herself. "He's losing his usual finesse."

Experimentally, Tim held the nose of his flamethrower upwards until it would have been visible from inside through the broken window, at which point it was almost knocked out of his hand by a much sturdier hardwood arrow that went spinning into the jam.

"We can't do anything while he's in a strong holdout position," said Tim, who also played strategy games. "We need to flush him out."

"Where're we going to get that much water?" I asked.

Tim rubbed his eyes, exhausted. "Okay then, we'll just do something that makes him leave the shop."

"Yeah, that's a much better idea," I said.

"I'll just blast a bit of fire into the window, just as a warning," thought Tim aloud. "Give him something to think about."

"Are you sure you want to surprise him?" said Angela. "He might do something sudden."

"Good call. HEY! Y! I'm just going to fire off a warning shot now!" He touched the triggers. The first snapped the barbecue lighter on and the second depressed the aerosol cans.

Tim conceded later that spraying fire at a shop full of wood, varnish, curtains, and strange hippie chemicals probably hadn't been the great idea it had seemed like at the time.

The ball of flaming gas dispersed around the top of the shop window display and set light to a billowing purple curtain that was attached to the ceiling. It had probably been bought from the same sort of place that all the children's pajamas on the torches had come from, because the fire swept along it like the Mongol hordes across the plains. This turned out to be the chintzy and tasteless fuse for the gigantic incendiary bomb that was the Knickknackery as a whole, because the entire interior was quickly bathed in flickering yellow light.

"Oh, shit," said Tim. "SORRY!" he yelled over the roar of the inferno.

"Y! GET OUT OF THERE!" advised Angela. Smoke was pouring from the door and broken window and we could no longer see anything inside but a merciless lake of fire.

"Should I grab a fire extinguisher?" I asked. The mall had been diligent on health and safety and I could see at least four just from our current position.

Tim considered this. "I see what you're saying, but I think that might send out mixed signals. Don't want to confuse the guy."

"I can't see him," said Angela, now carelessly on her feet and standing at the doorway, scanning the raging interior. "He might need help!"

We all jumped in fright as the other window shattered outwards. Y burst out in a midair storm of glittering fragments, surfing on what appeared to be an emergency exit door torn off its hinges. Some of his pouches and bits of webbing were still burning, but he either hadn't noticed or had felt they would look more intimidating, which was certainly the case.

Even before his door had finished clattering to the ground, Y launched himself off it and made for Tim, who was nearest. In one smooth movement, he grabbed the end of the flame-thrower in one hand and drove the elbow of his other arm into Tim's throat. Tim fell backwards, choking on his own cartilage.

After that, Y had his back to me. I knew I'd never have a better opportunity, so I made to wrap my arms around his treelike neck. He sensed me coming and effortlessly ducked out of the way, flipped my helmet off my head with one hand, caught it with the other, and shoved it into my solar plexus as hard as he could. I joined Tim on the floor.

That left Angela. She took up her double-bladed pool cue with her nonfilming hand and jabbed it clumsily towards the advancing figure. I didn't even see him move. I saw him raise his right arm, then I think I must have blinked, because the next thing I saw was Y holding the spear and Angela midslump.

"What's going on up there?" yelled Don from below. "Have you retarded him to death yet?"

Y skipped nimbly to the rail and readied the pool cue to throw like a javelin. I heard a terrified squeak from Don's direction. From my position on the ground I could see Don through the gap under the railing, standing waist deep in the jam with his hands over his mouth, metaphorically pinned to the spot in fear of soon being actually pinned to the spot.

But then Y froze, the ends of the weapon quivering as he held it horizontally. His steely gaze was locked with Don's petrified stare, but neither of them moved. He was like an actor freezing up as he forgot his line in front of an audience filled with his in-laws.

Then I realized that one of the smoldering bits of his webbing had set Y's ThunderCats pajama pants alight. His lower body was rapidly engulfed in a hellish pair of fire trousers. He collapsed onto his back and began slapping madly at the flames.

"Put him out," croaked Tim.

I scrambled to Y, transitioning from crawl to upright run on the way, and began stamping out the blazing parts. I was too flustered to notice exactly which blazing parts I was stamping out, and Y made a very curious noise when I felt my heel come down on the soft collection of objects around his lower trunk.

A single blackened hand folded around both my ankles and pulled my feet out from under me. I landed spine first on the solid tiles and a wave of pain pushed all the air out of my lungs. There was a flurry of movement around me, and something warm and leathery fastened tightly around my neck. I felt a nice comfortable high as Y began to cut off the flow of blood to my head, but through the welcoming red fog an urgent bell sounded, and it occurred to me that Y was about to twist my head around like a difficult beer bottle top.

"Y! Stop!"

My head cleared like a balloon being let out as X's shrill voice cut through the clouds.

"Stand down. Let him go."

Y didn't move, or reply. I could hear his heavy breathing in my ear, rattling coarsely in his throat.

"That's an order, sergeant," said X, with slightly feeble menace.

He let go. I scrambled over to Tim and had to stop myself from clinging to his leg. Y was on his knees, hanging his head, having fallen into standby mode like a Terminator with his head chip removed.

"What the hell is going on?" said Angela suddenly. "Who are you people really working for?"

X was kneeling in front of Y, stretching his eyelids out to check his pupils. She hung her head, heaved a deep, quivering sigh, and turned to Angela. "What?"

"Do you deny that you've been having him . . . silence people since the moment we arrived at this mall?"

"He's not silencing people!" insisted X. "He's just following the orders I gave him!"

"To silence people?" said Angela, losing self-confidence in the face of X's emotion.

"All I did was give him standing orders to establish a firm position with whatever party held the most sway. It's those lunatics at the Hibatsu building. They promised him a free ticket for us both if he did what they told him to. And they told him to come and . . . do this."

"So why's he trying to kill us?" asked Tim. "And why didn't he kill Don when he had the chance?"

"Why is that an issue?" said Don.

X scowled, holding Y's head like an owner comforting a beloved hound. "S . . . Y is not some kind of soulless assassin droid. Do you really think all this hasn't gotten to him? He is one of the most professional soldiers I have ever worked with, but when his orders are conflicting with what he knows is right, of course he's losing control!" She met Angela's dubious gaze. "And he was a heavy smoker, okay?"

"Ah!" Don clapped his hands. "Who called it?"

"The point is, there's no damn conspiracy!" concluded X.

"Except for Hibatsu conspiring against the plastic people," I said. "That's technically a conspiracy."

"All right, yes. There is a conspiracy to that extent. But there's no government cover-up and the jam was not released by the American military!"

"So who did release it?" said Angela.

X made a frustrated noise, clawing at her face. "No one released it! Not deliberately! You people, you just can't cope unless you've got someone to blame! Sometimes things just happen for no reason!"

"Well, speaking of having someone to blame," said Tim, "what are we going to do now? The plastic people are waiting for us to say we've sorted all this out."

"Haven't we done that already?" I said.

"Uh, we didn't do shit," said Don, who had now taken the escalator back up to our little conversation. "Just keeping that out there."

"Y, your orders have changed," said X to her huge, murderous puppy. "You are just my bodyguard again, okay? Your only task is to keep us both safe from physical harm."

It seemed like a little red light died in Y's eyes. "The Hibatsu settlement gave me orders," he said quietly, shoulders sagging. He spoke of *orders* in the way he'd speak of a child of his own.

"Don't you worry about Hibatsu," said Tim. "I'm going to offer them peace as soon as I'm the leader of the mall. But that all hinges on telling the people that their mysterious killer has been brought to justice, and I don't think they're just going to accept the assurance that he's calmed down now."

"I will not allow you to harm him," said X, standing in front of Y protectively.

"No, I guess not," said Tim uncomfortably, rubbing his chin in thought. "I think what we should do is bring him in alive. We can get hold of some cables from somewhere and tic him up."

"But then *they'll* kill him," I pointed out.

"I'll make a speech," said Tim. "Something about being the better men and not having to sink to the same level to prove our moral superiority. You know, all that kind of bullshit. It'd be a great opening for my declaration of peace with Hibatsu."

"I don't know about this . . ." said X.

"Sir," interjected Y. Even when speaking in quiet despair, as he was now, the echoes of his gravelly voice boomed around the silent mall. "It's okay."

The two Americans stared at each other in silence, a whole universe of different emotions bouncing back and forth between them.

Then Tim clapped his hands. "All righty then, let's get going. Oh, hang on," he added, as everyone started shifting their weight. "Travis, Angela, could you go fetch Crazy Bob and meet us back at the department store? They'll feel a lot more magnanimous if they can see he's all right."

"Can do," I said, relieved. I glanced over to Angela for confirmation, but she seemed to be lost in thought. Tim and X escorted Y towards one of the electronics shops like two zookeepers bringing a shamed bear to trial, Don following behind. Angela filmed them as they went, chewing on a knuckle. As they rounded a corner and disappeared from view, she slowly closed the viewfinder on her camcorder and let it fall to her side.

"She's probably telling the truth, isn't she?" she said. "Sometimes things just happen for no reason. There's no big conspiracy behind the jam."

"Isn't that sort of a good thing?" I said.

"Yeah . . ." said Angela, turning it over in her head like a taffy machine. "Yeah!" she added, with slightly more confidence. "It means we don't live in a world where people do that sort of thing to each other. That's a good thing." Her smile faded, and she looked at the floor sadly.

"Are you all right?"

She forced the corners of her mouth back up her face. "Yeah!" She laughed insincerely. "Stupid, really, when you think about it, isn't it? A conspiracy doesn't make the slightest bit of sense. There'd be too many people to swear to silence to pull this off. And there'd be no reason for the American government to do this to Australia rather than, you know, Iraq or wherever."

"Are you going to stop getting to the bottom of it now?" I asked hopefully.

"I guess we're as close to the bottom of it as we're ever going to get." She hugged herself. "Feeling a bit . . . lost, now. Come on, let's go get Crazy Bob."

I nodded, and took a step forward. My foot kicked something small and plasticky and it skittered across the tiles.

I looked down. There was a little white card on the floor, like a driver's license or a hotel room key.

"What's that?" asked Angela, not barking the question journalistically but only politely curious.

I sank to one knee and reached for it. "It's an ID card," I said. "It's got Y's photo. It must have fallen out of one of his pouches."

Y's picture had the usual fixed expression of mild shock, but his real name and most of the top half had been burnt off in the Knickknackery. What made my eyes boggle, though, was the name of the organization that had issued the card, written on the bottom-left corner in italicized block capitals:

HUMAN EXTINCTION PROTOCOL LIBRA

"H-E-P-L," I realized. "That was the name of the company X mistook us for when she first—"

I was interrupted by the loud *snap* of Angela reopening her viewfinder. A smile spread slowly across her face. "It's always the moment when you think the trail's gone cold, isn't it."

"If you say so."

"Let's go fetch Crazy Bob," she said, all energy returned. "We've taken the lid off the jam jar. Now all we need is a bagel."

"That's right," I said, jogging to keep up with her. "You used to work at Starbucks, didn't you."

DAY 6.1

"What's going on?!"

"We're just going for a little walk, Crazy Bob," said Angela with the warmth of a nursemaid.

"Don't talk to me like a child. Where's my tea?"

Crazy Bob was alive and conscious, whatever that was worth, but had apparently suffered some kind of hip injury and couldn't walk faster than a shuffle, so Angela and I each manned a shoulder and took some of his weight, braving the smell of armpit sweat and eucalyptus.

"Do you think this is right?" I asked Angela, behind Crazy Bob's head.

"What's that?"

"Exploiting a confused old man just to control the people who inexplicably worship him?"

She tossed her head back and forth pragmatically. "Isn't that basically how the monarchy works?"

Tim and the others were already back at the department store by the time we arrived. The shutters were open and the crowd was clearly of two minds as to whether to pack tightly around Tim or give Y as wide a berth as possible. The big soldier was trussed up so tightly with networking cables that he looked like he was wearing a big blue girdle. X was standing between him and the crowd, limbs uncertainly arranged in a defensive position.

The plastic people were making some unpleasant noises when we arrived, and Tim was trying to maintain order. "No, no, no, listen," he said, showing his palms to the crowd. "We're not doing anything to him."

"He killed like a million of our guys!" said a member of the mob.

"And that's why we're not going to kill him," insisted Tim.

"Oh, yes," said a pale Lord Awesomo, who was being propped up by Princess Ravenhair in front of a small legion of his loyalists. "Your logic is so clear to me now. Oh wait, no, it's the complete opposite of that."

"Look, if we kill him, then we sink to his level."

"And what level's that?" said Awesomo, as if the live debate had never been interrupted. "The level of *winning*?"

"I know he cost us a lot of good people," said Tim, retaliating by slipping right back into speech mode. "But we have a responsibility. We could well be all that remains of the human race. And if we let compassion and civility abandon us in these fragile early times, then it could be a very, very long time before humanity gets back on its feet."

"He's right," said Princess Ravenhair sadly. "Enough people have died already, Gerald."

As always, her feelings immediately shifted the mood of the entire populace. Lord Awesomo looked around at the shame-filled faces of the former lynch mob. "Oh, come on," he appealed. "I'm not asking to have him hung, drawn, and quartered! It's only one little kill and he got to do loads before he came over all pious. It's hardly fair!" He wasn't gaining any ground, so he went for the trump card. "Plus, he killed Crazy Bob!"

"No, he didn't!" said Angela grandly, as she pulled Crazy Bob and me out of the shadows and into the circle. She beamed at the gasp of wonder that subsequently went up.

"Defilers!" cried Lord Awesomo desperately over the appreciative murmur. "They sully Crazy Bob's holy body with their filthy hands!"

"Are you the silly prat who's been making all the noise?" said Crazy Bob. Lord Awesomo's fearsome image was taking quite a beating tonight. "I've a good mind to call the police."

"Travis," said Princess Ravenhair, noticing me on Crazy Bob's other armpit. "Did you save Crazy Bob?"

"Um." I sought an honest answer. "A bit."

"I'm not happy with the service at all," said Crazy Bob, unheard under the appreciative murmurs of the crowd who had apparently already decided what story they wanted to believe.

"Yes, Travis and Angela are my right-hand men," said Tim, seizing the opportunity to gain even more points, putting a hand on my shoulder. "They fully endorse my candidacy. And we'll be holding the elections tomorrow as scheduled." Lord Awesomo, defeated, seemed to slump as far as he could without actually falling to the floor. "My associates and I will guard the prisoner until we can get a cell ready."

"Well," said Don, who had been lingering around the outside of the circle in an I'm-not-involved kind of way. "If we're all quite finished with the returning hero thing, maybe I can finally go and get some damn sleep."

It wasn't quite the moment when everything fell apart, but it was the moment the first crack showed. Crazy Bob's cardboard face turned to scrutinize Don, and his gnarled arm unfolded to point accusingly. "You! It was you!" squawked Crazy Bob, furious.

Don froze, pinned to the spot by the bony finger. "What?"

"You're the one who knocked me down and dinged me hip the other night!" he rubbed the side of his pelvis to illustrate. "I'm an old man!"

"That was you?!" said Tim, as the plastic people turned to Don with suspicion.

"No, it was not me!" said Don, with desperate but apparently convincing contempt. "Look at him. He's senile. He couldn't tell his own goldfish from the Bee Gees."

"And you were there, too!" Crazy Bob turned to me. I was still holding his arm, so I received a lungful of breath that smelled like cheese and onion crisps. "You, the silly boy with the Goliath birdeater."

And that was the moment when it all went to hell. It was as if someone had sat on the keyboard of a church organ, sending out an ominous chord that silenced the room.

"What did you say?" said Princess Ravenhair, her tone of voice perfectly level.

"Nothing," I said quickly, putting my hand over his cardboard mouth. "Just an old-man burp."

"*Goliath birdeater?!*" continued the princess.

"Yes, that bloody horrible great spider," continued Crazy Bob, not muffled enough. "And it said some very rude things to me as you ran past, too."

"Travis, look at me," said the princess sternly. My heart almost pounded right out of my chest as I did so. "Is it true?"

The sweat flooded into the furrows of my brow, creating little flesh aqueducts. They were all the answer she needed. It was a terrible sight to behold, all the good cheer being washed from her face by a dark cloud of betrayal. A pile of apologies and assurances welled into my throat but tripped on the way to my mouth, leaving me stammering. Princess Ravenhair dropped her gaze, then turned slowly away and disappeared into the crowd.

Someone else came the other way, shoving their way to the front. A female plastic person in an opaque head bag. She grabbed Lord Awesomo by the bandaged shoulder, making him wince hugely, and pointed to Don and me.

"That's them," she said, fearfully. "I remember. Those are the two guys I saw outside. The ones who knew the killer."

"Well," said Lord Awesomo, clasping his hands and injecting several pints of delighted menace into a single syllable. "Suddenly this is all starting to fall into place, isn't it. Everything's fine, then you people turn up. Then something starts killing us, and all of a sudden one of you is using the deaths as leverage to take over the mall."

Having eagerly surrounded himself with a crowd of adoring followers Tim was quickly realizing what a terrible position that became if that crowd somehow transmuted into a hostile mob. "Hey," he protested. "You've got nothing to tie *me* to the killings."

"Hm," said Lord Awesomo with mock consideration. "No, I guess we don't. After all, quite a lot of people joined the settlement that day, didn't they. Of course, not all of them just declared themselves BFFs with someone who collaborated with a murderer and fed Princess Ravenhair's favorite pet to a giant spider."

I covered my face with my hands as the increasingly moblike crowd drew closer. Tim didn't say anything.

"So," wheedled Lord Awesomo, taking a step forward. "I suppose the question is this. Do you stand by your right-hand man?"

Tim looked at me, and I looked at him back. I could see in his eyes that it would take more than a few weeks of laundry duty to make up for putting him in this position. We both understood that confirming any connection between us would obliterate his election hopes like a biscuit under a heel stomp. But we'd known each other since primary school, and all those years of mutual reliance was a lot to throw away for the sake of a shopping mall full of nutters in polythene.

"I have known Travis," said Tim, "for a long time."

I realized what he was doing as soon as the words tripped slowly out of his mouth in single file. He was going to try and have his cake and eat it.

"If he has committed a crime, then I know he must have had a good reason to do it. And what I said about the human race still stands. If we are to survive, we cannot allow our emotions to cause us to self-destruct. We'll investigate Travis, and Don, and all the others, we'll find out why they did what they did, and we'll try to understand."

An exchange of divided looks and murmurs swept throughout the collective. For a moment, I thought he might have actually done it.

"And besides," he added. "You can't possibly equate the life of a human being with someone's bird."

Even though he'd come damn close to becoming their leader, it was obvious to me that Tim had never truly understood the ways of the plastic people. He was genuinely surprised at the gasps of horror and distaste, and the fragile bone-china teacup someone threw at his head.

"Hey, just putting this out there," said Lord Awesomo. "Let's throw them all down the Pit."

The Pit turned out to be a stairwell in the middle of an open area of the food court which led down to the very lowest level of the mall. I remembered when we first came to the Briar Center via the lowest entrance in the southwest, access to the majority of level B—which contained one large budget store and a few food retailers too gauche even for the main food court—had been closed off with shutters. We'd gone straight up the escalator to the level above. The few times I'd asked about level B, the plastic people had come over fearful and quiet or answered with more irony than usual.

We'd barely been given time to meditate on our upcoming sentence before Lord Awesomo had ordered us marched to the Pit's entrance, lashing our hands together behind our backs with some of the seemingly limitless duct tape the plastic people had lying around. Except me—my hands were taped together in front of me so that I could hold Mary's box. She was very nearly claimed by the jam as a guard shoved me roughly down the escalator into the jam-filled food court.

Tim followed after me. Lord Awesomo had made the extremely wise move of taping his mouth shut, but the baleful despair in his eyes when I looked back at him said it all. Don was next in our little chain gang, grumbling through tight, bitter lips.

Y was fourth, still swathed in network cable, trooping without complaint down the escalator before the procession was halted by X, who was fifth.

"He's not wearing plastic bags!" she cried. Indeed, after catching fire earlier, he wasn't wearing very much at all. And it seemed odd that he hadn't been the one to mention it. "You can't make him go into the jam!"

A few members of our plastic escort argued her point, but Lord Awesomo, already waiting in the food court, spoke over them. "Take him back to the store," he announced. "I'm going to take my time and think of a more interesting fate."

Y was led back up the mall, head hanging. "It's not his fault!" said X. "He was obeying orders!"

"Christ, she's like a broken record sometimes," said Angela bitterly, who was bringing up the rear of our procession.

"Ah yes, orders, I remember that excuse going down swimmingly at Nuremberg," said Lord Awesomo. "And these were the orders which you gave him, I understand?"

"It was the Hibatsu settlement!" said X indignantly.

"And they'll be next, I think," he said, wallowing in his newly restored status. Tim tried to say something urgently through his taped mouth before the nearest guard silenced him with the butt of the confiscated pepper-spray toy gun.

Our party of five moved through the jam in single file towards the ringed black hole that marked the stairwell, a sight that had once provoked slight amusement at its resemblance to a puckered arsehole, but now evoked an executioner's block. Behind our unhappy queue came most of the mall's population, following down the escalator in a seemingly endless multicolored train. As we stopped near the edge of the hole the crowd spread out into a circle, cutting off all possible exits.

"Fellow followers of the true way of Crazy Bob," said Lord Awesomo grandly, holding his arms at right angles to his body. "Today is a day for celebration, as we rid ourselves of the unsavory element that has plagued us for almost three days. Praise be to Crazy Bob."

"Hail Crazy Bob," went the crowd ironically, all rebellion forgotten. I cast my head back to see that there were two silhouettes at Crazy Bob's usual position. One in the cardboard mask and crown, and a shorter, female one in an aluminum-foil cape.

"Even in that short time these consummate villains have committed the following grievous offenses. One, a great number of completely deliberate murders. Two, conspiracy to commit completely deliberate murders."

"Why . . ." whispered X to herself. Or, again, she might have been saying Y's name. Perhaps we should have kept their code names the other way around after all.

"Three, spreading lies in an attempt to incite poor, innocent, misled citizens to revolt, including our beloved princess."

Tim moaned into his tape, wrestling with his bonds halfheartedly for a moment.

"Four, most blasphemous assault upon the divine person of Crazy Bob. Five, deliberate theft of sacred artifacts, to wit, one consecrated hard drive."

"Drinks coaster," growled Don to himself, like the first foreboding rumble before a catastrophic volcanic eruption.

"Six, fraternizing with criminals, harboring knowledge of their actions, and allowing them, through inaction, to occur unchecked."

"Okay, now that's reaching," protested Angela.

"And finally, perhaps their most heinous crime, consuming the actual body of His Tweetiness, Whiskers Ravenhair. And being an accessory to the consumption of said icon."

I looked up at Princess Ravenhair's shadow. "Don't do this," I said. She didn't move.

The end of a broom handle prodded me between the shoulder blades, forcing me to the edge of the puckered entrance to the jammy underworld. The rail around the stairwell had been removed, and the stairs bashed out, so only the hole remained. Jam ringed it like a stationary waterfall plunging into a fruit-scented blackness so complete it seemed to be sucking at my eyeballs. Mary pulled her legs tightly around herself as I held her over the drop.

"Does our first perpetrator have anything to say in his defense?" asked Lord Awesomo sincerely.

"W—"

"Too bad."

Something hard and wooden bashed the back of my legs, and I would have fallen to my knees, but my knees kept right on going. The mall blurred upwards to be replaced by a darkening red chimney. It was all I could do to keep my body arranged feet first, clutching Mary in both hands above my head.

The three feet of jam slowed my fall just enough to prevent both my ankles snapping like rice crackers, but my breathing hole came within inches of the jam's surface. I stood up as fast as I could, balancing Mary's box on my head as the first extended tendril of jam started to bat at my face like a curious cat.

At the bottom of the Pit was the smaller, secondary eating hall, the small collection of restaurants that had sold the cheapest, greasiest food in the complex. All of them had their shutters down. There were no torches, but from the remnants of the light shining down from above, I could see the entrance to the cheapo store across the hall, its windows smashed in and its stock of useful supplies no doubt exhausted.

And then a sparkle of reflected light caught my eye, and my gaze slipped down. The surface of the jam was completely covered in small shards of glittering glass, far too much to just be from the shop windows. I could also see scattered collections of knives and even a coil of razor wire. And as I let the focus of my gaze track closer to me, I could see a great number of torn plastic bags in the ring of the light.

I heard an angry yell from above and Don thudded into the jam. The word "ARSEHOLES" burst from his lungs as he landed, apparently as some kind of reflex action. "Oh god. I'm still alive."

"Hey," I said.

"Ugh." He straightened up. "So are you."

"I thought Tim was next?"

"Oh, I think Awesomo wants to get up in his grill for a while. Do I even want to know what's going on down here? Oh. Ohhh. That's a lot of sharp objects."

"I think the idea is they'll rip holes in our plastic bags if we try to move through them," I said.

"Well, Travis, it's nice to see the trauma of death row hasn't done anything to your razor-sharp reasoning skills."

X and Angela came next in a two-for-one pairing, Angela endeavoring to distance herself from X as soon as they landed.

"Yikes," she said, noticing the scattered array of cutting implements. Before anyone could stop her she moved to the edge of the safe area, picked up one of the razors in her bound hands, and started working away at the tape around her wrists.

"What are they going to do to Y?!" demanded X, staring up the Pit.

"You know what," snarked Don. "If I were the kind of person to worry about other people, I definitely wouldn't waste it on that steroid farm. He can take care of himself. Keeping ourselves alive is the hot-button topic for me."

Finally, Tim landed in the jam, almost on top of X. It seemed like it took longer than necessary for him to rise from his landing crouch, and when he did so it was with slow deliberation. He chewed tensely on his lip, surveying the thousands of glinting edges that surrounded us, then finally rested his gaze on me.

"Travis," he said. "None of this was your fault." The intensity in his eyes and the fact that he had even brought it up implied the exact opposite.

"Oh, don't start moaning," moaned Don. "Hibatsu's a much better-run settlement. This one was going out of its way to kill itself. Y was just speeding up the course of nature."

"There we go," said Angela, having freed her hands from the tape. She cut mine free next while I held the handle on the top of Mary's box between my teeth, then produced her camcorder from some custom pocket in her plastic lining and addressed it. "So, how will the party get out of this one? Could it be possible to get through the death jam if we just move really slowly and carefully?"

"Yeah, I bet all the owners of these thought something similar," said Don unhelpfully, lifting one of the emptied plastic bags with one finger. "Oh, look. That one made it almost six feet."

Tim moved his way to the front of our little huddle. He dug around inside his plastic vest and produced a small pocket flashlight, which he shone around the darkened eating hall. "There's the way to the underground bus terminal," he said, referring to a particularly deep section of the blackness over to the right. "Looks like the jam's clear there. They probably didn't think they needed to fill the whole floor with sharp things. We just need to get over about fifteen feet of death jam."

"Oh, well, as easy as that, is it?" said Don. "Anyone know the world long-jump record in a peat bog?"

Tim reached into his vest again and lifted out a coil of the same blue network cable we'd used to secure Y. Experimentally, he flung one end of the cable into the room. Fully extended, the far end reached about a foot past the death jam.

"If we had some way to secure the far end to something high up over there, like with a grappling hook," he thought aloud, "we could shimmy along the cable to safety without having to touch the jam."

"Where are you getting all this stuff from?" asked Angela.

"I thought it might come in handy. Haven't got anything like a grappling hook, though."

"Well, so much for that, then," said Don. "How about we eat Travis before we think about it some more?"

"What if," began Angela, with an enthusiasm that earned her everyone's undivided attention, "we swam under the jam?"

There was a silence as the rest of us digested this, which was broken when Don began slow clapping.

"No, seriously," said Angela. "All the sharp things are floating on the surface 'cos the jam won't eat them, but everything underneath that's safe."

"No it's not; it's jam," I said. "It'll suck our bodies out through our breathing holes."

"Not if we sealed them up," said Tim, one finger to his lips and supporting his elbow with the other hand. Terror struck me as I realized he was actually going to endorse this plan of action.

"Oh, even better," said Don. "So we'll have just enough time to enjoy the sensation of not being dissolved before we suffocate."

Tim hid his stress well, but I'd learned to recognize signs that he was getting tense. For example, rising to Don. "You know what, Don, you criticize everyone else's plans. Why don't you ever put forward any of your own? Since you're so much smarter than everyone else."

"Okay, here's my plan," said Don without hesitation. "We continue this conversation after a nice dinner of Travis. Garnished with spider legs."

"You wouldn't be able to breathe under there anyway," said Angela. She had produced her camera from inside her plastic wear and was taking in the death jam. "Get down, swim, come up, pull the bag off, needn't take more than thirty seconds at most."

"And only one of us needs to do it," said Tim. "They just have to tie the cable up so the rest can get across."

"I nominate Travis," said Don immediately.

"What?!" I interjected, as Tim nodded reasonably in agreement. "I can't . . ."

"Travis," said Tim, looking me square in the eye. "I don't want you to feel like you're obligated to do this to make up for anything."

His words were so much noise. The real meaning was in that look. Tim had once gotten depressed and eaten all of Frank's drinking chocolate, and when Frank had confronted us, Tim made up a story about extremely selective rats while shooting me a desperate look urging me to back up everything he said. This was that same look, times fifty.

"This'll do," said Angela, dredging a largely unbroken transparent bag from the cluster of abandoned outfits on the jam's surface. She pulled it over my head like a mixture of a hangman and a fussy mother on her child's first day at school. "This tape's still sticky, too. Take a deep breath."

"Wait!" I said as she came at me with the duct tape noose. "Could someone . . . hold onto Mary?"

Angela took the box as Tim repositioned himself carefully to keep at least one person between him and the spider. I checked my joins and filled my lungs, and then felt a friendly but firm hand seal a few layers of tape over my breathing hole, angle me towards the clear patch of jam, and push me down onto my knees.

Blood was rushing to my head as if trying to get away from the jam. The plastic flattened itself against my mouth again and again as fear took hold. I must have hesitated a little too long, because either Tim's hand or Don's foot hit me hard between the shoulder blades and I fell forward onto my stomach.

The jam usually repelled whatever it couldn't eat, but it had enough of a scent of my meat through the thin plastic to embrace me warmly. It was like swimming through an ocean of carnivorous worms, all fighting each other to get at me. The bag over my face wasn't quite taut, and I could feel jam trying to push its way into my eyes, ears, and nose. A horribly tonguelike extrusion was trying to wedge itself into my mouth like a nervous teenage makeout.

I half crawled, half swam my way along the tiled floor. With each movement my brain tried to convince me that I must have gone far enough by now and it was time to surface for some yummy oxygen, but I could still see light reflecting dimly off the broken glass above my head. Still, there was less and less the further I moved from the circle, and soon there was nothing but pitch darkness, omnipresent all-over massage, and no air.

My heart was beating so fast I must have been using about three idiots' worth of oxygen. It felt like I'd been under for at least an hour by the time I couldn't see anything glittering sharply overhead anymore. I pulled myself a few final inches, gathered my feet beneath me, and stood.

I was almost upright when I felt something snag my plastic, and it was too late to stop. There was a tearing sound like the universe ripping open. I looked down to see a line of plastic just above my navel drooping down towards a piece of barbed wire.

I unsnagged it just as the hole was falling open and slapped it against my stomach. I stood like Napoleon at attention for a second, waiting for my entire body to be yanked through a millimeter-wide slit. But the jam wasn't eating me. I'd risen a little earlier than I should have done, but I was safe.

Then my lungs seemed to twist painfully in my chest and I tried to inhale, only to feel plastic flattening against my open mouth. Hurriedly I shoved two fingers into my mouth to break the seal, and succeeded, but pushed a little too far and gagged. Bent double, I felt the hole by my navel falling open again, so I clasped it shut with both hands just in time for the second wave of puke.

"Was that Travis?" wondered Angela, from the illuminated huddle across the way. It must have been too dark to see me from there.

"Either that or the jam," said Don. "Maybe Travis is where it draws the line."

"Tie it up, Travis, if you can hear me," said Tim, throwing the cable out again.

I watched the cable's end plop onto the surface of the jam next to me. A thought occurred to me. They couldn't see me. They weren't sure I'd surfaced at all. And there was no reason I had to correct them. My stomach hurt, my face was covered in a film of tears, snot, and fresh vomit, and I was feeling more wretched than I'd ever felt in my life, which I'd incidentally just risked for someone else's stupid plan. And all my so-called friends could do was make snarky insults and order me around. I didn't need this. I could just leave them to it. Turn around and go. Make my own way through the underground bus way and start a new life.

Alone.

"Travis?" said Tim, with growing concern.

I picked up the end of the cable and began securing it to the top of a nearby speak-your-weight machine. "Yeah, yeah, give me a sec."

DAY 6.2

And so, two slackers, a game designer, a would-be journalist, a troubled American agent, and a giant spider made their way through the darkened underground tunnels away from the Briar Center. The bus way would eventually lead directly to the plaza by the Hibatsu building, near the bridge. The karmic wheel had, perhaps, decided to give us time to get our breath back.

After the others had crossed the death jam, we had continued in silence for some time, following Tim and his flashlight, trusting that he knew what turnings to take. Angela had stopped filming, and I had managed to seal the rip in my vest with some of the tape scavenged from the victims of the death jam. Mary was settled warily in the bottom of her box, probably thinking about what she had done.

Don clapped his hands brightly. "Boy, we really buggered things up back there, didn't we!"

Tim gave him an icy look. "*We* didn't."

"Oh, sure. You were stirring up the good kind of unrest."

"I wanted to help them!" said Tim unhappily.

"You can only help people who want to be helped," said Angela. "I heard that on a movie trailer once."

"If I could just have gotten them out of their horrible self-destructive mindset . . ."

"Well, it's a phase kids have to go through, isn't it?" I said.

Tim glared at me. "Why did you have to feed Whiskers to your damn spider?"

"I'm sorry," I said for what felt like the hundredth time that morning. "Mary's sorry, too."

Tim swatted the air and jumped away as I held out Mary's box for him to see. "Keep that thing away from me! It is not sorry!"

"Of course she's sorry. Look, she's cringing."

"She's poising to strike! Travis, listen to me. You need to stop projecting emotions onto the thing, before it bites someone's face off."

"It was your idea to bring her," I muttered sulkily.

"Travis," said Angela tenderly. "I do think the thing you have with that spider is very cute, but you are obviously projecting onto it."

"No, I'm not!"

"That's your case?" said Don. "Okay, here's my counter-argument: 'Yes, you are.' "

Tim had had enough. He stopped with a frustrated grimace and shined his flashlight at Don. "Why are you in such a good mood?!"

Don considered this, apparently uncertain of the answer himself. "I dunno. I guess 'cos we're not going to have to hang around so many people I hate anymore; that always cheers me up. And we've got a pretty decent excuse to go back to Hibatsu, where my build is."

"But we're going back to the mall," said X suddenly. She had been hanging at the rear. "We're going back to save Y."

Tim and Don both fell conspicuously silent to concentrate on wading, so it was left to Angela to respond. "Look, if the entire mall wasn't a match for him before, they won't be any more of one now their numbers have been reduced. I bet he's already waiting for us at Hibatsu. He'll probably have murdered everyone there by the time we arrive."

"I already explained why—"

"Yes, you say you've explained why he was murdering so much," continued Angela smoothly. "But somehow I don't think he's going to stop just because no one's telling him to anymore. Especially if the plastic people try to execute him."

"The rules are different now," argued X weakly.

We turned a corner and the road ahead was broadly lit with glorious summer daylight. The jam-covered bus way was a sparkling red ramp back into the surface city. As we trooped out of the underground we were hit by the kind of sweltering humidity I'd come to associate with an incoming subtropical storm, and sure enough, the next thing I saw was a huge cloud hugging the horizon like a black bedspread gathered at the bottom of a mattress after a restless night.

We were very close to the river again, on North Quay, which ran alongside Hibatsu and the plaza. The building itself was on our right, still thrusting powerfully upwards with the curious ring of risen jam around its base like a red skirt. We started wading towards it.

"It's even bigger than I remember," said Angela. She and Tim were the only ones who hadn't been inside the building before, I recalled (and probably X, although I definitely wasn't about to make assumptions there).

"What are they staring at?" said Don, looking ahead.

We were close enough to Hibatsu now to see the silhouettes in the windows again, watching the outside intently. Their posture seemed wary and defensive, but none of them was paying attention to us. I followed the average angle of gaze and found myself facing back towards the mall.

Specifically, one of the shops on the pedestrian precinct, just on the east corner of the plaza. I could just about see a multicolored cluster of indistinct objects on the roof like sprinkles on top of a cupcake. It was the entire population of plastic people. The frontmost group was carrying still-bound Y shoulder high.

"Where's she going?" asked Don.

X was pushing her way through the jam towards the multi-colored crowd, shoulders set like a mother hurrying towards a small child she's caught exploring its nasal passages with a kebab skewer.

"Crap," said Angela, hurrying after her.

"Just let her go," suggested Tim.

"No fear!" called Angela over her shoulder. She already had her camera out again.

"Yeah," sighed Don, following her. "Guess we shouldn't count on finding another American before the chopper arrives."

I opted to follow him. "Fine," said Tim. "I'll meet you in Hibatsu."

"Er, you probably won't," I called back. "Since me and Don and X are the only ones they'll let in."

Tim looked between Hibatsu and the plastic people a few times, weighing his options, before wading after us with a grumbling sigh.

As we neared the building the plastic people had chosen as their stage I could make out some finer details. Lord Awesomo was standing closest to the plaza with one foot on a vent. Nearby, Princess Ravenhair watched emotionlessly, with Crazy Bob on her arm.

The crowd dropped Y roughly on his knees. Lord Awesomo gave him only a passing glance. X had almost waded all the way across the plaza, but Awesomo showed no signs of having noticed her as he raised a megaphone.

"Greetings, residents of Hibatsu and consumers of dick," Lord Awesomo began. His amplified words rattled the still air of the deserted city. "We, the residents of the Briar Center and devoted followers of the true Lord, Crazy Bob, express our enormous thanks to you for sending an assassin to bring our settlement down from within." He paused to let them digest his words. "These are extremely *ironic* thanks. You think you're so great, don't you, sitting around in your tall building with your offices and your . . . windows. Well." Another pause. "You're not."

"No, no, no, the stupid bastard!" said Tim. He caught my questioning look. "He's declaring war."

A roll of thunder coughed its way across the plaza, a none-too-subtle reminder of the approaching storm. The Hibatsu building looked particularly sinister with the black cloud hanging about its shoulders.

"With the full backing of my people, I will now make my official rebuttal to your attempt to kill us all." He produced a knife from his pocket, its blade catching the darkening light. "I am going to rebut your agent right in the neck."

"No!" cried X.

She was close enough to be heard. I saw Lord Awesomo's gaze track to X, and then along the jam trail behind her to the rest of us trying to catch up.

"Idolaters!" he roared. "The heretics yet live! Ready projectiles!"

Plastic warriors took up position on either side of him. Most of them had apparently raided the armory of makeshift weapons and were wielding plastic crossbows and foam-pellet guns probably modified to fire flaming arrows or angry cats or something. But the soldier directly in front of Lord Awesomo was carrying, and god knows where he found it, a huge hunting rifle painted with unfriendly gray camo.

He glanced at Awesomo for a nod of confirmation, then began to draw a bead on the petrified X, and suddenly it was as if someone had pulled the cord on the little bathroom light in Y's head. He threw himself forward into an impromptu break dance, sweeping the legs out from under the three plastic people standing closest and using the momentum to flip himself onto his feet in a complex blur of gymnastics.

The sniper turned at the sound of his allies scattering to the floor like bowling pins and took a ringing heel kick to the chin. The end of his rifle flew upwards and a shot cracked harmlessly into the sky.

"Seize him!" ordered Lord Awesomo, before his own legs were swept out from under him.

Some of the plastic people must have seen those fight scenes in martial arts movies where the crowd of bad guys all attack in single file, but none of them had heeded the lesson they should have learned from them. One by one, they managed to summon sufficient courage to run forward swinging punches or big pieces of wood, only for Y to send them reeling back clutching their sensitive areas. It was particularly impressive considering that both his arms were still secured to his trunk.

Someone jumped onto his back, wrapping their arms around his throat. Y did a lumbering forward somersault, landing on his attacker with an eye-watering crunch. Lord Awesomo seized the opportunity to grab the rifle from its unconscious owner and aim the sight squarely at Y's forehead, scrambling back to keep out of the reach of his powerful legs.

"Jesus Christ!" panted Lord Awesomo. "I don't know what you run on, you mad bastard, but don't you ever run out of it?!" He cocked the gun.

I heard a sound behind me, distant but quite recognizable as straining rope and clonking wood. I turned around to see something large and mechanical being operated on the roof of the Hibatsu building.

I was one step behind everything that morning, because the next thing I heard was a catastrophic crash behind me. I turned again and saw a mangled filing cabinet slowly peel away from the massive dent it had just made in the wall of the plastic people's building.

Lord Awesomo stared up at Hibatsu, nonplussed. On the roof, the distant silhouettes of people were pulling back the arm of something large, mechanical, and catapult-like.

"They've got a catapult," I said.

"Actually, I think that's a trebuchet," said Don.

"The first shot is fired!" announced Lord Awesomo. He held his rifle above his head. "The battle will be ours! Charge, men! And women!"

Thunder rolled, and the long-promised storm began, skipping straight past the initial spitting to relentless sheets of rain. A couple of the braver plastic people readied their improvised weaponry and leapt straight off the roof, bouncing off awnings or counting on the jam to break their fall, while the majority filed disorganizedly through the roof access door, emerging shortly afterwards from the shattered ground-floor windows of the shop.

A photocopier with a missing lid descended from on high and landed squarely in the jam with a heavy thump. It bounced and rolled forward a few yards, knocking a handful of would-be besiegers aside like Skittles, but did nothing to slow the assault at large.

"Stop this!" cried Tim, his voice drowned out by the rain as plastic people charged by either side of him. I grabbed him under the armpits and dragged him behind the piece of statuary Don, Angela, and I had ducked behind when the fighting started.

"There's got to be something we can do!" he said. "This is insanity!"

"You only just noticed?" said Don. "Interesting question, isn't it. Who's more insane, the demonstrably mad people, or the guy who tries to reason with them?"

"But they're all going to be killed!" wailed Tim. "They haven't got a hope against Hibatsu!"

"How do you know that?" asked Angela, seeking the best angle to capture the slaughter from our hiding spot.

"Hibatsu have the higher ground, better weaponry, and an armored, defensible position," said Tim impatiently.

"Ooh, someone plays strategy games," said Don.

"And the plastic people are all standing around in man-eating jam," said Tim. His fingertips rattled against the metal of our cover in an anxious rhythm. "One slit in the plastic and they're done for."

It soon became clear that the busy workers of Hibatsu were already well aware of this. When the first few courageous fighters of the plastic army had slogged far enough across the plaza to start losing their blood rage and wondering if this was still the great idea it had seemed like five minutes ago, the windows on Hibatsu's fifth floor flew open with a grind of sliding plexiglass. A little heat haze belched out of the building, and tattooed, bare-chested office workers appeared, clutching improvised weaponry. The burlier characters had bows and crossbows made from ties and shards of desk, while others wielded handheld catapults twisted out of wire coat hangers and primed with elastic bands.

The plastic people weren't just outnumbered; they were the Celtic barbarians to Hibatsu's Roman legion, with no organization or tactics. Someone yelled a command from inside Hibatsu and every wielder of a long-range weapon fired simultaneously. A merciless cloud of box-cutter blades, glass shards, and sharpened DVDs rained down upon the front of the charge, scything through plastic and lodging upsettingly in flesh with soft thuds, although that soon became the least of the victims' worries when the jam did its part.

"A-yup," said Don. "Definitely not putting money on this one."

"We have to stop this," said Tim, as those waves of plastic people closest to the front line abandoned their charge and started fighting each other for what little cover there was.

"There's nothing we can do," said Angela.

"Where's the leadership?!" said Tim, peering at the roof where Lord Awesomo had been. I couldn't see anyone there anymore, partly because of the rain. It continued to fall hard and fast. The water sank straight down to the bottom of the jam, and I could feel it sloshing around my ankles.

"X!" yelled Don. With everyone distracted with the massacre in the plaza, the American agent was making a beeline for the shop entrance, too far away now to listen to reason through the storm.

Tim grabbed Don and held him back. "Travis, go after her. Find out if Y has left anything of the plastic people government. You have to convince them to sound the retreat."

"Me?" I said.

He conceded my point. "Angela, you go too. Don, you're going to get me into Hibatsu. I can talk to the leaders there."

Don shook him off. "Who are you now, plastic Jesus? Don't think you can order me around."

"Don," said Tim agreeably. "Do as I say, or I'm going to throttle you."

To my surprise, Don dropped his gaze and meekly followed Tim. For all his talk, Don still had the build of a video game developer, and while Tim wasn't exactly Herculean, he definitely had the edge from all the occasions he'd had to carry his own amps to gigs.

I went after X, Mary's box still swinging at my side, Mary herself trying to shrink unhappily from the rain that bled through the breathing holes. Angela was right behind me, trying to shield her camcorder.

X was already at the shop front, disappearing into the darkened interior. There were no more waves of plastic people to get in her way; they had all been wasted on that single, futile charge.

I kept moving towards X, but my bin liner costume had begun to hamper my progress, trailing oddly, gathering around my feet, and tripping me up. I looked at my hands, and saw the duct tape coming away from around my wrists. The moisture was reducing the stickiness, loosening the seals that kept the jam at bay. Another strike against the plastic army.

I tore away a trailing bag and picked up my pace. X had already gone up the stairs to the roof by the time we entered the store. We picked our way around the ruined shelving to the door at the back, which was still hanging ajar.

I hesitated at the stairs. Angela took the lead and was halfway up the flight before I spoke. "Wait," I said. "Do we have a plan?"

She turned. "I don't know. Do we need one?"

"Uh. You mean before we burst out onto a roof full of people who keep trying to kill us?"

"Hm." She looked up. "I'll just open it a crack, and then I'll tell you what I see, and we'll figure it out from there." She pushed the roof access door open gently, inviting a trickle of rain onto the stairs, and tried to poke her entire camera through the narrow gap for a second before giving up and putting her eye to it.

"Huh," she reported.

"What is it?"

"Well, everyone seems pretty distracted out there. Y's still alive. He's very, very alive."

"What do you mean?"

"Whoops! Look out."

She hopped back and flattened herself to the wall just as the roof door flew inwards and a plastic person, still clutching one of Jamie's modified pellet guns, tumbled backwards down the stairs. I stepped aside and he came to rest with his head halfway into the jam. He convulsed madly for a second as his breathing hole was invaded, then another man-shaped cluster of plastic bags flopped emptily onto the surface of the insatiable red glop.

I hurried up the stairs after Angela and was drenched by a fresh coating of warm summer rain. We'd managed to enter the fray completely unnoticed, partly because of the weather, partly because everyone was quite busy already. The first person we saw was X, standing a few feet from the door with her hands over her mouth. Princess Ravenhair was doing the same thing slightly further away. Crazy Bob was trying to hold his cardboard mask together in the driving rain.

Everyone was watching Y. He was engaged in battle with Lord Awesomo and Awesomo's two burliest goons, the ones with the gray bag covering. Awesomo himself was on Y's back, trying to gain a strong enough hold to choke him. Y was busy kneeling on one of the goons and head butting him in the face, while the other goon was hitting Y repeatedly about the torso with a baseball bat similar to the one I'd used on him earlier.

Y was obviously more than a physical match for Lord Awesomo or either of his goons, and probably would have been for about ten more on a level playing field. But Y was still only human—a human who hadn't eaten or slept in some time and quite literally had both hands tied behind his back, and the baseball bat was starting to take its toll. Y's attempts to shake Lord Awesomo off from around his neck had died down to feeble half twists, and the head butts he was pounding into the prone goon's face were barely making a dent.

The conclusion was foregone. Y put all his remaining effort into one last head butt, little more than a token tap of his forehead against the goon's chin, before slumping onto his victim in an awkward horizontal cuddle.

"Aw," said Lord Awesomo, panting through several broken teeth. "Sure you don't want to go a bit longer? I think I've still got a couple of unbruised bits." He rolled off Y and lay on his back in the rain, catching his breath.

"Y!" cried X. The big soldier didn't move. The goon beneath him patted him on the back rapidly in what was either a reassuring gesture or an urgent request for oxygen.

On hearing X's voice, Lord Awesomo sat up. He scowled at her, then moved on to Angela and me. "You're not supposed to be alive!"

"Tim says you need to call the retreat," I said.

"Oh, well, if Tim said that," he said ironically, crawling to his megaphone and holding it weakly to his mouth. "Come back, everyone! Mr. Important's back from the dead and ready to save us from our poor, helpless selves!"

"You haven't turned it on," I said, pointing to the switch.

"OH REALLY. THANK YOU FOR LETTING ME KNOW. IT'S NOT LIKE I WAS BEING TOTALLY IRONIC OR ANYTHING."

Lord Awesomo was reaching some kind of singularity, operating on so many levels of irony that he was impossible to reach. I tried anyway. "All your people are getting slaughtered," I appealed to Princess Ravenhair. "Princess. You can't let this happen." She sneered wordlessly at me, then looked away.

"Urgh. I can't believe what world-class intellects you people are," groaned Lord Awesomo, raising himself shakily to his feet. "The plastic people will lay down their lives in the service of Crazy Bob. Even if every single one dies, they will live on in the paradise He has built for us, where honey flows from the armpits of cherubs."

"You're insane," said Angela matter-of-factly.

Awesomo snorted. A little jet of blood and chunky bits sprayed from his left nostril. "You've never understood! No one like you could ever have led the plastic people! We're not doing any of this seriously! We're *ironically* waging a holy war! Don't you get that?!"

"But they're actually dying!" I said. Behind him, the jam of the plaza was becoming a colorful soup of discarded plastic outfits dancing madly in the powerful rain.

"They're *ironically* dying!" corrected Lord Awesomo at full screech. "And I'm so *ironically* sick of you!" He marched stiffly to the edge of the roof, where his hunting rifle was waiting. Halfway there, he tripped on his own plastic bags and stumbled. The rain was getting into his duct tape, too. His ankle bags had loosened around his feet like untied shoelaces. "Fan-buggering-tastic!" He thrust out his arms to stop himself falling flat on his face, and smoothly gathered up the rifle in the same motion. He endeavored to point the barrel at all three of us simultaneously, and we threw our hands up in the air.

"Don't do it!" said X.

"No!" called Angela suddenly. "Do it! 'Cos, like, we really want to get shot and everything. That'd just be peachy keen."

Lord Awesomo paused in the act of negotiating his loosened hand coverings around the trigger guard. He almost seemed impressed, but only for a moment. "Too little, too late," he growled, raising the sight to his eye and taking aim at X.

Later, I wondered if things would have happened differently if he'd chosen someone else for his first kill. Because all of a sudden he wasn't aiming at X, but at the chest of a newly risen Y, who had leapt to his feet with surprising speed.

Awesomo pulled the trigger. The single shot cut through the noise of the storm like an exclamation mark. Y's body shook, and Awesomo grunted with pain as the recoil slammed his wounded shoulder.

"NO!" yelled X.

Y's eyes closed for a moment as he absorbed the pain, then opened. It was his only change of facial expression. His mouth and nose were firmly set, not quivering. I saw blood appear among the knotted network cables that wrapped his torso and drip onto his austere military underpants.

At first, I thought he was falling forward, dead, but he put one foot forward and it became a lurch. He stalked towards Lord Awesomo with the inexorability of a giant boulder slowly rolling off the top of a hill.

Awesomo backed away, fumbling with the gun's mechanism. He fired again into Y's chest, barking animalistically as he took the recoil. I heard X make a little gasping squeal through her hands, but Y didn't even stop. He kept walking, getting faster with each step, as more of his own blood mingled with the rain. The latest shot had done serious damage to one of the important knots holding the network cables in place, and Y was able to free his arms. He brought his giant hands around and outstretched them like the kind of zombie this apocalypse was sorely lacking.

Perhaps the same thought had occurred to Lord Awesomo, because his next move was to aim for Y's head. Y was still a few feet away, but he was fast transitioning from a traditional zombie lurch to the modern fast zombie sprint. The pain was clearly getting to Awesomo, and his hand coverings were becoming looser and harder to work with, but he finally readied the rifle for another shot. He aimed the wobbling barrel and fired, screaming at length as he did so as if the extra air behind it could accelerate the bullet.

Something that belonged on the side of Y's head flew off in a spray of blood and bits of cartilage. Y ignored it. He pushed Awesomo's rifle barrel away with one hand while seizing him by the throat and lifting him off his feet with the other.

Even then, Y didn't slow down. He plucked the rifle out of Awesomo's grip, like a stern father confiscating an annoying water pistol, and cast it off the roof. Then he began tearing away loosened plastic wrappings and tape, which trailed in his wake like streamers off a wedding car, until Lord Awesomo's skinny, pale limbs and pretentious black T-shirt were exposed.

The rest of us could only watch, stunned. The gray-clad goon with the baseball bat seemed about to take another whack at Y, but he took one look at the big soldier's frozen face and lost his bottle.

Y finally slowed and stopped when he reached the very edge of the roof, holding Lord Awesomo over the jam as the scrawny young man clawed at the hand around his neck, and the last of his protective bags fell off his legs and fluttered down into the jam.

Only then did Y allow himself to die.

The strength in his outstretched arm began to sap and Lord Awesomo's weight pulled him off balance. The two men fell forward together, Y's grip still refusing to loosen, and they disappeared into the red.

It was as if a hypnotist had snapped his fingers and woken us all from a trance. X and Ravenhair ran to the edge first. Angela and I shambled up either side of X. The two gray-suited goons apparently had other things to do.

This should have been the point that we saw either Y or Lord Awesomo clinging to a window ledge or an extruding drainpipe or something. But that didn't happen. Neither of them was there. I could see Y's empty webbing floating on the surface, torn to pieces as the jam had claimed the organic rations stored within. Nearby I could just about make out an eyebrow piercing that had belonged to Lord Awesomo.

The storm was moving on. The sky had almost rained itself out and the deluge had simmered down to a gentle patter. A final peal of thunder rang out, gentle and distant, like a rumbling farewell. The weather was seriously overdoing the symbolism that day.

"Thus ends the never-ending battle that was Y's life," narrated Angela, pointing her camcorder straight down. "An ending with a lesson for all of us. That he who lives by the jam, dies by the jam."

"We didn't cause the damn jam!" yelled X. "Why didn't anyone stop him?!"

"Which one?" said Angela, pointing her lens in X's face. "The one with the gun, or the professional killer?"

"They're dead!" wailed Princess Ravenhair.

"Angela," I said quietly, urgently squeezing her upper arm. "They've both lost people close to them. Perhaps we should—"

"Are you telling me not to document this?" said Angela. "I should think a lot of people will be wanting to see for themselves the downfall of the two biggest murderers in—"

X and Ravenhair both simultaneously broke away from the edge and launched themselves at Angela, clawing at her face and neck. The two mourners were both babbling incoherent but obviously offended streams of high-pitched half words, while Angela's attempts to apologize were dissolved over and over again into pained shrieks.

X grabbed Angela by the shirt and hauled her to the edge of the roof so that her head and shoulders dangled perilously over the jam. The realization that I was going to have to attempt an intervention settled uncomfortably on my shoulders.

"Er," I began.

Any inspiring friendship speech I could have made was preempted by the voice that suddenly echoed across the plaza. "Attention, leader of the Briar Center survivors," it said. It was distorted through a loudspeaker, but recognizable as belonging to Kathy, the Hibatsu settlement's director of Acquisitions. "You are losing this battle to a degree my colleagues and I have elected to describe as *embarrassing*. We believe it would be in the best interests of your settlement to immediately surrender, ceasing the unnecessary squander of limited resources."

Plastic bags littered the square like blossoms under the moulting cherry tree of the Hibatsu building. Only a handful of the plastic people remained unjammed. They were huddled in small groups behind some of the modern art installations, asking each other if they knew what was going on.

I saw Lord Awesomo's discarded megaphone lying dented near the exit door. I grabbed it and hurried it to Princess Ravenhair in the hope of distracting her further from Angela. "You have to surrender," I said.

Ravenhair glanced down at the megaphone as I pressed it toward her, then squinted at me as if trying to make out my face in dim light. Then she shoved me away. "Leave me alone!" she barked. "Everything was fine until you and your friend showed up!"

I backed off, glanced at Hibatsu, then backed back on again. "I'm sorry!" I said. "How many times am I going to have to say sorry?!"

"You've only said it once," said Ravenhair, in the wet, shaky voice of someone trying to speak while blubbering.

"I'm sorry again!"

"Attention again, Briar leader," came Kathy's voice. "If you do not respond, it will be assumed that agreement has been made to resume hostilities. Obviously we would like to avoid this option if possible, and we assumed you would feel the same way."

"One second!" I called into the megaphone, before pressing it into Princess Ravenhair's stomach again. "Look, this is bigger than you and me," I said. "Your people are dying. More will die if you don't act. You have to be a leader now."

Overwhelmed, she dropped to the floor and hugged her knees, burying her face in the gap between them. I prodded her unmoving shin with the handle of the megaphone. Eventually she burst into life and madly swatted me away. "Leave me alone!" she yelled, before returning to fetal position.

"Deirdre, please," I tried.

"I'm not doing anything for you," came her voice, muffled, from between her thighs. "You killed my Whiskers."

"Oh, for christ's sake, grow up, you flaky bitch," said Angela angrily, now back on her feet and free of X. "Okay, so Travis probably was in the wrong when he fed your budgie to a giant carnivorous jungle tarantula, but a lot of people have died because of you going off about it."

Princess Ravenhair didn't respond, but she didn't react violently, either, so at least she was thinking about it. My next action would have to be carefully considered. I knelt down in front of her and laid the megaphone carefully on one of her feet. It slid off.

"Attention again, again," came the voice of Kathy from across the silent battlefield. "We feel it worth mentioning that a member of your ruling cabinet has already offered his surrender on behalf of your people, but our company policy does require that we have a unanimous decision before any official confirmation can be made. It's just a paperwork thing."

Finally, Princess Ravenhair untucked her face. "What did she say?" she asked, sniffing away tendrils of dripping mucus.

I strained my vision to its limits and peered into the windows of Hibatsu to get a better look. Now that I was looking for it, I saw it next to Kathy: a colorful plastic bag ensemble in the colors Tim had been wearing.

"I think Tim might have told them he's one of your leaders," I said.

"Now that's cheeky," said Angela, zooming in to the building as far as she could.

Princess Ravenhair stood up, taking the megaphone from her foot, and followed our gaze. She took in the Hibatsu residents, who were looking on dispassionately like schoolteachers watching one of their number administer a telling off. Then her gaze traveled down to the pathetic scene of the ruinous siege and the ten or eleven surviving plastic people looking to her for action. Then her gaze traveled down further still, and came to rest on Lord Awesomo's discarded piercing.

Not looking up, she took up the megaphone and held it to her lips. "We surrender."

The megaphone fell to her side as if pulled down by the sheer weight of responsibility settling on her. Her eyes closed, sending two final tears rolling down her cheeks, and she cast her head back to bathe her face in the light of the morning sun, newly peering from around the retreating storm clouds.

I coughed. "You need to turn it on."

Princess Ravenhair swore and fumbled the switch. "We surrender!" she repeated, tetchily.

DAY 6.3

"Okay, now that's over with, item two on today's agenda," said Gary the chairman, in the darkened meeting room at the very top of the Hibatsu building. "Finalizing the merger with the Briar Center. I believe we have the managing directors here?"

Tim and Princess Ravenhair were sitting at the big meeting table, gently sweating in the permanent humidity. Don and I were standing behind them, trying to keep up the stance of victorious insurgents guarding political prisoners.

"Now, just to confirm, you are both amenable to the surrender action?" asked Kathy, pronouncing the question mark as a momentary raise of pitch at the end of the sentence.

"Yes," said Tim. Ravenhair just nodded. She'd been sitting on her hands, staring at the varnished tabletop.

"Well, I must say," said Philip, the head of Agriculture. "You're a lot more coherent than the last person we dealt with from over there." I winced, and glanced at Ravenhair, but she didn't react.

"The Briar Center population that survived the siege this morning are being held in our Acquisitions department," said Gary, checking his paperwork. "A total of twelve individuals. I should mention that nine of them have already renounced their membership of your community and been inducted with us. I gather they were eager to stop having to wear plastic coverings with the, er, internal environment being what it is."

"Still working on it," said David the air-conditioning guy testily. "We're doing the best we can with the resources we have, but I'm waiting on Kathy to put together a dog acquisition strategy document."

"So really, it's over to you," said Kathy, pushing two handwritten contracts and pens across the table to Tim and Princess Ravenhair.

"Erm, I just have one question," said one of Hibatsu's directors whose name I didn't know. "It was my impression that company policy was to only hire new employees if they contributed enough resources to support them."

"And that contribution will be adequately made once the Briar Center resources have been acquisitioned," said Kathy, "as well as the plastic bags that remain at the site of this morning's merger." I had to wonder about people who used the word *acquisition* as a verb when *acquire* was much shorter and easier to spell.

"Transferring the resources to this building could be the first job of our new recruits," suggested Gary. This brought on a round of nodding.

Tim had already signed his paper. Princess Ravenhair seemed listless, so he carefully slid the pen into her hand and moved it around until something vaguely signature-like had been marked on the page. "So," said Tim brightly. "Since we will be donating our, er, resources and manpower, I would like to gain some understanding of how your settlement works."

"Mm, certainly a tour can be arranged," said Gary.

"And after that I'd like to talk to your leader."

The Hibatsu directors exchanged eyebrow-raising looks. If this was a job interview, Tim had just lost his place on the list of maybes. "We are the board of directors," said Gary.

"Yes, I get that, but who actually makes the decisions?"

"We vote. Any of us can put forward suggested changes to policy, and we debate whether they would be for the good of Hibatsu."

"But who exactly is Hibatsu?" asked Tim. I eyed him, wondering what he was getting at. He was leaning forward with chin between thumb and forefinger.

"We all are," said Kathy abruptly.

Tim nodded, his knee bobbing spasmodically. "So, since this is a merger, could I get a seat on the board of directors?"

"Certainly," said Gary. "Since you were the leader of your settlement, we can definitely bypass a lot of the requisites. All you'd need to provide is a statement of intention, written sponsorship from at least one existing director, and character references from either three citizens of your previous employment or one fellow leader."

After a slightly stunned pause, Tim glanced hopefully at Princess Ravenhair, who finally made some kind of response. She glared at him with a look so poisonous it would have caused a massacre if she'd directed it at the river.

Most of us new arrivals were assigned sleeping quarters in one of the many, many generic cubicle farms that filled the building from top to bottom. Ours was on level twelve and divided into open-plan sections, each of which had four cubicles facing each other, perhaps to give the office workers the small mercy of company. It had been left to us to create bedding from whatever vaguely soft objects we could find. I'd ended up using a mail sack full of scrunched-up printer paper which rustled annoyingly when I lay on it.

But on average, I was feeling quite positive, once I'd stripped off my plastic bags and trousers and let my T-shirt dangle from the waistband of my boxer shorts. I'd been straining my memory but couldn't think of a single reason why anyone in power at Hibatsu would want me dead, which was a vast improvement on my earlier position. Mary, her species indigenous to rainforest, was quite at home in the moist, tropical atmosphere. Princess Ravenhair—technically just Ravenhair, now, probably—was still angry, but at least all secrets had been aired, and it was only a matter of time before she got over everyone she'd ever known being dead and was ready to start forgiving and forgetting.

Few of my companions seemed to share my feelings. Don refused to go topless or trouserless and was shedding angry sweat copiously as he assembled his own bed. Tim had been sitting in silent thought ever since we'd gotten back from the meeting. Angela had sat down nearby to review footage, but after I'd turned my back to make my bed for a few minutes she'd moved on.

I spotted her hanging around another cubicle divider in the section next door, crouching weirdly with her arms and shoulders flattened against the felt. She'd taken her shirt off to reveal her increasingly sweat-stained bra, but had compromised with the jeans by simply rolling them up to the knee. The atmosphere around Tim and Don was starting to feel like a teacher's lounge on the first day back from holidays, so I left Mary to enjoy the afternoon sun and sidled over to Angela with my hands gathered behind my back.

She was trying to peer around the edge of the cubicle divider. "Whatcha doing?" I asked.

Her hand shot out, closed around my T-shirt kilt, and pulled me down into a crouch beside her. Her finger not occupied with the camcorder touched her lips meaningfully.

I peered over the top of the divider to see what Angela's camcorder was occupied with, and saw X. She was sitting in one of the communal areas, peering at the contents of—what else?—a plastic bag. Kathy's Acquisitions department had taken everyone's plastic bags and placed them in storage, so this was a little suspect already.

"What's she up to now?" muttered Angela to herself.

"Er . . ."

It turned out the question hadn't been directed at me. "There's something important in that bag," Angela said. "It's something she doesn't want us to know about, I'm sure. It could be the answer to all of this."

"Oh, for christ's sake, Angela," I moaned.

I had to concede, though, that X was definitely being weirdly secretive about the bag's contents. She glanced left and right, clasping the bag shut between her clenched fists. Angela and I tried to flatten ourselves another inch or two into the cubicle wall. X didn't seem to have noticed us, but she still looked uneasy. She got to her feet and marched towards the stairwell door, speeding up as she passed the small work force brainstorming ideas on fixing the elevator.

"Let's follow her," said Angela, rising and breaking into a jog. I did likewise; by now I was curious, too.

By the time we entered the stairwell we could hear X's sensible shoes clacking loudly on the concrete steps several stories above. I was barefoot and Angela still had her sneakers, so we were confident our footfalls would go unheard. Nevertheless, every time X's footsteps paused, the two of us would drop into half crouches and freeze.

After who knows how many stories, I was sweating even harder and beginning to feel considerable sympathy for the elevator team when we heard a door open and close. A heavy door. The roof access door.

X's footsteps were now inaudible, so we sprinted up the steps with renewed vigor. "She's going to the roof," said Angela. "Maybe she's had a working phone all this time. Maybe she's trying to get a signal."

I practically piled into her as she stopped to open the roof access door silently. We needn't have worried. The Agriculture team were all watching X suspiciously, and X was standing at the edge with her back to the rest of the roof.

She had her head bowed and was examining the contents of her plastic bag, which we couldn't see. We watched her carefully from behind the bare soil where the potato salad had been planted. With her back to us, all we could see was that X was either turning something over and over in her hands or wrangling an energetic mouse.

Then, without warning, she flung something off the building. Instinctively Angela and I ran forward and leaned over the edge as if to catch it, but to no avail. We watched the remains of Y's torn-up webbing until it dropped into the jam, out of sight.

"Hey!" said Angela. "Are you destroying evidence? Stop it!"

X was quite startled by our sudden appearance, and her mouth flapped wordlessly like an offended party host. She was still holding the plastic bag open, so Angela thrust her hand in and withdrew a set of dog tags.

X snatched them back hurriedly as if they were her unwashed underwear, then held them to her face reverently, which is where the comparison breaks down.

"Y's things?" I said.

"No one else is going to mourn him," said X, tucking the dog tags into her sensible bra. "I just . . . had to do something. But there's nothing to bury. This felt right. That's all." She looked up, and frowned at Angela's openly dubious face. "That's all," she repeated, with greater emphasis.

"How can we believe anything you say?" said Angela nastily, not dropping her camcorder. "Practically the very first thing you said to us was a lie."

X put on that slightly condescending half smile which was always the signal she was slipping into press-conference mode, but now there was a hint of desperation behind it. "I don't have any idea what you're talking about."

She wasn't helping her case. I sighed in irritation. "Look, we know that HEPL is a real thing. You can be honest with us."

"Travis!" Angela nudged me sharply in the ribs.

"Well, it hardly matters now, does it?" I protested. "Show her that thing we found."

X bravely maintained her half-smiling expression of feigned bafflement as Angela reluctantly went to her trouser pocket and produced Y's ID card. X's face froze and I saw a spark of strong emotion behind her patronizing eyes. I could practically hear the chill running down her spine.

She reached for the card. Angela warily passed it over, whereupon X flicked the card away over her shoulder without breaking eye contact. It spun through the air right off the building and out of sight.

"What the hell'd you do that for?!" shouted Angela.

"Do what?" replied X innocently.

"You threw our card away!"

"How odd, I don't remember that at all. If I had done such a thing there'd be a card around as evidence, but there isn't any." She was trying to keep looking smug and authoritative but there was desperation in her eyes. "If there's nothing else, I'll see you later."

It took until X was most of the way back to the stairwell door for Angela to become unstupefied. "You are beyond belief! You can't even be grown up about it!" X didn't turn around. "This is why nobody likes you people anymore!"

The roof access door slammed shut. X was gone. Angela glared at where X had been, then glared at me instead. "Nice thinking, there, Travis. Let's just wave our evidence around in front of her. We're a regular Woodward and Bernstein."

"The cigarette company?"

She sighed and sat down on the edge of the roof, dumping her face unhappily onto her fists, where it remained for all of half a second. "Well, it's not too much of a problem," she said, sitting upright again. "We know about Human Extinction Protocol Libra. We don't need the card to continue the investigation."

"Is that what we're doing?" I sat down next to her. "What do you think it is, then? HEPL, I mean?"

"Okay." She wriggled into a more comfortable position, holding her hands flat and parallel to each other in frozen pre-applause. "Let's pin down what we know. We know it's something to do with human extinction. We know X and Y landed on our building because they thought it was an HEPL outpost. And we know X and Y don't want us to know about it."

"Well, we know X doesn't want us to know about it," I said, stroking my chin. Each day without shaving made my fingers gravitate there more and more often.

"And why do you think that is?"

"National security?"

"Ah!" Angela waggled her finger. "I've been thinking about that. I'm not sure this is just an America thing. Because X and Y thought there'd be an HEPL outpost in this country. So that means it's international. Could be more of a corporate than a government thing. Did X or Y ever actually say they work for the American government?"

"Yes."

Angela waved a hand dismissively. "Well, they're liars. We've established that."

"It could be X is keeping it secret because if we find out the truth we'll be very angry and might beat her to death or something."

"Well, we'd only do that if it turned out she was actually personally responsible for the jampocalypse."

The word *responsible* echoed around my skull, with X's previous use of the word—in a conversation that had taken place on another rooftop—joining the chorus. Not for the first time I considered telling Angela. It seemed like a waste to keep the knowledge to myself, because I didn't have the first idea what to do with it. I tested the water. "You wouldn't actually do that, would you?"

"Course I would," she said, matter-of-factly. "I mean, we've never really talked about this, I think because it would just bring everyone down, but we've all basically lost everything. Our whole lives, people we loved . . . If someone is responsible for this, I hate them. There isn't a survivor in this city who wouldn't want to kill them, if they found out who it was."

She dropped her gaze, saddened by her own words. Now *I* was starting to want to beat X to death. "What if they didn't mean to do it?" I tried.

"Wouldn't matter. You don't want someone walking around loose if they can set off something like this by accident. They might get into another accident and blow up the universe."

"Excuse me, could you people please leave?" One of the farmers had been passive-aggressively tutting and trying to work around us, and had finally decided to abandon subtlety. We apologized and got up to head back downstairs.

That's when we heard the noise. A deep, rising roar like a slow tide. We'd heard it many times before, but it sounded very different from up here, heavily echoed by distance.

"Another tidal wave," I said, out of habit. When we'd first arrived I'd been quick to bring up the matter of the risen jam around the building, but no one in the community seemed to be that bothered by it, since it wasn't getting inside and hadn't risen any higher. By this time I'd adopted the Hibatsu attitude of bored defiance towards the jam. The wave was far below me, as small and insignificant as a ripple in a puddle.

Then I looked around, to see if Angela was watching, and felt myself fill with dread. The wave was coming towards the Hibatsu building from every direction. Up until then I'd assumed the waves had been heading towards the sea, or at the very least the river, but this wasn't the case. The waves converged simultaneously against the four walls of the building with a loud chorus of wet slaps.

After this violent crash, the jam settled back down. The sheath of jam around Hibatsu looked like it had risen slightly higher, but it might have been my imagination.

"What the hell was that?" I was pushing my head and shoulders as far over the edge as I dared to get a better look at the building.

"That's how the jam rose," deduced Angela. "The tidal waves have all been converging on this spot."

"Why?"

Neither of us had an answer. We met each other's confused looks, each trying to tell from the other if we were supposed to be scared.

"Are you going, or what?" demanded the farmer.

DAY 7.1

I was started from sleep at around seven in the morning by the sound of someone clearing their throat into a loudspeaker. I hauled myself sleepily up until I could see over my cubicle wall. There were two Hibatsu employees standing at the stairwell door.

"Attention, level twelve," announced the one with the loud hailer. "This is the daily test of Hibatsu's emergency fire alarm. Please do not evacuate on this occasion. This is only a test. Now beginning fire alarm sequence."

He passed his loud hailer to his placid-looking friend, who immediately began screaming at the top of his voice. "AAAAAGH! FIRE! RUN FOR YOUR LIVES! AAAAAAGH!"

"That concludes today's test of the level-twelve fire alarm," said the first speaker, taking his loud hailer back. "In the event of a real fire emergency, the alarm would have been sounding continuously and from several different sources. Thank you."

There was a grumble of rising human beings all around me then, and it seemed pointless to go back to sleep. I sat up, yawned, stretched, and took the lid off Mary's box. She chomped her mandibles in greeting, and I picked up an open can of cat food and dropped a spoonful onto her nest of cereal.

I'd chosen cat food on the basis that cats also eat birds. The people in the Catering department had been very eager to let me have a crate of it, because they were terrified that their supervisor might one day suggest padding the human food supplies with the stuff. As I watched Mary eagerly feed, I had the warm, comfortable feeling that I was beginning the start of a lovely, boring routine.

Even Don seemed upbeat. He was moving cheerfully towards the river of human traffic filing towards the stairwell. He saw me looking at him just as he was vanishing into the crowd, and he offered me a smile. It looked about as natural on his face as a moustache on the Venus de Milo. I had a feeling that his build was somehow involved.

"Have you seen Tim?" I asked Angela, who appeared to have been up for a while. She was standing by the window filming the streets, perhaps to monitor the jam for odd behavior.

"He had to go to Personnel to get his job assignment," she said, without turning around.

I nodded. That meant Kathy's department, so I joined the queue for the stairwell. After yesterday's discussion with Angela, I'd come to the decision to tell on X. The information was too big a thing to house in my small, humble mind, and Angela was right—everyone had lost a lot in the jampoca-lypse and that meant they had a right to know. Whether they had the right to murder X for it was still up for debate, which was why Angela was definitely not the person to tell.

Similarly, I couldn't tell Don. He'd had far too much of a stake in the previous civilization and was not a man who suffered his enemies gladly. I still had a vivid memory of him tied to a chair back at his studio, roaring and bouncing around the room. If he channeled all that energy at X she'd probably get blasted through a wall.

Another option had been X herself. There was the chance she would break down and confide the full story, then I would become the friend she badly seemed to need after the loss of

Y. I decided against it because that was the best case scenario, and the worst involved her making a call to have the entire city nuked from orbit.

So it had to be Tim, now removed from power and considerably more approachable. Of all of us, he was the least bothered by the apocalypse itself. If anything, it had given him a whole new lease on life. And he was still my best friend, as far as I knew.

I met him in the Acquisitions department just as he was emerging from Kathy's office. His new lease on life was a bit ratty, going by his slouch and darkened eyes. I gradually shifted my cheerful bounding to a sympathetic saunter as I approached. "Hi, Tim," I said. "What did you get?"

"Scavenge," he spat.

"Oh, like me and Don?"

"Yes, like you and Don. In fact, you, me, and Don now have to take the *Everlong* back to the Briar Center and start loading up their food stores. I get to be the head of our division because I used to be a *leader*."

"Oh, that's good."

"No, it is not *good*. It's humiliating."

"Um. I hate to bring this up, but you were never officially a leader."

The look he gave me made it very clear that I had to dial my good mood down a notch. "Where's Don?" he asked.

"I dunno. I saw him heading upstairs."

"Let's go meet him."

Tim started walking towards the stairwell, shoulders hunched and hands tucked into the waistband of his underpants. I scampered after him.

"Tim, I need to talk to you about something," I said. "I found something out and I just need you to know about it. Do you promise not to tell the others? I'm afraid of how they'd react."

He paused with one hand on the stairwell door and looked at me, concerned. "You're gay?"

"No, no, no. It's about the jam."

"What have you found out about the jam?"

I waited until we were in the concrete stairwell and for a brief lull in the human traffic. "I overheard X say she felt responsible for it."

He froze in midstep with his back to me. He hesitated long enough for me to start regretting my decision, then I saw his shoulders untense. "Wait, you honestly thought she was being literal?"

"Well . . ."

"I had the same conversation with her a while back. I said we all have to take responsibility for the disasters that befall us because it was our way of life that brought them about. And she got this faraway look in her eye and she said that really spoke to her in a lot of ways."

I thought about pressing the point, but had lost confidence in my plan. I let it go, telling myself I'd have another attempt tomorrow, the same miserable assurance I'd given myself every single morning in high school after failing to ask out Tricia McGee.

We met Don coming down the other way, apparently from quite high in the building, since he was even sweatier than normal, and in the already pungent atmosphere of Hibatsu he was the center of a particularly armpitty little aura.

He was still in an uncharacteristically good mood, though. He smiled with both rows of teeth on display like an entire team's worth of cricket bats speeding through the air towards us. "Well, if it isn't Simon and Gar-dickhead," he said. "Look. I have found more fulfillment than you will ever know in several of the pathetic, drunken jigs you call lifetimes."

"And how's that?" asked Tim, not sharing Don's glee.

Don reached into his back pocket, then produced his hard drive, which he displayed for us between his fingertips like a glorious sunflower. "See how it shines," he said reverently.

"It's your build," I said.

"And look, no coffee stains," said Don, smug satisfaction making him virtually unrecognizable, lovingly fondling his prize like the delicate buttock of a beautiful girlfriend.

"Right," said Tim, as we headed for the stairs. "Except that if there isn't any civilization left anywhere it's just a chunk of plastic and metal that's really easy to scratch."

The Don I knew returned instantly, the frown sweeping over his face like a forest fire. "Cock."

Someone had taken the trouble to pull the *Everlong* from Queen Street to the Hibatsu plaza, and no sooner had they finished than we were preparing to take it all the way back again. We'd suited up into some of the plastic bags Hibatsu had recovered from the battlefield. They smelled unpleasantly of fresh duct tape and death.

Don stood at the back of the boat, pushing us along with the poles. I did my best to steer. Tim was sitting on the deck, deep in thought.

"So what do you think of Hibatsu?" I asked him, once we were out of the building's judgmental shadow.

"I have some concerns," he said.

"Oh, do you," said Don unpleasantly. "God forbid anyone run things differently to how his worship wants them. After all, he's already got experience with completely cocking up one settlement. Two, if you count whatever the hell that thing at our old apartment complex was."

"The helicopter messed that one up," I said. "To be fair."

"Yeah, but I didn't see Tim trying to wave it off."

"Do either of you have an actual point you want to raise?" said Tim sternly.

Don rolled his eyes. I coughed. "Why do you have concerns about Hibatsu, Tim?"

"Well, I might need a little longer to get the full picture, but my main gut concern with the Hibatsu settlement is that they're evil."

He let the word sink in for a moment. "More or less evil than the plastic people?" I asked.

"I can't decide if actual evil is better or worse than ironic evil. But at least when Lord Awesomo killed people it was because he placed some importance on them, like they were a threat to him. Hibatsu treat their people like machines. Or boxes of pencils. It's really corporate thinking."

"They were a corporation," I pointed out.

"I know. I have a really bad feeling about any society that started out as a corporation. I'm seeing Nazi jackboots in three generations."

"Bam!" said Don suddenly. "Called it. I god damn knew the moment you started talking that you were going to mention Nazis at some point. It's exactly the kind of lazy comparison I'd expect from your kind."

"What the hell does that mean, *my kind*?"

"You know what I mean. I've figured out what you are, now. You're a communist."

Tim kept his mouth tightly shut at Don's statement, and I knew why. I remembered that student society he'd joined in high school that had almost gotten all its members expelled for holding a rally outside the tuck shop.

"No, actually, that's too dignified a word for it," added Don. "You'd probably call yourself a communist in high school but really you're just a whiny kid who hates anyone who's powerful or has got a real job because it underlines how frigging worthless you are."

"You know, Hibatsu almost killed you, too," said Tim serenely.

"So maybe I'm not the kind of guy who bears a grudge." Tim and I both snorted with barely suppressed laughter. "All right, shut up. The point is, you only had power over the plastic people because they were idiotic sheep and you were marginally smarter. And now you resent Hibatsu like a big fat baby because everyone already knows what they're doing."

"But what they're doing is oppression," argued Tim. "There's no individuality. Everyone just does whatever it takes to keep the corporate entity going. Absorbing other settlements, stealing supplies . . . When you run things by committee, there's no one human soul running things who accepts responsibility for the actions. You become a monster."

Don sighed, bored of the argument. "Well, whatever. Why don't you just set up another revolution? There's always room on your resumé for another cock-up."

Tim's face was scowling, but thoughtful. That's what worried me.

DAY 7.2

After completing the rather ghoulish business of looting the now-silent mall, we returned to Hibatsu without incident. I was on level three helping the Acquisitions team unload when I glanced through an internal window into a conference room, much like the one where I'd first been interred, and saw Princess Ravenhair sitting alone.

There was only one door, and it was being held shut by a deeply tanned guard with the build of a gym enthusiast. I remembered what Tim had said about Hibatsu being evil, and that didn't put any kind of positive spin on why they'd be holding someone prisoner.

"Is that Princess Ravenhair in there?" I asked, peering at her through the blinds. She was sitting at the table with her head in her hands.

"Mm-hm," said the guard, bored. "Refusing to cooperate."

I bit my lip. "Is she . . . lashing out?"

"No. She's not cooperating, and she's not lashing out. Truth be told, she's not been doing much at all."

"You're not going to . . . terminate her or anything?"

"Nah, apparently not," he said, rolling his eyes in contempt for red tape. "Diplomacy and all that. Most of the ex-plastics in here still think she's like the Dalai Lama or something."

"Can I talk to her?"

"Sure, if you think it'll achieve something." He peeled his naked torso away from the door, leaving an elongated stain like the trail behind a slug. I wrapped my hand in my T-shirt skirt and turned the handle.

Ravenhair (I kept forgetting to mentally subtract the *princess* part) glanced up at my entrance, then just as quickly glanced down again. I kept my hands behind my back, using them to sheepishly push the door closed.

For several minutes neither of us spoke, or moved. The air of civility in the room felt a little fragile, and I spent some time internally debating the best way to open the conversation. *Hello* felt too neutral. *Hi* felt too facetious. *How are you feeling?* was out, because I didn't much relish the answer.

The fourth minute of silence began. I had to pick something, because otherwise she'd think I only came in here to eyeball her for five minutes.

"I am very, very sorry," I said.

She sighed at such length she sounded like a leaking air bed. "Could you please stop apologizing?"

"Sorry. I mean, er . . . not sorry."

"I know none of it was your fault." Her voice was small and heartbreaking. "I shouldn't have used Tim to get at Gerald. I should have stepped in when he started declaring war. I shouldn't have gotten so . . ." She formed something small and bird shaped with her hands. "I just wanted to say I forgive you for . . ."

She trailed off. I tried to think of a tactful way of putting it, but for some reason it was getting harder to think, and all I came up with was, "Tweet tweet chomp chomp?"

"He was only a budgie, after all," she said. "You were worried about Mary. I might've done the same thing. You care about her just as much as . . ."

"Um, yeah," I said, remembering that I hadn't checked on Mary since I'd gotten back. "Deirdre . . ."

"And who knows, maybe I feel free for the first time since this all began. Now that no one's expecting me to be a leader anymore. Does that sound terrible?"

"No, no, I get it," I said quickly. "But what are they doing to you?"

She frowned and looked up, finally meeting my gaze. "What are who doing to me?"

"Hibatsu. Are they being evil?"

"Evil? Not really. I've talked with some of my . . . former subjects, and they're all really happy with the way things are being run." Her eyes glazed over slightly. "Happier than they'd been in some time, actually."

"But why are you being held prisoner?"

"I'm not. I just came in here to have a think. I don't know why that guard's standing there. I think there's a breeze."

The door I was standing in front of flew open with such force that I was hurled into the nearby wall. I half crawled away, clutching several bruised joints, and saw X. She was standing with clenched fists hanging down at her sides and her entire body thrumming with emotion.

"They were lying. About having. A phone," she said, visibly fighting an urge to burst into frustrated tears.

Deirdre immediately stood up, went to her, and hugged her gently. I watched, feeling like a voyeur. The two of them had gotten rather comfortable with each other since I'd seen them last. Perhaps they'd found common ground, such as the loss of a male friend, or a mutual desire to strangle Angela.

"Did you really think they had one?" asked Deirdre without malice. "I mean, they'd have used it themselves by now, surely."

"Y said they had communication with the outside world," quavered X into her shoulder. "It turns out it was just their stupid corporate speak for the sign they put on the side of the

building and Y wasn't creative enough a thinker to realize
and now it's all been completely pointless . . ."

I coughed. X seemed to notice me for the first time, and
detached from Deirdre, embarrassed. She sniffed wetly, and
quiveringly put on that mellow, press-conference stance.
"Hello, Travis."

The tension in the room went up a couple of notches. "Er,
hi. I was just leaving." I left, neatly proving my point.

I retired to our sleeping area, feeling oddly drained by the
day's events, and sat hugging my legs on my makeshift bed,
staring fixedly over the space between my knees. Nothing
more was being asked of me that day, so I was taking the
opportunity to rest and picture all the clever, insightful, reassuring things I could have said to Deirdre and X.

I was broken from my daydreams by the short, harsh sound
of something expensive being tormented. At some point Don
had arrived on the scene, and was hunched over one of the
dissembled work stations. He was holding a screwdriver in one
hand and a hammer in the other, and had the sick expression
of a clingy mother leaving her child for its first day at school.

He smashed his makeshift chisel a second time and, with
another heartbreaking crack, successfully pounded a hole
through the plastic housing around his beloved hard drive. I
watched curiously as he attached a lanyard and dropped it
smartly around his neck. It was evidently heavier than his
spine had been anticipating, but he absorbed it manfully.

"What're you doing?" I asked.

"Isn't it obvious?" he spat. "I'm going to wear it around
my neck from now on."

"You don't think that's a tiny bit neurotic?"

"I dunno. Are you a tiny bit retarded?" He tapped the
casing and winced as the impact shot up his neck. "I am never

letting this out of my sight again. Because . . ." His face twisted with loathing even before the concession was out of his mouth. "Because Tim had a point. While we're still trapped in Brisbane, the key to my future happiness is just an uncomfortable pointy object. Anything could happen to it before we're rescued."

"Or we just won't get rescued at all because this is a total jampocalypse," I said.

"And I've told you before, if that's the case I'm going to wrap myself in bread, throw myself off this building, and get turned into a jam scroll. So it doesn't matter." He rubbed his eyes. "Christ, if I just had a working computer. And half an hour of Wi-Fi. I could just upload the build to my FTP. After that I could stick this hard drive in a woodchipper and take a shower in the bits."

"There's bound to be a laptop in Hibatsu that's still got charge in its batteries," I suggested.

"That's only half the issue. Stop trying to help—it just makes me more annoyed. God, why am I even talking to you about this?"

"What's that supposed to mean?"

"It means, Travis, that the closest you ever get to a good idea is when you successfully get to a toilet before pissing yourself."

"Oh, I'm sorry," I said, hotly. "I didn't realize your head didn't have room for any more ideas because you've pulled so many out of your big fat arse."

My mind only processed my own words after I saw Don's stunned expression.

"Did you just sass back?" he said, astonished.

"No!" I squawked. Then I ran away.

DAY 8.1

I slept in a different, unused cubicle just to be safe and woke at around five when the early morning sun scythed out from between the neighboring buildings and struck me directly in the face. When I crept sheepishly back to our living space the others were still asleep, Don pressing his cheek against his hard drive, so I sat nearby and waited for them to wake.

As I waited, I mulled a few things over. Ever since yesterday's outburst, I'd wondered what had gotten me into such a mood. Not that I was ashamed—I was still tottering from the strange energy I'd been filled with as the anger surged, like a virginal schoolgirl discovering orgasms. Was this how people like Don felt all the time?

For some reason, my thoughts kept returning to Deirdre. I'd been in a generally crabby mood ever since speaking to her on level three. Plus, I'd just woken from a rather upsetting dream in which I'd been beating upon the outside of a sound-proof box, inside of which Deirdre and X had been getting up to some very indecent things.

At around seven thirty Don finally coughed himself conscious. In the very next second, he was on his feet and displaying the flats of his hands in some improvised karate stance. "GET THE HELL AWAY FROM—oh, it's you."

I rose cautiously out of my terrified flinch. "Yes. Hello."

All his muscles relaxed at once and he almost collapsed again. "I was having a horrible dream about drinks coasters." He fingered his hard drive sleepily for a moment, then suddenly directed a raised eyebrow at me. "Wait. Why are you watching me sleep?"

"Just didn't have anything better to do," I said nonchalantly.

He eyeballed me. "Oh, well. Nice to know I'm your last resort for entertainment." He kicked Tim sharply in the leg. "Oi. Salvage time."

"I'm awake," said Tim. "You woke me when you screamed the room down. Why did you kick me? And why are you still kicking me?"

"If you have to ask, you'll never know," said Don. He gave Tim one more friendly boot after he'd gotten to his feet, and the three of us set off for the boat.

"Why are you in such a good mood?" moaned Tim, rubbing his eyes.

"Oh, god, I have no idea," said Don bitterly. "I've actually been looking forward to going salvaging. That scares me. I think I might be getting acclimatized."

"You don't get acclimatized after three days," said Tim grumpily.

"You know what I mean. I'm relishing any distraction I can get from the nightmare of my life. Like Albert Speer with his garden in Spandau Prison. Or maybe I'm just looking forward to getting out of the damn greenhouse for the day."

By now we were in the stairwell and tramping our way down to level three. "Wanting to get out of this building I can understand," said Tim.

"You still don't like Hibatsu?" I inferred aloud.

"I'm still not sold." A few tribespeople coming the other way smartly climbed past us, and Tim turned his head to watch them go. "Look, that's my point. Their faces are so . . . blank. Even the guys with plastic bags over their heads had some emotion about them. This is like a Catholic school."

Don was on point, and half turned his torso to address us. "Hey. Not everyone feels the need to run around with big stupid grins on their faces all the time. At least Hibatsu is efficient."

"Nazi Germany was efficient."

Don made a vocalization that was hard to transcribe. "PFFGLAH. There you go again, comparing things to Nazi Germany. It's such a pathetic argument."

"You brought it up first."

"No, I didn't—oh, come on, Spandau Prison references hardly count. Anything after the Nuremberg Trials—"

"DON, LOOK OUT!" I grabbed his gesturing arm and pulled him back so hard the two of us sprawled diagonally up the stairs in a tangled clinch.

"What the hell are you doing?!" he said, pressing a knee into my chest as he struggled to get away.

"J-m," I choked, unable to breathe.

The stairs descended into jam. I thought we must have accidentally miscounted and gone all the way down to the lobby, but the sign on the wall read *3*, bold as brass. The stairwell door was open and I could just about see the jam continuing through there. The stuff must have risen during the night.

"We left our plastic outfits on the *Everlong*, didn't we?" said Tim uncomfortably. "Someone take my hand. I need a better look."

I fastened my hand around his proffered wrist and he leant over the jam to take a better look through the door. Then he had to lean a little bit further, so Don took my free hand and the two of them proceeded to stretch my upper body quite painfully.

"Yeah," said Tim. "The whole level's flooded. Three feet. Looks like it came in that window you two broke."

"Oh, christ," wailed Don. "Suppose I should blame myself for this one. I knew it was a mistake to say I was looking forward to going outside. Jinxed that up the arse, didn't I."

"Do you think the Acquisitions department got out in time?" I said.

We exchanged glances, then the three of us wordlessly raced up to the next level. There, we stopped dead. None of us had registered or drawn attention to it on the first walk past, but now I could see there was a lurid red light spilling into the stairwell from around the edges of the door. It was a startling effect, like a doorway to hell.

Tim took the initiative. Ready to slam the door shut again at the first sign of imps and flaming pits, he tentatively pulled it ajar, affixing his eye to the crack. Then he let the door open fully, letting his jaw settle at around knee height.

Every window on the fourth floor was red. My first thought was that someone had put red cellophane over them all, perhaps for some therapeutic reason, but then I saw the red covering flex and pulsate around the window joins like seaweed swaying on the ocean bed. The jam had continued to rise thinly around the outside of the building but, lacking a broken window, hadn't gotten inside.

I felt myself breathe a sigh of relief when I saw Kathy and several other familiar faces milling around, shaken but undigested. But there was still a nagging question hanging over the entire situation.

"Why is the jam rising?"

"It's got to be something to do with how this place is being run," said Tim, thinking.

"Oh, you'd love that, wouldn't you," growled Don. "It's jam. Who says it has to be rational? Maybe it's eaten so many people it's just having a great big burp."

The argument might have continued, but we were rudely interrupted by something banging loudly against a nearby window. We glanced over like startled meerkats and saw the upper portion of the *Everlong*'s mast waving drunkenly back and forth.

The *Everlong* was extending horizontally from the building like a flapping white ear, wobbling crazily in the wind. It was still anchored to a window frame that was now under jam, and the boat teetered like a seesaw on the peak of a jam mountain.

"Ah, I was about to send someone to fetch you," came the voice of Kathy. Don, Tim, and I turned to see her flanked by two large, burly tribesmen, and suddenly our being backed up against the window took on something of a firing-squad quality. "Do you have any explanation for this?"

"Why are you asking us?" said Don.

"You do regularly leave the settlement and interact physically with the jam," she said, with infuriating tact. "We were wondering if you could think of something you might have done to activate it in some way?"

"Oh, good god," said Don witheringly. "You think because we've splashed around in it a lot that we're some kind of jam whisperers now?"

"You do have the most experience with it."

"I'm sorry. We're as lost as you are," said Tim tightly, folding his arms.

"Of course, you were the ones who broke the window on the third floor in the first place . . ." said Kathy. She never spoke in anything other than understanding concern, but the merest hint of threat hid in that last ellipsis like a troll under a bridge. "Well, anyway, the workday must continue. Come with me; we need to go over your salvaging agenda for the day."

"You still think this place has good leadership?" whispered Tim challengingly, as we followed her swaying hips.

"So they've got bad intelligence," answered Don levelly. "I'd have thought you'd be glad to find some common ground at last."

Kathy led us into the department where her new office was apparently located. With the eerie red glow, the sticky heat, and the partially disassembled cubicle farm, the place had started looking like a postmodern hell.

"All right then," said Kathy when the three of us took the three prepared seats in front of her desk. "We have had to increase our quota for food supplies, now that the community has absorbed the surviving Briar Center refugees. Fortunately, our lookouts and Intelligence department have put together a rather detailed map of food sources throughout the nearby city that should still hopefully be well stocked."

She spread a road map of the city center over her desk. It was sprinkled with red crosses, which had all additionally been circled with green highlighter, because there were a lot of people in each department who were constantly looking for ways to look busy.

"Your best locations for today would be the food court at the top of the MacArthur Center and the restaurants on the upper level of the Wintergarden," she said, pointing them out. "Now, there's a pet shop directly between those two. David would be grateful if you gave it a quick once-over for dogs or anything large enough to run a treadmill."

"What if we find another survivor settlement?" asked Tim.

Kathy's pen rattled rapidly against the map as she considered this. "That would obviously depend on whether or not they are infringing upon our territory."

"And what consists of our territory?"

She examined the map, then swept her open palm across the whole thing in a circular motion. "Pretty much all of that. But you should definitely take a diplomatic approach at first."

"At first?" Tim folded his arms. "So don't break out the napalm launchers until we get the order?"

"That's right," said Kathy, oblivious to sarcasm. She returned her finger to the location of the pet store. "Now, even if you don't have any luck with meeting the dog quota, the Agriculture department have also asked if you wouldn't mind keeping an eye out for something they could use as fertilizer—"

A sudden, short, sharp, cracking sound put a full stop on her sentence and stirred me from a light doze. At first I thought Tim had lashed out at the idea that he, a former pseudoruler of a rival settlement, should rummage around in the bottoms of guinea pig cages for bits of dried-out shit, but he hadn't moved. Then there was another *krk* and all three of us jumped and pointed at the window behind Kathy.

A stark white line, curving and bending weirdly like a bolt of lightning, crawled across the glass. By the time Kathy had turned around far enough to see it, it had bisected the entire window. At several points along its length, tiny bubbles of jam appeared and began to swell. As we stared, they expanded into peas, then olives, then gumballs, then stopped, quivering as if ready to burst.

Kathy made the mistake of reaching out a finger towards the closest one, perhaps responding to some inbuilt instinct to pop bubble wrap. When it caught the scent of her flesh, the bubble deformed and became a horizontal stalactite, straining itself forward to reach her.

Then four more cracks appeared all at once, forming an X in the glass around the pointed bubble. They scuttled rapidly along the window, and at the moment they touched the frame, the glass shattered.

A wave of jam forced its way into the room, sucking Kathy into its depths as if it were popping a boiled sweet into its gaping mouth. The rest of us were already off our overturned chairs and backing towards the door, as the jam slurped its way along the carpet toward us, eating up Kathy's meticulously made bed and the papers on her desk.

The intrusion hadn't gone unnoticed by the mentally keener members of the Acquisitions team. Most of them were already making for the stairs. Cracks were appearing on every window in the level, like partially completed spider webs. I heard metal groaning like a sleepy bear and another window gave way in the north wall, flooding hastily vacated cubicles with a second wave of jam, which spread lazily through the room like honeymooners making themselves comfortable on a hotel bed. It didn't take long for the south wall to bow to peer pressure.

With jam encroaching from all sides, it was getting very crowded around the door to the stairwell. Even life in the saunalike environment of Hibatsu had done little to reduce the doughy, bell-shaped builds of the topless office workers. A heaving mass of sweating flab had formed and was now attempting to shrink away from the expanding jam like a drop of water on a hot stove, but a middle-aged secretarial woman and a bespectacled IT sort had become wedged in the door frame.

Don, babbling incoherent, angry syllables, took a risky step away from the mass, then shoulder barged the human lump like a Japanese train guard. It quivered, but refused to give. The safe area of floor had shrunk down to about seven feet across, a circle of institutional gray in a vibrant crimson carpet.

Don and Tim exchanged nods, then both of them took a step back and, on the count of three, threw themselves at the blockage. A tidal wave of struggling limbs and pale flesh tumbled out into the stairwell. Everyone was fighting to get up the stairs, struggling over each other like bees in a hive. I saw Tim crawling over the mob, madly bringing his fists and feet down to push back the others as he clawed ahead, which would have been pretty damning if he had any political ambitions left.

"Tim!" I called, grabbing the banister and pulling my entire body up the steps. "What are EEP."

Someone's hand grabbed my ankle as I planted it in the human quagmire. I yelped, pulling in vain at the vicelike grip, before it suddenly relaxed. The jam had reached the door, and had started with the base of the pile before it moved on to the topping.

In the end, all but four or five bureaucrats were able to jump away and get up the first set of stairs, where we paused to watch the jam. It gradually leveled out about four steps up, expanding downstairs to hook up with its manifestation on the third floor.

But then it kept moving. A miniature wave appeared in the surface and threw itself against the next step up. Then another, and it caressed the top of the sixth step.

"It's still rising," I said aloud.

No one needed further encouragement. Within seconds the surviving members of the Acquisitions department had sped upstairs en masse, leaving me alone with Don and Tim. As the crowd thinned down to the three of us, the jam ceased climbing the stairs, one last wave flopping poutily backwards.

"Well, this all puts rather a dampener on things, doesn't it," said Don with grim annoyance.

"I'm gonna go talk to X," I said.

"Why?" asked Tim, hugging himself.

I was already climbing the stairs. "She knows something about the jam. Maybe she knows why it's doing this."

"Great idea," sighed Don, still staring at the jam. "I mean, she was evasive about it for the first ten million deaths but I reckon five more will tip it."

I was quite glad that Don and Tim didn't join me on my quest to interview X. The fact that she knew about the jam seemed to be an open secret to everyone but her, and I was afraid she'd lock up if I didn't speak to her alone, especially if I had to bring up the whole "responsibility" business.

I found her on the roof. I wasn't sure if she'd been assigned a job, but if she had it must have been a pretty lackadaisical one. I strongly suspected she'd been given some kind of diplomatic immunity, like what Deirdre had. I found her staring down into the jam, head bowed.

"X!" I called. She turned and watched me approach, confused. "X, listen. I need to know what's going on with the jam. It's doing something weird."

Each part of her face shifted one by one into a carefully neutral expression. "I don't know why you'd think I'd know more about the jam than anyone else."

I put my hands on my thighs and panted, still out of breath from the run up the stairs. I didn't need this. "X, please, be serious. The jam's rising. Some people have already died."

Her eyebrows rose, shocked. They waggled subtly for a few seconds as if engaged in some silent debate, before they both settled back down. "If that's the case, then you should stop wasting time trying to get me to—"

"I know you're responsible for the jam."

I'd gone with a sudden instinct, fearing the conversation was ending too quickly. Every single part of her turned to slightly reddened stone. I chewed my lip guiltily, as if I'd just yelled out a swear at a funeral.

"What did you say?" she quavered.

I considered backtracking, but for better or worse I was in this, now. "I know you're responsible for the jam. Or at least you think you are."

"How do you . . ." She stopped for a deep breath. "What makes you think I think I'm responsible for the jam?"

"I overheard." Like a runaway truck speeding down a hill towards a puppy and duckling farm, I told her about the entire conversation I'd overheard on the roof of the Briar Center, where Y had assured her that Hibatsu would provide for them and she'd made her confession. She listened placidly, but I noticed her eyeballs bulge by about a millimeter every five or so words.

"I-I don't recall saying . . ." she began.

"Don't, just . . . just don't," I said.

"So now that you have this information, what do you intend to do with it?" she asked. The foot on the end of her crossed leg was jiggling spasmodically.

I sighed. "I don't intend anything. I wouldn't know what to do with it. I can't even imagine what I could blackmail you for. I just want to know why the jam is rising and I think you can tell me."

"I would have thought it would be obvious," she said in a suddenly much lower and more resentful voice.

I was momentarily stunned by her directness, but recovered quickly. "Erm. Apparently not."

"You've observed that the jam can extend parts of itself towards organic material, right?"

"Yeah, I noticed that."

"The effect amplifies the more organic material it can sense, especially living material. When you have a lot of living things clustered together in the same place, the jam finds it a lot easier to detect them. That's why the jam has risen around this settlement. It's designed to prevent pockets of resistance—" She stopped herself and reddened. "I mean, it looks like it would have been designed to . . . I mean, this is all an educated guess, obviously."

In my private thoughts I speculated about the exact nature of that education. "So why has it suddenly risen now?" The answer hit me before she could reply. "Oh god. It's because of us, isn't it. Now the plastic people have been absorbed, the Hibatsu population's gone up far enough . . . Hang on, how come we never noticed any of this happening back at the Briar Center?"

"Because the residents there were all moving around in the jam already. It would only have been trying to move sideways, and that wouldn't be noticeable. Here there's a huge cluster of humanity hovering just out of the jam's reach. Of course it's going to rise. It's like blotting paper in water. What exactly has the jam done?"

"It's gotten as high as level four and I think it's going to keep coming."

"Okay. Take a quick look down there and tell me if the jam has risen any further since you saw it last."

I stepped to the edge of the building and looked down, obeying with flustered excitement before remembering how many stories lay between me and ground level. The vertigo swam about my head and stomach like a pair of cackling ghosts, but I forced myself to focus on the jam. It was so far down it was impossible to tell if it'd risen any higher, since the fourth floor and the fifth floor looked pretty much the same from—

"There you are!" came Angela's voice.

I spun around. Angela had just emerged from the stairwell door, but the slightly more pressing detail was that X had silently moved directly behind me, and was frozen with surprise at my sudden turn. For an instant I saw that her hands were splayed out as if preshove before she clasped them together into a more neutral arrangement.

"What are you doing?" I said.

"Me? Nothing!"

Angela was now beside us, filming as always. "Hey, we've been called to a meeting with the board of directors. That's us three, Don, Tim, and a few other lads. Right . . . now . . ." The space between her words lengthened as she noticed that I was staring at X with tight-lipped terror. "What . . . what are you doing up here?"

"Is this something to do with the jam's behavior?" said X, very deliberately turning away from me and towards Angela.

"Oh, don't you even pretend you don't already know this. It broke all the windows on level four."

We started on our way to the top-floor conference room. "It broke windows?" said X, as we descended the stairs. "I never even considered that." She stroked an invisible beard nervously. "I suppose the jam must have risen to the point that it acquired enough of a constricting effect to cause damage to the building's—" She stopped when she noticed Angela watching and listening intently.

"Ye-es?" she said, from behind her omnipresent camera.

"I mean, it's just common sense," said X defensively. "Common, everyday intuitions like normal people have."

When we were on the director's level, Tim and Don were already waiting outside the main conference room door, along with a group of around twelve former plastic people.

"Ah yes, normal, everyday people like the ones who work for places called Human Extinction Protocol Libra," said Angela in a deliberately conspicuous voice. "Have you told everyone about that card we found, Travis?"

"Oh, give it a rest," snapped Don. His arms were still as folded as they'd been in the stairwell and appeared to be locked in place with shock.

"This is all part of the scheme, I know it!" said Angela. "They're not satisfied with just silencing the people; they've got to silence the whole building, too!"

"Um, could someone please tell me what's going on?" asked Deirdre petulantly.

The meeting room door opened slightly and a young man who had apparently been nominated Kathy's understudy poked his head out. "We're ready for you all, now."

Our rather ungainly group filed in and took up position in a cluster against the wall. There was a tension in the air, like the pause between the words *aim* and *fire*.

"Thank you for coming in on such short notice," said Gary. His fingers were interlaced like the jaws of a steel trap. "I expect you already know what this is about."

"No, I don't," exclaimed Deirdre, glancing up and down the line. "What happened? Did someone die?"

Gary coughed meaningfully and she shut her mouth. "The loss of level four is going to be difficult to bounce back from. And it seems like an appropriate leap of logic to assume that the jam is rising because of our recent sudden population growth."

A cold lump was gathering in the pit of my stomach. I risked a look over at my peers, and judging by their faces, something similar was interfering with their digestive systems, too.

"The motion was carried that we should systematically reduce the population by one individual each evening and measure the jam level each morning," said Gary matter-of-factly. "Continuing until the jam has stopped rising or begun receding. This should effectively minimize the number of terminations."

"Terminations?!" I cried.

"Thrown from the roof. We're going to do it in a sort of sacrificial way," said Philip excitedly. "Don't worry; the jam makes for a pretty soft landing."

"Now, we don't expect anyone to volunteer for this," said Gary. He paused lengthily to give someone a chance to defy his expectation, but no one went for it. "That's why we'd like all of you to talk it over amongst yourselves and nominate one of your number democratically."

"What? Why us?!" barked Don.

"We decided to go through candidates according to reverse order of arrival," said Gary. "All of you were very recently inducted into our community as a consequence of the conflict between our settlement and the Briar Center."

X put up a hand. "I nominate Travis."

"What?!"

Gary put up his hands. "Now, now, please let this be a group decision. Can we leave this with you and ask that you come back with a unanimous decision by around six o'clock?"

Everyone looked a little stunned. Tim stepped forward. "Look, you have to have realized this isn't necessary. We'll just leave. All of us, we'll just get in the boat and go. We won't be a problem anymore."

"Of course we considered that option," said David. "But our feeling was, we've only just gotten rid of one rival settlement within our territory, and planting the seeds for another would just be counterproductive."

"So, six o'clock, then?" said Gary, shuffling his papers in a finalizing kind of way.

I glanced along the line and noticed everyone else doing the same, waiting for one of us to light the fire of defiance under the rest. But lighting the fire was taking too long and Gary's papers were being shuffled with more and more meaningful violence with each passing moment, so the former plastic man nearest the door took the initiative and walked morosely out of the room. The rest of the group started following without haste.

"All right, next item on the agenda," said Gary, adjusting his ridiculous headdress and finding the right paper in the well-shuffled mess before him. "The aircraft carrier that has been spotted drifting at the mouth of the river."

X's head snapped around like a loose hinge. "What did you say?"

"Don't let us keep you," said Gary testily, poised and ready to start shuffling again at a moment's notice. "You have big decisions to make."

"You said there's an aircraft carrier?"

"Look, just go up to the roof if you want to see it," said David. "We've got a lot of items on the agenda and you're not part of them anymore."

X bolted from the room. The rest of us followed.

Hibatsu was the tallest building in the city, and the view from the top was spectacular. The inner city spread out below us, framed on one side by curving red hills like the contours of a sunburnt teenager's face, and on the other side by the red-filled river. Brisbane's center was just far enough from the coast to deter holiday makers, but the sea was still visible from the top of Hibatsu.

And there, spoiling the picturesque horizon, was the awkward, angular shape of an aircraft carrier, run aground and tilted ever so slightly to the left, but otherwise completely undamaged. It was far enough away that we probably wouldn't have seen it had we not known to look.

"Oh, finally," breathed Don as we took in the majestic sight of it. "I told you rescue would be coming. Now everyone can grow their sanity back." He shoved Tim.

"Don, I think it's run aground," I said, shielding my eyes. "I don't see anyone moving on deck."

"Shush," said Don, shutting his eyes and covering his ears. "Just let me believe it. Just for a moment. I need this."

Angela turned her camera to X, who was groping her invisible beard with more and more ferocity. "Look familiar?" wheedled Angela.

It took a moment for me to realize what she was getting at. "Is that the aircraft carrier you and Y came on?" I asked.

"That's it," she said. "The USS *Obi-Wan*. But it couldn't possibly . . ."

"I thought you said the jam took it over?" said Angela. "Another in a long line of things you said that we can't trust?"

"The jam was all over it," said X, bewildered. "It was sinking when we left. All the crew were absorbed, we barely got off in . . ." She glanced down at the risen jam still sucking on the Hibatsu building's lower half like it was a giant licorice stick. She turned her head towards me, away from Angela, and lowered her voice to a mutter. "The jam is all one swarm. After it cleaned out the *Obi-Wan* it would have had no reason to stay there. It must have withdrawn when it began concentrating on attacking Hibatsu." She then looked Angela square in the camera and spoke at full volume. "I have no explanation for this."

"You're saying," I said, "that the jam pulled out of the ship once it couldn't find anything more to eat in it?"

"Yes, that theory you just came up with on your own sounds perfectly feasible, Travis," said X loudly.

"I've got a question," said Don, putting up a hand like a schoolboy.

"Yes?"

"*Obi-Wan?*"

X looked embarrassed. "It was a PR thing. There was an Internet poll to decide on the name, some website flooded the votes, by the time anyone found out all the signs had already been painted." She peered at the ship again. "I have to get to it."

"Why?" said Don. "If Travis is right, which is admittedly a pretty vast assumption to make, then it's already been cleaned of survivors and food. It's just floating scrap metal, now."

"It has its own generator that should still be functioning," said X.

"Oh, okay, so what's the proposal here?" snarked Don witheringly. "Sail the big horrible thing up the river, lean it up against Hibatsu and plug in the air conditioning?"

"One of the things the generator will power . . ." said X. From the quiet smugness in her voice I could tell she was preparing some devastating move. "Is the onboard computer network with satellite Internet access."

Don went very still and quiet for a few moments, his disdainful expression frozen. When he spoke, the words slid shamefacedly out of his flattened mouth. "I suppose we had better get over there, then."

"Okay, here's what I'll do," said X. She marched decisively towards the stairs and spoke as she walked, the rest of us half jogging to keep up like yes-men following a brainstorming Hollywood director. "I'll take the sailboat up the river and board the *Obi-Wan*. I'll make contact with the outside world, arrange a properly organized rescue, and get back to you guys before six o'clock."

Tim grabbed her shoulder and stopped her. "We're all going."

"Oh?" Slightly panicked innocence radiated from X's voice and eyes. "I wouldn't want you to put yourselves out. I won't really need any help and it'll just be very boring."

"We're totally all going," said Tim.

"Yeah, boring is good," said Angela, smiling devilishly. "I love boring. Gives you plenty of time to talk about things, doesn't it. Things like jam."

"Could someone explain what's going on?" said Deirdre unhappily. "Do we think X knows something about the jam?"

"No," said X.

"Yes," said everyone else.

"Try to keep up, dear," said Don.

DAY 8.2

"We really should have thought about this sooner," said Don.

"You mean we shouldn't have crossed this bridge when we came to it?" I said—rather cleverly, I thought.

We were on the now rather sparsely populated fifth floor of the building, the new front in the struggle against the jam, and were deforming our faces stupidly against the windows along the west wall. The *Everlong* was below us, still tied to a third-floor window now buried in jam. The boat protruded horizontally from the wall and the very top of the mast was swaying back and forth a few feet below our vantage point.

"At least we won't have to worry about guards," said X.

I glanced around at the floor, which was deserted but for our party and the occasional individual running in and out to grab some possession as quickly as possible. "What's with that, anyway?" I asked.

"I guess everyone prefers to be as far from the jam as possible, now," said Angela.

"But now everyone's getting more clustered together higher up," I said, looking at X. "Won't that make it easier for the jam to sense them?"

"Maybe," said X. "Or maybe they'll be far enough from the jam up there that it won't be an issue. Either way, perhaps some of you should stay behind to make sure—"

"No," said Tim and Angela in unison.

Tim ran his hands along the window directly above the boat and found the catch, wrenching it open with only slight difficulty. The window fell ajar and a breath of cool air scythed blissfully through us. But when he pushed the pane out until the opening was wide enough to fit through, I suddenly noticed a thin piece of wire originating from somewhere around the ceiling becoming taut and then becoming slack with a little snapping sound—which is a scenario unmatched for creating a sudden hushed atmosphere of *oh shit*.

From the level above we heard something covered in bells collapse jangling to the ground, and it was a fair bet that anything with bells on was designed to be listened to. "It's an alarm," I realized.

"They must have installed measures to warn if any windows near the jam . . ." deduced Angela.

Don, who had been excitedly bobbing up and down on his toes ever since the notion of acquiring an Internet connection had penetrated his cynicism, shoved everyone aside and hopped up onto the window ledge. "Whatever!" he declared sagely. "Alarms just mean move faster!" Then he dropped onto the *Everlong*. Judging by his face he only realized the depth of this decision's badness in the moment after he'd thrown himself off.

He hit the mast hard and his weight caused the entire *Everlong* to swing down, her keel slapping wetly against the vertical wall of jam, before coming back up like a pinball flipper and dislodging him from the mast. When he hit the deck it went down again for a second round, and he had to cling to the rear handrail as it went fully vertical, legs kicking frantically over the drop.

"Are you all right?" I called down, once the boat was horizontal again and Don lay panting and spread-eagled on the deck.

"SPIFFING," he replied, pronouncing the *P* like an armor-piercing bullet. "You should all come down and have as much fun as I'm having."

We could hear voices from the stairwell and large numbers of feet slapping down the steps towards us. Tim started lifting his legs onto the open window. "Act, don't think," he chanted to himself nervously. "Act, don't think."

"Yeah, that's our bloody motto now, isn't it," said Don, bracing himself at the rear handrail as Tim dropped onto the boat and made it lurch again.

X went next, with one last insistence to the rest of us that, no really, it was probably just going to be really boring and we could stay behind if we wanted. That only made Angela more determined to go next, very nearly shattering her camcorder against the mast as she landed.

I couldn't help noticing that all the weight that had been added to the *Everlong* so far was making it less and less horizontal each time it came back up from a dip. Everyone sliding down to the far end of the deck wasn't helping, either. I was now going to have to drop onto a forty-five-degree slant. Mary, whose box I had insisted on picking up on the way down, champed nervously on some leftover cat food.

The footsteps had reached the stairwell door, so I took Tim's mantra to heart and switched from thinking to acting. Mary and I were perched on the window and ready to drop when Deirdre laid a hand on my arm.

"Travis, what's going on? Why are we doing this?" she asked. She looked like she was close to tears.

"I'll explain everything," I said, sweating as I heard the door handle turn. "Just follow me." From some neglected part of me came the words, "I swear I won't let anything happen to you."

There were already people spilling out into level five, looking for whatever had disturbed the windows. I clutched Mary's box to my chest and jumped.

As my weight was added painfully to the growing pile at the rear of the *Everlong*, there was a small but incredibly foreboding *snap* from somewhere within the jam behind me. For the second time in as many minutes, I felt the sudden burst of panic that comes from the sensation that something previously taut has suddenly gone slack.

Whatever had been keeping the *Everlong* tied to the third-floor window frame had thrown up its hands and abandoned us. I had only a moment to look up and see Deirdre being pulled away from the window by rough, sweaty hands before gravity stopped daydreaming and the *Everlong* fell.

The five of us, screaming like theme park patrons, clung to whatever railings, edges, and limbs our flailing hands could find as the boat slid down the wall of jam. The boat flew down the slope and shot out across the horizontal plain, mast rocking madly back and forth.

With gravity shifted ninety degrees we were all now lying on the deck in a complaining pile. The boat still had quite a bit of momentum to use up and was wobbling its away along the jam, spinning as it went.

Once it had come to rest, no one spoke for some time. We crawled off each other and lay panting, waiting for our pounding hearts to use up the adrenaline.

"Is it over?" I said, timidly.

"I hope so," replied Don. With superhuman effort he rose to his knees, rested for a moment to get his breath back, then threw his partially limp arms onto the rail and pulled himself up until he could see over the side. He took one look, then groaned and collapsed. "Whoops. Jinxed it again."

I heard the boat creak. The jam didn't seem to be as flat as it should have been. Somehow I'd slid over to the front of the boat, and out of fatal curiosity I climbed up to look down the prow. I found myself staring down into the jam-covered river, and the boat was tilting forwards again.

"Ugh," I said wearily, bracing myself.

"What is it?" asked Angela.

"Uh. Round two, I think."

The roller-coaster scream went up again as the tilting boat made its mind up and slid forward. The *Everlong* careened down towards the river like a sledge on an icy hill, shaking and jumping as the jam's contours rose and fell with the uneven terrain of the riverbank.

Just as we reached the base of the slope the *Everlong* hit a rise with sufficiently ramplike qualities to send us flying a good six feet over the surface of the river jam. I was still attempting to dig all my toes into the hardwood deck when we hit the river.

The boat landed prow first and the point sank a good six feet into the welcoming red quilt. I was being crushed against the front rail by a balled-up mass of Don and Angela, and the jam was barely a foot away from hoovering the eyebrows right off my face. The boat remained stuck in that position, rear end sticking up absurdly, before the jam noisily sucked at the prow like a pensioner with a boiled sweet and began to crawl along the hull towards us.

"Everyone to the back!" commanded X.

With the varnished deck and the steep angle this proved quite a skillful climb, but in a five-part storm of grabs for handholds, masts, and each other's limbs, we somehow managed to roll up to the rear in an undignified mass of humanity. Losing our scent, the jam gracelessly spat out the inorganic hull and the boat settled back into the horizontal. The five of us fell to the floor again, making twitchy invisible snow angels.

"Well, that works," said Angela with forced jollity, filming the Hibatsu building as the wind picked up and it slowly retreated. "Now we just have to follow the river out into the bay."

"Yippee," said Don quietly, his face pressed into the deck.

"Do you wanna take the rudder?" said Angela, adjusting the sail.

"In a minute," said Don, rubbing his chin. "I think I might have swallowed some fillings."

DAY 8.3

I couldn't stop checking my watch, even though it hadn't been working properly since back at Briar. I had to keep glancing back at the Hibatsu building to make sure it was still there. By then it was just another drab corporate tower in a skyline full of them, except with a coquettish jam miniskirt that I swear was getting longer every time I looked at it.

The river valley was pretty windy and we were making for the coast in good time. The USS *Obi-Wan* had been visible on the horizon for a while now, but we still had a way to go.

"They won't kill Deirdre, will they?" I asked.

Don was on the rudder, the length of the journey causing his initial excitement to gradually slip away like dandelion seeds in the wind. He shook himself from a doze. "Who's Deirdre?"

"You know. Princess Ravenhair."

"Oh, that. Would they kill her? By *they* you mean a community really big on capital punishment who believe their very survival depends upon a few scheduled murders, and by *her* you mean one of the scheduled murders in question who was just caught assisting a bunch of the other scheduled murders to escape their extremely necessary fate?" He puffed out his cheeks. "No, no, I'm sure they've already given her the Order of Lenin."

"No, but wait, they wouldn't, would they? The only reason they scheduled murders is because they needed to reduce the population. And we've already done that by running away."

"You do have to understand you're dealing with middle managers, here," sniffed Don. "If the board of directors command them to jam pencils up their noses and head butt their desks, they won't even think about disobeying until an interdepartmental memo tells them to."

"But they can't kill her," I said, shakily. "I promised her she wouldn't get harmed."

"Oh, well, in that case, she's got nothing to worry about, has she."

"Did you really promise her that?" asked Angela. She had been at the front of the boat filming the upcoming aircraft carrier, but now turned around to focus on me.

"Just before we had to leave," I revealed.

"Oo-ooh."

"What the hell does that mean?" interjected Don. "Was that a suggestive coo? You're not honestly implying Travis has something going on with that bint? He's not that dumb." He only had to take one look at me. "Oh, for christ's sake."

"We don't . . ." But that was as far as I got.

"Why don't you get married?" said Don spitefully. "We'll have a lovely ceremony on some rooftop and serve up some peanut butter and cat food for the guests. Maybe Mary could be the maid of honor and Whiskers could be the best man. Oh, wait. You murdered him."

Mary hissed savagely from her box by my knee. I patted the lid mollifyingly. "She forgave me for that. Mostly."

Angela closed her camera viewfinder with a snap, then walked all the way across the deck to my position. Then she placed a hand on my shoulder with slow deliberation, and gave me a patronizing look. "We'll get you back to her," she said.

I hung my reddening head. "Thank you." I wished I hadn't said anything.

Tim appeared on deck, ascending the steps slowly and

deliberately like a schoolmaster walking grimly into class to announce who was getting the cane that morning. "Erm," he said, in that very loud way people use to make sure you pay attention to the rest of their sentence. "Does anyone have any idea why X would hide inside the fridge?"

The three of us all turned towards him as slowly as possible to give us the most time to think of a response. I went with "No."

"No," echoed Don. "I would call that pretty irrational behavior."

"Unless she was trying to cover up something inside the fridge," said Angela bitterly.

"Yeah, that's pretty much what I thought," said Tim. He coughed. "X is hiding in the fridge."

His sentence was punctuated by the snap of Angela opening her camera viewfinder again. I wasn't sure I entirely trusted the smile on her face. "Scoop," she said, simply, before trotting down the steps.

"Did she explain why she was in the fridge?" I asked, making to follow.

Tim walked alongside me as I descended the steps. "She's just being evasive and pretending everything's normal."

"She sounds fine to me."

When we reached the gloomy kitchen, Angela had already moved past excitement at the possible deepening of the ongoing conspiracy and arrived at concern that X might genuinely have gone right around the garden path and up the rabbit hole. She knocked tenderly on the side of the weirdly large chest freezer, camcorder at bay. "X, we're not angry or anything, we just want to know why you're hiding in the fridge."

The lid opened a crack and X's voice floated out. "Really, there's nothing to worry about," she assured us. "It's not turned on."

"Er, that wasn't exactly our concern," I offered.

"Yes, yes, I can see you're thinking this seems like totally irrational behavior," said X. She was pausing between each word in a stalling kind of way. "But I can quite easily put this whole matter to rest with the very simple and straightforward explanation for it."

The last ten or so words had taken close to half a minute. "Well?" said Angela.

"Honestly, it's hardly worth stating the explanation I'm about to give because you'll all realize how massively obvious it is when you think about it."

Angela banged her fist on the side of the fridge, frustrated. "How can you be a secret government agent when you're so bad at lying?!"

"I'm not a secret government agent," said X, lying badly.

There was a whistle from above. We saw Don's skinny form silhouetted against the light coming from above. "Oi! Fathead parade! Come back up here a second."

We left X quietly refrigerating herself and filed up the stairs in neat single file. The *Everlong* was closer than ever to the *Obi-Wan*, which was already blotting out the sun. We were close enough to start thinking about points of entry. The column of handholds forming a ladder seemed like the best bet.

"How long do you think it'll take to reach at our current speed?" asked Tim, spellbound by its massiveness.

"At our current speed?" said Don, amused. "Somewhere within the ballpark of eternity."

It was only then I noticed that the *Everlong* wasn't moving at all. And not for lack of wind, either. Our hair and beards were whipping merrily and the sail was fully puffed out.

"Did we run aground?" said Angela, filming over the side.

"Don't see how we could," said Tim. "Grab the poles. We'll just have to push out of it."

In the middle of the river, there were no inorganic objects to push off of. I was concerned that our poles wouldn't be long enough to go all the way through the jam, through how ever much river water there was underneath, and push off the riverbed, but I hit bottom with my hands a good two feet above the jam's surface. With me and Tim both pushing, the boat was dislodged like a loose tooth and the wind took us again, resuming our journey towards the supercarrier.

I looked back. I thought I saw an indentation in the jam exactly the size and shape of the *Everlong*'s hull. A moment later I looked again and the jam was perfectly flat. I wondered if it had been a mirage.

"So, did we figure out why Agent Scully was hiding in the fridge?" asked Don conversationally as the hull of the *Obi-Wan* drew ever closer. "Is she sulking because you won't let her be a bridesmaid?"

"She said she had a good reason," I said. "She never got around to telling us what it was."

"She's such a bad liar," said Angela unhappily. "It's not fair. If absolutely everyone knows you're full of bullshit then you're not allowed to try to keep it going. It's like April Fools'."

"Oh, it hardly matters now," said Tim dismissively. He was looking up at the *Obi-Wan*. The base of the gray steel wall was mere yards away, now. "I wonder what we'll find up there."

"I bagsy first go on the Internet," said Don, batting his dangling hard drive like a cat.

"All right," said Tim. "Just tell me this. What will you do if you start up the Internet and there's nothing there?"

"Then I will assume the onboard Internet connection is not working at present," said Don reasonably.

"Okay," said Angela. "So what if the Internet is working but none of the sites have been updated in, like, twelve days except for a few blogs that are all going, 'Oh no the whole world is in a jampocalypse and we're going to be eaten a second after I'm finished writing this'?"

Don remained phlegmatically tight lipped until she was finished. "In that case," he began, "I will concede that Tim was right all along, shake him humbly by the hand, and throw myself out the nearest porthole."

"No you wouldn't," said Angela.

"I totally would. Unlike you people I have no illusion as to my usefulness in an actual apocalypse, and believe me, death holds no fear in a world without cappuccinos. No, the most I can hope for is to die in a pose that confuses future archaeologists."

"Why have we stopped moving again?" said Tim from the front of the boat. He took up a pole and tried to touch the ladder on the side of the *Obi-Wan*, but it was too short by about six feet.

"Erm," said Angela, filming all around. "Is it my imagination, or are we sitting a little lower in the jam than we usually do?"

I looked over the side. The surface was definitely closer than I remembered. I saw the bit closest to me start to bulge in preparation for extending, so I quickly backed off.

"Push off from the ground again," said Tim, who had also noticed this. He picked up a pole.

The boat split. There was the slightest creak of warning, then a deafening, crunching snap. The front and back ends both tilted crazily towards the middle and the mast fell sideways, hitting the jam with a harsh slap. The jam tossed a lazy tentacle across the boat's middle like a sleeper throwing their arm around a bedmate.

"OH JESUS BLOODY BLEEDING OUT THE ARSE," yelled Don, apparently involuntarily.

"What was that about death holding no fear?" said Tim, backed up against the handrail.

I only became completely terrified when I realized that I'd been cut off. Circumstance had contrived to place Tim, Don, and Angela all on the front half of the boat while I was on the rear. I thought about taking a running jump over, but the river of jam suddenly widened with another tortuous crack and began to crawl up the deck with rows of thin, spidery limbs.

"HELP!" cried Angela, practically standing on the front handrail.

"Oh, come on," snarled Don. "Who exactly did you expect to be listening to that, Angela? There's—"

Don stopped suddenly as something bonked him squarely on the top of the head. It was, of all things, a rung. One of several rungs attached to two lengths of nylon rope.

"A rope ladder?" identified Tim correctly. He looked up. It was a long one leading all the way up to the top deck, colored in the stern dark gray of military issue. "Who sent that down?"

"Dunno. Wait here and I'll go ask," said Don, wasting no time in grabbing the ladder and beginning to climb. The ladder swung and jerked sickeningly as he kicked his way up. Tim followed as close as he could without getting a kick in the face, then Angela, who was the only one to remember me.

"Travis!" she cried, reaching fruitlessly towards me as whatever had extended the ladder suddenly began to retract it. She maintained eye contact with me right until she was too high to be seen against the bright afternoon sun.

I stood miserably on the rear half of the *Everlong* like the last, unnoticed teaspoon in the washing-up bowl. I remained frozen until the questing jam caused the boat to shift hard enough for me to stumble.

Against all odds, my mind suddenly started working. And the first thing it came up with was a genuinely rational reason that someone would hide inside a fridge.

Fortunately I was on the half of the boat with the deck hatch and the kitchen. Grabbing Mary, I descended the stairs. The boat was tilting far enough that the stairs were now a vertical wall, which gave me a painful washboard treatment as I fell into the kitchen, sprained my ankle on the tilted floor, and almost rolled straight into the sprawling red soup that used to be the sleeping area. I yanked the fridge door up to find X still there, hugging her knees and glancing up politely.

"Erm . . ." was as far as she got before I got in the fridge with her, wedging my feet either side of her and bending almost double to fold the rest of me in. The chest freezer's lid slammed down heavily with just a little coercion, sealing in place.

We remained silent in the cramped pitch blackness as we felt the jam tearing the boat apart and surrounding us. The walls creaked metallically as the jam took up its usual three-foot depth around us.

After several seconds of total silence, the first few twinges of back pain set in. "Er," I said. "I'm actually quite surprised at how big this fridge is."

"But in many ways, not big enough," said X curtly.

She had a point. It was very stuffy inside the fridge. It got even stuffier when I realized I was sharing the fridge with a woman who, with no opportunity to change outfits since leaving the greenhouse that was the Hibatsu building, was wearing little more than a bra and skirt. The stuffiness ramped up another notch when I remembered that X wanted me dead. And I could think of no better place to secretly murder someone than inside a fridge. Well, actually there were probably several better ones, but none came to mind at the time.

"Guess you knew this was going to happen, huh," I said, to fill the silence. It was hard to think of how it could have been more awkward, unless I, say, sprouted an erection.

"N—" began X, moving immediately to deny, but then she sighed in a way I found quite discouraging. "Yes. Of course I did. The jam weakens the boat more and more when it sails with too many people in it."

"And that's why you and Y didn't want to ride on the boat when we first found it."

"Yes."

"Ah." I fidgeted with the edge of my T-shirt. "You could have told us this."

A pause. "I didn't want anyone to suspect that I knew something about the jam."

My joints really were starting to hurt. I tried to shift my position, but I felt parts of me rub against soft, warm parts of X and I didn't want her to get the wrong impression.

"Travis?" said X softly.

"Yes?"

"Is your spider in here?"

A familiar skitter against tupperware somewhere between us in the darkness answered her question. I laughed nervously. "This really is quite a big fridge, isn't it."

"The air is going to run out very fast," said X without emotion. "We're probably going to die in here. We're going to die because I couldn't bear anyone suspecting I'd killed everyone else in this city." A mirthless chuckle. "Guess I've no right to complain, do I."

Her words scared me, but at the same time they were quite calming in the face of death. "So you are responsible for the jam."

"Yes."

I let out a long, rather wasteful breath. "People might have understood if you'd just apologized."

"I'm sorry, Travis." It was a little too late, but she meant it. I felt her moving, and after some rather difficult shifting of position she put her arms around my torso and buried her face in my shoulder. I could only sprawl, frozen, watching the spots form in the blackness as the air began to move hoarsely in and out of my lungs like a saw stuck in tough wood.

The next thing I noticed was gravity shifting. Something was tugging on the further portion of the fridge, and after a moment's ambiguity the fridge tilted forward onto its end. The lid sealed closed even tighter as the jam pressed it inwards.

Then, all of a sudden, I was vertical again, upright and in a clinch with X. Her skin pressed warmly into mine. I could feel her hot, labored breathing on my neck. Mary grumbled jealously at our feet. The situation threatened to reach maximum awkwardness.

"What . . ." she whispered.

Something was pulling us upwards. The jam held onto us with all its tentacular limbs like a clingy child but couldn't maintain its grip, and the fridge detached with a noise like a giant boot being withdrawn from thick mud. We swayed groggily back and forth as we ascended. From somewhere above us I heard the clink of heavy chains.

"I think something's rescuing us," I said. The fridge knocked jarringly against something large and metallic which must have been the hull of the *Obi-Wan*. I pushed on the fridge door. It only opened half an inch, revealing that a chain was wrapped around it, but it was far enough to flood the tiny space with glorious, cool, fresh air.

"We're not going to die," said X, with a curious joylessness.

"We're not going to—"

My reiteration of her sentiment was cut off when I felt her hands clasp tightly around my throat. Ridiculous half syllables burbled from my lips. I felt my face redden and throb as the blood vessels in my neck were constricted.

X pulled herself languorously up my body and rested her forehead on mine, pinning my arms to the back of the fridge with her knees. Ten seconds ago I'd been resigned to death, but that was swiftly forgotten as I jerked my hips and kicked my legs into hers as hard as I could, to no avail.

I went limp. X renewed her grip. With the meager light from the cracked-open door I could see her face. Darkness was encroaching around my vision and it was like looking at her through a hole in a curtain on the far side of a dark room, but I thought I could see tears in her eyes.

My head felt like a balloon full of scalding hot water. My lungs rattled in my ribcage. I could feel it coming, now, the final crescendo when the balloon would burst and everything would stop. X's face was further and further away. My wrist was pinned, so with my last ounce of strength I patted her shin reassuringly.

This was how I would die. Strangled by an attractive, seminaked woman inside a fridge with a giant tarantula in the middle of a sea of carnivorous jam. As I blacked out, all I could think of was a fortuneteller I'd spoken to a few years ago, and how full of shit she'd turned out to be.

DAY 8.4

"He's dead." Don's voice was neutral.

I made the effort to moan. I coughed through what felt like an entire hard-boiled egg lodged in my throat.

"Oh, guess he's not, then. Hush my mouth."

I opened my eyes, and was greeted by the night sky. I was still lying in the fridge, and the faces of Don and Angela were looking down with mixed degrees of concern.

"See, this is what happens when you lock yourselves in a fridge with a limited air supply," said Angela, helping me to my feet. We were on the deck of the *Obi-Wan*, which extended massively in all directions. It was utterly devoid of people or aircraft, which somewhat undermined its status as aircraft carrier.

"Mm, you two were just spread-eagled over each other," said Don, standing with arms folded lest he accidentally make some friendly gesture. "Hope you realize I'm going to have to tell your future bride about it."

"You're lucky the crane thingy up here was still working," said Angela as I picked up Mary's box. "Only thing that does, mind. Tim's gone to look for the generator."

"It'd better be there," said Don ominously. "And X had better know how to get it working or she's going to be an ex-X."

"Weak, Don," said Angela.

"Where *is* X?" I asked, one hand straying to my tender neck.

Immediately Don and Angela both looked at an empty patch of the runway, which they seemed to find rather disturbing. "Where'd she go?" said Angela.

"You were supposed to be watching her!" snarled Don.

"She was unconscious! I thought you meant, you know, make sure she's lying on her side so she doesn't choke on her lungs or whatever! Why would she just run off?"

"Angela?" I said.

"What?"

"X is responsible for the jam."

It was like I'd flicked her off switch. Every muscle on her body hardened. Her face was trapped in a single moment of mild annoyance. After a few seconds, she brought her camcorder up and snapped the viewfinder open with a smooth sequence of very slow, deliberate movements. "Say that again."

"We thought we were going to die. She admitted it. She said she was sorry."

"Urgh. This had to happen when I was this close to an Internet connection, didn't it," growled Don. "Couldn't you have had desperate life-affirming sex instead?"

"I knew it!" said Angela, awkwardly trying to simultaneously film us and run around in circles looking for X. "Didn't I say right from the start she knew more than she was telling?"

"Everyone knew that," said Don testily. "She's not exactly Mata Hari."

"But I was the only one who cared!"

"You're still the only one who cares. What are you even going to do with this information now you have it? Right here and right now the most you can do is go up to her and go nyah-nyah-nee-nyah-nyah."

Angela turned on him and seemed about to fly off when, at the worst possible moment, our attention was drawn by a metallic clatter some distance away. X's head appeared momentarily out of some kind of maintenance trench that ran alongside the main runway, then dropped hurriedly out of sight.

"Hey!" yelled Angela. She had time to take one single step in pursuit.

A gunshot crackled through the still night air. Something struck the tarmac-like surface of the aircraft carrier's runway and threw up dust and shards a couple of feet away from Angela, who froze in place.

"Oh my god, I'm so sorry," called an educated man's voice from some distance away. "That must have seemed like I was trying to shoot you. I'm really not. I was just trying to look at you through the scope on this thing. It's very powerful."

Another bullet ricocheted off the prone fridge. For some reason that was what made us finally unpetrify. The three of us all jostled for a crouching position behind the fridge. Don shoved the fridge door open for the extra cover it gave.

"Okay, yeah, I think I've figured out what's making it do that," said the flustered sniper. "Look, I was the one who sent the ladder down. I thought you might have been someone I knew. Then I saw you weren't, so I just thought I'd watch you for a bit before I introduced myself. Wait, does that still sound a bit threatening? It does, doesn't it."

"Dr. Thorn!"

X had suddenly reappeared from wherever she'd been hiding and was standing fearlessly in the open a few yards down the runway from the fridge. Not only was she not afraid, she looked like it was taking all her power to resist jumping up and down for joy.

"Yolanda?" said the sniper as if he'd spotted her at a high-school reunion. "Is that you?"

X waved both her arms in that really enthusiastic crossing-uncrossing way. "It's me!"

"Hold on. I'll come down." Yet another gunshot sounded and a bullet whizzed by some way above us. "OW. Ow. Sorry, put it down too fast."

X was already running towards the tower. When she was halfway a figure burst out the hatch in the tower's base and ran to meet her. I could almost see them go into slow motion and hear the music swell. Crucially, the sniper rifle wasn't in evidence, so we came out from behind the fridge and headed over awkwardly.

By the time we were close enough to converse they were only just breaking off from a hug, holding hands and bobbing up and down like high-school girls catching up after a long summer holiday.

"Oh my god, I thought you were dead!" said X.

"Oh my god, I'm not!" replied the man she had addressed as Dr. Thorn. He was middle aged, with touches of silver hair at his ears. He was wearing a white lab coat over a T-shirt for some Japanese cartoon. "I thought *you* were dead!"

"Oh my god! I'm not either! How did you survive when the jam came aboard?"

"I hid in the freezer! Hey, does this mean you were the one who took off with the helicopter?"

He didn't seem too offended, but X hung her head apologetically. "I didn't . . . I mean, if we'd known you were still alive we would never . . ."

"Oh, forget about it; it'll all even out in the end. Do you know those guys?"

"Oh yeah, this is Don, Angela, and Travis," said X, shifting back into her monotone professional voice now that we had reentered her zone of perception. "I've been . . . traveling with them. We were trapped in the city for several days. Things have deteriorated somewhat among the locals." The dismissive way she pronounced *locals* made Angela bare her teeth.

"Oh, sure, hey guys. Sorry about all this."

"Is the generator still working, Dr. Thorn?" asked X, anticipating the question Don had already opened his mouth to ask.

"The generator? Oh, sure, I turned it off right after I got out of the freezer. Didn't want to waste power. You want it on for a bit?"

"My companions would like to make use of the satellite Internet," said X in a hushed tone.

"I can understand that," said Thorn. "Do you want to use it too, Yolanda? I'd've thought you'd want to check in with HEPL at least."

X (or Yolanda) covered her eyes with a loud, painful-sounding slap, a gesture that completely sailed over Thorn's head. I heard a funny noise come from the back of Angela's throat.

"HEPL?" she asked, after a cough.

"Yes, Human Extinction Protocol Libra," said Thorn, beaming with the pride of a Boy Scout giving his troop number. "We're the idiots who caused this whole mess, but I'm sure Yolanda already told you that."

"Let's take a look at that generator," said X, grabbing Thorn very firmly around the arm and propelling him towards the main hatch at the base of the tower so fast that she had slammed the heavy steel door behind them and turned the wheel lock before any of us got there.

Angela, the reactionary, was already sprinting to the door. Without a word she tugged the wheel around as hard as she could, so I ran up and helped. Don held back, never having been one to give in to enthusiasm.

The instant the door was wide enough for her to fit through, Angela slid inside, not waiting for us. I was just in time to see her rattle down a flight of metal steps, and was going to follow her when I felt Don's hand on my back.

"Computers," he said, simply, pointing to an open door opposite the main hatch which led through into a small office with a couple of laptops and an old-looking bulky desktop machine.

"So?" I said, mindful of Angela's fading footsteps.

He tapped his hard-drive necklace. "I'm gonna get set up. Let me know if there's any problem with the generator."

"Don't you want to find out about . . ." I attempted to gesture towards the entire city and the ocean of red horror it was sitting in.

He swatted me away. "Give me the abridged version later. I'd rather just sort out this albatross."

"I thought it was a hard drive."

He opted not to respond and set to work cracking open the desktop case, so I hurried after Angela. The carrier's interior was cramped and metallic enough that I could still hear the echoes of her sneakers being carried throughout the corridors.

I caught up with her, along with X and Dr. Thorn, in what I presumed was the generator room, because it was full of massive pieces of machinery that left me utterly bewildered, with everything connected by pipes that seemed specifically designed to get in everyone's way. The two Americans were by a control bank at the far end of the room, Thorn lighting the scene with a battery-operated lantern, and after negotiating our way around the labyrinth of pipes Angela leapt into the circle of light like Batman confronting two creeping ne'er-do-wells.

"You caused the jam!" she yelled.

"Yes, I said sorry," said Thorn openly, as X's hands snapped back over her eyes. Thorn studied Angela's gobsmacked expression and added, "Oh, we didn't mean to. Is that what you were thinking? It was an accident. Ooh, are we on camera?"

"You didn't mean to?!" Angela's camcorder hand was shaking, but then she'd probably never been in the running for any major film awards. "You're called Human Extinction Protocol and you didn't mean to cause human extinction?"

"Well, the fire department doesn't go around starting fires," said Thorn, still smiling but slightly nonplussed. "You don't call them the Spray Water All Over the Place Department. HEPL was set up to specifically control, analyze, and suppress the usage of any technology that might cause artificial human extinction. Excuse me a moment." He turned and pulled a large switch on the control bank behind him, and the generators whirred to life, fading in the ceiling lights. He strode cheerfully out into the corridor away from the increasingly loud noise, and the rest of us followed.

"Yes, been a lot more call for this sort of regulation," he continued, once the hatch had shut and we could hear ourselves think again. "What with all this top-secret nanotech research that's been going on. You know, gray-goo scenarios and whatever. Are you all right, Yolanda? You're making some very strange noises."

X stepped close to him and mumbled directly into his ear, not quiet enough to go unheard. "My feeling was this information exists on an official need-to-know basis."

"You haven't told them anything?" He clicked his tongue. "Personally I think I'd have a need to know about things that had destroyed my home and everyone I've ever met. I've always said you're a bit too neurotic about this, Yolanda." He turned to us. "You know, we used to go to this little bar by the river after work, and Yolanda used to insist we pretend to be substitute teachers. Good times. We had fun in this city. Shame about what happened to it."

X was starting to look like a teenage girl whose embarrassing dad was jovially telling her friends all about her culpability in crimes that carried the death sentence. Angela was still staring at Thorn with open-mouthed disbelief.

"You . . . you were here before the jam hit?" I asked.

"Of course. We brought the jam here, on the *Obi-Wan*," said Thorn. "It's been anchored out in the bay for months. We were doing tests on the stuff, trying to create a neutralizing agent."

Angela adjusted her camera. "So that's what this was? Some American government test? And Australia was the nice, dispensable country to act as a test ground?"

"Well, yes," said Thorn, with the obliviousness of a lifetime in the academia bubble. He blinked as he analyzed her accusatory tone. "Oh, well, we didn't intend it to get released in any populated area, if that's what worries you. We had a special test zone on a patch of dead ground in the country somewhere. The whole area was cordoned off with plastic barriers going right into the ground. We took every care to stop it getting out."

"But it did get out," I said.

"I know! Don't even know how. One day the testing went on, same as always, we put the jam back in its containment unit, put it away with all the rest of the equipment, and set off back to the city. When we unpacked everything on the *Obi-Wan* the containment unit was missing. And the next day, the jam hit the city. That's as far as I know."

"Could you have left some of it behind?" asked Angela.

"No, it doesn't work like that. There's only one swarm, it can't separate into smaller ones, and we take every precaution on site. It was probably just stolen by terrorists. That's what normally happens."

"What about X—I mean, what about Yolanda?" I said.

"What about her?"

"She said she was responsible for the jam."

"No way! She said that?" He reacted with excited glee as if I'd said she'd found a new boyfriend. "You didn't actually say that, did you, Yolanda?"

Our foursome in the cramped corridor had, at some point in the conversation, been downgraded to a threesome. From somewhere not far away I heard an interior door slam.

"Where's she going?" said Thorn.

"God damn it!" cried Angela, immediately sprinting after the newly identified Yolanda.

Thorn and I watched them go. When their footsteps had faded away, I became suddenly, depressingy aware that I was now alone with the bizarre scientist. He rolled his eyes at me and smirked like we were watching our nine-year-olds kick each other's teeth in on the football pitch.

"Did you really create the jam?" I asked.

"No no no, not at all," he displayed his hands openly. "They just gave it to us to study and wouldn't tell us where it came from. Need-to-know basis. Apparently it wiped out an underground research facility in New Mexico, but I don't know if it was created there or if they were just studying it as well. Did she really say she was responsible for this?"

"Yeah," I said, rubbing my neck uncomfortably. "I don't think she was lying. There wasn't much of a reason to lie at the time."

"Hm," said Thorn, scratching his head. "No, I think you must be mistaken. I know Yolanda quite well. I don't see any reason why she'd admit to doing something like that. I wouldn't discount her doing it, you understand—christ knows she's wound tight—but I definitely don't believe she'd admit it."

"I'd better . . . check on my friends," I said, attempting to drift away.

"Oh, sure, I'll come with you," said Thorn eagerly, drifting right along with me. "Of course, if she is a terrorist, that puts a bit of a dampener on the jam neutralization project. Shame. We were so close."

I'd been attempting to block him out but his words burrowed right into my head like an agitated mole. I stopped and spun on my heel. "Did you say you can neutralize the jam?"

He grinned impishly. "Certainly can. Isn't even that hard. Obviously it works on a molecular level, since it can convert matter into other matter, so we formulated a compound that effectively turns its molecular disassemblers on themselves. Turns the whole swarm into water. Theoretically."

"Where is the compound?" I barked, before he could digress too far.

"Ah. Well, I say *theoretically* because we never actually made any of it. We were going to call it 'Peanut Butter.' "

My built-up hopes promptly dashed me down. "Oh."

"I should be able to make some with the *Obi-Wan*'s facilities, though. I'd just need the test data."

I very cautiously let my hopes start building up again. "Where's the test data?"

"I gave it to Yolanda just before the outbreak, on a USB stick." He stroked his chin again. "Hm. That might have been a bad decision, mightn't it." I was halfway through deflating again when he suddenly added, "Oh wait. I remember now. She gave it to her bodyguard for safekeeping. I forget his name."

"Y," I breathed.

"I dunno. I guess because he wasn't very memorable?"

My hopes had been inflating and deflating like an accordion throughout the conversation but they'd ended on a slight net gain. Y had been claimed by the jam, but we knew where it had happened, and a USB stick was inorganic. The most the jam could do was give it a polish. There might have been a few waves since then that would have pushed it away, but it was still a hope of some kind.

We approached an open doorway leading into what looked like a small cafeteria, and both stopped short as Tim suddenly appeared at the entrance to the extremely well-polished kitchen, a certain wildness in his eyes. I made the introductions, and Tim gave Dr. Thorn only a momentary glance as if I'd merely pointed out my new set of self-assembly bookshelves. "Travis, come look at this," he said, before racing back into the kitchen without even waiting to see if I was coming.

I stepped through and found him in a storage room, making the kind of hand gesture usually accompanied by the exclamation *ta-da*. I looked around, but it was a perfectly ordinary pantry with militaristically clean floors and large catering-sized cans of food on every shelf. Then I started. There were large catering-sized cans of food on every shelf.

"Food?" was all I could say.

"Canned, jam-safe food," said Tim like a proud parent. "Enough to keep an entire settlement going for a very long time."

"Oh, sure, take whatever you need," said Dr. Thorn, just behind me.

"But how're we going to get it all back to Hibatsu?" I said. "We lost the *Everlong*."

He gave me a look that made me wonder if I'd turned over two pages at once. "The Hibatsu building's going to tear itself apart. What we have here is a ready-made settlement in itself. Food, water, power, and transport. It's absolutely perfect."

"I guess," I said, scratching my head. "But how're we going to get everyone from Hibatsu to here?"

"Do I get a say in this?" said Thorn, to fill the unpleasant silence.

Tim wouldn't look me in the eye. "I don't think the Hibatsu settlement needs to know about this." I heard myself make a sound like an upset puppy and he continued. "Travis, this is what we've wanted right from the start. A settlement of our own. Look, we already know we can't have too many people on the ship at the same time. That's why the jam killed the whole crew the first time, right? We have to keep our numbers small."

"But we can take it out to sea," I said breathlessly, thinking on the fly. "Past the jam. Then bring them all in on small boats. You said yourself the building's about to tear itself apart; we can't just leave Deirdre to that!" I checked myself. "And everyone else!"

"And what makes you think the jam hasn't spread all the way around the world? And would that be so bad? We could become adventurers traveling the jam seas on our own aircraft carrier. It'll be awesome."

"It's possible," said Thorn, tapping his chin with a strange regular rhythm like a slow metronome. "We never tested it on seawater. I suppose there might be enough life forms to sustain its growth."

Tim looked Dr. Thorn up and down again. "Who did you say this was?"

"He's a friend of X's and he knows more about the jam than anyone else," I said. "That was the other thing I needed to tell you. He might be able to destroy the jam."

"He . . . what?"

"We need to get his test data back from where Y died but when he gets that we can turn all the jam into water."

"Actually, we could turn it into whatever liquid you want, hypothetically," piped up Thorn. "Water, vodka, milk, whatever you're into. I was thinking it might be best to turn it into regular, non-maneating jam at first so everyone can be let down gently."

Tim didn't reply straightaway. He walked slowly out into the cafeteria, barely acknowledging our presence as we moved out of the way of the pantry door, and seemed to be heading for the exit when he tottered drunkenly and turned to us again. "You realize that'll flood the city?"

"I like that better than what we've got now, Tim," I said, slightly loudly. "We've got a dam for floods. We don't have a dam for jam."

"Yes, yes, I get that." He resumed drifting to the door. "I'll see you up top later."

"I am really not making a good impression on all these new visitors," sighed Thorn, hands on hips. "Are there any more?"

"Don," I said. "Don was just . . . I need to find out if the . . ."

I left the sentence where it was and ran from the room. The power was on now, I realized, and we could already have access to the outside world. After several minutes of wrong turns I eventually reached the computer room at the base of the control tower. Dr. Thorn didn't seem to be following me anymore, which I noticed with mixed feelings.

"Don, I—WAAGH," I exclaimed, jumping back from the doorway.

He looked up slowly. "What's wrong with you?"

The ceiling lights were off, but the computers were on, and the blue-green light of the monitors deepened every crag and shadow on Don's perpetually angry features. For a moment I'd thought the room was haunted by the ghost of my old head teacher.

"Sorry," I said. "Is the Internet working?"

"I don't know."

"You don't?"

"I can't bring myself to open the damn browser." He rubbed his eyes violently. "This is when we find out, isn't it?

Whether or not everything can go back to normal. If the whole world's gone, then I said I'd kill myself. You can't just go backsies on that sort of thing."

"You could if you want. You know that guy who was shooting at us? He says—"

"You do it." He swiveled the monitor around and looked away, covering his eyes. "Just tell me if there've been updates in the last eight days. And if there haven't, I dunno, just lie and say there have."

I leaned around him to the keyboard and entered the address for my favorite news site, BadNewsFromKittens.com, in which the latest negative bulletins were displayed in speech bubbles on photos of nonplussed cats, in order to create a softening effect. I pressed Enter, and waited.

My heart seemed to be standing still at a point just below my tongue as the lonely radio graphic in the corner of the screen slowly animated. Don's breathing was getting faster and faster the longer the silence went on.

The error page came up like a vicious smack in the chops. My heart plunged down my torso and landed in my stomach like a turd in a toilet bowl.

"Well?!" barked Don.

"Er . . ."

"Oh god, I knew it."

"Hang on," I leaned closer. "Oh. Sorry, I put a comma instead of a full stop. Let me try again."

The cruel bastard of a browser seemed to wait even longer this time, but then the reassuring salmon-pink backdrop of Bad News From Kittens filled the screen, followed by the last few updates. In the most recent entry a tabby kitten attempting to sit on a volleyball meowed petulantly about the CEO of some investment company on Wall Street running off with his company's pension fund. I checked the top left corner.

"It's dated today," I said aloud. "It's been updated today! The jam hasn't reached America!"

Don shouldered me aside and hunched over the keyboard again. He flashed a single dirty look at me for my choice of news source before turning back and madly rattling the scroll bar up and down. "Oh, thank christ." His good mood didn't last long. "Damn it, this computer doesn't have TransferAGoGo. Going to have to download that before I can upload my build. Bloody government issue."

"Wait!" I grabbed his mouse wrist. "What's that?"

I scrolled down a little to see the entire picture that had caught my eye. It was an image of a tortoiseshell cat, sitting and staring up reproachfully at the cameraman, who had undoubtedly been the one to dress it in a miniature Akubra hat with corks around the brim. The speech bubble emerging from its unhappy mouth was decorated with Australian flags.

"*Miaow, cobber!*" it read. "*Australokitty is so sad to hear that there is still no transportation or communication to or from Australia since the country was devastated by a massive meteorite strike two weeks ago. A spokesperson from the US Navy announced that they will maintain a perimeter around the country until they are sure that there is no risk of space radiation, and only then can rescue efforts be mounted. Miaow! Does that mean Australokitty doesn't get to chase kangaroos around the outback anymore? Fsst fsst!*"

"Meteorite?" I said.

"Perimeter?" said Don.

"Space radiation?" I added.

"Those cheeky bastards," said Don, astonishment in his voice. "They're actually trying to cover this up. Where's X?"

"Angela's chasing her somewhere. Thorn told us that the Americans brought the jam here on this ship and ran tests on it in the countryside and Angela thinks X might have set the jam free on purpose."

"Hate to say it, but Angela might not be far off the mark." He read the screen again. "Almost impressive, isn't it, the audacity of it all. Oh well." He resumed searching for somewhere to download his favorite file-transfer software.

"What about bringing America to justice?" I said, just to test the water.

He looked at me. The frightening effect of his ghostly face hadn't diminished much. "Travis, no one got punished for Iraq. No one got punished for the Bay of Pigs. No one will get punished for this. Just stop caring. It'll make you feel better."

It was clear that Don was going to be hogging the Internet for a while, so I took the opportunity to aimlessly explore the *Obi-Wan*, stomping around with my hands in my pockets, looking for someone to take charge and dictate the next course of action. Occasionally I heard running feet, which I presumed to be the ongoing X-Angela pursuit, but it had always moved on by the time I got there.

Finally I climbed a hatch in the ceiling of a storage room full of inflatable life rafts and found myself outside again, at the side of the runway. I peered out to sea and tried to spot the edge of the jam, but it was the middle of the night, the moon was drifting unhelpfully over the land, and the landing lights that now lit up the entire deck like a Christmas tree certainly didn't help, either.

Dr. Thorn stood near the other edge, watching the city through a set of high-power military binoculars. There couldn't have been much to see at midnight with the power still off, but he seemed to be getting something out of it.

"Oh, hello again," he said, hearing my approach. "Do have to say, it's nice to have people around again. I've spent the last eight days on my own here and I actually think I might have started to go a little bit peculiar."

"Can you really destroy the jam?" I asked.

"Definitely, definitely, certainly yes. We'd created a small amount of Peanut Butter at the end of our last field test session."

"And it worked?"

"No. But given another couple of hours I'm sure I could have ironed that out. Sixty to seventy percent sure, at any rate." He turned back to the city, then almost immediately turned around again. "Hey, have you seen that sniper rifle?"

"The one you were shooting at us with?"

"Yes, that fellow. It's not mine, you see. I was going to put it back in the locker where I found it."

Afterward, I couldn't tell which had come first: hearing the shot, a hideous, penetrating noise pounding through the air like a giant pneumatic hammer, or seeing Thorn flinch. A hole no bigger than a dollar coin appeared in his T-shirt, and I heard a collection of wet, slippery objects splash upon the tarmac behind him.

He rocked on his heels. His brow creased and his mouth opened, as if he was about to start complaining about the unfairness of it, but then he spat up blood and slumped to the ground.

For a moment, I felt like all the bones in my legs had simultaneously stabbed downwards about three feet, pinning me to the ground. It was only when I saw a glimmer of moonlight reflected off a rifle scope on the roof of the control tower, winking like the green on a set of traffic lights, that I broke into a run.

There were no more shots, and I managed to get through the tower hatch and slam it closed with my entire body weight. My ongoing shriek faded like an inflatable running out of air as I slowly slid down onto my arse.

"What's gotten into you?" called Don from across the way. "It's something to do with all that blood down your front, isn't it."

I glanced down. Dr. Thorn's arterial spray had left a flower of gore across my upper chest. I stumbled drunkenly into the computer room and collapsed into a chair. Don had already started the upload of his build, and now appeared to be composing a lengthy and profane e-mail. "Thorn's been shot," I said, my lips feeling numb and alien as they formed the words.

"Who's been shot?"

"Dr. Thorn! The guy who was shooting at us with a sniper rifle!"

He took a moment to digest this. "So what's that, karma?"

"Please take this seriously! There's a murderer loose!"

"And who do you think that would be?" He still wasn't looking away from the screen.

"I don't . . ." I forced myself to think through the fog of shock. The killer definitely wasn't me, unless I'd finally snapped in some extremely complicated way. And Don would have had to be an Olympic-level sprinter to get down from the roof in time for me to have met him here. Of the remaining candidates, only one had recently been strangling me to death in a kitchen appliance.

"X, it's got to be X," I said aloud. "She's trying to silence us all."

Don whistled. "Guess we'd better not say anything about what Australokitty just told us."

"I'd really appreciate it if you started panicking like a normal person!"

"Don't pressure me." He quickly checked the progress of his upload. The bar was about a tenth of the way across. "This is the first good mood I've been in for quite a while. The world isn't jammed and I'm uploading my build. I'm sorry;

it's going to take a while for me to come back down to your level."

At that point we heard a scuffling from out in the stairway and Angela appeared at the side of the doorway, walking backwards. She shuffled her way into full view with some difficulty, dragging X along with an arm around her neck, and jumped a little when she saw Don's ghostly face. "Oh, it's just you two."

"What are you doing?" I asked.

She released X's throat and booted her into the room with an irreverent kick. X fell onto all fours and made no effort to stand, keeping her gaze fixed on the floor.

"Go on, tell them," commanded Angela, summoning her camcorder mysteriously and planting it firmly to her eye.

"I'm responsible for the jam," said X, barely audible. Her voice was so plaintive I almost felt guilty for being in the audience.

"I knew that," I said.

"Yeah, I thought we all knew that," said Don, recrossing his legs.

Angela was not to be disheartened. "And tell them why you did it!"

"I released the jam deliberately because I was ordered to by a secret conspiracy within the American government," said X. She was still keeping up the press-conference tone even as tears ran down her face.

"There!" said Angela, panting with the adrenaline. "I've been saying it all along and there's the proof. I did it. I uncovered the truth."

"Where did you just come from?" I interjected.

"Below decks, I've been chasing her around a table in the cafeteria for about half an hour," said Angela, puffing theatrically. "Is that your blood?"

"So she can't have shot Dr. Thorn!" I concluded.

"Ezekiel's been shot?!" cried X, suddenly rising to a kneel and clasping her hands as if in prayer. "Did he survive?!"

"Yes. Well, at first. For like a second. But then he died, so I guess no."

X emitted a tortured howl that set everyone else's teeth on edge and planted her face against the floor, clutching the back of her head in two clawed hands. Angela coughed, clearly uncomfortable, but kept filming.

"Where's Tim?" asked Angela, voicing my own sudden worry as the suspect list rather drastically narrowed.

"He couldn't have . . ." I began.

"Are we absolutely sure there was no one else on this ship when we came aboard?" said Angela quickly.

"Well, it doesn't exactly go unnoticed. There could be any number of survivors lurking around," growled Don, hands behind head and legs folded comfortably. "Or, y'know, Occam's razor, Tim did it."

"How can you say that?!" I said, clutching at the air.

" 'Cos he passed by my door a few minutes ago. Heading up those stairs. I was going to tell you when you calmed down and let me get a word in edgeways."

I pushed past Angela, poked my head out the door into the stairway, and called upwards to where presumably the bridge and the roof access were. "TIM? ARE YOU UP THERE?"

The only response was an elongated metallic groan, echoing from all around us. As it rose in volume and shifted into an ongoing hum I felt a rising vibration in the floor. Then the entire carrier lurched hugely and I was pulled from my feet.

"TIM!!" I yelled, dangling from a banister that was suddenly at a very awkward angle. The hull shifted again.

"Someone's trying to start the engines," realized X. "Someone in the bridge. It's just up . . ." She attempted to run for the stairs when Angela shoved her back down.

"You are so not going anywhere," she said sternly, producing a length of thin rope she'd picked up somewhere for presumably this very purpose. "Travis, go up to the bridge. Find out what the hell Tim's playing at. If it is Tim."

X didn't resist as Angela began binding her to a chair, and I charged up the steps three at a time, which proved unwise when the ship lurched again and I tripped on the top step, slamming into the hatch at the top of the stairs. It didn't give at all. I wrestled with the locking mechanism but something was blocking it from the other side.

"Tim?" I hammered on the metal door. "TIM? Is that you in there? Everyone wants to know what the hell you're playing at!"

There was no answer.

I hammered until my fist ached too much to continue. "Can you hear me? You've got to stop. You can't drive this thing!"

As if in response, the carrier gave one last violent shift, then leveled out. Glancing out a nearby window, I could just about see from the meager moonlight that the land had started moving away from us. He'd successfully pulled out of the sand and was heading out to sea.

"Okay, so maybe you can drive this thing," I said uncertainly. "That still doesn't mean you should! And you definitely shouldn't shoot people, either! That was very unhelpful! Why did you even do that?!"

I was talking to myself. I was sure Tim would have responded to me of all people, if only to tell me to just leave it. It couldn't have been him.

That was at the same time a massive relief and incredibly terrifying. I tried to force myself to think clearly and compose theories as to the identity of the unseen murderer I was currently doing my best to annoy. If Thorn had held out then another member of the crew could also have done so, perhaps another soldier like Y who had been driven slowly insane by—

The hatch opened about six inches. Tim's face appeared in the gap, looking rather pale and heavy around the eyes. He was still clutching the sniper rifle in one hand.

"Travis," he said, outwardly calm. "Just leave it." Then the hatch slammed shut again.

DAY 9.1

I kept knocking for a while, but Tim didn't emerge again. I slunk back to the computer room, chin on chest. Angela seemed about to ask me how it had gone, but decided against it after seeing the look on my face.

I sank down to the floor with my back to the wall, knees drawn up to my chest. X appeared to be asleep in her cozy-looking rope waistcoat, while Angela filmed her vigilantly. Don hadn't moved.

"I've got it," said Angela suddenly, after half an hour of worried silence. "All we have to do is turn the generator back off. The engines'll be cut and Tim will have to—"

She was silenced by a vicious slap of hand against desk. Don had suddenly leaned forward, his easygoing mood gone as swiftly as it had arrived. "If anyone touches that generator before my upload is finished . . ." He paused for dramatic effect. "I will ram my thumbs into their eye sockets and jiggle them around really hard."

"We can't just sit here," protested Angela.

Don leaned back into his chair. "Why not? I was going to go straight back to America anyway. What's left for us back there?"

"Hibatsu!" said Angela.

"Deirdre!" I said, simultaneously.

Don rolled his eyes. "Oh, come on, they're all adults." He casually lifted his foot to rest it on the seat of his chair.

As he did so, one of the many nagging suspicions I'd accumulated in the last few days started hammering on the alarm button. His trousers were bathed in the glow from the monitor, and the way they completely didn't go with his *Mogworld* T-shirt reminded me that he had stolen them eight days ago from Y's unconscious form.

The words *the Sunderland issue* suddenly bubbled up into my conscious thoughts. On two occasions back at the mall, Y at his most kill-crazy had refrained from attacking Don while Don had been standing in jam. They hadn't seemed like last-minute twinges of guilt. Could there have been something he didn't want to lose?

It couldn't possibly, said the back of my mind. *There's no way it could be in there so stop thinking it before you get disappointed.*

"Don," I said, wetting my lips. "Have you gone through all the pockets in Y's trousers?"

He gave me one of his looks. "What possible interest do you have in the contents of Y's trousers?"

"Just tell me! Have you?!"

"No, not all of them," he said, arms folded. "Have you seen these things? I don't know what those military types think anyone's going to use all these pockets for . . ."

I was standing up, now. "Could you turn them all out? Right now? Please?!"

He frowned, but I'd sounded crazy enough that he didn't argue. He stood up and went through each pocket, depositing a great deal of tiny, scrunched-up bits of paper and tissue on the floor before reaching into one of the least convenient thigh pockets and hesitating. I could see his fingers beneath the camouflaged material groping interestedly at something.

He held it out for us to see. It was a USB drive, a small, black, unassuming one that couldn't possibly contain something important.

"This is what now?" asked Angela, turning her camcorder onto Don.

"Dr. Thorn said Y had some data they had on a compound that can turn the jam into water," I recounted, glancing excitedly back and forth between Angela and Don. "He said if we could just get this to him he could make . . ." A nagging thought finally got through and switched the track on my train of thought. "Nothing, because he's been killed. Oh, god."

"But it'd still be *something*!" said Angela, still buoyed.

Don was turning the little electronic nugget over in his fingers. He came to a decision, and worked the connector into one of the ports on the side of his computer. "Let's see what's on it, first."

It was only when the USB connector slid home that X stopped feigning sleep. With a violent scrape of chair legs she turned to Don menacingly. "Do NOT look at the contents of that device," she said, like a Wild West poker player putting a hand to their gun.

Don met her severe gaze, surprised. A few seconds of silent tension passed. Then he very suddenly jabbed a finger into the keyboard, opening the contents of the drive in a central window.

"I AM WARNING YOU," roared X, hopping up and down in her chair. "If you take ONE look at ANY file on that drive, I will do EVERYTHING in my power to ensure that you are all imprisoned and prosecuted by the government of the unmmmtmm mmmmmmm mmmmm."

Angela wrapped one arm across X's mouth and the other across her torso, pinning her to the chair. "What's on there?" she asked.

Don picked through the directory. It was filled mostly with rather dry-sounding documents. Don opened one at random and found a scanned image of a notebook page, covered in complex molecule diagrams and idle doodles, side by side and virtually indistinguishable, except for a rather hilarious cartoon of X off to the side with a speech bubble reading, "NAG GNAG GNAG."

"Don, aren't you a programmer?" I said, behind his shoulder.

"Designer. I write spec documents. I couldn't make head or tail of this."

"Wait." My eye flew to the screen. "What's that?"

"Text document," said Don, as if it were obvious.

"But it's dated the day after the jam hit."

He put a finger to his mouth and leaned forward. "Well spotted, Watson."

X suddenly went berserk. She shook like a rodeo bull and mooed through Angela's hand like the rodeo bull's wife, trying to escape her bonds. For the merest second she was able to shake Angela's hand off and get a single sentence out: "IT WAS MY FAULT!"

Angela wrapped both arms around her face. On the screen, a window filled with text appeared. "What is this, a diary?" said Don.

"Dr. Thorn's diary?" asked Angela.

"No, it's . . . it's not a diary. It's more like a statement or . . ." he trailed off as the words seized his attention. His eyes darted left and right with increasing speed.

Then he started laughing. His lips had been moving as he read, and they'd been gradually sliding apart into a grin. When he reached the end, he expelled all the air from his lungs in a single guffaw. Then he sucked it all back in and did it again.

I wasn't as fast a reader. I reached the end a few seconds later. Then I started laughing, too. X sank in her chair with a high-pitched whine like a deflating balloon.

"What?" said Angela, concerned. "What's so funny?"

I was in the middle of sinking to my knees. Don gradually expelled the mirth from his system, giggle by choking giggle, then wiped his eyes. "You want to know why X released the jam?"

"That's in there?" said Angela dubiously, but readying her camcorder.

"Oh, it's in here. All the deep, dark motivations spelled out in incriminating detail." I'd almost calmed down, but that set me off again.

"Tell me!" demanded Angela, coming very close to stamping her foot in frustration.

"After the last day of testing, Dr. Thorn put the jam in a containment unit and handed it to X and Y. Their job was to drive it and the rest of the sensitive equipment back to the *Obi-Wan* overland, in her car." Don bit the inside of his cheek as his grin threatened to take over his face again. "And that's when her sinister plan was put into motion."

"What plan?"

"Y put the containment unit on the roof of her car while he packed everything else away," said Don, picking through his words with the care of a minesweeper. "And then they very sinisterly forgot about it and drove off."

Angela was silent for a long time, then drily said, "What." The comic timing was so perfect that it set off another storm of chuckles. By then I was curled up on the floor clutching my head.

"The jam got into the forests! Chased them all the way back to the ship!" crowed Don. "They didn't even realize until they were back on deck!"

Angela left an unresisting X where she was, pushed Don's convulsing torso off his chair and read the text for herself. It was all there, in Y's unmistakable, clipped tone: A confession written on the assumption that it would only be read after it was too late to matter. Angela glanced at X, who was hanging her head in shame. "It was . . . just Y's stupid mistake?"

X sprang back to life. "It was not Y's fault! It was mine! It was all me! I should have . . . I should have exercised greater discipline."

"Why are you covering for that big, dumb android?" asked Don.

"He was NOT an android!" screamed X. "When he saw what the jam had done to the city, he almost . . ." She deflated again. "I had to . . . It was destroying him."

Angela's face was awful. The corners of her mouth seemed about to dive bomb for the floor. She slowly closed the camera's viewfinder, unstrapped it from her hand, and watched it sit on her upturned palm for a moment. Then she hurled it at the wall above X, where it broke apart with an apocalyptic clatter. Fragments of lens sprinkled across the American's slouched shoulders like dandruff.

"Oh, real mature," said Don, unmoved. "So much for all that footage."

"The batteries ran out on day two," said Angela, sitting in the corner and drawing up her knees. "I don't know why I kept . . . I thought I was achieving something."

"Erm, I'm just going to check on Tim," I announced, as the atmosphere of embarrassment became too stifling to stand. I speed walked out, not daring to meet anyone's eyes.

I hammered on the door to the bridge for a good five minutes and didn't even get the courtesy of a quick *go away*.

"Tim, we found out the rest of the world hasn't been jammed," I relayed through the unfeeling metal. "And it was Y who caused it. But it wasn't on purpose. Did you know Angela's camera hasn't worked since day two?"

Silence.

"What are you planning?" I asked. "Everyone seems to be okay with us going to America. If that's what you're doing. There's no reason we can't all talk about it. And I'm sure we'd all understand your reasons for shooting Dr. Thorn if you told us them. If you did shoot him."

Still nothing. I sat with my back to the door, contemplating my dramatically shortened list of reliable friends. It was as I realized that only one name remained that a guilty sensation socked me in the gut. She'd always offered unconditional love, and like a swine I'd left her in a box in the bottom of a fridge.

I trotted back down to the runway. The wind was strong and very cold and I was still mostly dressed for Hibatsu climate. I wrapped my arms around myself and hurried to the fridge, hoping that spiders don't catch colds.

Mary was snoozing away, perfectly fine. The combination of her hair, the fridge, and the tupperware had shielded her from the elements. I picked her up and she shivered in irritation when the wind hit. I held her box close to my face so she could bat at my nose.

"You okay, Mary?" I asked, as she turned away from me frumpily. "Are you cross because I've been distracted? I'm sorry. We're going to America. But we're probably going to come straight back to rescue everyone at Hibatsu. You like Deirdre, don't you?"

Her abdomen shook and her head lowered. I fancied I heard an irritated sigh, but it was hard to hear much over the noise of the keel ploughing through the jam sea.

"Don't tell me you're jealous?" I interpreted. She didn't respond. "Mary, come on. There's room in my life for a girlfriend and a spider." I tried to work a finger in one of the breathing holes to stroke her, but she backed away, and I realized that she wasn't avoiding me, but watching something on the horizon.

It was still the middle of the night, but suddenly some of the stars looked a little off. There were several extremely bright ones gathered in a cluster, and some of them were rather lurid shades of red and orange.

At first I thought Tim had had a change of heart and was taking us back to the city, but the city didn't have power, and as far as I remembered, its skyline didn't feature so many funnels and turrets.

They were ships, lining the horizon as far as I could see. My first instinct was to run a few rather pointless steps forward and wave my arms frantically to get their attention. Mary, her box handle still dangling from my left hand, raised her forelegs in imitation. There was no answering signal, and I let my arms drop to my sides.

The ships were starting to remind me of the two guys from the opposite rooftop we'd encountered and fought with over the *Everlong*. They weren't going out of their way to be noticed. They were waiting for developments, watching us like hawks. Or American eagles.

It had to be the perimeter Australokitty had mentioned. Which meant they weren't going to be thrilled with the idea of us trying to get through it, not if they really were going to try and keep this all hushed up. And they definitely wouldn't be impressed by the stolen vehicle we were attempting to escape in.

I ran back inside, up the stairs, and didn't decelerate when I reached the bridge door. I threw my entire body against it, which seemed like the most urgent way to knock.

"TIM! THERE'S SHIPS!" I screamed.

No response.

I tried a different tack. "THERE'S SHIPS, TIM!"

"Yes, Travis, I see them," came Tim's voice, almost inaudible through the heavy door.

"What are you going to do?!"

"I'm going to keep going," he said. "What can they do to stop us?"

"Tim, every single aspect of those ships is specifically designed to stop us."

"They won't shoot at refugees," he said firmly. "Especially not while we're on one of their own aircraft carriers."

The second point I was most dubious about, because even from a single distant glance at the perimeter I knew that the US Navy could very comfortably lose one aircraft carrier and still have shitloads left over.

I gave up on him and returned to the computer room. Don was still unblinkingly watching his upload's progress bar, while Angela and X were still sitting in their respective sulks.

"What were you yelling to your boyfriend about?" asked Don.

"We're heading straight for the perimeter! There's gun!"

"There's gun?"

"Ships! Gunships! What do we do?"

X suddenly looked up, her arms still securely tied behind the backrest of her chair. "Does Tim know how to stop this ship?"

"He doesn't intend to," I said, wringing my hands worriedly. "He's just going to try to plough through."

"Then there's no other option," said X. "We have to shut off the generator."

Don was on his feet so fast his chair was practically catapulted into the wall behind him. "No one's touching the damn generator! Getting this build uploaded is worth more than your pathetic lives!" The progress bar on the screen was at 70 percent.

"If the *Obi-Wan* continues towards the perimeters at this speed, it may be interpreted as—"

In the distance, there was a shot. It suspended X's sentence like a semicolon. Then the scream of something overhead served up a tortuous ellipsis, before the exclamation mark hit with an ear-shattering blast.

"Hostility," finished X.

The ship swayed deeply, recoiling from the hit, and Don was bashing the keyboard with absolutely zero consideration for government property. "Connection failed? What the hell?!"

"They must have hit whatever receives the satellite Internet," I thought aloud.

"The satellite receiver," said X. "Angela, could you untie me now?"

"BASTARDS!" yelled Don in the general direction of a nearby porthole. Angela was on her feet, tearing at X's bonds. Another shot went off, followed by a visceral squidge of jam.

"First shot was probably a warning. Hitting us was a fluke," said X. "If we advance much further, their aim will improve considerably. We have to shut off the generator."

"No. No no no," said Don, sweating like an ornamental fountain and patting his trousers desperately. "I can save this. I've still got my phone. It's got international roaming. I can rig up a connection. I can do this."

"Come on," commanded X, now freed. She strode boldly for the stairs that led down, Angela following meekly.

"One hour!" shrieked Don after them, desperately trying to prise his phone apart on the edge of the desk. "Give me one hour!"

Another shell shook the jam sea, causing me to stumble as I made to follow X and Angela.

"Thirty minutes!" called Don. "Or I'll sue your arses off!!"

"Don says to wait thirty minutes," I relayed, after I'd caught up with the two women in the cramped passageways in the *Obi-Wan*'s belly.

"Tell him it's out of the question but he will be fully recompensed," said X, not slowing.

"Or just tell him *up yours*," added Angela, with genuine spite.

We followed X through a bulkhead hatch and found ourselves on the clanky gantry that ran along the perimeter of the generator room. X began to descend a ladder to the main engineering level. "Stay here," she told us. "It won't take long."

Angela and I leaned over the gantry railing and watched X navigate the bewildering array of components, pipes, and cables to the main power lever. She pulled it. The lights died, and a moment later the slightly eerie emergency lighting flickered on. Don's angry outburst was clearly audible even through the layers of bulkheads.

"Hopefully, this will be enough," said X.

There was another explosion, perilously close, and the ship rattled like a china teacup. The echo of the blast faded, and was replaced by a high-pitched rushing sound. I saw water arcing thinly from about three different spots in the hull, and heard a couple of rivets ping merrily off something metal.

"Get back!" yelled Angela.

We had all been frozen in place. X snapped out of it first, and began navigating the maze back towards the ladder.

There was a creak of metal; then a pause; then the wall exploded.

A hole like the mouth of Satan yawned open, admitting torrents of seawater that smashed expensive hardware aside like Lego bricks. A huge curved blanket of the jam flopped in on top of the water and began to swell.

X made a desperate leap for the ladder, but it was too far. She fell short by several feet, and was instantly blindsided by a raging white wall of water. By the time the first rush had settled and the sea had started concentrating on rising, X was no longer anywhere to be seen.

"X!" yelled Angela.

"There!" I said.

She was floating on her back above the main generator, not moving. She must have hit her head on something; with the way the room was laid out, not doing so would probably qualify her for some Olympic swimming award. As the water continued swirling into the room, she drifted in a circle, momentarily coming within arm's reach of the ladder.

Angela was already climbing down the rungs, reaching out to catch her.

"Angela!" I said. "The jam . . ."

"It wasn't her fault!" she replied. "It was just a stupid accident!"

"Don't go into the water!" I yelled.

The jam had already filled the entire corner of the room nearest the hole and was expanding fast, the incoming water pushing more and more of the red goo inside. It wouldn't be long before it reached us. Angela climbed down as far as she dared, with the rushing water just up to her knees, then held onto the ladder with one hand and reached towards X. Her hand just managed to brush the hem of X's skirt, but she couldn't get a grip.

"One more time," muttered Angela, ascending a couple of rungs as the water level rose. She strained as hard as she could, keeping a grip on the ladder with her fingertips, her body almost fully horizontal, watching X circle around again.

This time, she came close enough. Angela's hand clamped tightly around X's wrist, and a triumphant gasp escaped her lips.

Then the jam struck.

I'd been too busy watching Angela to notice how far it had swelled. A thick slab of jam flopped hungrily around the American agent's midsection. She disappeared into the red mass, her hand tearing from Angela's grasp so violently that Angela lost her footing and tumbled into the raging water.

She managed to grab one of the many nondescript pipes that ran through the room before the swirling current could pull her into the jam. She clung to the creaking metal with both hands as the red nightmare pulsed and burbled inches from her feet.

By then I was halfway down the ladder, stretching towards Angela as hard as I could. My arm was too short by about two feet.

"Angela!" I yelled over the noise. "Do you think you can hold on while I go and fetch a stick?"

Before she could respond, there was another cataclysmic scream of metal and the gash widened further. A sea of jam brutalized its way into the room and the whole mass of the jam ballooned insanely. It wrapped itself around Angela's legs and kept going. The extending cylinder of jam came all the way up to the pipe and sucked her hand off it like the last bit of frozen orange on a popsicle stick.

Once she was gone, the massive red appendage flopped obscenely into the water, wobbling in bloated satisfaction. I slowly placed both hands back on the ladder, and when the jam popped up a single periscope-like tentacle, hunting for me, I scrabbled up as if my trousers were alight.

I had just dragged myself back into the hall when the horizontal shifted about twenty-odd degrees to where it'd been earlier, and I almost toppled right over the railing and back into the jam's clutches. The *Obi-Wan* was going down.

The sounds of explosions and rushing water were all around me as I ran through the narrow corridors below deck, stumbling as tremors threw me into the many unsympathetic walls, door frames, and fittings.

The roar of the water was joined by a raging, crackling backing track the closer I came to the computer room, and my nose was hit by a thick stench of smoke. Fire.

There must have been a direct hit on the tower. The stairs leading up to the bridge were wreathed in flame. Most of the objects in the computer room were burning merrily away. I was about to move on when I saw that Don was still inside, still in the same chair and staring fixedly at the dead screen.

"Don! Get out of there!" I yelled.

"Half an hour!" he responded, not looking away.

"The power's off!"

"No it isn't!" He pointed to the screen, on which the burning items on the shelf behind him were reflected. "Still lit up!"

I covered my mouth and dove through the flames to grab Don's shoulder. "We have to go!"

The fire glimmered in his eyes for a moment, then he shook me off and set about the computer case on the desk. "All right, hang on, let me just get the hard drive . . ."

I grabbed him around the armpits and yanked him off his chair. I was amazed at how light he felt. He thrashed at me weakly as I dragged him out into the hall, knocking burning furniture into our wake and leaving the place an impassable inferno. I paused only to kick Mary's box out into the hall, apologizing as I did so.

Once everyone was out and safe, I let go of Don. He jumped up and shoved me roughly in the chest. "God damn it, Travis! If I can't recover my build now I'm going to—"

He was interrupted by a small but no less stunning explosion from the room we'd just left. Judging by the white vapor that was now mingling with the smoke, the fire extinguisher on the far wall had exploded. Don grabbed both sides of the doorway and stared. The chair on which he'd been sitting now had several greasy metal shards embedded in it.

"Oh, buggering bum bollocks basket," he breathed. "I was sitting there, I would have . . ." He flailed furiously in my direction. "You complete bastard! You saved me!"

I was on the floor, partially curled up. "I couldn't find a stick," was all I could say.

"You what?"

"Angela and X, they . . ." I flapped a hand at the stairs leading down, from which roaring water was becoming increasingly audible. "I couldn't find a stick."

"Is that your braindead-yokel way of saying they're dead?" asked Don, but the spite was gone from his voice. He listened worriedly to the rushing tide. "We need to get off this damn ship. Are there lifeboats?"

"There's inflatable ones," I said. They had been in a little alcove just under the main deck that wouldn't have flooded yet. "But wait. I've got to find Tim first."

"Don't be stupid, Travis," said Don, pausing in the act of running for the stairs. "He made the bed; he can lie in it. We need to go, now."

I shook my head and picked up Mary. She twitched at Don defiantly. "I'm not letting anyone else die."

Don hesitated for a moment, then a familiar angry scowl broke out on his face. "Well, I'm not waiting for you. Enjoy the rest of your life." Then he was gone.

The fire that had been blocking the stairway to the bridge appeared to have died down, probably as a result of the exploding fire extinguisher. I stuck Mary's box under my arm as I stamped out what few flames remained, then started up the dented metal steps.

Looking up, I could see what remained of the bridge, my view framed by mangled metal and extruding bits of broken pipe and wire. I called Tim's name, to no response. Through the smoke, it was hard to tell if he was even there.

I kept climbing. When I ran out of stairs, I climbed the wreckage, finding handholds in the newly exposed infrastructure. When I reached what had been the top of the stairwell I paused for a moment to catch my breath, clinging to part of the twisted handrail, and that's when I saw Tim.

He was running across the airstrip towards the jam, clutching one of the packaged life rafts under one arm. At first I thought it was Don, but then another near miss lit up the scene and I saw Tim clearly as he recoiled from the blast.

"TIM!" I yelled. He didn't turn. Without thinking, I swung myself towards him as hard as I could and let go.

I scraped my backside unpleasantly on the ragged remains of the wall, and Mary's home took a rather severe knock. Then I found myself slipping onto the side of the lower, intact portion of the tower. I scrambled to find footing, but gravity sent me into a cartwheel, bashing Mary's box a few more times against the metal. I flew the last few meters to the tarmac, twisting my ankle rather badly on impact and bouncing onto my chin.

Tim had already inflated his life raft. It was circular, with a red canopy almost as vivid as the jam. I wondered if it was made of the kind of rubber that the jam liked to eat, but Tim wasn't letting the same thought bother him. It looked like he was getting ready to launch.

Every part of my body was registering a screaming complaint, but I forced myself onto my hands and knees. I went into a crawl and felt Mary pat my back encouragingly through a crack in the side of her mangled box as I transitioned it with painful difficulty into a bipedal run-limp.

"TIM!" I called again.

He didn't turn around, but I was almost certain he hesitated. The sniper rifle he still had dangling from one hand twitched momentarily. Then he started pushing the life raft towards the jam, running behind it like a bobsledder.

I put everything I had into my legs, so that everything above my waist seemed to stream limply behind me like an unfurled windsock as I concentrated on reaching him before it was too late.

The life raft slid out onto the jam. Either it wasn't rubber or it was too heavily processed and treated to be of interest to the jam. Satisfied, Tim leapt into the entrance flap. The jam-filled gap between the sinking airstrip and the raft was expanding rapidly with every—

I jumped. My twisted ankle shrieked and time seemed to slow down to let me savor the pain for as long as possible. Below me, the jam quivered in excitement.

I flopped down onto a yielding surface of bright red. My mind had already started up the first reel for the scheduled flashing of my life before my eyes when my senses tactfully reported that I'd landed not on the jam, but the life raft's canopy. A human-shaped lump struggled out from under me and Tim's face appeared around the flap.

"Travis," he said. "Thank god you're all right. Get in here." He did a very good job of sounding genuine.

I crawled inside but paused at the flap to watch the scene we were quickly drifting away from like a puck on an air hockey table. Most of the *Obi-Wan* had sunk below the viscous waves. Only the last portion of the airstrip and what was left of the tower remained visible. The lights on the American ships that marked the perimeter hovered dispassionately like hyenas circling a dying man in the desert.

Tim grabbed me and pulled me back, zipping the flap closed with his other hand. "Keep it down," he hissed. "Hopefully this thing's red enough that they won't see us."

A tiny battery-operated light in the roof of the canopy illuminated the raft's interior. Tim leaned back against the opposite flap. I leaned back against mine, letting Mary's crumpled box fall gently to the floor. It was intact only in the broadest possible use of the word, but Mary was flexing her legs, uninjured.

"So much for that," said Tim, after we'd sat panting for a while.

"So much for what?" I said. "Tim, what the hell were you thinking?"

"That was going to be our settlement. We would've been living like kings in the new age."

"There is no new age. The jam only covered Australia and Dr. Thorn could have gotten rid of it. Until you shot him. And by the way, why *did* you do that?"

Tim's hands were clenched together in front of his face, pushing his mouth shut. He took a deep breath through his nose, then lifted his head. "Travis. Have you ever considered that maybe, overall, in the long run, the jam was a good thing?"

I screwed up my face. "No! No, that never crossed my mind! It killed everyone!"

"But what were they doing? Nothing. Just . . . stuff. Shifting numbers and papers around at stupid office jobs or hanging around at the mall being ironic. The jam took that all away; it gave us back the chance to fight for our existence. It gave us the chance to be human again. You agree, right?"

"Tim?"

"What?"

"Just stop."

There was a slurping sound outside, and the canopy fluttered as if something had struck it. The floor began to tilt, and I felt the inflatable walls deform oddly.

Tim carefully unzipped the flap behind him, and I did the same to the one behind me. The raft wasn't moving. It had sunk a couple of inches into the jam, which was visibly puffing up towards us.

"It's trying to get in," reported Tim from his side.

"Small raft, two people close together," I thought aloud. "It can sense us. What do we—"

When I turned around, Tim was holding his sniper rifle again. He was sitting staring at the space between his legs, with the gun across his chest. "Travis," he said.

"Tim?" I replied, clutching my knees.

"I think, Travis, if one of us were to . . ."

"Yes." I didn't want to hear him say it. "Yes, I know. But . . . Angela and X, they've . . . I don't want anyone else to . . ."

"It's going to be either one of us, or both of us." His voice was maddeningly steady and he still hadn't looked me in the eye. "It doesn't make rational sense for both of us to . . . So we have to decide."

The boat shifted again, and sank another inch.

"Well, logically," said Tim. "It should be you."

Finally I met his gaze, and his eyes stabbed coldly through his fringe. Unconsciously I drew my legs up into a defensive position. "What do you mean, logically?!"

He inched closer, and I tried to inch into the wall. "Because, really, we wouldn't be in this position if it weren't for you, would we. You jumped onto my life raft. There were loads of spare ones, more than enough for one each. You should have gotten your own."   •

"There wasn't any time!"

Tim rose to his knees and pointed the sniper rifle at my

chest. "You won't feel anything. It's a big bullet. Just put the end in your mouth."

I tossed my head left and right like a toddler refusing a spoonful of mush. "No! Stop being crazy!"

"Crazy?! This is what makes sense! You agree this is all your fault, right? If it hadn't been for you we wouldn't have been kicked out of the mall and none of this would've happened. Why do you have to be such a dick about it?"

"Tim, please!" The barrel was against my cheek, still smelling of the shot that had killed Thorn. He steadied the gun with one hand and reached for the trigger.

My arm moved. In some desperate animal response, I threw the first thing that came to hand.

Mary's box had taken some punishment on the way down the tower, but even I was surprised when the lid and most of one side flew off on impact with Tim's throat, sending several plastic shards pinging away.

Tim backed off. The barrel of the rifle lowered to the floor. The broken box rolled noisily away, empty, and Mary leapt to Tim's face.

A shudder ran through his entire body, catapulting the rifle out of his hand. He clamped his eyes and mouth shut as Mary's claws sought purchase on his cheeks, and blew sharply out through his nose. He madly tossed his head back and forth and left and right, but when she was finally dislodged she grabbed his collar on the way down and took up position on his chest.

He backed away in a panic and swatted rapidly at his chest with his fingertips, wanting to scratch her off but unwilling to touch any more of her than was necessary.

By the time she fell, landing on her back with a muffled squeak, Tim was already too far to catch his balance. He plunged straight backward through the flap behind him and disappeared from sight. I heard a yell cut off by a wet slithering noise, then some kind of amorphous belch as I felt the jam retreat from around the life raft as it fought amongst itself over a meal.

I lay where I was. There didn't seem to be any point in moving.

DAY 9.2

The next time I opened my eyes, daylight was meandering in through the open flaps. I could hear the sound of waves. My limbs were slightly numbed from exertion and sleep, so I pulled myself exhaustedly to the nearest flap and hung my head loosely over the side as if about to throw up.

Water. The raft was floating in good, old-fashioned, honest-to-goodness water, rolling away in all directions with a gentle swell. I looked down, and saw the ocean's depth falling away into reassuring blue-black. Besides the life raft itself, there wasn't a single square inch of red to be seen.

When the raft was at the peak of the swell, I could stick my head out, strain my eyes, and just about see a few distant funnels and masts belonging to the US Navy's perimeter, but they must have been literally miles away. I'd drifted unnoticed out of the jam. I'd escaped.

I flopped down on the floor of the raft. Mary was on the other side, picking through the remains of her box for scraps of cat food. I looked over my shoulder at the sea again, and the blue-black infinity of the undrinkable water was less reassuring than it had been a moment ago.

"At least we're safe from the jam?"

"Forgive me if that doesn't make me turn little happy somersaults," said Mary.

I blinked. She looked up innocently.

"Mary?" I said, after a minute.

She sighed. "Okay, look, usually I'd draw this out a bit longer, but frankly I'm starting to feel sorry for you. I'm not your stupid spider talking. I'm just a voice in your head."

"Am I going insane?"

"No. That's the most pathetic thing. You just think going insane is the sort of thing you're supposed to do in this situation, so you're pretending. You're not even doing it right. The voice is supposed to be in your head; you don't speak it out loud."

"Yeah, I thought that might be it." I fiddled with my fingers for a bit, then stopped. "Everything's going to be all right now, isn't it? We'll just keep going to America."

"Yes, we'll just do that trip that takes months even if you've got an engine behind you, with no food or water. Everyone else who got lost at sea and died obviously just wasn't trying as hard as we will."

"Getting to Hawaii or somewhere would take less time, though, wouldn't it?"

"Well, there was me thinking you weren't on top of things. Guess we've got nothing to worry about. You just sit back and relax so you don't have to think about all the people you killed."

I gave her the death stare. "I didn't kill anyone. You killed Tim."

"I didn't throw myself at him, did I? And I wasn't the one who dillied around while X and Angela bought it."

"You were the one who ate Whiskers," I pointed out. "That's what ruined everything at the mall."

"If you're going to go that far back, let's just blame all our mothers for giving birth to us. Whoever's to blame, you've got precisely zero friends left and now you're going to die alone in the middle of the ocean."

"Shut up!" I croaked, clamping my hands over my ears. "You're not Mary!"

"And another thing, this relationship you've imagined between me and you is really weird." She groomed her legs languidly, the way a human woman might examine her nails. "The way you project all these emotions onto me because you desperately want to think something actually loves you . . ."

I hit her. I crossed the short distance between us in a flurry of limbs and backhanded her across the raft. She landed on her back and skidded into the inflatable wall. I stared at my hand, shocked at myself. Mary uprighted herself laboriously and cowered back, gathering her legs.

"Real big man," she said. "Is this how you're going to make yourself feel better? Picking on a poor, defenseless tarantula?"

I crawled slowly and calmingly to Mary and extended a hand. "I'm sorry," I said, chin almost scraping the floor. "I'm just under a lot of—"

She bit me. She wrapped a few legs around my hand in an almost romantic gesture, then sank her fangs into the webbing between my thumb and forefinger. I shook her off with another backhand and she tumbled away, dazed. I clutched my hand. It wasn't that much worse than a bee sting, but a bee sting wouldn't have left such an emotional wound. And a bee sting also wouldn't have released urticating hairs. A horrible burning itch began to spread across my hand and arm.

"Just an animal," said the voice I'd been attributing to Mary. "Just a dumb animal that eats what's put in front of it and bites what threatens it. It doesn't love you. It's scarcely even a pet. Birdeaters are notoriously aggressive. It's not like those orange-kneed things you can train to sit on your head."

Perversely, my stomach rumbled again as I scratched madly at my hand. I hadn't been marooned at sea for long, but I hadn't eaten anything since my last rationed Hibatsu breakfast, and that had just been a juice box and half a tin of beans. With nothing to distract me, my hunger was a dark, sucking leech digging its teeth into my stomach walls.

Mary was still dazed and making no effort to right herself. I glanced around in case I'd somehow missed an obvious, convenient box full of survival rations, then stared at her again, quivering with revulsion at my own thoughts.

The Mary voice laughed unpleasantly. "What's so disgusting about it? It's probably a delicacy with natives around their natural habitat; the big horrible insects usually are."

"Tim had this theory," I murmured. "That the word 'delicacy' means 'the food that it's most hilarious to try and fool foreigners into eating.' "

"Oh, man up. Just try not to taste it on the way down."

I picked up Tim's rifle and toyed with the idea of shooting my prey hunter style before a quick glance at the inflatable wall gave me second thoughts. I spun it around and prepared to bash the remainder of Mary's life away with the butt. A single plaintive twitching of her upturned legs gave me cause to hesitate.

"Spiders aren't choosy either. I won't think twice about sucking down your blood like a cherry smoothie the moment your backhand gets too weak."

I raised the gun, closed my eyes, and concentrated on the throbbing pain in my hand.

"Vwooooo."

I opened my eyes. "Did you just say vwooooo?" Mary didn't have a comment.

I heard the sound again. It was coming from outside. Deep, groany, and faintly metallic. It was either some kind of horny walrus inside a tin bath, or . . .

I ran to the flap. A gunboat, painted in militaristic gray with an American flag decal on the side, bobbed in the nearby waves. A burly sailor stood on the side, one leg propped confidently up on the edge. He was holding out a hand to me and saying something I couldn't hear.

"One second!" I shouted, holding up a finger, before popping back inside. Mary was still on her back, faintly twitching. Miserably, I gathered her up in my arms, clasping her scratchy warmth to my chest.

"Come on, buddy," said the American sailor as I appeared again. The boat was now pressed right up against the side of my raft. The sailor withdrew his hand at the last second when he saw what I was carrying, and I would've fallen into the sea if he hadn't recovered and grabbed my wrist with the lightning-fast reflexes of military discipline. He pulled me over and I stepped onto the reassuringly solid floor of the boat.

"We done here?" asked the sailor, directing his question over his shoulder.

"Yes, this is the one," said Don. "Take us back to the mother ship. Or whatever you people call it."

"Don?!" I exclaimed.

He scowled at me. "Don't say a bloody word. Don't start going off on banal thank-yous. This is just straight backsies for pulling me out of that explosion. Don't read too much into it. And stop breastfeeding your damn spider on deck."

"Thank you, Don." He bridled huffily. "Is this the navy?"

He drummed his chin theatrically, surveying the sailors all around us. "I think so, Travis, yes."

"Weren't they trying to silence us earlier?"

"Let's just say they're having to cut a few losses," he said. He smugly reached into his pocket and showed me a small, black USB stick I'd last seen protruding from the computer on the *Obi-Wan*.

A FEW WEEKS LATER

I woke up one morning to find that my entire body had been covered in a three-inch layer of old newspapers.

I sat up, rubbing my back. I knew I shouldn't have tried sleeping on the bench by the little news agent at LAX. I'd thought about curling up in a booth at the fast-food place, since I'd seen a lot of people leave half-finished milkshakes around, but the news agent had seemed more convenient for bedding.

I dragged myself to the departures board and looked it over. I'd slept for longer than I thought; boarding commenced any minute now. Idly I glanced at the arrivals list; another plane from Australia was landing soon. More survivors were popping out of the woodwork every day—

"Where the hell have you been?" barked a voice from behind.

I turned on my heel. He was clean shaven with neatly combed hair, and was wearing a hoodie and sweatpants probably taken from the pile of charitable donations, so it took a moment to recognize him. "Hello, Don."

He glared firstly at the state of disarray my hair was in and secondly at the newspaper sticking to the sole of my bare foot. "Why aren't you staying at the hotel? It's on the government's dime."

"I was afraid I might oversleep and miss—"

"Yeah, whatever," he interrupted. "I've been looking for you. We're leaving for DC tomorrow."

I cocked my head sleepily. "We?"

"Yes, Travis, for the hearing." He produced a pair of boarding passes from the pocket of his hoodie and waved them under my nose. "Remember? Half the American navy are lining up to dob in their superiors?"

"Oh. Yeah." Very few of the ships in the blockade had been happy about the orders they'd been given. A few strategically placed satellite phone calls had blossomed into several hundred as large numbers of officers demanded to know what the government was playing at. Don had done an exclusive phone interview for every media outlet on earth by the time our ship had docked at Long Beach.

"After that, we're going to Bellevue," he said. "That's in the other Washington."

"We again?"

"It was Brian at Loincloth Bellevue who suggested my transfer to Loincloth Australia in the first place." He grinned maliciously. "And now there is absolutely nothing I could ask for that the company won't provide. So . . . corner office, I'm thinking. And a desk I don't have to share."

"But why we?"

He looked down his nose benevolently. "I've gotten you a job. Quality assurance. Entry level, of course, but from tiny acorns do mighty—" He looked me up and down for a moment. "Well, do trees of some kind grow, anyway."

"Don, I can't . . ."

"And before you say anything, I'm just trying to do something useful with you. So don't thank me. You know I can't stand all that pathetic, moisty-eyed—"

"Don, I'm going back to Brisbane."

His mouth stayed open, but no sound came out. I could almost see his tonsils frozen in the act of snark. I dug out my own wrinkled boarding pass and showed him.

An announcement was made over the tannoy, and another batch of bedraggled Australian refugees started trickling into the lounge. Some were greeted by friends or relatives; others were directed to the processing center by some hassled-looking security guards with two-way radios. I scanned each face as it passed, waiting for Don to find his words.

"Why the hell are you going back to Brisbane?!" he said, aghast. "There's nothing there! Even the jam's been washed away."

"Ah, well, actually, a lot of survivors are staying. Look." From my other pocket I produced another wrinkled piece of paper: a newspaper clipping. "It says the economy's booming. They've had so many tourists booking holidays they're having to turn people away. There're whole survivor communities coming together to run some of the hotels."

"Apocalypse tourism," read Don aloud. "Christ, I should've guessed. A bunch of rubberneckers wanting to wander around a deserted city and pretend they're in *Mad Max*."

"They're saying it's like Pripyat without the radiation poisoning. And look, there are studios queueing up to use Brisbane as a shoot location," I said, pointing to the relevant paragraph. "The writers can't put out zombie scripts fast enough."

"Bloody vultures," sneered Don. He finally looked away from the article and caught me staring at the new arrivals. His eyebrow raised. "And that's why you're going back, is it? To open your very own souvenir shop?"

I coughed. "Partly."

"And surely the other part is nothing to do with certain below-average specimens of femininity? Christ, Travis, don't tell me you're still picturing your fairy-tale wedding."

I dropped my gaze. "It's not because I . . . I just need to know." I looked at the floor. "After Tim. And Angela. And

Frank. And X and Y, I guess. I just need to know that at least one other . . ."

My voice trailed away. Don folded his arms and sighed through his teeth, irritated by his own emotions. "You really are hopeless, aren't you."

"Not anymore."

Another tannoy announcement cut through my reverie, nasally informing me that my plane had commenced boarding. I glanced left and right, then back to Don. "Actually! Yes! Since you're here. Could you come this way for a second?"

He followed me uncertainly as I jogged back to my sleeping spot and picked up a military storage crate I'd borrowed from the boat. I pressed it into his unresisting arms. "Do you mind?"

Don was shaking his head back and forth, still trying to figure out what floor my mental elevator had stopped at. "The hell's this?"

"She likes cat food. I was worried about getting her on the plane, but this is probably a better idea."

He peered through one of the holes in the lid and reared back at the sight of hairy legs. "Jesus Christ! Travis, do you have any idea how much you're inconveniencing me? We've got a hearing! And I promised you to QA! And I hate buying pet food—the shops always stink!"

I awkwardly put my cheek to the crate and gave it one last squeeze. "Goodbye, Mary. Look after Don." I started to leave, but stopped myself before I'd gone six feet. "Don?"

"What?!"

"Thank you very, very much."

I turned and jogged away, his angry swearing lost among the clamor behind me.

ABOUT THE AUTHOR

Ben "Yahtzee" Croshaw is the sole creator of Zero Punctuation™, a popular weekly game review on the Webby award-winning *Escapist* online magazine, for which he also earned the Sun Microsystems 2008 IT Journalism award for Best Gaming Journalist. He has also worked as a game designer and dialogue writer for various studios. His first novel, *Mogworld*, was released in 2010. He was born and raised in the UK and now lives in Brisbane, Australia.